# Mental Distortions

By Jean Grandbois

ISBN 0-9730522-0-1

**Author's note**

This is a work of fiction. Names, characters, places, and incidents either are the products of the author's imagination, or are used fictitiously, and any resemblance to actual persons, living or dead, events, or locales, is entirely coincidental. Some well-known people, such as Tibet's missing Panchen Lama, make cameo appearances in these pages, but this is a work of fiction and the usual rules apply : none of these events ever happened.

Cover artwork by Thunder Art (http://www.bythunder.org)

Written in Montreal, Canada, 1999-2002.

*For my wife, forever beautiful.*

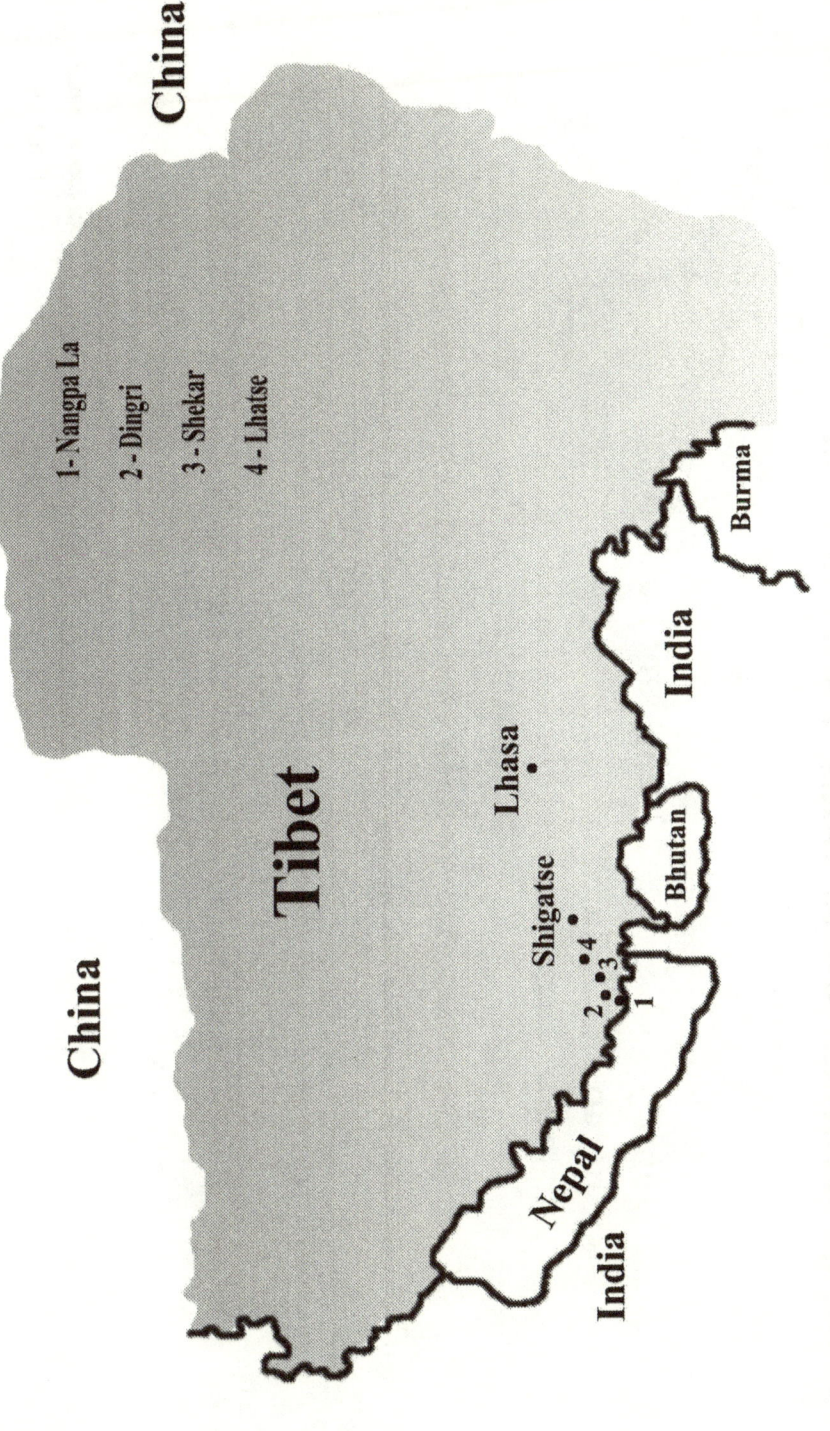

China

China

Tibet

1- Nangpa La

2 - Dingri

3 - Shekar

4 - Lhatse

Lhasa

Shigatse

•4

2 •3

1

Nepal

Bhutan

India

India

Burma

200 miles

Note: Political boundaries are approximate only,
and not recognized by all nations involved.

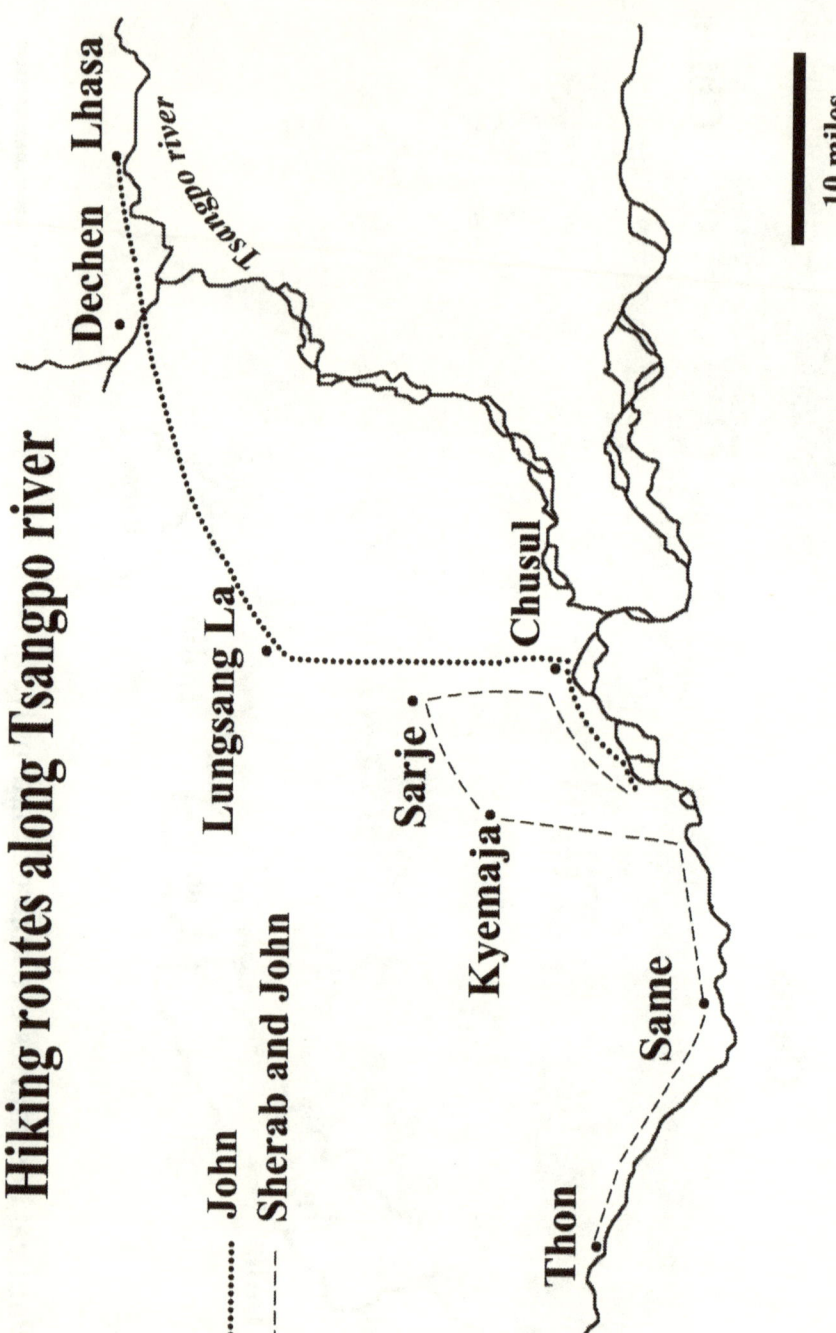

Hiking routes along Tsangpo river

............ John

– – – Sherab and John

10 miles

"According to Buddhist belief, every sentient being has a mind whose fundamental nature is essentially pure and unpolluted by mental distortions.  We refer to that nature as the seed of enlightenment."

- His Holiness the Dalai Lama, from "Human Rights on the Eve of the Twenty-First Century", Paris, 1999

# Chapter 1

The cool breeze rustled through the tall grass, stranding him in an ocean of thin, swaying blades. There were no warm breezes this high on the Tibetan plateau, the wind always seemed to originate from the Himalayan range on the horizon. His eyes feasted on the idyllic postcard backdrop. He was alone, or at least he thought he was alone, admiring one of nature's gifts prepared just for him. He had dressed warmly for the climate, but that midmorning breeze still chilled him to the bone. He did not think much of it then, but he would remember it all too clearly later. Even in a relaxed setting, some inner survival mechanism never sleeps. The instinct that tells you someone is watching, or that makes you decide to shoulder check before switching into the same freeway lane you drive in every day. That morning, the survival instinct inside his body chilled him despite the warm clothing. He ignored the instinct this time, for nothing happened in postcard settings, after all.

He clapped his hands together to beat off the chill, stood up, and headed back for his campsite. A one-night stand in a lean-to might not have qualified as a campsite, but it was his home for the day nonetheless. Logically he knew that camping out there alone was dangerously foolish. No white man could wander off into the Tibetan landscape unescorted. He supposed that he might find himself pleading with a Chinese prison guard for a call to the Canadian consulate. But he had paid dearly to wander through these isolated plains. He had paid not only with money, but also with his job, and with a very interesting, and now very confused, lady back home. Of course, she would not be the first one he had left in a confused state during his impulsively shallow adulthood.

Some may say he had it all. John Pearson was a successful stockbroker in a booming economy. His attractive 36-year-old body naturally attracted equally beautiful women. He maintained the adventure level of a twenty year old, with backcountry trips, canoe trips through rapids, heli-skiing, even parachuting. Perhaps all these outdoor activities had caused his thirst for life beyond the downtown Toronto rat race. Sure, Toronto was not New York, but it certainly was not a Tibetan landscape either. So what made a man like him throw it all out and run off to the Himalayas? He truly hoped to find an answer to that question during his solitary journey. He did not plan on becoming a Buddhist monk, but he could use a little of that inner peace, thank you very much. He'll take that with a side of contentment, and make it to go please. You can take the guy out of the city, …

He had to admit that fate had played a role in this little excursion as well. At a time when he felt a need to do something irrational, all the right political stars were in alignment to allow a crazy Canuck to wander into Tibet with just a backpack. Tibet had recently experienced unrest worse than had been seen since the 1959 uprisings, and subsequent Chinese crackdowns. The various Free Tibet organizations all over the world had a field day with the Chinese military response to the protests in Lhasa. The Chinese government then hatched a great plan to ease the situation. They opened up Tibet to foreign tourists, making way for new public relations with the rest of the world. While some powers in Tibet resented the foreign intrusion, others recognized the economic benefits of tourism to this impoverished land. China brilliantly improved its oppressor image in the world's eye, while dividing the Tibetan leaders into two factions.

One of the major new concessions to tourists was the back country, free roaming hiking. Previously, foreign visitors were only allowed into Tibet through tightly controlled tours. With the new Chinese resolutions, a foreign visitor could apply for a back packing permit. After some background check, the permit was usually approved. However, the government insisted on visitors never traveling alone, a Chinese guide always had to accompany them. The Chinese justified this regulation using the safety of tourists as their prime concern. Most people could see through this thin veil and understand that an unescorted foreigner might run into things that were better left unseen by the outside world.

He left his guide, Mr. Yu, behind three days ago. Fortunately for him, Chinese guides are just as human as anyone else. A few days out of Lhasa, and they were in total isolation. An offer to double his wages if he let John go on alone broke any resistance Mr. Yu might have had to the idea. The guide knew that there was virtually no chance of his crime ever being discovered in this no man's land. He could double his wages and avoid a week of marching through the wilderness. Who could resist? Yu danced the amusing dance of indignation at being bribed before he accepted. Yu then gave careful instruction of directions to avoid because of villages or monasteries. They agreed to meet in twelve days, and then Yu would escort John back to Lhasa.

With a last lingering look at the Tsangpo river, John headed back towards the campsite. Perhaps ten minutes passed before he froze mid-step. He had not been aware of his surroundings, as one is apt to be when thinking of past events. He turned to his right, where he had seen a blur of a movement out of the far corner of his eye. The world in one's peripheral vision always seemed to consist of blurs. He stared for several seconds, which felt more like several minutes. He absently reached for his camping knife, knowing it offered laughable protection against the thieves that were rumored to roam in the countryside. Coincidentally he stared at the same postcard image as before, only this time instinct did not have to chill his body for him to feel the danger. No, his instinct knew to leave things well alone when the people upstairs in his brain were aware of potential danger.

He saw no further movement, and wondered if it could have been his imagination. Was that not always the most comforting thought? Yes, the peripheral vision was faulty, always blurry, and sometimes imagined things. But he knew he had not imagined anything, which left three possibilities. Either the sunlight reflected on the water, or an animal darted in the grass, or he was not alone. Logically, if he had company, it was to his advantage to find out now instead of at the campsite in the middle of the night with a knife against his throat. Or worse, perhaps with a knife through his throat, and the life running out of him.

Grudgingly, he began to advance towards the approximate location of the blur. David, armed with a pocketknife this time, faced Goliath. He might have smiled at the analogy if he had not been sweating with fear.

"Hello? Who's there?"

Never mind that if anyone could hear, they probably did not know a word of English. He could not stand the thought of people jumping at him unseen until the last moment, he much preferred trying to get them to come out now. At least then he would know in which direction to run away. No movement, no response. Slowly, he continued his careful advance. He was within ten yards of the shore now, with little room left for a would-be assailant to hide. The wind continued to rustle through the grass, whispering a hushed warning for him. The swaying grass moved all around him, giving him the urge to drop the knife and run like a madman. Five yards. With a primal scream he rushed the last distance to the shore, knife held out in front of him like a spear.

The river lapped at John's feet as he struggled to regain his balance after nearly running straight into the water. He rapidly swung around to face the attacker he knew had to now be behind him. The grass continued to sway from side to side, like the arms of the biggest cheer leading squad in history. Were they mocking him or cheering for his panic induced bravery? No hordes of Chinese thieves came down on him. He made his way perhaps twenty yards along the shore, looking for footprints or any other sign of a presence. Finally he began to feel foolish walking alone in a desolate area with a pocketknife tightly clutched in his fist.

The sweat had dried off his forehead by the time he arrived at his campsite. He still felt unnerved by his experience, but he began to accept that he would not be receiving any uninvited guests that evening. Being alone could often cause paranoia.

He sat down for his evening meal of dried meat and dried fruit. No wood could be found for a fire in the area. Even if he had carried his own wood, only a fool would start a fire in this tinderbox of grasslands. Although he expected nightmares of Chinese thieves descending upon him, he slept the dreamless sleep of the exhausted that night.

There are mornings where you wake up from a peaceful sleep and stretch out lazily. The next morning John's instinct kicked him in the head, making his eyes snap open. For no good reason he gave up the warmth of his sleeping bag and quickly stood up in panic. The Tsangpo river sparkled under the brilliant morning sun. When his eyes adjusted to the shimmering light, he saw the monk-like figure by the shore. He didn't think he made any noise, yet the figure turned towards him as soon as he stood. Then he saw her eyes.

How long did they stare at each other? One second? Ten seconds? Five minutes? John had no idea. His brain registered that her eyes were the only feature that distinguished her from a man at this distance. Her age was impossible to determine, she could be twenty or fifty. The absence of hair, the dirty, loose-flowing robe that had once been white, sufficiently masked both her age and her sex. The eyes though, they told everything. Her large brown eyes spoke to him of the beauty that once was. "Look here" they said, "don't look at the rest". They also told him that they had seen a lot, more than a woman or man should have to see in a lifetime. They looked tired, alert, and frightened all at the same time. They also had a very calculating look, as if experienced in evaluating critical situations.

If it were not for those eyes he might have noticed earlier that she carried his backpack. She obviously had the same survival instinct that he possessed, which was probably what had alerted her to the fact he stood up in the first place. She hunched down and bolted to her right, seeming to disappear in the tall grass. John wasted another ten or fifteen seconds looking for his boots before realizing she must have taken them too.

He sprinted in the general direction where she was headed, on his bare, tender, city feet. He quickly lost site of her among the weaving grass, but she left a clear, trampled path in her wake. Head down he followed as fast as he could without losing the path that pointed in her direction like an arrow. The tough, sharp blades of grass began to cut at his aching feet. Ignoring the growing pain, he resolutely maintained his direction along the path. Then it ended. Damn, how could her path suddenly end? He stood up and tried to peer into the areas of grass around him, perhaps she had leapt just a few feet to cause a break in the path. He trampled around for a few precious moments before realizing that she might have backtracked. Between his bare feet and his need to follow her path, he must have been going slower than her. Perhaps she used the extra distance to buy some time to confuse the trail. For the first time he wished he had added hunting and tracking to his list of regular outdoor activities.

As he returned along the path at a slow, steady jog, this time he held his head high looking for new paths along the side of the main path. No sooner had he begun the search that he saw it, perhaps five yards from the end of the path. She indeed had run back along the path, and then jumped a few feet off to the side and continued her escape. What a smart, brave woman. The short distance between the end of the path and this new path encouraged him. She must not have been too far ahead of him or she would have backtracked further down her original path. But she had indeed bought herself precious seconds with her trick.

With one look at his bleeding feet, his will to catch her redoubled. Her new path seemed to go in a fairly straight line. If he tried carefully following her path, she would outdistance him. Time was on her side, he could not go much longer on his lacerated feet. Gambling, he sprinted headlong in the straight line of the path. He knew he would miss any more tricks she might have planned, and he would lose even more time if she suddenly made a sharp turn.

After a few breathless minutes of running at full gait John caught a glimpse of her ahead. She tried to run low, but he was near enough to see her bobbing head and she made her way through the grass. As he neared, she turned back once and opened her eyes wide with fear and surprise. He could ignore the pain in his feet, but she could not ignore the weight of his backpack.

With his lungs bursting for air John sped up to shorten the distance between them. His heart thundered in protest, and his stomach began to cramp. But the distance did close between them. When he was almost close enough to tackle her, she turned once more. Her eyes had changed, they were no longer afraid or surprised. In fact they seemed nothing at all, perhaps resigned, perhaps dead. Whoever said that the eyes were the windows to your soul must have seen a woman like this.

Before he could launch his final grab at her, she just collapsed on the ground. Without time for him to stop, he ran right over her, tripping on her body and tumbling forward. Dazed, he stood up as quickly as his shaky legs allowed. He felt sure that she had tricked him again and was well on her way once more. But as he turned around, John was stunned to see her lying motionless at his feet.

She had curled herself up into a ball, and trembled like a frightened rabbit. Up close he could see many more details of his thief. Her skin was a dark tanned brown, with the slightly wrinkled look of too much sun exposure. Her legs were bent at the knee, and were far too skinny to be considered attractive. Her emaciated arms protectively covered her head and neck. With a shock it dawned on him that she had the position of a person trying to avoid serious injury in an imminent beating. What had this woman been through?

His interest in the stolen boots all but disappeared as he slowly knelt beside her. When he gently laid his hand on her shoulder she shuddered.

"It's OK, I won't hurt you. Do you speak English?"

This time she cautiously raised her head and looked at him. His sweat-drenched face must not have conveyed the sorrow he felt for her, but he was certain that she saw no signs of anger and revenge. Perhaps he sent her the wrong message when he gently stroked her arm and shoulder again, because the fear, mixed with fury this time, entered her eyes once more. Oh, she was quick this one, John did not even see the rock in her hand until it was inches from his temple.

***

She never thought he could have run this far without his boots. Blood dripped from an ugly gash on the side of the man's head. She dropped the stone limply, studying the effect of her work. She bent cautiously to see if he was still breathing. Dizzy from exhaustion, she almost fell over him. He's a foreigner, and a man; he deserves what he got. Her bitter inner voice helped squelch the rising guilt invading her senses as blood continued to seep down the side of his head.

Like most pigs, he had tried to take her when he had caught up with her. She did not understand the words coming out in his foreign tongue, but she recognized the soft touch on her shoulder for what it was. He wanted the same thing that they all wanted from her. But she would die before letting another man take what he wanted. The bloodied stone, and the prone body at her feet proved that her conviction was more than idle words. This was the new Sherab Choezom. She might not live much longer, but she would live freely.

The pain in Sherab's stomach reminded her of why she had robbed the foreigner in the first place. She debated whether to forage for food in his backpack now or to distance herself from him. Wisdom dictated that she push her starving body a little further, away from the white enemy. Her numbed and tired mind threw one last insightful spark when she thought he might have more goods back at his campsite. With that plan in mind, she resumed her dull, animalistic stride through the grasslands.

Sherab enjoyed walking through the fields. She could shut down her thought processes, and concentrate on the path ahead of her. Always alert for signs of other humans, she felt like a lioness on the prowl. I am a proud lioness, she thought with amusement, holding her head up a little higher. A lioness without a past, only with a future. This impersonation allowed her to forget her inner torment, leaving her with nothing but physical pain. She welcomed the pain of weak, exhausted muscles, and of an empty stomach.

Halfway to the campsite she gave in to her hunger. No longer a proud lioness, the hungry scavenger dug through the stolen backpack with enthusiasm. The dried meat looked mildly revolting but she adored the sweet, dried fruit. Careful not to overstuff herself, she crunched on a small handful of nuts before reluctantly conserving the rest of the precious food. She smiled when she noticed that the man had been kind enough to include a full water gourd in his pack. She drank deeply, and appreciatively splashed the cool water on her face and shaven head. With an abundance of fast flowing water in the nearby river, she could afford to waste as much as she wanted. Feeling somewhat refreshed, she resumed her march towards the man's campsite.

The lean-to remained in place after the man's hasty departure that morning. With barely contained excitement, she slid into the man's bedroll. The comfort and warmth brought a relaxed smile to her face. Sherab knew she could not linger at the campsite for very long, for the man was sure to return as soon as he woke up. She rummaged around his small site, and gleefully poked her head into a spare food bag. She had missed it during her stealthy search while he slept.

It was time to move on, she had already stayed at the campsite too long. She walked quickly to the river to refill the drained water gourd. She stuffed the food bag into the already distended backpack, and hefted it onto her shoulder. The pack's weight threatened to crush her. She looked longingly at the bedroll, but knew she could not add it to her burden. A few weeks from now, if she lived that long, her body might have the strength to carry more of the man's belongings. But for now, she accepted the limits that her frail body forced upon her.

The man's eyes were deceptive. She knew what he wanted when he touched her, but his eyes tried to trick her. It took a while for her mind to sort out exactly what feelings those eyes induced in her. His soft brown eyes seemed to want to help her, to take care of her. She shook her head in disgust at her weakness. Not since she lost her parents had anyone cared for her. She quickly shut out those memories, trying in vain to protect herself from the unwelcome pain. No one would ever care for her, especially not men. As long as she remembered that, she would be free.

With considerable effort she cleared her mind once more, and continued her march into the late afternoon. Her body trembled with exhaustion from the added weight of the backpack. She knew she should walk until dusk, but as usual, she lacked the strength to do what needed to be done. She despised her weakness. Sherab could not be sure who she hated more, herself or the rest of the world. She would welcome death like a lover when it came, for it would kiss away her misery.

She sat down heavily, choosing her resting place for the night. While she caught her breath, her eyes naturally gazed towards the majestic Himalayas. Ever since she left Lhasa several days ago, the mountains always seemed less than a day's walk away. Her objective lay halfway between her current position and the Himalayan foothills. The odds that they would let her get that far were terribly slim. Yet Sherab knew that she herself had no choice but to follow her destined path. She would fight as hard as she could to make it. But fate had already chosen the outcome, and Sherab had to wait to witness its fickle decision.

The early evening breeze blew colder, reminding her of how thin a robe she wore. She pushed away images of the man's abandoned bedroll, and searched through his backpack for some clothing. A warm flannel shirt promised to help her cope with the night's plummeting temperature. The shirt could not make her warm, but it would reduce the previous night's numbing cold. The man's scent permeated her senses as she wrapped herself into the large shirt.

The shirt hung down almost to her knees, and the sleeves flapped loosely over her hidden hands. The smell continued to assault her mind, almost making her throw the shirt away. Even his deceptive smell tried to trick her, she thought. She stomped her foot in rage, and began taking the shirt off. Sherab stopped herself with the shirt half off her right arm. Succumbing to the comforting smell was a sign of weakness. But not being able to deal with it, and throwing away the shirt's promised warmth was even weaker, and stupider. With an impatient tug she rewrapped the big shirt around her.

Sherab recognized her mounting anxiety and took a deep breath. Until she learned to control her anger, she knew she would remain in this most unpleasant realm. She wished she could consult with a monk to determine her place in the six Buddhist realms. Given the amount of suffering she continued to endure, she felt she had to be in either the hellish realm of the hungry ghost realm. The former sounded more appropriate for how she felt, given its emphasis on pain. The latter, characterized by constant deprivation of food and drink, was probably more accurate.

"Om Mani Padme Hum." Her own voice startled her briefly, after the prolonged silence of solitude. With practiced ease she cleared her mind, and concentrated on reciting her favorite mantra. She rested her left hand on her lap, and laid her right hand on top of the left, with both thumbs touching. Her lips moved automatically and rhythmically to the sound of the mantra, while her mind explored its meaning. 'Om' symbolized the contrast between her own impure being and that of the exalted Buddha. 'Mani', or 'jewel', represented her intention to become enlightened, which would lead her to the higher realms. 'Padme', or 'lotus', symbolized the wisdom required to carry out her intentions. 'Hum' spoke of the indivisibility of wisdom and intent, both were required to reach towards nirvana.

Gradually the tension eased out of Sherab's troubled mind. She welcomed the inner peace the mantra never failed to bring her. With a soft smile she settled down on the cold bare earth. Hugging the oversized shirt for warmth, she fell asleep dreaming of the higher realms.

# Chapter 2

John never knew that one could dream when knocked unconscious. He dreamt of her eyes. In the darkness surrounding him, her eyes shone like twin beacons of light. She held him prisoner, and he could do nothing but follow the eyes through the darkness. He smiled when they were at peace, cowered when they were angry, and cried when they were sad. But he always followed, sometimes stumbling on unseen obstacles, but never stopping. They drew him towards her with the unrelenting force of a hurricane wind.

The early morning sun had nearly completed drying the dew off his clothes when he awoke. He tried to find some part of his body that did not ache, but failed. His face stung with what must have been a dreadful sunburn. He had begun his little adventure mid-morning on the previous day. That meant he had lain beneath the sun all afternoon, at a considerably high altitude. He had no doubt that his face would peel. The throbbing in his head seemed to take attention away from his feet, which felt like they were slowly roasting over hot coals. As he sat up to examine his feet, the increased pain in his head almost made him vomit. Determined not to lie back down, he sat there trying to figure out if he was going to die, throw up, or just remain in this hell of pain.

John's gaze turned absently to his feet. What must have been a dense criss-cross of small cuts managed to merge themselves together to form one large, raw wound on each foot. The underside of the feet thankfully did not seem as bad as the tops. The skin was not only tougher, but the tops of the feet had been the ones whipping through the tall grass as he ran.

His hand gingerly touched the rock's point of impact on his temple. A blinding flash of pain rewarded his effort, along with some caked blood on his fingers. He would have to wash the wound soon, or risk infection. The local hospital would certainly sew in some stitches if he were home. Somehow clean, white hospital sheets sounded so comforting at the moment. John felt lucky that the thief looked half starved, otherwise he might never have woken up.

The hunger pains in his stomach finally got his attention after thinking of the half starved rock lady. He had to go back to his campsite to eat, if she had left him any food. Most of his supplies were gone with the backpack, but he did have some food laid out in a separate bag for yesterday's meals. Hopefully she had been nervous and rushed enough when she stole the backpack to overlook the food bag. His worries intensified when he remembered that she had not been rushed enough to overlook his boots.

Ignoring the pain in his head that increased with every movement, he took off his shirt. With the help of his teeth John tore it in half, and began to protectively wrap his feet. The pain was intense, and some of the deeper wounds re-opened, staining his shirt with fresh blood. How long he sat there after bandaging his feet, John could not tell. He knew that the thought of standing, much less walking, frightened and discouraged him.

With a grunt of pain he stood, somewhat wobbly at first. For a moment it was not clear if his legs would hold him or if they would drop him back down on his bottom.

"One step at a time," he murmured to himself, as he began his old-man shuffle back down the path. Despite the discomfort he managed a smile when he thought of his assailant. She did not quite fit the image he had of the roving bands of Chinese thieves in these areas.

John wondered what his ex-wife would think of his situation at the moment. She had always resented the way he selfishly clung to his youth, while putting her in second place. He had vehemently denied her accusations back then. But over time, as women entered and left his life, he began to understand what she had meant those many years ago. She would probably laugh if she saw him now. Not out of malice, but more because of how predictable his lifestyle had become. Some of her resentment came from being left alone too often, but some of it came from watching him take unnecessary risks. Eighteen months later, she changed the locks on their door while he was gone on a canoe trip.

An hour went by as he slowly worked his way through the path. Yesterday's chase could not have lasted more than thirty minutes. With his current walking speed, he did not know if he had another hour to his campsite or another day. Gradually his feet grew numb to the pain, and the throbbing in his head seemed to subside. John's thoughts were empty, he simply followed the trail and tried to ignore his various aches and pain. He lost track of time, and enjoyed the unexpected surprise of stumbling into his campsite without warning. The joy did not last long.

She cleaned me out, he thought. The lean-to over his head, the bedroll under him, and a few cooking utensils were all she left behind. Even his spare shirt had vanished with the missing backpack. His water gourd, boots, knife, and food bag: all gone. His water supply would not run out because of the potable river water. Food would be a problem. He could head back to his guide, but that meant traveling away from the river. He might last three days without food, but not without water.

The thought of water awakened the latest lament of his body, his mouth felt full of sand it was so dry. John struggled with the idea of walking to the river for a drink and a bath, versus the bliss of curling up under the shade of his lean-to. His feet made the decision, as he collapsed to his knees and rolled himself under the lean-to. Sleep came to him without a struggle.

He did not know how long he had walked, or how long he slept. The stars shone on him when he awoke. Thirst had taken first place in his list of problems. He needed to go to the river urgently, but dared not try to get there in the dark. In his present state of mind he could so easily become disoriented and wander off in the wrong direction. He felt feverish, and for the first time began to fear for his life. Until now John had known he would find his way out of this predicament with some discomfort, and perhaps a bruised ego. But as he lay under the Tibetan night sky, shivering in the cold, sweating with a combination of shock and fever, he realized he might not get out alive. He drifted back into a fitful sleep, filled with dreams of angry, mocking eyes.

The pre-dawn gray sky brought no soothing warmth when John awoke the next morning. His arms and legs were stiff with cold as he clumsily made his way out of the lean-to. The first order of business was to get to the river, there was no debate this time. The throbbing in his head had diminished to a dull, but persistent, headache. His feet still hurt tremendously, but he thought they screamed a little less loudly than the day before.

By the time he knelt on the shore, the sun had risen and his limbs had loosened up. John drank slowly, remembering that filling up such an empty stomach would probably cause violent retching. When he dunked his head into the cold river, feeling a sharp sting on his wounded temple, all thoughts of death left him. The coolness eased the pain of his burned face, and made him smile with contentment. Next came off the rags, to let the cool water work its magic on his abused feet. After the initial shock and sting subsided, the cold water indeed numbed his feet. After a moment he gently washed most of the blood off them, and observed the interesting roadwork of cuts. Fortunately most cuts were quite shallow, and closing up nicely.

The cold water did not allow John to completely immerse himself. He contented himself with lying back on the shore to let his feet dry. His refreshed mind began to analyze the situation, so that he could begin to find a way out of this mess. His day and a half without water convinced him that he had to stay near the river. Tibet was an isolated area, but if there were any settlements nearby, they would also logically be near the river.

He decided to head west along the Tsangpo, towards the distant mountains. From his dim recollection of a few Tibet maps, there were cities east of Lhasa along the river. Whether they were a day's march or a week's march away made no difference to him. Heading west he knew there were cities, heading east he knew nothing. The west at least held some hope, no matter how small.

His mind made up, John started back to the campsite. He shoved the fork and spoon into his pocket, thinking he may have a use for them later. The bedroll he decided to bring to keep warm at night. He debated whether or not to carry the lean-to. It would be very awkward to carry without a backpack to attach it to, especially in his weakened state. However it would provide shelter from wind, sun, and rain. In the end he decided he would not be able to carry it very far before being forced to abandon it in exhaustion. The rest of the cooking gear he also left behind. Without food, the cooking gear had little value. Armed with his fork, spoon, and bedroll, John began his western journey along the southern shore of the Tsangpo river.

With frequent stops to rest, he managed to walk most of that day. As the sun began to set, hunger induced dizzy spells forced him to stop for the night. He removed the bandages from his feet and washed them again. Only the wounds along the creases of the feet remained opened. Each step he took prevented these from closing up. Despite the headache that continued to assault him, and despite the ever-increasing hunger pains, he curled up in his bedroll and was fast asleep.

The next morning found John in the worst condition yet. The hunger was incapacitating, he had been without food for almost seventy-two hours. The pounding in his head also increased its tempo, and seemed to inflate his head with each beat. He became certain that the pressure would explode his brain matter all over the shore at any moment. John put his hand to his temple, and gasped with shock when it felt wet and sticky. With a sinking feeling, he thought he was bleeding again. With horror he looked at his hand and saw it covered with a yellow-green slime. No, he was not bleeding, but infection had set into his skull.

In a panic he crawled to the water and began washing his head. The cool water revived him somewhat and he managed to bandage his feet and get up once more. He did not march west, he stumbled and shuffled west. John lost all track of time, his mind was a numb blank as he made his way along the shore. When he collapsed for the final time, the sun still hung high in the sky. He could not be sure if he walked until late morning or early afternoon. He did not partake in his ritual of washing his feet. John just lay there, feverish and in pain, until he fell asleep moments later.

He woke up under a dark sky. John crawled to the water to quench his thirst, and almost passed out with his head in the water. He dragged himself away, feeling nauseous from the dizzying spins he experienced. He could not make it to his bedroll, just out of reach of his outstretched arm. He fell asleep, or passed out is probably more precise, lying on his stomach, with the water lapping at his feet and his hand less than a yard from the bedroll.

\*\*\*

Life is suffering, Sherab thought. She had no problem remembering Buddha's first Noble Truth, for it applied very well to her experiences. But she often had trouble with the second Noble Truth, identifying the cause of suffering. The wonders of freedom had left her ever since the encounter with the white man. She no longer enjoyed her walks through the open grasslands. During the day she often stopped to meditate, trying desperately to stifle the anxiety that grew within her.

On this second night, after reciting her mantra countless times, Sherab thought she knew the cause of her present suffering. In her anger, she had made the white man suffer. Contrary to all Buddha's teachings, she had harmed another. She could not even try to use self-defense as an argument. The man had not yet done anything to harm her, but she struck him down. In all likelihood, he would have harmed her. But without proof, the guilt rested on her shoulders. Now she would suffer until his suffering ended. It would take days for his wounds to heal. Plus, she had left him without food.

What if he died? Sherab's eyes snapped open in terror at the thought. How many more lifetimes of misery would she endure for killing this man who had chased her after she robbed him of his only food? She began to tremble then, fearing for him, and for herself. She had to go back and help him, or at least ensure his survival. But after having robbed and assaulted him, Sherab had a good idea of the kind of reception she would get from him.

She would have to use stealth then. She would retrace her steps, and then try to track him down without being detected. She had done it once before, but then the man had not been on his guard. No doubt he would now be distrustful of his environment, and watchful for any new intruders. Of course she could not replace the food she had eaten. But if she did get near him, she could leave his backpack somewhere that he was sure not to miss. And afterwards, leave as fast as she could in case he decided to track her down.

Fear took second place to the overwhelming peace of mind that came from knowing how to partially right the wrongs she had done. She settled down more comfortably in the man's shirt now, aware that she would have to return it along with the backpack. Sleep came to her easily, despite the chilly evening breeze that blew over her, and up under her robe.

The next day Sherab marched long and hard back towards the campsite. Already she felt the effects of decent nutrition and hard exercise. Her legs carried her further and with less protest every day. Her back still ached from the backpack's weight, but even that pain seemed to subside over time.

On the morning of the second day she had covered the distance that had taken her a full two days previously. She stumbled unexpectedly into the campsite, and immediately crouched down into the tall grass. She waited several minutes for any sign that the man might be about. The area remained deserted, she could sense the emptiness around her. Cautiously, she stood and made her way into the center of the campsite.

The man had left behind the heavy lean-to, but had brought his bedroll with him. The missing bedroll filled her with hope. The man could not be seriously injured if he had been able to come here to get his bedroll. She considered leaving now, and accepting this piece of evidence that he would survive. His lack of food prompted Sherab to go on. She would never know the outcome of her attack until she restored his belongings to him.

Sherab had the man's water gourd, which meant he was forced to stay close to the river. She walked to the water, and began examining the sandy shore. A jumbled set of prints seemed to lead in all directions. She walked eastward for perhaps twenty yards, but could not find a visible trail leading in that direction. Traveling westward, Sherab continued to make out an occasional footprint, or disturbance in the sand. Although large stretches of shore lacked any signs of trespassing, the occasional clue led her to believe she was on the right path.

Her heart nearly stopped when she found him the next morning. The frigid water lapped at his bloodied, bandaged feet. His naked back took on a sickly white pallor, like the underside a dead fish out of water. The ugly gash on his head, the gash she had caused, oozed pus over the encrusted blood smears. His utter stillness projected an image of rotting corpses along a war torn beach.

Holding her breath in tormented awe, Sherab slowly walked around the fallen man. As she drew near his turned face, his closed eyes mesmerized her. She had closed his eyes, bloodied his feet, and traumatized his head. Her hands trembled as the broken body held her guilt-stricken gaze with unrelenting cries of outrage. Sherab slowly sank to her knees, wetting them on the shore's damp sand. She held a quivering finger near his mouth and nose, hoping to feel a faint breath. Nothing.

Her hands recoiled at the touch of his cold, rubbery flesh when she bent to turn him over. Gritting her teeth to fight off the revulsion, she pulled on his shoulder until she rolled him onto his back. A low groan escaped his lips, causing her a frightened intake of breath. She quickly put an ear to his chest, and heard his slow, but steady heartbeat. Suddenly she no longer faced a corpse, but rather a life to save.

Sherab stood behind his head, put her hands under his arms, and began to drag him away from the wet sand. She hastily stripped off his shirt from her body, sat him up awkwardly, and managed to dress him with the shirt. She then took off the wet rags from his feet. The wet, wrinkled skin underneath looked like it belonged to an old man. She dried his feet as best as she could with her robe, and then retrieved his socks and boots from the backpack. How absurd that she had kept his boots, she thought. Perhaps part of her knew she would have to come back. Sherab smiled, thinking that some inner part of her might know the path to enlightenment after all.

He really needed a warm fire, but she had no suitable fuel to burn. She briefly considered lending him her only robe, but realized that she could not last long in this temperature without any clothes. With great difficulty, she managed to get his uncooperative body into the bedroll. Fortunately it had enough space for her to crawl in as well. She lied on top of him, transferring as much of her body heat as she could. At first his cold body seemed like it would win the battle, but eventually her body produced enough heat to warm them both.

She studied his face carefully. He had handsome features, for a white man. The thought made her suddenly feel very uncomfortable lying on top of him. She forced her mind to concentrate, and observe him some more. His lips continued to have a bluish hue, despite the warmth seeping into him. Their flaking dryness alarmed her more than their color. She would have to make him drink to overcome his extreme dehydration.

She turned his head slightly and examined the wound more closely. The ugly gash had not closed itself yet. The cut would leave a permanent scar, and should have been stitched days ago. The best she could do for his head is keep the wound clean, and apply a soothing poultice to prevent further infection.

Sherab pressed the palm of her hand on the man's forehead. In contrast to his cold limbs, his head felt too hot. He would have to fight off the fever by himself, for she could do nothing but keep him warm. She let her head rest on his chest, and remained in this lover's embrace until his body heat returned to normal.

Sherab reluctantly climbed out of the warm bedroll to attend his wound. She took the rags that had wrapped his feet, and washed them in the river. His eyes remained shut when she gingerly cleaned the wound, but they flinched in unconscious pain. An anguished moan escaped his lips as she insistently cleaned the entire length of the gash with the rags. Fresh blood began to seep out of the open wound. She gathered a few large leaves from the nearby vegetation, and applied them to the wound. She wrapped his head loosely with the wet rag, to keep the makeshift poultice in place.

Finally, she had to get him to drink. She brought him into a sitting position, and had him lean back on her. She poured some water on his face, letting it run over his dry lips. He opened his mouth, letting some of the cool water splash onto his tongue. She brought the gourd to his lips, and tilted it just enough to let a small amount of water trickle out. At first he managed a few small swallows, but she soon had him coughing and sputtering with too much water in his mouth. She started over, more slowly this time, until he drank a few mouthfuls of precious water.

The fields around her held plenty of edible grains. Sherab decided to prepare a soupy gruel that the man might be able to swallow. She crushed barley grains inside his metal cooking pot, and added small amounts of river water. Sitting him up again, she tried feeding him a small spoonful of the gruel. He began to gag and cough when she pushed the food in towards his throat. She quickly poured some water into his mouth. This caused him more choking, but at least it cleared away the food particles from his irritated throat. It was no use, she could not feed him until he regained consciousness.

She spent the rest of the day alternating between making him drink, warming his bed, and preparing grains for herself. She had decided to stop eating his dwindling food supply, and to begin surviving off the land. Before nightfall, she cleaned his wound and changed the poultice. With some apprehension, she slid into his bedroll to sleep for the night.

# Chapter 3

John didn't know how many days he lay on that shore, thrashing with fever and chills. His days and nights were filled with dreams of the thief with the haunting eyes. The eyes were never angry. They often hovered near his face, seeming to soothe him just with their gaze. He dreamt that he ate a feast, again with the eyes just out of his reach. The eyes whispered to him, but he could not understand what they were telling him.

The first thing he noticed when he regained consciousness was that the throbbing in his head has lessened once again. John felt a slight pressure around his head. When he reached up with his hand, he found some sort of cloth had been wrapped around his head. Then he noticed that his hand was sticking out of a sleeve, he was wearing his spare shirt! He quickly tried to sit, but only managed to prop himself up on his elbows. He could not see her, but she had obviously returned. Nearby a small pot, one of his camping pots, he noticed, held some kind of liquid. It reminded him of chicken soup, and he hungrily reached for it. He was half way to sitting up before the dizziness overcame him, and he lay back down abruptly. John slipped into an unconscious sleep once more.

Nighttime. He looked side to side, but did not try to get up. He saw only shadows, no movement. He felt starved. Somehow she had kept him alive, he thought. Hell, more than kept alive, she was nursing him back to health. "But why?" he wondered. If she thought John was a rich foreigner, perhaps her and her band of thieves were planning to get a ransom for him. These disturbing thoughts could not prevent him from drifting off to sleep again.

The sun shone brightly in his eyes when he awoke the next morning. Perhaps it was the sun that woke him, or perhaps it was the small metallic clinking noise he heard. John turned his head towards the sound and saw her for the first time since she had knocked him out with a rock. Alarmingly, she once again had a rock in her hand. But this time she used it to grind some kind of grain inside the cooking pot. Still unaware of being watched, she added more grains and continued her rotating, grinding motion with the rock.

He took advantage of his undetected awakening to study her further. He felt foolish for thinking she wanted him for ransom. She barely looked like she could keep herself alive, much less hang out with a gang of thieves and kidnap foreigners. Thankfully her eyes were lowered towards her work in progress, otherwise he might get lost in them once more and fail to see the rest of her.

Her head was not bald as he previously thought, in fact there was a short crop of dark hair growing. The scalp also seemed dark, as if she had been bald until recently. Above her left ear, a patch of ugly white scar tissue prevented hair from growing. Perhaps she had suffered a serious accident which caused a head injury, he hoped. At the moment, he preferred not to think of the way she cowered at his feet when he had stood over her an eternity ago.

As she bent over the pot, John guiltily looked down the top of her robe. She had removed his old shirt from his feet, and managed to cover herself with some form of undershirt. He concluded this was for warmth, and not modesty. Still, with a trickle of sweat running down the length of her neck, and into his old shirt, he could not help thinking about her as a woman. Fortunately he was weak enough that there was no visible physical response to his lecherous mind.

Her bony arms continued to pound the grain with a force that seemed unnatural for such thin muscles. He could see her small calf muscles working as well as she squatted in front of the cooking pot. She held the rock with both hands, although her small finger on her right hand stuck out at an odd angle, hooked like a talon. If her other fingers had been similarly malformed he might have guessed that she suffered from some form of arthritis. But the broken finger formed one more piece of the ugly puzzle that was her life.

"Good morning," John croaked from his dry voice box.

She let out a startled gasp, dropped the rock, and spilled her pot of grains. She fell back from her squatting position into a clumsy sitting position with legs spread out. He caught a glimpse of where he should not have, before she recovered, got on her knees and quickly picked up her rock. This time the rock's target was not the pot of grains, she was threatening John once again.

"Please, no!" he said as his outstretched arms prepared to fend off any missiles she might throw his way. It only took her a moment to calm down and see how weak he was. She waved her hand at him and spoke in a rapid singsong oriental voice. John had no idea what she said, or even in which language she spoke. In typical western arrogance he had entered this country without understanding a word of its language.

"I don't understand," he said, shrugging his shoulders in what he hoped was an international gesture of ignorance. She ignored him then and began picking up what crushed grain she could salvage.

This woman had saved his life. Even though she originally caused his problems, he still felt indebted that she returned to care for him.

"Thank you," he said. She looked up at the sound of his voice, to see him pat his heart and extend his hand to her. He felt a little foolish, in some ways it looked like he was saying "I love you". John hoped she understood that he felt gratitude and that he knew that he was alive only because of her. She studied him without expression for a moment, before returning to her grains. But not before he caught a small light in her eyes.

When she had ground a sufficient amount of grain, she added river water to the pot. This time she used her fingers to stir it up into a coarse dough-like substance. She approached him with the pot, offering an evening meal.

"Tsampa" she said, with a small smile on her lips. Her head bobbed side to side, with the body language that suggested what she had was only an approximation of tsampa. He happily understood her, for tsampa was a staple food of the Tibetan people. It was a kind of dough made with roasted barley flour mixed with tea and yak butter. He was not familiar enough with grains to know if she had crushed barley or not, but the river water in place of tea, and the absence of butter, made this dish a far cry from tsampa. John could not believe it, she had gone from thievery, to assault, and now she cracked a joke! He could not help but smile, because of the humor and because they had achieved some form of communication.

"Tsampa!" he replied, nodding his head and smiling. Rather than accepting the pot, he reached into his pocket and pulled out the spoon he had rescued from the campsite. After dropping it into the pot, John gently pushed the pot back to her. Her eyes struck him then. She not so much stared at him, but stared into him. At first he did not know if he had violated some custom by giving her a chance to eat before him. After a moment she lowered her eyes, perhaps conscious of how naked he felt under her gaze.

"Thu-chi che" she said softly. John did not need to understand Tibetan to understand her meaning, the tone said thank you. She briefly studied the spoon before awkwardly scooping up some pseudo-tsampa and eating it. She ate perhaps one quarter of the mixture before passing him the pot. Ignoring his ravenous hunger, John carefully ate the same amount before passing it back to her. This time she was the one to refuse the pot and gently push it back to him. He gave in to his hunger and nearly finished the entire pot before lamely trying to offer her the last few spoonfuls. She declined with a firm shake of her head. Only a strong act of will stopped him from licking every last grain out of the pot.

John lied back down, and patted his stomach with a satisfied look for this morning's cook. It seemed pointless for her to know how unsatisfied he was, John felt he could have eaten ten more pots of those grains. She must have sensed his hunger, because she prepared an early lunch, and took the time to prepare much more grain than the breakfast had.

After lunch, she brought John his backpack, and with downcast eyes she knelt before him. He tried to understand what she meant by this gesture. Did she regret having stolen from him? Had she decided that she needed him to survive and therefore restored his goods? The latter seemed hard to believe, by now she knew his lack of survival skills in her country. Perhaps she wasn't a thief after all, but simply a hungry, desperate woman.

"It's OK," he told her, "I forgive you." Again he had to rely on the tone of voice and body language to convey what he meant. As he uttered the words, John gently placed his hands on both her shoulders, trying to comfort her. He touched her without thinking of the consequences of the last time he had touched her like this. No stone came ripping at his temple this time. Instead she looked up at him with disappointment and sadness in her eyes. As the tears began to flow she lay down on the grass before him, hiked up her robe and spread her quivering legs invitingly.

Seeing her spread-eagled in front of him stunned John for several seconds before he understood what she was thinking. God, did she think I was such an ass, he thought? Did she think he expected sex as a payment for forgiving her thievery?

"No!" he shouted, perhaps too harshly. A frightened, wary look came into her eyes as she closed her legs and backed away a little bit. "No need for that," he said more softly this time, trying to relax the tenseness in his facial expression. He walked up to her, knelt, and pulled her robe back over her legs. He needed to make her understand that touch did not mean sex. He held her shoulders once more, with his hands moving slightly up and down her arms as he simply gazed into her eyes. Unable to help himself, John knelt closer to her and brought her into a hug. Great racking sobs engulfed her then, she lay like a child in his arms, soaking his shirt with her tears.

This seemed to go on for perhaps twenty minutes before she cried herself out. At one point John had to shift his weight, his legs were cramping from being in a kneeling position. Eventually he sat, and she leaned against him to cry.

When she recovered she slowly backed away, never lifting her eyes to meet his. John felt so frustrated at their inability to communicate. Who was she? Where was she headed? What had happened to her to get her into this poor physical and emotional state? He had so many questions to ask this strange, beautiful woman. He was startled to realize he now thought of her as a beautiful woman. Her current physical appearance was anything but beautiful. John thought her eyes helped him see her as she was before her body had been wasted away.

During the afternoon he felt well enough to get up and walk a little. When she left to gather their evening grain, John followed her and tried to assist. She gave him that penetrating look again when she realized he came to help. He began to wonder if help was an unaccustomed event in her life. She showed him how to strip the grain from the stalk. Before long he got the hang of it, but at about half speed of what she gathered. He also needed to take a few breaks, his bout with fever and infection had left him severely weakened. After perhaps thirty minutes of gathering, she uttered a few words in her language and headed back to their campsite. John assumed she meant they had gathered enough for supper. Along the way she stopped to pick up a few more plants. He had not seen her prepare these before, and thought they might enjoy a bit more flavor in tonight's menu.

While she prepared the supper grains John took out some of the dry salted meat he carried in his backpack. She gratefully accepted some and put down her grinding stone. They chewed in silence for a while, occasionally stealing a glance at each other. He wondered if she felt the same frustration at not being able to speak to him. She resumed her grinding, and soon served up another pot of grain mixture.

After supper she came to him and gently removed the bandage around his head. He reached up with his hand and found it had at least stopped leaking pus. She gathered the plants he had presumed were herbs for their dinner, and prepared a kind of poultice, which she then applied to his head. John let her work on him as she saw fit, she had the confidence of someone with experience in treating wounds. She carefully wrapped his head once again, tucking the ends in on the uninjured side of his head.

"My name is John Pearson," he told her. She studied his face, trying to grasp his meaning. He felt like he was in an old Tarzan movie, "Me Tarzan, you Jane".

He patted his chest with both hands, "John Pearson" he repeated.

Her eyes lit up, she understood. "Ja Peywsan" she repeated.

He smiled, and discarded the last name. "John" he repeated slowly, patting his chest again. This time she managed to pronounce it reasonably well. He then moved his hands to her, palms held upwards.

"Who are you?" he asked.

"Sherab Choezom," she said, patting her chest. "Sherab", she repeated.

That was pretty easy. "Sherab," he repeated. They now knew each other on a first name basis, he thought with a smile. Two weeks ago he could never have imagined spending an evening with someone called Sherab.

The setting sun brought on the cool night air. John felt a sudden discomfort as he began to wonder what the sleeping arrangements were. The falling temperature was too harsh for him to sleep without his bedroll, yet how could he let this thin robed figure sleep without covers? Surprisingly, she took charge of the situation by getting the bedroll herself. He watched her quizzically, wondering what social graces demanded in this situation. She spread the bedroll near his side and motioned him to lie down. Now he was the one that felt like a child. He meekly went over and lay down as she indicated. Without hesitation she curled up against his back and threw the rest of the bedroll over them.

John's entire body stiffened with shock and embarrassment. How could she sleep with him so easily? She felt his rigid body, and tentatively brought her hand on his shoulder, mimicking the times he had touched her. After a moment he began to relax. John supposed that living in harsh conditions had led her to sleep with others quite frequently. The need for mutual warmth against the cold nights quickly did away with the social implications of sleeping together. His first active day since the fever struck had exhausted him. He soon fell into a deep and untroubled sleep.

They repeated this restful pattern another day as his strength returned. On the following day he decided to begin the trek back to his guide. John and Mr. Yu had agreed to meet ten to twelve days after separating. Assuming that he had been unconscious with fever for about two days, then John had left the guide thirteen days ago now. How long would the guide wait for him? Since Yu risked punishment for letting John go alone, John thought the guide would patiently wait for him, and perhaps start walking in the direction he had left.

Other than getting him back home, the guide also offered John the chance to help his new friend. Yu represented the closest thing to the authorities that John had encountered. If Yu could not help Sherab, at least he would know where to bring her for help. At a minimum, they must speak the same language, so Yu and John both could put their minds to helping her out. That she needed help, John had no doubt. Someone had mistreated her, and that someone was going to pay.

With the return of his backpack, John and Sherab now had the resources to travel inland. The easiest way to explain to her that it was time to leave was to simply start packing up. It did not take her long to catch on, and she helped John pack up the few remaining items, and attach the bedroll to the backpack.

The unaccustomed load on his back left John momentarily dizzy, this would be a short hiking day. He headed inland towards his guide's location. It was shorter to go directly to the guide rather than picking up his lean-to at the old campsite. For the few remaining days he had left in this primitive wilderness, John could do without the lean-to. His desire to be in a warm, soft bed brought urgency to his plans.

After a few steps he looked back to ensure that Sherab remained in step with him. He saw a very anxious woman looking at him, she had not moved from the campsite. John had feared Sherab might not know if she should follow. Rather than trying to explain it to her, he deliberately started walking away.

"Come," he said, beckoning her with his hands, "John will help".

A visible relief swept over her face as she quickly jogged up to him. The poor thing had no way of knowing how he would react now that he was healed. It really was all her fault, he thought with a smile. She had stolen from him, and then struck him with the rock. But he saw the tenderness in her when she nursed him back to health. He knew she had robbed him out of desperation, not from a lack of morals.

John smiled at her, and continued to walk. A firm hand on his shoulder stopped him. Sherab shook her head when he turned around, and pointed to the Himalayas. His confused stare made her take his arm and start walking towards the mountains. If he had any doubts before, they all but disappeared when she forcibly dragged him. He could not understand why she wanted to go to the mountains, but this Canadian had endured quite enough camping.

"No!" John exclaimed, planting his feet in the ground. She stumbled after his sleeve slipped out of her grasp. She began to speak excitedly to him in her language, all the while pointing to the forbidding mountain range. John had no desire to climb Mount Everest before he came to this country, and he certainly had no interest now.

"No!" John repeated emphatically, and took a few steps backwards. He stopped shaking his head when he felt a headache returning. Even as she kept jabbering at him in her foreign tongue, John turned around and resolutely marched in the direction of his guide. The pitch of her voice briefly rose before she gave up. The rustling of the grass underneath his boots only deepened the silence of her abruptly cut off voice.

John stopped again a moment later. The need for her to come with him over-powered his senses. Sometimes there are feelings he could not explain or ignore. This woman had to come with him to Mr. Yu. He turned again and watched her agonized confusion. She wanted the mountains, but she also wanted the safety of traveling in twos.

He gave her his most confident look and told her: "Come with me, I will help you." One hand lay over his heart and the other hand waved her towards him. She seemed to weigh her alternatives carefully before hesitantly coming towards him.

Sherab seemed emotionally exhausted as she drew up next to him. John put his hand on her shoulder once more, leaned down and put his face just inches away for hers.

"It's OK," he said to her, almost in a confidential whisper, "John will help you".

She nodded briefly, understanding that he meant well. With a last lingering look at the mountains, she headed off in the direction towards the guide.

John calculated that they had a healthy two and a half day march to the guide's location, given that they were bypassing the original campsite. Add to that another half to full day for the fact they were anything but healthy. On the other hand, with some luck Yu was already heading their way.

They traveled most of that day, with plenty of rests. That night John had Sherab lie down on the bedroll first, and took the pleasure of holding her from behind as he went to sleep. It had been a long time since he had held a woman like this. They still had a platonic relationship, but they lay there with the comfort that only years of marriage can usually bring. He smiled contently as he felt Sherab back up and press herself into him. For the first time she fell asleep before him. John felt warmth inside him as she slept soundly in his arms. If he could, John would have stayed awake a long time to enjoy the feeling. But by next morning, the short-lived moment seemed more like a dream.

# Chapter 4

Sherab did not understand this strange man. She had caused him so much harm, yet he treated her like a queen. When she had returned his backpack, she was sure he had asked for compensation. Despite her vow to remain free, she had decided to pay for her crime, in hopes of absolving herself of the suffering she had caused. But she remembered well how his eyes had turned soft again, penetrating her defenses with ease. Sherab still felt somewhat ashamed of the way she had cried in front of him. She worked hard to hide her weakness, but this man, this foreigner, somehow reached deeply into her. She felt exposed in front of him, and allowed herself the luxury of comfort while she cried in his arms.

On this second day since they had left the shore where she found John, they continued marching with hardly any breaks. She suppressed a small smile at the thought of his silly sounding name. John pushed hard, making them walk until hunger or fatigue forced them to stop. Her life seemed to have been turned upside down since she met this man. Not only did she fail to understand him, but also she no longer understood herself either. She had allowed him to lead her in the opposite direction of where she had to go. Why? She shook her head in bewilderment.

Against all logic, she trusted John. Perhaps she was too tired of surviving on her own. Allowing him to lead gave her a mental rest she desperately needed. Also, John seemed to have confidence in his decision. He had a purpose in mind, and kept urging her to come with him. Surely he knew she was in some kind of trouble, so he might have a way to protect her with his foreign contacts. In fact she was quite surprised to have found a foreigner traveling alone. It was disconcerting to find evidence of changes since she had last been free. What else had happened while the world moved on without her?

What were John's motives? He could have forced himself on her at any point in the last few days. That eliminated the possibility that he was bringing her somewhere to take advantage of her. If he had enough money to travel all the way out here, then he was probably a rich foreigner. It was unlikely that he wanted the token reward he would get for turning her in to the authorities. She hated mysteries, and she hated having to put her life in this man's care. She had vowed to remain free just a week ago, and already she had become dependent on another. Every time she considered simply leaving him, he would smile at her with twinkling eyes, or help her prepare the barley grains, or offer her food, or find her a comfortable place to sit for their meal. She felt humiliated by her weakness, but still she could not leave him.

That night John seemed exhausted as he put down the bedroll and flopped noisily onto it. Fortunately he was not looking in her direction as she failed to suppress her wide grin. In so many ways he reminded her of a child. After having had a tiring day, he simply fell into his bed, ready to enter his dream world. She remembered his shyness the first night that he had been awake when they shared the bedroll. She was sure she would lose control and burst out laughing. His body had become rigid like a statue, and yet he did not turn to look at her or speak a single word. She would probably have embarrassed him so much if she had let her laughter loose on him. To ease his tension, and take her mind off the comedy in front of her, she had stroked his arm and shoulder. She finally had been able to release some of her laughter when, like a child, he had swiftly fallen asleep under her soothing touch.

Before John could fall asleep this night, Sherab knelt in front of him and gently pushed him backwards. She had enjoyed being in his arms last night, and wanted the same feeling tonight. The look on his face told her that he did not mind at all. That boyish grin returned to his face as he lifted his arm in anticipation of holding her next to him. This felt like her spot now: his arm draped around her, and his body pressing against her back. As she drifted into a deep sleep, she wondered if John enjoyed it as much as she did.

On their third day out, a Chinese man called out to them. He took them by surprise. They were dazed in a mid afternoon fatigue, heads hanging down, when they heard him. Sherab could instantly recognize the look of self-important authority that the man carried with him. She had seen these kinds of men before, and seen what they were capable of doing in the name of the law.

Before she could react, John happily shouted a greeting back to the man. Sherab froze in terror as the man jogged towards them, one arm raised in a friendly salute to John. Unwanted memories flooded her terrified mind like a ruptured dam.

John turned to her with bright eyes and a relieved smile on his face. His expression became clouded with uneasy inquisitiveness as soon as he noticed Sherab's panic stricken face. Sherab grabbed his arm, and violently pulled him away from the oncoming man. John stumbled a few steps in her direction before shaking her off.

"He is one of them!" Sherab screamed in exasperation. "We must run, please hurry!" Frustration built up in her like a revving engine. John's puzzled expression reflected the problem of communication they had faced from the start. He could not understand a word she said.

To make matters worse, John began speaking to her in his strange tongue. As he spoke, a determined look came over his face. The same stubborn expression had convinced her a few days ago to come in this direction instead of towards the mountains. She hesitated but for a moment. The Chinese man approached them rapidly, and she was wasting precious seconds. Although she would have preferred staying with John, she could not risk being interrogated by the authoritative man. With a last lingering look into John's eyes, she sprinted away from both men.

She heard John call out to her, but she could not turn back to look at him. She heard approaching footsteps just before someone collided with her and sent her sprawling onto the ground. She landed hard, but uninjured. She spun around to face her assailant, and saw John speaking rapidly to her. The idiot! Why was he stopping her? Perhaps she had been wrong to trust him, he might be working for the Chinese. Or he might simply be greedy, and hoping to get a reward.

"Get off me you lying, dung-eating pig!" she cried in frustration. Sherab pummeled the arms pinning her down. Her small fists seemed useless against the heavy man's chest and muscular arms.

"I will die before going back there. You can't do this to me!" She tried twisting under him, looking for some way to get out of his clutches. John began shouting at her, trying to drown out her desperate voice. They struggled for a minute or two in this way, shouting incomprehensible words to each other. Then the other man arrived.

Before Sherab could escape John's clutches, the Chinese man took a length of rope out of his backpack and approached her. Pushing John aside, he expertly flipped Sherab onto her stomach and began fastening her hands together. She tried kicking out at him, but he brought his knee down hard on the small of her back. The man's strength and obvious experience quickly overcame her efforts to free herself.

Once her hands were bound to his satisfaction he let her go and stood up beside John. She spun over onto her back and lay there panting. John spoke rapidly to the man, while pointing at her. The man ignored John and stood looking down at her. He wiped the perspiration off his forehead and tried to regain control over his heaving chest. His short, almost military, black hair glistened under the afternoon sun. A trickle of sweat ran down the side of his thick, powerful neck. His callused hands still shook a little from the exertion. A thin, tightly shut mouth underscored his angry brown eyes as he glared at Sherab lying at his feet.

Sherab looked at John's face expectantly. She hoped to see her salvation there, but instead John merely looked back at her in confusion. The Chinese man turned to John, smiled, and shook his hand. She could not believe what she saw. What a fool she had been! She had trusted John, and he had delivered her to this new captor. Her whole body collapsed like a rag doll, as she wept silently, ashamed of her weakness once again. After having sworn to remain free, she was now bound at the feet of a new jailer.

John and the new man exchanged words for a few minutes, with John doing most of the talking. Sherab guessed that he must be explaining her attack on him, and how he had led her so easily into this situation. After asking a few questions, the man seemed to nod his satisfaction to John. His smile disappeared as he approached Sherab.

The man hauled her by the shoulders into a sitting position. He switched to Chinese when he addressed her.

"I am Tzyy Cherng Yu," he began, "a hired guide for this foreigner." He indicated John as he spoke to her.

"Now you will explain to me where you have escaped from, and you will answer all my questions."

How typical, she thought. He immediately assumed she was guilty of something, and wanted her to confess.

"I have escaped from nowhere, I am a free woman."

"Free like the rest of your country?" he asked derisively.

"Why have you tied me? I have done nothing."

"This foreigner says you robbed him. He is filing charges against you when we get into Lhasa. Only a criminal like yourself would rob a wounded man."

Sherab's mind was reeling. John had indeed planned to bring her in for her crime. But Yu had said she robbed an injured man, why did John lie about the cause of his wound?

"Answer me!" Yu growled at her. "Where do you come from?"

"Lhasa," she responded truthfully.

"What is your name?"

"Sherab Choezom." There was no point in lying, since John already knew her name.

"What were your crimes before this latest robbery?"

"I am not a criminal!"

"Listen carefully to me Sherab Choezom. You feel safe right now in front of this foreigner. But he won't be with you when you're in a Lhasa prison and I repeat these questions. I've noticed your finger, and the scars on your head. Yes, and that look in your eyes right now. I think you know what it's like to be asked questions in the privacy of a jail cell, don't you?"

Sherab could not answer him. She simply stared at her inquisitor, trying desperately to shut unwanted memories out of her mind. Yu smiled when she began to tremble.

"The more difficulty you give me now, the more time I will spend with you in Lhasa. Now I repeat, what are your previous crimes?"

Sherab tried to control the quivering stammer in her voice. "I once was arrested for attending a peaceful demonstration." She hoped this lie was close enough to the truth to convince Yu.

"A political prisoner!" he exclaimed triumphantly. "How did you escape?"

"I was released, I swear I didn't escape. All of my family is dead, and I was starving. The authorities gave me nothing when they released me, what could I do? I was only going to take a bit of food and return his bag to him."

"So we release you, and you immediately return to a life of crime. That's not a very encouraging sign to release you again, is it?"

Sherab felt some relief that he had bought her story. But she was terrified of where she was headed with this new lie. Most accused criminals lied about their political activities. How ironic that she lied about her real situation and pretended to be involved in a political demonstration. Once again she reflected on what she might have done in a previous life to deserve this level of danger.

"How long ago were you released?"

She brought her wandering mind back to focus on the immediate dangers. "A week ago," she answered slowly.

"Show me your papers."

"They gave me no papers."

"Liar. All political prisoners are given release papers."

Was he trying to trick her? Perhaps they did give papers now. She hesitated wondering if she should stick to her story or tell him she lost her papers.

"Maybe they made a mistake with me, because I didn't get anything when they threw me out."

That answer seemed to throw him off his line of questioning. It still left her uneasy, waiting for the next trap to be sprung.

"Where are you headed?"

She almost blurted out her real destination, but then realized she had been traveling in the opposite direction with John. He saw her hesitation, and pounced.

"Are you having trouble making up lies fast enough? Should I slow down with my questions for you"

"No, no. No lies. I don't know where I'm heading. I told you my family is dead, I don't know what I'm going to do."

"Well, I can answer that question for you. You're going to go to Lhasa with us. You will face charges of robbery, lying to an officer, and escaping from prison. You will confess to all of these crimes, and then we can put your miserable hide back in jail where it belongs."

"No! Please!" Sherab cried out. "Why are you doing this to me? I have done nothing to you."

Yu took a quick look towards John, noting his curious and perplexed expression. John obviously spoke no Chinese.

"Very well, I will tell you why. You are ugly, and you are Tibetan dung. And by robbing this white barbarian, you have made me late in returning him to Lhasa. Just like the rest of your worthless comrades, you are nothing but trouble. Now at least I'll have an excuse for being late, I caught an escaped political prisoner. Is your curiosity satisfied now, ugly one?"

His faced blurred behind the tears she could not contain. If he brought her to Lhasa, he could probably extract the truth out of her. Then her best outcome would be a swift death. Why had she returned to John? She tried to focus on the state of her karma. Had it been worthwhile to return the stupid backpack? Certainly not for this life, for she now faced more suffering and then death. She prayed that her next life would be better, since this one now seemed over.

Yu waited a few seconds after uttering his last question. Sherab had nothing more to add. As a final punctuation, he spat on the ground beside her before getting up and going to see John.

***

The animosity Yu displayed towards Sherab continued to baffle and surprise John. He knew that Yu was angry with him for being late, but that did not explain Sherab's mistreatment. John regretted having admitted that she had stolen his backpack. Yu's eyes had brightened cruelly when he heard that information. But he recalled how Yu had seemed almost disappointed when John explained to him that he had taken a fall, and Sherab had helped him recover. John emphasized how she had been returning the stolen backpack at the time. In his opinion, he told Yu, she had more than made up for stealing the food she so desperately needed.

Before leaving her side, Yu seemed to study the horizon for a few moments, apparently lost in thought. John gave him an inquisitive look, shoulders raised, palms held upwards, as he finally approached.

"China thanks you Mr. Pearson," he began. "You have helped capture a dangerous criminal." John could not help looking at the frail woman lying on the ground, hands bound behind her back. Dangerous criminal? That description did not fit well with what his eyes saw. He let Yu continue uninterrupted.

"You are not her first victim, she is indeed a professional thief. Her, and her group of bandits, travel the countryside and victimize tourists, Chinese, and their own Tibetan people alike. They mainly rob them of food and valuables, but will not hesitate to kill."

At this point John had to jump in. "No, she was alone. There was no band of thieves in all the time I was with her."

"Of course not," the guide replied, with the tone of a patient teacher explaining the obvious to a slow student. "Two weeks ago she was separated from her group during a raid on some Chinese tourists. Unfortunately for her, the tourists were mainly a group of vacationing Chinese military. Several in her band were killed, the rest scattered with the wind. She was lucky not to be killed, and you are very lucky she did not kill you."

John's mind tried to cope with this new information. The woman he had allowed to sleep with him would have killed him instantly, if she had not needed him for survival. He remembered how quickly and surely she had moved when she whacked him with the rock. How could he have been such a fool? He looked her way and their eyes met. John's projected disappointment, almost betrayal. Sherab's only conveyed sadness and despair. Her eyes confessed the truth to him, John thought.

"What will happen to her now?" he asked dully.

"She will be punished under Chinese law Mr. Pearson. Rest assured that she will spend many years in prison for her crimes. Now, are you well enough to travel? We must hurry back to Lhasa."

"I can go a little further" John replied, "but I can't last much longer. My head injury weakened me quite a bit."

"Very well," Yu answered, his polite guide-voice having returned. "We shall continue for one hour and then stop for the night. I extend my deepest apologies to you Mr. Pearson, on behalf of China. As you are well aware, all countries have problems with criminals. I am sorry that you had to experience ours in such a personal way."

That being said he barked some orders in Chinese to the prisoner. She began to scramble to her feet, but not fast enough for Mr. Yu. He grabbed her arms and painfully hauled her up on her feet. With a push on her back he began the march towards Lhasa.

That night they camped under a small grove of trees. Only after tying her feet together did Yu untie her hands so that she could eat and drink. As soon as she finished eating, he tied her hands again, without bothering to untie her feet this time. He dragged her bound body to the nearest tree, and lashed a long rope around her waist, securing her tightly in a sitting position against the tree. He walked back to their eating area with a small, satisfied smile on his lips.

"Do you intend to leave her like that the whole night?" John asked disbelievingly.

"Yes," he replied curtly. "Now we can sleep in peace."

"But the nights are cold, she'll freeze like that!" His voice was indignant, John could not contain his building anger at Yu's mistreatment of her.

"Mr. Pearson," he began with barely controlled fury, "she is no longer your concern. She is my responsibility. She will not die from the cold, trust me. I will admit that if she did, it would not be a great loss to China. But I am here to see that she is brought to justice, not to kill her. In China we may not treat prisoners with the same royal softness western nations do, but that is not for you to judge. Now please kindly stay out of what is a Chinese internal affair." Realizing how angry he was, Yu quickly got up and walked off into the approaching darkness before John could even begin to reply.

He was right, John thought. This was none of his business. John may not have liked what he saw, but this was how it happened every day in this country. All he wanted now was to go home, he had enough adventures and exposure to 'internal affairs'.

When Yu returned half an hour later, he had visibly regained his composure. They did not speak again that night, neither of them wanting to upset the peace. John felt a small tug at his heart as he unpacked the bedroll. He would have no warm companion this night. He snuggled into the bedroll, feeling guilty for Sherab sitting against the tree, no doubt feeling the cold already creeping into her robe. She is a murdering thief, he thought to himself. She deserves what she gets.

No matter how he tried to convince himself that this situation was acceptable, John could not fall asleep. Soon the guide began to snore softly. He obviously did indeed sleep peacefully once Sherab was secured to the tree. John briefly considered untying her, but realized how dangerous and foolish that was. He looked over in her direction. By now full darkness had descended on them, he could barely see her. With her white robe she looked like a faint ghost watching him. Without realizing what he was doing, John quietly got up and went to her with his bedroll. No, Mr. Yu would not approve, but he covered her as best as he could with the bedroll. Murdering thief or not, John could not leave her exposed to the night air like this.

She looked up gratefully at him, not daring to speak a word out loud. As John wrapped her, he could feel that she had already begun to shiver. He resisted the crazy impulse to kiss the top of her head, and went back to his sleeping area in a confused state. He untied the backpack and took out the extra pair of pants he had. These he wrapped around his chest as a makeshift blanket. He curled his legs around the backpack itself, looking for something against which to build up warmth. His mind felt more at peace, and he started to drift off to sleep.

John woke up the next morning, frozen and stiff. The cold and the hard ground had joined forces to make him feel awful. He opened his eyes and saw Mr. Yu a few feet away still sleeping. He painfully sat up to see if Sherab was awake. All thoughts of his own discomfort disappeared when his eyes took in the scene before him. Her lips were almost blue from the cold. Her body lay limp and shivering against the tree. Her tear streaked face looked vaguely in John's direction, but without really seeing anything. The bedroll he had carefully tucked around her lay just a few inches away from her outstretched feet.

The monster! How could a human being want to deliberately impose such suffering on another person? John got up, shouting: "Mr. Yu! What is the meaning of this?"

Yu woke with a start, and quickly sat up to appraise the situation. "What do you mean?" he asked with a smile, when he understood the nature of John's anger.

"You know what I mean," John replied hotly, "I gave her my bedroll last night and you deliberately removed it! Chinese internal affairs may not be my business Mr. Yu, but what I do with my bedroll is none of yours."

Again, that small smile of his stayed on his face as he answered in an all too calm voice: "I slept the whole night Mr. Pearson. Perhaps China's winds were seeking justice when they blew your bedroll off her."

If John disliked Mr. Yu yesterday, he absolutely hated him at this moment. It was pointless to argue with the man. John walked over to Sherab and re-wrapped her in the bedroll. This time there was no gratitude in her eyes, her entire face remained blank. He turned back towards the guide, and caught his look of pure contempt. Yu's eyes might have been looking at an insect in his soup, one that he would gladly pluck out and crush.

As John began to take out some food for breakfast, Yu immediately got up and went to her. He ungraciously threw off the bedroll. John was about to start in on him when he saw the knife in his hand. Yu looked at him, smiled, and said: "Don't you want her to join us for breakfast?"

John became furious and frightened all at once. This was not his country, and he wanted to get out badly. He became convinced that his guide was somewhat deranged. Without answering Yu, John continued to prepare the breakfast.

Yu reached around Sherab and cut the rope from her waist. Her body slumped over on its side. He then untied the rope from her bound wrists. He barked an order to the prone figure at his feet. Sherab had barely started to move when he kicked his booted foot hard into her thigh.

She screamed in pain, while John jumped to his feet in shock. "Mr. Yu! That is quite enough you sadistic bastard!"

Yu turned to John with a dangerous look, and pointed his ugly knife in his direction. "That is quite enough from you Mr. Pearson. I am telling you one last time, you stay out of our internal affairs! Even western tourists are not above Chinese law I will remind you. If you continue to interfere with my arrest I may have to arrest you too!"

'Come visit Tibet, the land of friendly people', the travel brochure had read. The tourist bureau had wisely not included a picture of a maniacal, knife-wielding guide on the front cover of their travel magazines. John felt like he was in an episode from The Twilight Zone, could all of this really be happening?

He thought about arguing with Yu that basic human decency ignored political boundaries. However, one look at Yu's eyes told him it was once again time to calm down.

"Look, she is obviously a burden to you. May I help you and take care of feeding her breakfast?" John thought that he had cleverly disarmed the guide then.

"No!" Yu replied sharply, bursting John's bubble of hope. "She will feed herself or not eat at all."

"Why are you so mean to her?" John asked. His tone was not angry or accusing, but defeated and quizzical.

"I am not mean to her, Mr. Pearson. For your sake I am treating her more kindly than she deserves." He looked at John piercingly then, perhaps wanting to shock him. "Her prison guards will not have the same reservations as I have."

John swallowed hard, not sure if Yu was deliberately exaggerating to make him angry. He didn't think so, he believed Yu was simply telling the truth. The motive remained the same, Yu wanted to make John angry and make him understand that he had no influence here.

Their exchange of words had given Sherab time to get on her feet. She stood unsteadily next to Yu. He gestured graciously for her to go to the eating area. His eyes mocked her as she began to hobble towards the breakfast area. John turned back to the breakfast preparations, and heard her yelp again. He looked up quickly to see her fall forward onto the hard ground. Yu laughed and said "I guess her feet are not quite awake yet!"

Though John could not prove it, he knew Yu had tripped her.

This time the look in John's eyes told Yu not to interfere as he got up and went to help her. Yu backed away a few steps and let John lift her and help her make it to the breakfast area. Yu had relished his victory, and letting John carry her these last few steps meant nothing to the guide.

John did not know at which point in the day his subconscious mind decided that he could not be a spectator any longer.

# Chapter 5

Throughout the day Yu verbally abused Sherab. He had no qualms harassing her in front of John, who spoke no Chinese. Whenever Yu noticed that John was turned away, he would strike out at her. Sometimes he would trip her, making her fall to the hard ground with her hands tied behind her back. Once he had simply delivered a mighty kick to her thigh. The hard hiking boot felt like a baseball bat, making her leg instantly collapse underneath her. Each time she hit the ground, Yu would be standing over her with a smug look on his face and a barely suppressed smile. John would help her up, while casting angry, suspicious glares towards Yu. She saw Yu shrug his shoulders innocently as he gave some sort of lame explanation to John in his language. John's eyes seemed to glaze over during the day, as he repeatedly was forced to pick her up off the ground. She could tell he tried hard to always keep her in his view. But Yu was a crafty tormentor, and he never missed an opportunity.

She could smell Yu's foul breath as he leaned over her to tie her to another tree for the night. He gave her a sick, lustful smile, which brought her back to the previous night's horrors. Yu had removed the bedroll that John had so thoughtfully given her. He had kneeled over her legs, and tried to kiss her. He had grabbed her hair with one hand, while the other painfully squeezed her breasts. He punched her breast after she spat in his face. The pain had been enormous, bringing her back in time to her previous captivity. She thought of John then, and threatened Yu that she would cry out. He claimed not to care, but after a few more slaps and cruel pinches, he had backed off.

"Perhaps we can play again tonight," Yu told her, from behind her tree. He pulled on the rope until it painfully cut into her abdomen and restricted her breathing.

Already the cold air was working on her legs in her thin robe. She looked at John hopefully, not wanting him to sleep before Yu. John seemed to totally ignore her tonight, as he curled up comfortably into his bedroll. Would he try to keep her warm again, or had he given up in the face of Yu's cruelty?

Sherab relaxed as much as possible in her cramped and cold position. Yu's snores could be heard above the night breezes. John had indeed fallen asleep before Yu, but thankfully the guide had been too tired to come to her, yet. She tried sleeping, but knew it was pointless. The rocky ground numbed her sitting body. Her back ached against the tree, and her arms and stomach burned from the biting rope. The cold was the worst, inexorably creeping into her. The cold brought discomfort this early in the night, but she remembered well how it tortured her with shivers and stiffness as the night went on.

Her heart began to race when she heard the unmistakable rustling sounds of one of the men moving about. A dark shape stealthily approached her. Her eyes grew wide in terror when the faint moonlight glinted off the blade of a knife. She had trouble recapturing her breath when John's familiar face became discernible in the darkness.

Motioning her to be quiet with a finger over his lips, John reached around and cut her from the tree. He then quickly cut the ropes tying her hands and feet. Free from her restraints, she stood up with his help. She could not believe what he had done for her. She beamed her gratitude at him, wishing desperately she could speak to him. She did not understand why he was freeing her after having led her to Yu.

"John helped," he whispered to her with a grin on his face. She had learned to recognize this phrase, for he used it whenever he surprised her with his kindness. He had the grin of a naïve child not realizing the trouble he had gotten himself into. She understood then, and felt her heart go out to him. He thought like a child, and must have mistakenly assumed Yu would help her. Perhaps she had been wrong to think he had wanted to put her in jail. She would not be shocked if Yu had lied about John's intentions to have her arrested in Lhasa. One look at his twinkling eyes and silly grin gave away his western innocence.

His face then registered some sadness as he backed away a few steps, and motioned her to go. She frowned in confusion. Surely he did not think he could stay with Yu now. She beckoned him with her hands to quickly come with her. John shook his head, no.

Her eyes opened wide in panic when she saw that familiar stubborn look come over his face. She grabbed both his shoulders and tried to physically force him to go with her. She became afraid that their scuffling noises would awaken Yu, but thankfully John let himself be dragged a few feet away.

He whispered urgently in her ear, but 'no' was the only word she recognized. She stopped then, with her face a mask of frustration at not being able to speak to him. She thought a moment, and then began her sign language. She held her wrists out together, like they were shackled. He nodded his understanding. She then pointed to Yu's sleeping form, then the wrists again, and then she pointed to John.

She hated to lose that little boy look in his eyes, but she did feel relieved to have finally induced panic into his face. Yu would certainly arrest him for setting her free. She had no idea what international laws protected him in this kind of situation. She hoped that he had heard enough horror stories of westerners held in various foreign prisons across the globe to know that he was in very real danger.

Adrenaline is often referred to as the 'fight or flight' hormone. The adrenaline flowed freely through her body at that moment, and fight was the furthest thought from her mind. John's knees literally began to shake as he digested her new information. Until now she had been willfully stopping herself from running away from Yu at the top speed her legs could carry her. While John stood there trying to deal with his panicked mind, she quietly went to retrieve his backpack and bedroll.

John stared dumbly at her, as if he did not know what to do. She tried using his language on him.

"Sherab help," she whispered to him.

He nodded uncertainly, and shakily put the knife in his pocket. John took the backpack from her. She quietly slipped away into the darkness, sure that he would follow.

When they were out of earshot from Mr. Yu, Sherab spoke out of habit, even though she knew he would not understand.

"Let's run for a while, he will chase us tomorrow." At least he knew she had tried to explain her actions to him when she began to jog away. Despite the exhaustion from the day's march, she picked up the pace and let John jog after her. With burning lungs and screaming legs they jogged through most of the night. Sherab tried in vain to ignore the pain by focusing on her prayers. She recited her favorite mantra numerous times in her head. At one point, when she was sure she could not go on, they stopped briefly.

John had not recovered from his bout with fever. She knew he would collapse soon if they did not stop. She decided to carry the heavier backpack for a while, and handed him the bedroll. He looked almost frightened when she handed it to him, as if he would fall over from the extra weight. But he started to protest when she began to remove the backpack from his shoulders. John tried to knock her hands away.

"We need to go further and you're about to fall over!" Sherab tried to use her sharpest, most commanding voice to break through his resistance. Her gamble paid off, for he became subdued, too tired to argue or put up a fight with her. Only his male ego must have rebelled at the idea of her carrying the heavier load.

They were soon forced to stop for the short remainder of the night. John had no sooner put out the bedroll that they were fast asleep, she in his arms once again.

Sherab woke up early, despite the pitifully few hours of sleep they had been given. She decided to let John sleep longer, while she prepared a makeshift breakfast. When she shook him awake, he blinked at the early morning sun a few times before recognition came to his eyes. Before he could sit up, she handed him some dried meat and the bowl of grains she had prepared.

"Tsampa," John said, rather grimly. This brought a small smile to her face. It was a game now, "tsampa," she repeated.

He seemed starved, and eagerly filled his spoon with grains. Sherab was taken once again by his sweet innocence. Was he aware that he had become a fugitive in her country now? She did not think he really understood it, the way he dug into the cold grain mixture like he was at a famous restaurant buffet. She could not take her eyes off him, and wondered what this strange man was doing to her.

He caught her gaze while his hand was halfway to his mouth. She looked at him, studied him with great intensity. She wanted to understand how he continued to affect her behavior so much. She suddenly felt bad for him, for her stare seemed to have frozen him into a comical position. His mouth gaped open, and a dripping spoon of grains hung near his mouth. She walked towards him, and knelt in front of him. She never released him from her stare as she put her hands on his shoulders. She tried to will him to see the depth of her gratitude for freeing her. Sherab kept him as her prisoner this way for perhaps thirty seconds. On impulse, she leaned forward and softly kissed his forehead. She got up quickly before he could see the embarrassment creep into her flushed cheeks. She had felt a small jolt of electricity as she pressed her lips to his head. Sherab did not feel comfortable with the way he was changing her, she did not normally act so out of character. To quell her bewildered mind, she busily continued packing up for the day's hike.

After a moment, Sherab risked an embarrassed glance in John's direction. His mouth still hung open as he watched her work. She broke into a surprised and hearty laughter for the first time since they had met. In fact, she could not remember the last time she had truly laughed. She self-consciously covered her smile with her hand, stifling her laugh in the process. She continued to look at John, and waved at him with her other hand. "Eat!" her hand tried to say, and she made spooning motions. This jolted him out of his stupor, now it was his turn to be embarrassed. He lowered his gaze to the food bowl and ravenously began to eat. She let her smile return to its full, uninhibited self now that he looked away.

Sherab finally pinpointed the strange emotion she felt around John. It had taken her a while to recognize happiness.

Their sudden and apparently mutual happiness did not last long, as their tired legs protested to the morning march. By midday they looked liked zombies, their bloodshot, tired eyes stared ahead as they slowly continued to move westward. Obviously, the need to distance themselves from Yu was paramount. Still, she began to wonder if they had made a mistake by thoroughly exhausting themselves through the night. It seemed like they were going to be able to walk through most of today, but at such a slow pace. Yesterday's panic gave way to a listless shuffle towards the mountains. Tonight she would insist that they sleep well, or they might not be able to continue tomorrow.

When Sherab stopped to prepare lunch, John did not immediately join her in gathering the grains. Out of the corner of her eye, she curiously watched him examine his supplies of dried meat and fruit. After looking at the dwindling remains, he sighed and began gathering grains with her. They were fortunate that Tibetans had sowed so much barley in these areas. Barley was the grain of choice for growing in this climate, and Tibetans had cultivated it for centuries. It was not surprising that they found wild barley in most places that they walked.

In the late afternoon they came across a small stream. John took the opportunity to replenish their water supply. They both enjoyed washing up in the stream, even though the cold water numbed the skin. The stream must have originated in the Himalayas, and no doubt fed the Tsangpo. She was encouraged to have found the stream, for they would likely run into more of them as they traveled closer to the mountains. Leaving the Tsangpo had caused her to stress over their now limited water supply.

In the early evening John wearily began to gather their supper grains. She did not think she could move again if they stopped now. She walked over to him, gently took his hand and continued walking westward. He dropped the small handful of grains in his hand and followed her without resistance. Most of her body was numb with exhaustion. The only part of Sherab that felt alive was her hand, easily cupped within his. Once they began walking, she could have let his hand go. Likewise, he could have removed Sherab's hand and walked alongside her. But neither of them let go, they continued their slow moving march hand in hand, drawing energy from each other.

They traveled perhaps another hour before she reluctantly let him go. They had to stop for the night before one of them simply collapsed. Their usual barley porridge fell far below its usual standard. Neither of them had the strength to crush the grains properly. If not for the total exhaustion, she might have laughed at the crunching noises they made as they tried to eat the coarse grain.

They quickly finished dinner, and took out the bedroll. Neither of them stood up during that time, they simply crawled around to find what they needed for the night. They soon curled up for what she hoped would be a long and peaceful sleep.

Yu split her lips as he forced the gun barrel into her mouth. She woke from her sleep with a start, but Yu's hand held her to the ground with his hand on her throat.

"If you make a sound, I'll blow your head off," he whispered into her ear. "Then I'll shoot your new, treacherous boyfriend's kneecaps, and leave him here to die slowly. Do you understand me?"

Sherab nodded quickly, her teeth knocking against the metal barrel in her mouth. Its oily taste, mixed with blood from her lips, made her want to gag. Yu made her nausea worse when he grabbed her hair, and pulled her head up to shove the gun deeper into her mouth. Her jaws ached from being forced apart so widely.

"Come on," he whispered, as he fiercely yanked on her hair. She stumbled along helplessly, without even being able to glance at John's sleeping form. She shivered in the cold night air. This physical response truly woke her up. The loss of John's comfort and warmth brought this new harsh reality into focus.

Yu knocked her feet out from under her, and she fell hard against a small tree trunk. Keeping the gun trained on her, he looped a rope around her neck, and then tied it securely to the tree. He pulled hard, choking her in the process. Once she was helpless, he put the gun down and secured her hands behind the tree as well. Every time she swallowed, the tightly wound rope rubbed painfully against her throat.

Her only hope now lay with John. She prayed fervently that Yu's disturbance had woken him up.

***

The stars shone brightly that night. John could even see their reflection on the gun barrel held firmly against his forehead. Normally he would have jumped with surprise if someone woke him up abruptly during the night. But when held down by a revolver pressed against his head, a strange sort of calm enveloped him. A logical part of his brain that had never shown itself before told him to remain calm. No sudden movement, no surprised shouts of fear.

John's eyes blinked several times, in the absence of his hand to wipe the sleep out of them. He tried to focus on Mr. Yu, and to use his peripheral vision to evaluate Sherab's state. Yu's voice soon interrupted John's analysis of the situation.

"You are a very foolish man Mr. Pearson," Yu spat out at him through clenched teeth. "I will satisfy your curiosity about our justice system. You are now under arrest under Chinese law. You may keep your whore company at night, I will be kind enough to tie you both to the same tree." He added this last comment with a smug, satisfied look.

"My government will demand my return." John tried to put confidence in his shaky voice. "And the world will hear about my experiences here!" John took a chance, knowing it was foolhardy of him to goad Yu like this. Perhaps his gamble paid off, because Yu did not kill him. Chinese officials were very much aware of world opinion lately. They may have despised the fact that they needed to worry about such external views, but they were smart enough to understand the significance to their own economy.

John wondered where Sherab might be at the moment. If only she could awaken and get Yu to move that gun off his head, they might have a chance to overwhelm him.

"Roll onto your stomach now, and slowly please." Despite his choice of words, there was no mistaking the warning behind Yu's order. "I could easily bury you here Mr. Pearson, and no one would ever find your body."

John could see Yu's smile inside his head, as he slowly rolled to his stomach. The barrel never left his head. John felt it scrape along the side of his head as he rotated his body. As he turned, John noticed that Sherab was gone. This filled him with hope, had she heard Yu and escaped before he descended upon them? Would she rescue John? But then he remembered Yu's comment about tying them to the same tree. She must already be caught, he thought glumly.

"Hands behind your back," Yu barked at John. He put each hand into the slipknots at the two ends of a rope, keeping his gun pressed against the back of John's head. He was then able to secure John's hands tightly by twisting the rope several times. Only when his hands were bound did the gun come off John's head. Using both hands now, Yu tied John's feet together, with perhaps six inches of rope between them. Yu then returned to John's hands and tied a more permanent knot to replace the twisted slipknots.

"Get up slowly," Yu told him. Yu was not one to waste words, John thought humorlessly. He felt the gun against his back as one of Yu's hands painfully yanked on his arm, almost lifting John to his feet. They walked a short distance to a nearby tree, as Yu had promised. Sherab stared silently at John as they approached. She also must have wondered why John had not woken up, he realized.

Yu had John sit on the opposite side of the tree from Sherab. After Yu had tied him to the tree, John discovered that the trunk was small enough for his and Sherab's fingers to touch. They began to stroke each other's fingers as Yu settled down to sleep a few feet away.

"I'm sorry," John spoke out into the night, wishing the woman behind him could understand. He heard her reply with some words in her own strange language. He could not understand her, but he sensed the comfort that the words meant to bring him. Despite the cold and the uncomfortable position, John soon fell into a fitful sleep.

John had a beautiful view of the mountains when he woke up. The sharp pain in his back, the numbness in his buttocks, and the cramps in his arms confirmed that he was not viewing these lovely mountains from a hotel suite. The cold night air had stiffened every limb.

Sherab must have sensed that he woke up, for he soon felt her fingers move against his. He craned his neck and saw Yu was still sleeping in under the gray pre-dawn sky.

"Hey, how about some breakfast!" he shouted. It was a childish impulse. John did not want Yu getting rest while they were awake. Sherab's fingers froze in panic against his, since she obviously had no idea what John was shouting about. Yu sat up quickly, looking in their direction to see if they were escaping. An angry look came over his face when he understood John's purpose.

Yu looked up at John without expression then. He was slightly downhill from them on a gentle slope. He walked quickly towards John. John began to fear that Yu was going to kick him for the unwanted wake-up call. John shut his eyes expectantly as Yu walked right over his outstretched legs. He could not suppress a sigh of relief as he heard Yu's boots crunching past him. Yu stopped perhaps five feet upslope from them and turned to face his prisoners.

John could not believe his eyes as Yu unzipped his pants, and began urinating on the ground in front of them. Soon a small rivulet of his urine began running down the slope towards them.

"You fucking pig!" John screamed as he felt the first wetness creep through the bottom of his pants. A few undoubtedly profane words from Sherab brought Yu's stream to her direction. They soon were both shouting at Yu loudly, while he laughed lustily.

Yu was still chuckling to himself as he walked back to his sleeping area. He carefully walked out of their kicking range, as they sat in his puddle of urine, thoroughly humiliated.

They watched Yu eat his breakfast in silence. The gnawing in John's stomach told him to stop torturing himself by watching Yu eat. John could not turn away, and his hunger soon turned to revulsion as he watched Yu eat his breakfast. Yu must have been on his best behavior when John was the innocent tourist. Apparently he no longer felt a need to impress anyone. He shoveled food into his open mouth, never ceasing to chew. Partially chewed food occasionally dribbled out of his mouth and into the food bowl held a few inches below his chin. It was the open mouth chewing that got to John. It left an impressive view of the food being processed inside his mouth as well as the food stuck in his teeth.

With a few healthy belches of satisfaction, Yu put the half full bowl of food down at his feet.

"You may finish my breakfast," he told them in mock grandeur as he walked back to their tree. After untying them from the tree he led them bound hand and foot to the breakfast area. They both limped along on their stiff, frozen limbs. John winced when he saw an ugly purple welt across Sherab's throat. No wonder she had been up before him, he thought, she could not have slept much with a rope strangling her all night. Once they were sitting down Yu released their hands, but not their feet.

John gazed in disgust at Yu's food bowl, seeing untouched food as well as the morsels that had escaped his mouth. While John's still too civilized mind studied the food, Sherab again surprised him with her speed. Before Yu had safely backed away to watch over them, she whipped her hand down, grabbed the bowl, and swung it behind her in a long arc. At the apex of the arc her hand was perhaps two feet from Yu's face. His eyes had time to open wide in surprise as she released the bowl.

The bowl's edge struck the bridge of his nose with the distinct snap of a broken bone. The contents flew out of the bowl and into his left eye, temporarily blinding it. His hands reached for his agonized face and he fell back into a sitting position. Before John could react Sherab was on him, pounding at the side of his head with her tiny fists.

John's slow reacting body finally kicked into action. As he swung around and headed for Yu, he saw Yu's right hand form a fist and drive itself deeply into Sherab's abdomen. The blow was powerful enough to physically lift her a fraction of an inch off his body for a moment, before she collapsed back onto him. Her mouth was open and gasping for air, her face a mask of agony.

John began to raise his foot to stomp on Yu's exposed ribcage. Yu was not able to move because of Sherab's weight on his body, but he was already preparing for John's attack. John overshot Yu's side, and brought his boot down towards his chest. Yu's right fist swung around the back of John's leg as it descended. John put his full weight behind this kick, and could not stop his fall when Yu deflected his boot. Rather than trying to stop his kick, Yu had knocked his foot forward so that it landed above his shoulder. This threw John off balance, and he fell into an awkward sitting position. His legs spread apart, he sat partially on Yu's chest and partially on Sherab's back.

Yu's hand still formed a fist as it now shot forward between John's legs. Vomit rose to his throat as he fell backwards off Sherab and Yu. Doing his best to ignore the pain in his testicles, John got up to face Yu again. When his eyes focused on Yu, the angry guide had cast off Sherab's body and took a step towards him. Alarms began to go off in John's head as he saw that the pistol had made its way out of Yu's waistband and into his hand.

Thinking that Yu was going to hold him at gunpoint, John did not raise his hands to attack or defend. His eyes followed the barrel of the gun even as it completed its arc towards his temple. At the last second John whipped his head away from the gun, but not soon enough to avoid the blow. John did not think Yu had struck him at a random location. He had carefully aimed to strike at the very same spot Sherab had hit John two weeks ago.

The blinding flash of pain hid the ground rushing at him as he fell. At that moment he wished for the blessing of unconsciousness that refused to come. He never imagined pain could be this intense. He could not even feel the pain in his testicles anymore, for his head injury paralyzed the rest of his body. With no movement possible, John was at Yu's mercy.

Yu studied John for a brief moment and then turned back to Sherab. She was still immobile, clutching her stomach and gasping for air. John watched in horror as Yu began to unbutton his pants. Tears welled in John's eyes, from the pain as well as the frustration of being incapacitated.

With his pants down around his ankles Yu stood over her and began to lower himself. Using a reserve of strength John could not have guessed that she possessed, Sherab kicked straight up between the legs about to straddle her. Yu bellowed in agony as his legs collapsed and he landed clumsily on top of her.

Yu's cry of pain turned into a scream of rage at Sherab. He dropped his gun and fell forward, hands clamping down on her throat. Her feet thrashed as his powerful forearms pressed his hands around her neck, cutting off her already short air supply.

Still paralyzed, John painfully turned his head away, unable to watch any longer. His eyes lost focus for a second before he saw it. Nothing in the world is so plain and unassuming as a rock sitting in the dirt. This rock had the same indistinguishable mixture of black and gray that only a geologist could decipher. Perhaps one third of its form was beneath ground level. A few crystal-like specs twinkled under the morning sun. It sat about a foot away from him, one more rock in a world with millions of similar rocks.

He wondered how such a common object could have so much influence in his life during the past two weeks. The human thought process was so blindingly fast at these moments. Time seemed to stop as his brain analyzed the color and content of a rock, and pondered the implication rocks had on his life. No more than a split second passed while John's brain processed this wealth of useless information.

He drew strength from this rock, thinking back on the rock that had first thrown him into Sherab's life. His eyes did not leave the rock as his hand shakily reached for it. He heard Yu and Sherab struggling behind him. John saw nothing but the rock in his hand as he fought to get up on bound feet. He saw nothing but the rock as he turned and shuffled towards the sounds of conflict behind him. He did not think he could continue if his eyes left the rock. Only by concentrating on it could he put off the unconsciousness he had longed for moments ago.

He placed a second hand over the rock, carrying it like a precious jewel. Only when he stumbled on either Sherab or Yu's foot, he wasn't sure which one, did he look down towards their bodies. John's world began to spin as he searched for the back of Yu's head. He found it, and let himself fall towards it. Rock held out in front of him, John put what little force he had, and all his weight, behind it.

By some miracle he connected squarely at the base of Yu's head, just above the neck. John's hands released the rock, and he rolled limply off Yu's body. He saw Yu's body slump onto Sherab before losing consciousness.

## Chapter 6

John came to, sputtering water out of his mouth. When his eyes focused, he saw Sherab leaning over him, concern written all over her face. She held the now empty food bowl, dripping with water. Angry, red welts stood out on her throat, he could clearly see the imprint of Yu's fingers. The thought of Yu made him scramble into a sitting position.

A small puddle of blood had formed under Yu's head. He wondered if he had killed him. Sherab moved aside as he crawled towards Yu. He put a hand under Yu's swollen nose. To his relief, he felt a faint breath coming from Yu.

John began to take in more details of his surroundings now. Sherab had cut the ropes off their feet. He had not even noticed when he crawled to Yu. The backpack was ready to go as well, complete with bedroll. Judging from the pain in his head, he could not have been unconscious for long, but Sherab had been busy preparing for their departure.

She helped him to his feet, and he began walking towards the backpack. His brain was just starting to function when he heard a loud, sickeningly wet, thumping sound behind him. He turned and saw Sherab standing over Yu with the same rock he had used to knock Yu out. It took but a moment to notice a fresh wound on the side of Yu's head, at the same moment that she raised her arms to strike again.

"Sherab! No!" he cried out. "Don't kill him!" She paused, her hands in mid-air, and looked at John stumbling towards her. "Please," he said, one hand on his heart. She dropped the stone then, tears welling in her eyes. "Please," he repeated, "don't turn us into murderers".

Yu had a stubbornly hard skull, because he continued to breath regularly when John checked him once more. Sherab tugged at John to get going. He began walking with her but then stopped when a thought occurred to him.

"Wait a minute," he told her as he held her arm to stop her in mid-step. She looked at him quizzically as he returned to Yu yet again.

John had seen too many movies where the good guys, or the victims, run away without grabbing the gun just sitting there. "Grab the gun stupid!" he had spoken out loud so many times as a young boy.

He muttered to himself as he bent down to retrieve Yu's pistol. "And you can be damned sure I won't go into the basement if I'm ever caught in a haunted house."

John was not a firearms expert, but he had enough experience to check the pistol's clip. Yu wasn't fooling around, this was a fully loaded weapon. He bent towards Yu once more, and opened his jacket. As he suspected, Yu's utility belt held a spare ammo clip, which John gently removed. Yu was out cold, but John still feared waking him up as if he was a sleeping giant. While he was there, John also relieved Yu of his knife, which was a good two inches bigger than John's.

He stood up, caught Sherab's eye, and smiled. He then bent down and began unlacing Yu's boots. Again he looked up at her and now she had a distinct blush on her cheeks. She had taught him first hand how to slow down a pursuer. Just as she had done to him, he removed Yu's socks as well, stuffing them into the boots.

Now they were ready to leave. John tied the boots together and swung them over his shoulder. Once more he stopped, this time he had spotted Yu's canteen lying next to the backpack. They were two people drinking out of John's water gourd, so a canteen would supplement their supply very well. He was proud of his survival instincts. They had arrived a little late, but they were certainly earning their keep now.

Yu's backpack yielded a few more treasures. John replenished his meat supply. Yu only had less than a two-day hike to Lhasa, he would survive without the meat. In a small zippered pocket John counted about four hundred Chinese Yuan, roughly the equivalent of fifty US dollars. His eyes opened wide in delight when he miraculously ran into a small bottle of what seemed to be painkillers. He forgot how well prepared a guide had to be.

He showed the bottle to Sherab, unable to decipher its foreign label. As she examined it, John pointed to his head and effortlessly put a look of pain on his face. She nodded, opened the bottle, and handed him three small tablets. He quickly swallowed them using the water in their new canteen.

John's movements were jittery, he was anxious to put distance between them and Mr. Yu. He noticed Sherab also seemed to bounce lightly on the balls of her feet. He shoved the bottle of pills into his pocket, along with Yu's money. The spare ammunition clip went into his other pocket. The gun he stuffed into his belt, in the small of his back as he had seen countless actors do. Swinging the canteen over his shoulder, John started walking once more.

He had to admire Sherab's strength in all this. Although she had perhaps half of his body mass, she continued to display more endurance and survival skills than he ever would have. He felt uncomfortable letting her take the backpack, but he could still feel a trickle of blood leaking from his newly opened wound.

Perhaps the painkillers took effect, or perhaps he simply got used to traveling in pain, but somehow they managed to walk for the rest of the morning. By the time they stopped for lunch, his concerns for Mr. Yu began to fade. He knew enough about bare footed pursuit that he did not think they would see him again. Before he sat down to eat, John untied Yu's boots. He flung one boot as far to his right as he could throw. He turned and threw the other boot in the opposite direction. He was glad to be rid of the extra weight.

With the immediate danger of Mr. Yu removed, his mind began to think about what their next step might be. The ultimate objective was to get out of this country. He was a wanted man now, he thought grimly, a fugitive of justice. Once Mr. Yu made it back to Lhasa, every border crossing would be alerted with John's name, passport number and photograph. Even if they could make it to a border crossing before Yu rang the alarm, he could not get through without his guide. His travel permit explicitly stated that he was on a backpacking trip, which meant that his guide had to check him out when he left the country.

All right, he was getting somewhere now. Eliminate border crossings from the list of possibilities: he had to leave the country through illegal means. He had less than twenty-four hours of experience at being a criminal. His mind drew a blank when he tried to plan an illegal escape from Tibet.

What about Sherab, what was her plan? She seemed determined to keep heading west towards the mountains. With a sudden insight he guessed that she must have been searching for her gang of fellow thieves. According to Yu, a bad raid had split the gang up. Although several had been killed, the rest must have gathered at their regular hideout. It made sense that they would live in the lower mountainous regions. These areas were remote, and provided good shelter from prying eyes.

He was definitely uncomfortable at the thought of being led to a band of criminals. If Sherab had any status among the thieves, then he was sure she would be his guardian angel among them. But if she had little say in the group, he did not know if she could protect him at all.

She would not be so eager to rejoin them if she had been badly treated, John concluded, stretching his thread of logic as far as it could go. Besides, who better to seek out than criminals when he needed an illegal escape? Between Mr. Yu's money and his own, he had close to one thousand Yuan. One hundred and twenty five American dollars did not sound like a lot of money, but it might be enough to buy their services for a short time. Perhaps with the combination of the money and Sherab's good will, the thieves would get him out of the country.

John's mind was made up then. He would let Sherab lead him into her unknown world. The first dream he had of her eyes came to him then. He remembered how he followed her eyes through many obstacles in the darkness around him. The world he was entering now was indeed a dark mystery outside of his life experiences. Nothing in his upbringing had prepared him for running from Chinese law in remote Tibet.

After eating lunch, John began packing up for their departure. Sherab came to him and held his arm to stop his preparations. Puzzled, he watched her rummage through the backpack until she came out with the empty linen sack he had used as a temporary food bag long ago. The need for the sack had all but disappeared as his food supply decreased. She then emptied out the contents of a much smaller sack, and handed that one to him. She stood up and motioned him to follow.

She pointed to a small mountain range to their right, dwarfed by the Himalayas in the distant background. He looked, but saw nothing unusual. She impatiently wiggled her two fingers, symbolizing a person walking, when she saw that he did not understand her.

"So we are changing course," he said to himself, studying the mountain range with more interest now. He could not think of a way to ask her what their final destination was. He simply nodded to her, and watched her begin filling her food sack with grain. They would need to carry their own supply of grain into the higher elevations. Wearily, he began filling his smaller sack. He wondered how his tired legs would react to an ascent into the nearby mountains, which did not look so small any longer.

By the time they were ready to move out, the pounding in his head demanded a new dose of Yu's painkillers. They left behind what seemed like a well-worn trail, and began to head out of their little valley. As they climbed that afternoon, the vegetation changed around them. They soon left barley fields for short, tough scrub grass. The rocky soil crunched and rolled under his boots, increasing the difficulty of the climb. The dry, stunted underbrush provided some reasonable handholds as they struggled upwards. The wind was quieter up there, without grass to whip around. Soon their labored breathing and their crunching footsteps dominated the sounds in his ears.

Midway up the mountain, they reached a small plateau. Sherab wearily put down her load, and he gratefully followed her lead with the backpack. On the northern edge of the plateau a small stream trickled down from the upper elevations, and cascaded over the edge of the plateau. They had their own miniature waterfall to enjoy. They did not waste too much time looking at it before getting under its icy stream. John's first order of business, after removing his only dry shirt and boots, was to rinse off Yu's urine from their clothes, which had begun to reek. John let the water run over his aching head. The cold both shocked and numbed him, and provided a soothing, cleansing feeling.

They stepped out of the stream, shivering in their wet clothes. With some embarrassment, John stripped down to his underwear, and laid his wet pants against a nearby rock. He quickly put on his shirt, grateful for having removed it before taking his freezing shower. He reached into his backpack for his spare pants, and then spotted Sherab standing by the water in her wet robe. Of course, she had no change of clothes. He looked longingly at his pants, which seemed to promise him warmth beyond his heart's desire. Self conscious of his semi-naked appearance, John walked over to her with the spare pants.

When she heard him approaching, she began to turn towards him. The sun behind her made its way through her wet robe to provide a stunning, and provocative profile of what the robe tried to concealed. Her legs formed an upside down 'V' as she carefully turned herself around on the rocky soil. A dark patch above the notch of the 'V' reminded John that she was very much a woman. Her robe clung to her small breasts, the cold nipples dotting through the cloth, calling his eyes. He felt a familiar stirring between his legs, and quickly lowered his eyes.

"Put these on," he told her needlessly, handing her his pants. He could not bring himself to look up and meet her eyes. He just stood there shivering in his underwear, waiting for her to take the pants. After a moment he felt her hand pushing his back, she was refusing them.

"Please, take them," he said, and then simply dropped them at her feet. Since he had nothing to offer her as a top, she would have to keep his old ripped shirt that he had used as bandages. The shirt remnants were also wet, but would dry more quickly than her robe.

For the first time that day John felt sudden joy. The ground on the plateau was mostly rock. No doubt stones had broken off the mountain above for centuries, and many had landed on this plateau. The dried and dead bushes left thin branches strewn all around him. Tonight they could have a fire! This thankfully took his mind away from Sherab, and he began gathering wood for the fire.

John foraged for wood in perhaps a forty-foot circle around their new campsite. He kept his eyes on the ground, for he did not know how to handle

Sherab yet. With each armful of branches, he returned to a growing pile of firewood. On one such trip he noticed that she had moved his wet pants onto some rocks near the future location of the fire. She had laid the pants out carefully to dry, next to her robe. His mind shut down, he compulsively continued to gather wood, despite the growing pile.

"John," she finally said, stopping him in his tracks. He loved the sound of his name with her Tibetan accent. How ridiculous he must have looked standing there in his now dirty underwear, holding an armful of dry branches, with his head pointing straight down at his feet.

"John!" she repeated, more insistently. He cautiously looked up, knowing what he would see yet unable to prepare himself for it. She stood a few feet away from him, holding out a bowl of their "tsampa". He could not prevent the sharp intake of breath as he took in her bare stomach below his stretched shirt remains. His all too baggy pants were tied low around her waist with some spare rope they carried. She heard him, and her smile vanished into an embarrassed look, as she now turned her eyes to the ground.

John dropped the wood he was carrying and quickly took the bowl to release her from this moment. She stepped away and began clearing a small circular area for the fire. By the time he finished eating his bowl of grains, she had prepared a small mound of branches in her makeshift fire pit. He put his bowl down where he stood, and went to find matches in the backpack. They seemed to be doing a good job of keeping themselves busy at different locations.

As he lit the fire, he guiltily noticed that she was preparing herself a bowl of grains. "Idiot," he muttered to himself for not having even thought of sharing the first bowl with her. The warmth of the fire on his bare legs soon pushed all other thoughts away. He had never appreciated a fire more in his life. Sherab sat on the opposite side of the fire and ate her food. He shut his eyes and let the warmth soak in.

He had to stop thinking of the backpack as "his" backpack, John realized as Sherab started looking through it. She soon removed a small pouch of plant leaves he assumed she had gathered days ago. He recognized some of them as she began to mix them in water. Before she knelt beside him, John already knew she was preparing to dress his head wound once again.

He sat rigidly still as she tended his wound. He looked straight ahead, trying to ignore her bare arm inches away from his naked eye. The pain of his wound could not mask the gentle touches of her fingers on other parts of his scalp. When her breasts accidentally brushed his shoulder, John lost his ability to control a very typical male physical reaction. He prayed she would not notice, all the while wondering how she could possibly miss it. His breathing became quicker as he imagined her hand dropping down there and squeezing him. "Please," he thought, "finish what you're doing and leave before I go crazy!"

She soon finished applying her care to his wound, and left his side. John breathed a sigh of relief, not knowing if she had even noticed his excitement or not.

"Thank you Sherab," he told her once she was reseated. The fire between them hid his lower body, so he could look at her without more embarrassment. He held a hand against his wound as he thanked her. She looked up and smiled an acknowledgment to his appreciative words.

Although the sun had not set, they both were ready to sleep for the night. He now felt relief at having left behind the trail. Yu would not be able to track them down to this plateau, even if he did have boots. John added more wood to the fire, and went to get the bedroll. He stood a few feet away from the fire and spread out the bedroll in front of him, nice and close to the fire.

Sherab watched his preparations eagerly. He had no sooner motioned her to come lie down that she was on her feet and headed his way. His intention was to have her lie facing the fire, and he would curl up behind her. He should not have been surprised when she lay next to his feet, facing away from the fire. She expected him to be the one closest to the fire, with his back against it.

A naughty smile crept onto his face when he saw her lying there expectantly. She had as much tenseness as he did with this awkward situation. Before he lost his nerve, he quickly bent down, grabbed the edge of bedroll under her, and pulled up with a great force. With a startled scream and flailing arms she rolled over towards the fire. He had meant to just roll her onto her side, but she twisted all the way around and landed on her stomach. She looked stunned, with her arms and legs spread apart.

John's laughter finally made her look his way as he came down on the bedroll, away from the fire. The laughter was infectious. Once she understood what he had done she joined him in his laughter, with a small slap on his shoulder. When they had recovered, he turned on his side to face her, and propped up his head. He was not ready to sleep yet, and he wanted to spend another quiet moment with her.

She lay on her back then, her hands absently covering her breasts. His eyes made the mistake of drifting away from her content smile to her shining eyes. She mercilessly stole his soul again, as he lost himself in their depth. With a blink she turned her head and looked at the setting sun, releasing him of her grip.

He felt sorrow when he saw the welts on her neck from Yu's fingers as well as from last night's rope. His eyes drifted down to her stomach where Yu had delivered his terrible punch. There too a purpling bruise left a reminder of Yu's beating.

He saw her wince with pain when she turned towards him once more, her hand pressing on the very bruise he had just noticed. He reached to move her hand off the bruise, and gently began to stroke it. His fingers lightly touched the purple skin, almost tickling it. He felt her body relax, as she shut her eyes. A small tear formed on the corner of her eye, unable to decide if it should dry up or run down the side of her head. If Yu was with them right now, John might just sit and watch her pound his head into jelly with the rock.

John's arm began to feel like lead, it was time to sleep. He gently moved over to her side, and pressed himself into her exposed back. He was nearly asleep when he felt her hand reach between them. For a brief moment he thought she was fulfilling his earlier dream and reaching for him. She reached behind her back to untie the wet shirt covering her chest. John removed his arm around her to give her room to work. Never turning his way, she struggled out of the shirt and put it down near the fire to dry. Their legs were still in contact, but he could not bring himself to put an arm around her now bare chest. After a moment she reached behind her again, searching for his arm. Her hand first touched his thigh causing him another intake of breath. He quickly gave her his arm, before she could make another mistake. She brought his arm over her, resting his hand on her stomach. His tenseness soon dissolved and John's exhaustion knocked him out for the night.

They had lunch on the other side of the mountain the next day, shortly after crossing the peak. While they ate, John pointed out small plumes of smoke in the distance, perhaps four or five miles away.

"Kyemaja," Sherab answered him. He assumed that this was the name of the town or village generating this smoke. Or it was the Tibetan word for 'smoke', he thought wryly, a smile breaking onto his face. He decided to test this theory. He wiggled his fingers and moved his hands up and down, trying to symbolize the smoke.

"Kyemaja?" he asked. Sherab smiled and shook her head. Pointing at his hands she said "Dud". She thought for a moment, then pointed roughly to the east and said "Lhasa," swung her pointing finger to the source of the smoke nearby and finished with "Kyemaja".

John had never heard of Kyemaja, but judging from the few wisps of smoke, it must be a small village. Sherab pointed to her and John, then pointed west and said "Shigatse". His eyes opened wide in surprise. He knew Shigatse was one of the larger cities in Tibet. From his scant knowledge of Tibetan geography, it was about two hundred miles from Lhasa. Sherab studied his face gravely, as if trying to decipher what he was thinking.

The more information she managed to convey to him, the more questions he had. Why Shigatse? What answers to her puzzle would he find there? Was that the central location of her group of thieves? If so, she had strayed pretty far from it. To ease her mind he nodded, repeating their destination out loud. Sherab looked grateful that he would follow her so far. He began to wonder if Shigatse was their final destination, or if it served as just another stop in her unknown plan.

Sherab led them down towards the valley, but avoided going directly to Kyemaja. Perhaps some of its citizens had been victims of her gang, he thought nervously. As they neared the valley floor, he noticed a small river flowed along the bottom. The current ran southward, so the river probably dumped into the Tsangpo.

Although the ground distance over the mountains could not have been more than ten miles, the rugged terrain made it seem like twenty-five miles. The sun hung low over the horizon as they reached the river on the valley floor. He estimated that they had overshot Kyemaja by perhaps three miles upstream. Sherab must have considered this a safe enough distance for them to camp for the night.

The ground was damp near the river, and John felt safe lighting a fire for the night. However, Sherab stopped him when he began gathering branches. She shook her head, and pointed upstream. Still shaking her head, she said "Kyemaja". Fine, he thought, another cold night. At least this night they were able to wear all their clothes.

The next day they followed the small river southward. Mid morning they skirted around another village, called Tona, according to Sherab. In the late afternoon they had made it back to the Tsangpo. As he thought, the small river fed the much larger Tsangpo river. It was still early to stop for the day, so they pushed on westward along the Tsangpo.

Despite all the days of walking John had done since first leaving Yu outside Lhasa, he did not think they were very close to Shigatse. They had gone back and forth a few times when looking for Yu, then running from Yu, and then marching as Yu's prisoners. In all they had traveled far less than one hundred miles from Lhasa, perhaps even as little as fifty miles. He began to feel depressed, thinking that Sherab intended them to walk all the way to Shigatse.

Darkness had crept in around them when they finally decided to stop for the day. Their strength and endurance had grown considerably in the last few days. John was happy to realize he had not taken any painkillers since the morning meal. All in all, he felt pretty good when he sat down with Sherab for their late supper. He reflected on how it did not take much to make him happy after recovering from a miserable situation. He was dirty and tired, eating a cold grain soup, sitting in the frigid night air. Yet, other than the ability to speak with Sherab, he could not think of anything in the world he really wanted at the moment.

John made love to her in his dreams that night. Their bodies rolled in the damp earth along the river's shore. A blazing fire warmed them as they gave each other pleasures beyond compare. Her eyes roamed over his body, examining every inch of it. He regretted having this dream, for it would make the next several nights very difficult for him to sleep next to her.

The next morning he looked guiltily at Sherab, as if she had witnessed his dream. Time soon dissolved this ridiculous feeling, as they continued their westward march. Mid morning he heard the distant rumbling of a heavy vehicle. They were near a road! He took Sherab's arm excitedly and pointed to the sound at their distant left. She nodded, and put her hands up on an imaginary steering wheel. He wanted to drive to Shigatse, not walk. He took her arm and started to trot towards the road.

John was not entirely surprised when Sherab put the brakes on his plans. She yanked back on his arm, nearly spilling him over. She shook her head, eyes staring at him wildly. Ominously, she then made a gun out of her hand and held it to her own head. She would be killed if caught, John realized. All along she must have known about the road, but had chosen to walk parallel to it rather than try to hitch a ride.

With a glum nod he turned back to their original path, and continued walking. They walked for the rest of that long and uneventful day.

Sherab seemed restless that night, like she did not want to stop. John, on the other hand, felt quite content to rest his tired legs. His dream returned vividly to his mind when he saw Sherab bend over to spread out the bedroll. Only with great self-control did he lie down next to her, being very careful where he put his hands. The days of hard physical exertion saved him in the evenings, helping him sleep despite his uncomfortable thoughts.

The sun had not cleared the horizon by the time he woke up the next morning. Sherab was noisily preparing breakfast. This was unusual, he thought. She always managed to wake up before him, but never had she deliberately made noise to wake him up. He watched her busying herself, running back and forth between tasks. Her nervous energy affected him, and he soon got up and began helping her. He wondered what was making her so jumpy, as he ground up barley grains.

By mid-morning John received the answer to his question. As they climbed a small hill, he began hearing noises in the distance. The noises grew in intensity as they approached the hill's summit. Sherab sprinted the last short distance ahead of him, and stood at the top of the hill. He ran to catch up with her.

Below them lay the first significant sign of humanity since John had left Lhasa. This was not a small village, but an actual town. The first outlying structures were perhaps half a mile from them. The town sprawled along the river for perhaps another two or three miles. At the far end he saw a dirt road intercept the town's central road. This must have been the highway access road whose traffic he had heard yesterday.

Sherab interrupted his study of the town. "Same," she said proudly. Her eyes shone with hope when she looked at him. They began their descent towards the town, approaching it from the rear. He was overjoyed that the town of Same could bring so much hope into Sherab's eyes in such a short moment. John soon found out it could rip that hope out of her beautiful eyes just as quickly.

# Chapter 7

Same was one of countless small towns in Tibet whose population or location justified a Chinese administrative office. The town was often referred to as 'Same Qu', the 'Qu' designating it as a town with a Chinese office. Typically these offices were near a town's temple, where the Chinese expected religion-inspired political demonstrations. Small and unassuming, the gray, nearly windowless building sat in sharp contrast to the nearby colorful and exotic temples or monasteries. Its threat of power was not in its architecture, but in the red flag flying above it. The flag usually hung over the main entrance, where an ever-present armed soldier emphasized the vision of power.

The centers of Chinese authority logically followed the old Tibetan centers of religious authority. Towns with smaller temples became 'Qu' towns. Larger towns with more powerful monasteries became 'Xian' towns. Xians housed a more central government office that controlled a region of 'Qu' towns.

Invariably, the access highway into a town came very close to the administrative office. Since the Chinese built most of these roads, they designed them to provide high mobility between offices. All government related construction seemed designed to combat possible uprisings of native Tibetans. This apparent architecture did nothing to comfort a fugitive entering the town.

Same's layout followed an economic pattern seen throughout Tibetan towns. The temple proudly displayed itself as the jewel of the town. The wealthiest establishments surrounded the temple. The impressiveness of a structure was inversely proportional to its distance from the temple. As a result, when you entered a town you first encountered the huts and tents of the poorest inhabitants.

Fortunately, these inhabitants were not overly curious to see a Tibetan woman walking furtively with a white man. They all looked up at them, but then quickly turned away, not wanting any involvement with their strange appearance. Now Sherab hoped John understood why she had packed Yu's pistol in the backpack that morning. She knew that John drew some comfort from having it close at hand, tucked into his belt. But she certainly did not think it would be wise to walk around a town with a visible Chinese handgun.

The few small fences in the area were used to keep in livestock. Sherab could not see any visible property divisions. The structures seemed to be randomly distributed, as if a giant had flung handfuls of tents and huts into the area. A few chickens clucked nervously as Sherab made her way around the coops. The chicken clucks were the only sound generated by John and Sherab's presence in the village.

When the huts became more affluent wooden houses, she led John further into the outskirts of the town. They were soon walking parallel to the town's development, but behind the nearby tree line just outside the town's boundary. The closer they approached the town center, the more stealthy Sherab's movements became. John soon followed her pattern of walking bent low towards the ground, stopping to rest behind the larger trees and bushes.

They reached a crossroad in their path. Sherab stopped while they were still under the cover of the shallow forest. On the other side of the street sat the temple of Same. What the temple lacked in size, it more than made up in splendor. What might have looked gaudy in a western city managed to look majestic in this rural Asian setting.

The temple's main structure consisted of a square, two-story building. The walls were painted bright red, to immediately attract one's eye. A white stripe separated the two floors, while a thinner white stripe decorated the top of the walls. Three windows per floor provided natural light through the sides of the building. Curved, wooden awnings, painted in white and gold, capped each window top like a hat. At each corner and at each midpoint along the wall, small golden spires adorned the roof.

The front of the temple provided a spectacular entrance into the holy building. A white staircase of perhaps ten steps covered the entire length of the temple's front wall. At the head of the stairs stood two rows of four red pillars, decorated with gold trimmings at the top. Behind the pillars were the temple's three main doors. The pillars supported a golden overhanging platform on which rested an extension to the second floor. The extension was no more than five feet in depth, more like an enclosed balcony. At the top of the extension ran a long golden border, with another set of spires at both ends. At the center of the border a golden circle jutted into the sky as the highest point on the temple. This was the Buddhist Dharma Wheel, the wheel of life. Its eight spokes represented the Noble Eight-Fold Path.

Sherab had not seen such a beautiful temple in many years. She felt enraptured as she stared at the golden wheel. Her eyes automatically scanned through each spoke, speaking the eight steps of the path to enlightenment. The first spoke: right understanding. One had to first understand the Four Noble Truths of Buddha. The second spoke: right thoughts, or kind thoughts. The third spoke: right speech, or refraining from lies and slanders. The fourth spoke: right action, which meant no killing, or stealing. This made her cringe, for she had almost done the first recently, and she had definitely done the second. The fifth spoke: right livelihood. This meant avoiding jobs that dealt in various undesirable industries, such as firearms, animal slaughtering, drugs or poisons. The sixth spoke: right effort, or endeavoring to promote good and suppress evil. The seventh spoke: right mindfulness. This one was giving her trouble as well. She was supposed to be aware of her own words and thoughts, yet John kept confusing her mind. Finally, the eighth spoke: right meditation. She had been lax here too, not finding enough time to properly meditate.

Sherab breathed deeply, feeling refreshed and relaxed after having concentrated on the great wheel of life. She understood where she had to improve, and would try to focus on those areas. Her renewed determination to improve her standing in the next life would help her get through this difficult situation. She returned her attention to the temple and surrounding structures.

On the left of the temple sat the Chinese government office with its required soldier at the entrance. Although the young soldier had a rifle slung on his shoulder, his relaxed demeanor suggested that he expected no trouble in this town. He leaned back casually against the gray wall of the office, all the while smoking a cigarette. He looked like a very bored young man. Many Chinese stationed in Tibet feared for their health. They believed that the higher altitude expanded their lungs, and caused heart problems. Sherab absent-mindedly wondered if this chain-smoking soldier complained about the ill effects of high altitude.

The soldier must have heard the approaching footsteps, because he suddenly stood at attention, and crushed his cigarette under his boot. A moment later an older, stern looking soldier marched out of the building, heading for a nearby jeep. This man carried himself with authority, and brushed by the young soldier without even looking up. He carried no rifle, a strapped sidearm was his only weapon. He jumped into a jeep with a waiting driver. She heard him bark out some orders to the driver, who had already started backing out the jeep. Within seconds after the jeep roared off, the soldier at the entrance was once more leaning on the wall, lighting a new cigarette.

That activity was the most significant they observed during the hour that they watched the temple. The lack of movement seemed to reassure Sherab, as she led them towards the right of the temple, away from the office. Perhaps fifty yards to the right, a busy market crowded both sides of the street, barely leaving room for a single passing car. Sherab knew that the market would provide the necessary cover for them to cross the street unnoticed by the soldier.

She scanned the area for any other Chinese authorities, but could see no one suspicious. They came around the back end of the market, putting as many people between them and the Chinese office. Sherab pretended to look at a merchant's goods, while furtively stealing glances towards the soldier. John tried to hide his white man's face behind her body. Sherab suddenly moved towards the other side of the street. As she left, she noticed something on the other side of the office caught the soldier's attention. For the moment, the soldier's face was turned away. John quickly followed Sherab, drawing a few curious glances along the way.

Finally they were on the same side of the street as the temple. As they had done on the other side of the street, they made their way behind the market. At the edge of the market, Sherab noticed that the path was clear between the market and the temple. They could not walk down the last fifty yards without being seen. Sherab could tell John was watching her expectantly, as she studied the temple from afar.

She made up her mind then, and reached to take John's hand. She had barely touched his hand when she dropped it with a nervous, guilty look around her. They were no longer alone in the wilderness, a Tibetan woman holding a white man's hand would draw much more attention than they needed.

People's reactions to her holding John's hand concerned Sherab less than the ease with which she had taken his hand. She felt close to him. That was an understatement, she thought with an inward smile. She recalled so many little details of her last days and nights with John. His extreme shyness when he stood before her in his underwear up on the plateau had made her want to hold him in her arms and kiss him. She blushed at the thought. She tried to focus away from that particular memory, because she knew she wanted to do more than kiss him.

She felt ashamed of her physical desire for John. Only once had she felt anything close to this for a man. She had been much younger then, and very idealistic about life. She had turn the nice young man away, so that she could pursue her destiny. It hurt her to think of that boy, just like it hurt her to think of losing John. But a man did not fit into her life of devotion as a Tibetan nun.

Sherab's forced captivity had thus far prevented her from being ordained as a nun, but that would change. She was free now, and she would pursue her studies once again. This is what she had dreamed of over the last lonely, desperate years. So why did John's face keep appearing in her mind when she thought of becoming a nun? This was just another sign of her weakness. Now she felt the pull of her desire wanting to take her away from her true purpose in life. Sherab vowed to be strong, and not give in to John's charms.

Sherab felt grateful that John could not see inside her. She could feel his desire for her, and it drove her mad with lust. There were times when she had been ready to give herself to him. She felt so ashamed when she recalled how she had taken her wet top off as they went to sleep after washing. She tried to make it look innocent, but her thighs throbbed at the thought of John touching and kissing her nakedness.

She shook her head, clearing the blasphemous image away. Fate had brought her together with a noble man whose greater strength had saved her until now. She had tried to give herself, and he held back. But he was indeed a man, for she had seen obvious signs of that many times. How much longer would he last? She had to take control of herself, and behave like the nun she was becoming.

Perhaps she was being tested. She no longer doubted that she would ever find a man like John again. In the early hours of the morning, as she studied his sleeping face, it brought tears to her eyes. He was the one. John was the man for her, and she was throwing him away for her predestined fate. She would serve Buddha for this life, hoping to make up for her sins. Perhaps in another life she would be blessed with a man she loved.

John touched her arm, waking her from her reverie. She felt embarrassed, as if he had read her thoughts. They left the road, and headed towards some nearby houses. Sherab wanted to go around a few houses and reach the temple from the rear. She was not yet sure how she would get inside the temple once they reached the back wall.

They had to be more careful around these houses. In all societies, wealthy citizens were more likely to report strange sightings to the authorities. She had no doubt that John and her sneaking around in someone's backyard qualified as a 'strange sighting'. Fortunately, the first house they passed had drapes covering the one window on the side wall. As they rounded the corner, she noticed a path between the houses that would lead them to the temple. She counted three houses that they had to pass before safely making it to the temple.

She could not believe their luck, no one stood outside the three houses. They walked carefully along the path, trying to be quiet despite the absence of people. The market noises diminished behind them, making her more conscious of their own muted footsteps. As they approached the second last house, a small noise on her right caught her attention. Looking over, she saw a woman kneeling on the ground, tending her flower garden. Sherab froze, grabbing John's arm.

If the woman looked up, she would see them. If they walked another ten feet, they would enter her narrow field of vision from her kneeling position. The seconds ticked by, as they stood frozen like deer caught in headlights. Fortunately the woman was far too absorbed in her garden to look up at them. Sherab thought she heard the woman humming lightly to herself. The woman's garden must have been an escape from her everyday life, a time to lose herself in the beauty and innocence of flowers. These peaceful thoughts were a sharp contrast to the panic racing in Sherab's mind, urging her stubborn feet to run as fast as she could.

Glancing over her shoulder, Sherab saw that the opposite house seemed deserted at the moment. Even through the open window she could see no one. Taking John by the elbow, she slowly began backing away from the woman, towards the house on the opposite side. She could not prevent the woman from looking up at them at any time. All they could hope for was to get out of the woman's current field of vision, and pray she did not hear them, or decide to sit up and stretch. Both of them kept their eyes on the woman as they backed away. When they had backed as far as they could, John and Sherab began a sideways, shuffling walk towards the temple. Only when they reached the last house did they turn their bodies and begin a faster walk to the nearby temple.

They cleared the third house uneventfully. With a glance in either direction, Sherab was about to break into a short jog to the temple wall. That was when she heard a man's voice behind them. She could not help jumping at the sudden sound. How guilty she must have looked with that reaction. For the first time since entering Same, she wished John's gun was within easy reach.

Sherab and John turned around as one, facing this new danger in their journey. Shutting the door behind him, a small, middle-aged man stepped out of the house they had just passed. His eyes, though not unfriendly, pierced into them, trying to determine who they were. Sherab assumed he was evaluating their potential threat to the temple, for his long, flowing red robe clearly identified him as a Tibetan monk.

***

Sherab had been amazing, John thought. She had led them through this unfamiliar town right up to the temple. Luck had finally turned against them when the monk exited the house behind them. The monk spoke a few words to Sherab, as he continued advancing towards them. His bald head glistened with sweat under the midday sun. His eyes moved constantly, darting between Sherab and John, and also glancing at their immediate surroundings. As the monk turned his head, John noticed a small scar above his left ear. He had a slight, almost unnoticeable limp in his stride. His hands seemed disproportionately large for his small body. The hands of a working man, John thought.

Monks were among the more educated people in Tibet. Perhaps this one would understand John.

"Do you speak English?" John asked hopefully.

The monk turned to John, a look of annoyance on his face. Before he could answer anything, Sherab spoke to him in Tibetan. They exchanged a few sentences, before he nodded, and motioned them to follow him. The area around the temple remained deserted as the monk led them towards the back of the temple.

The monk brought them to a small door cut into the temple's back wall. Reaching into his robe, he pulled out a large, ancient looking key. He opened the door, and led them into its dark interior. Inside, a short hallway led to a large door at the end. On their immediate right was another door, which the monk opened for them. The first thing John noticed in this room was a cluttered desk with stacks of papers occupying every inch of space. A small bookshelf above the desk held an array of books, all in Tibetan. Some of the books must have dated back a hundred years, while others had not yet lost their glossy appearance. A few chairs and a small table completed the room.

Another entrance carved out a hole in the opposite wall. No door separated the two rooms. John could see half of a tidy, well made bed. Its rough woolen blanket was carefully tucked under the thin mattress. The room's emptiness and orderliness provided a sharp contrast to the busy office they stood in.

John jumped when the monk spoke to him.

"No one will disturb us here, please sit down." He spoke slowly, with visible effort, in a clear but heavily accented English. "My name is Regra Konchog, I welcome you to this temple. I will speak to this lady first, and then to you. It will be easier for me this way to understand your story."

John was overjoyed to have a friendly, English voice on their side. Knowing he could not ask about Sherab yet, but unable to stop talking, he asked: "Is this where you live?" The moment the question left his lips, John felt foolish. What a dumb question.

"Yes," Regra replied simply.

"But you came out of that house, I thought perhaps you lived in a nearby home." John tried to recover from the poor impression he must have made so far.

Regra looked at John for a moment, trying to form the correct sentences. "The couple who live in that house are too old to come into our temple. Now I must go to them to give them the comfort they need."

That was enough small talk, John thought. He nodded and remained quiet, letting Regra settle down with Sherab. John was normally a patient man, but their two-hour conversation was undoubtedly the longest two hours of his life. Regra's voice ranged through every emotion as they spoke to each other. At times he was sad, at times angry, at times surprised. Sometimes he spoke softly, other times he raised his voice. All the while Sherab spoke in a controlled, low voice. She often had her head down, as if speaking to someone under the table. Several times her voice started to break, and tears formed in her eyes.

At one point near the end John heard her mention his name. They both briefly glanced at him, and then continued to speak. John felt like a father anxiously waiting to hear about his child's birth from the doctor. How long would he have to wait before they were done?

A long pause in their conversation made John look up hopefully. They sat looking at each other, and then Sherab asked him a question. Regra firmly shook his head, and took her hand. John detected rising panic in her voice as she spoke again. It was the first time she raised her voice in the entire conversation. Regra lowered his eyes and kept shaking his head, muttering something in a low voice. Sherab became hysterical as she ripped her hand away and stood up before him. Then he became mad, standing up as well and motioning her to be quiet. They stood facing each other, anger in their eyes.

Sherab broke first. With a sob she sat back down and put her face in her hands. Regra took her elbow and gently brought her to her feet. Her face never left her hands as he began leading her out of the room. They had already passed John when he recovered from his stunned reaction to this last exchange.

"Wait!" he said to Regra. "Where are you going? Please, tell me what's happening!"

Regra paused a moment, then turned to John. "I'm sorry, I cannot help you." He spoke in a low voice, and seemed to be ashamed at his inability to help.

"Look Sir," John began, having forgotten Regra's name, "I have been running for the last week with this woman, and I have no idea why or from what we are running. Please, if you can't help at least tell me what is going on."

As John spoke, Regra kept walking, and they were soon standing by the back entrance to the temple. The monk spoke again, as he opened the outside door.

"Mr. Pearson, for your own safety, the less you know, the better." He gently pushed Sherab out the door as he said this. John stood in shock, not believing that Regra refused to speak with him.

"Please!" Regra said, motioning John to go outside. "If half of what she said is true, then you will not be allowed to leave this country alive." That stunned John enough that Regra was able to lead him outside like a child. As John watched the door begin to shut behind them, he quickly reached out and grabbed it.

"Please Mr. Pearson, I cannot help you!" Regra's voice sounded desperate now, he was anxious to be rid of them.

John looked at him, trying to put as much strength in his voice and eyes as he could. "Go hide in your temple if you must," he started, trying to play on the shame Regra felt. "But first at least tell me where I can find her band of thieves. Maybe thieves will help us where a monk cannot."

Regra's eyes looked confused when he heard John. He shook his head and said: "This woman is not a thief Mr. Pearson."

Regra's tone told John that the man had lost some respect for him. John thinking that Sherab was a thief almost seemed like a personal insult to Regra. Both his tone and his words broke John's resistance. Regra pushed John's hand away and slammed the temple door shut. They stood silently, facing the closed door of their hopes.

John's mind was reeling with all the implications of what he had learnt. If Sherab was not a thief, then why had Yu fabricated all those lies about her gang's raid on Chinese military tourists? Was he simply an evil man taking advantage of their language situation? John could not believe such a simple explanation, there had to be something about Sherab's past that Yu did not want him to know about.

His frustration at all the unanswered questions became anger directed at the monk inside the temple. He stepped up to the door and started pounding on it and shouting at Regra.

"Monk! We're not going away until you explain to me what is going on! Monk! Get out here now!"

Sherab spun him around as she pulled on his door-pounding arm. At first John thought the anger in her eyes was directed at Regra for not helping them. But then the intensity of her stare and the hardness of her whispered words to him told John otherwise. He had compromised their safety by making so much noise.

He looked down the alley they had walked and noticed a few heads sticking out of doors and windows. He did not think Tibetans would willingly tolerate a foreigner banging on their temple.

It was time for them to disappear before they attracted any more attention. Or, more accurately, before John attracted any more attention. Either side of the temple led up to a main street, they could not go there. Neither could they return the way they had come, for too many people were watching them. Going in the opposite direction would bring them behind the Chinese office, which did not seem very wise. That left them with heading directly away from the temple, towards the town boundary.

Resisting the urge to run, they walked away from the temple. They only had two houses to clear before they were once again isolated in the safety of the surrounding thin forest.

"I'm sorry," John told Sherab, hoping she would understand his tone. He had let his anger endanger them, and he would never let that happen again. Sitting in the safety of the trees around them, Sherab no longer looked angry with him. He asked himself again who this woman could be. What had she seen or done that would make Yu want to arrest her without telling John the truth? What secrets did she possess that would make a Tibetan monk throw them out of a temple? What did she know that made Regra fear for John's life?

John felt ashamed that he had believed Yu's story. Sherab looked defeated after their encounter with Regra. He took her hand in his, reached over, and kissed her forehead.

"I wish I knew what mysteries lay behind those beautiful eyes," he told her.

She smiled at him, comforted by his kiss if not by his words. She squeezed his hand with her thumb and three good fingers. He released her hand and gently stroked the broken, deformed finger. He brought it to his lips, kissing it tenderly.

"Shigatse?" he asked her, while they touched hands. He did not know if the monk was part of her plan or not. He wanted to know if their faraway destination had changed or not.

"Shigatse," she replied, nodding at him. Her eyes moistened as he stroked and kissed her hand. The tears welled in her eyes, threatening to spill onto her cheeks.

With his new information about Sherab, John wondered once again why they were headed to Shigatse. He had assumed it was to join up with her band of thieves, but that was obviously not the case. John smiled when he realized that the very reason he had decided to blindly follow Sherab's plan was to use her thieves to get him out of the country. Although he no longer had a good reason to follow her, John lacked a plan for himself. He would continue to follow her, partly because he had no better idea to get out of the country, partly because he wanted her company. If he could help her by going along, then it was worth his while.

"Shigatse," Sherab repeated with a sigh, as she stood up to go. John stood up beside her, and then remembered the market they had passed. This would be a good time to replenish their food supplies. Ignoring Sherab's questioning look, he put the backpack on the ground and began rummaging through it. He found the money, and held some out for Sherab. With his right hand he made eating motions, while pointing his head in the general direction of the market.

Her eyes lit up briefly when she understood. She took some of the money, and started walking towards the market. John shoved the rest of the bills in the backpack and scrambled after her. Sherab stopped at the sound of his approaching steps and turned around. She put a hand on his chest, stopping him from going further. She pointed him back to the trees they had been sitting under. Of course, he thought. He could not accompany her to the market. They had managed to sneak by it without drawing too much attention. But now she was going there to actively buy products. A white man hanging around behind her for that amount of time would definitely raise inquiries, perhaps even at the administrative office.

John hesitated to let her go alone. They had a long trip ahead of them, and badly needed the supplies. However, separating now seemed unwise. What if she were arrested, how would he ever find her? Before he could try arguing either way with Sherab, she was already gone out of the forest and towards the market. He glanced at his watch, and made up his mind to go find her in thirty minutes if she had not returned. He knew it made no sense for him to go alone into the town, but at least it made him feel better to have a plan.

Putting down his backpack, he stretched out on the ground, forcing himself to rest. He shut his eyes, and thought about all the events that had led him here. Never could he have imagined his getaway trip to Tibet would have turned out this way. He was in an unknown town, heading for a city he knew only by name, accompanied by an unknown Tibetan woman wanted by the law.

After a length of time he estimated to be thirty minutes, John glanced at his watch once more. Eight minutes had gone by. John stood up and began pacing, nervously awaiting Sherab's return. After what seemed like hours, thirty minutes finally passed by. Faced with his expired time limit, he decided to give her another fifteen minutes before going in after her. His arrival into the town was sure to be a disaster, so he decided to give her a chance to make it back on her own.

Perhaps ten minutes later, approaching footsteps rewarded his patience. Throwing caution aside, he ran in the direction of the sounds. John's heart leapt for joy when he saw her familiar figure walking towards him. She smiled when she saw his face. He ran to her and hugged her fiercely. His heart hammered in his chest, making him wonder just how much he cared for this woman.

"Where have you been?" he asked her, knowing she could not answer him. With a beaming smile she handed John a rough sack of goods she had bought. He opened it up and saw a small loaf of bread, some dried fruits, dried meat, and a small pat of butter. John assumed this to be the yak butter Tibetans cherished so much.

"This is great!" he said to her, hoping to show appreciation for her efforts.

She still had that crazy grin on her face. It had not changed since he took the sack of goods from her. Then John noticed she still had one arm behind her back. She looked like a child, anxious to show a surprise. John smiled, and pointed at her hidden arm. Her smile grew, and she teasingly shook her head, taking a few steps backwards. He dropped the sack, and jumped the short distance between them. She squealed with delight and surprise when he caught her by the shoulders.

"Give it to me!" he said, smiling at her face. She slowly brought her arm around then. Her hand held a paper wrapped mound of dough, which she pushed towards him.

"Tsampa!" she said happily. She looked a little embarrassed by her child-like behavior then.

John was so moved by her gesture. After all the cold grain "tsampa" they had shared, she wanted him to try the real thing.

"Thank you," he said after an awkward moment of hesitation. His stomach growled, reminding him that they had not eaten lunch yet. Before he could taste it, she pinched a small amount of dough with her thumb and forefinger. She tossed it into the air, and looked at John expectantly. Unsure of what custom they were following, he pinched a piece of dough and tossed it like she had done. She smiled then, and motioned him to eat.

He pinched off a larger piece of tsampa, and gingerly put it into his mouth. It was delicious! The roasted barley mixed with the rather sweet butter gave it a wonderful nutty taste. It tasted somewhat like a moist nut loaf.

"Mmmmmmmm," he said, rubbing his stomach appreciatively. She sensed his contentment, and smiled happily. John handed her the tsampa, and she ate some as well. They soon finished the dough, and continued their feast with some buttered bread. He felt like a king after such a royal banquet.

After lunch they sat under the trees, looking at each other, wanting to speak but unable to. His hunger was more satisfied than it had ever been since they had first met.

John wanted to be well away from the town by nightfall, it was time to leave. He took a deep breath, and stood up. "Shigatse," he told her one more time. She nodded and stood up as well.

They kept behind the tree line running parallel to the town. After passing the busy area near the road and highway intersection, the houses were soon replaced with huts and tents. Not long after that they began a short ascent up a hill overlooking the town. That is when he noticed that the town was nestled between two hills, the one they had come down when they had entered, and the one they were climbing as they left.

At the top of the hill John turned around to look at the town. Its busy market area continued to bustle with people. Its temple still stood as gracefully as it had when they entered. He saw a small red figure in front of the temple. At this distance John could not tell if it was Regra or not. Sherab soon joined him as they looked down on this town that refused to help them. With a final longing look at the temple, Sherab turned around and continued walking. John adjusted the backpack on his shoulders, and turned his back on Same. Ignoring his fears, he followed Sherab into the unknown once again.

# Chapter 8

When the evening sun began to set, they had walked approximately four miles out of Same. The hours slipped by in silence, each of them lost in their thoughts. Neither of them could know that their first meaningful communication was so close at hand. They might have pressed on and walked during the night if they had realized it. With a look at the lowered sun, Sherab called a halt to their day's march.

While their evening meal lacked the same quality as that day's lunch, it was still superior to the food they had throughout their days before Same. They finished the last of the buttered bread, and skipped entirely the cold grain soup they usually ate. Tomorrow they would return to their regular diet, in order to preserve their supplies.

That night they slept facing each other, drawing comfort in each other's arms. Sherab felt her short hair rub under John's chin as her head rested against his chest. Her arm fell over his waist, while his lay on top of her arm, just below the shoulder. John pulled her gently with his arm, and she dragged herself closer against him, their legs now touching. Her body stiffened when John kissed the top of her head.

He was doing it again, she realized. John's tenderness had a way of knocking down all her defenses. She longed to remain in his arms, feeling kisses on her head, for the rest of her life. Each time she wondered if he was intentionally seducing her. But even though he won each time he tried, he never claimed his prize. He had her again tonight, if he wanted her. She hated herself for feeling this way, but one touch is all it would take.

Maybe he never took her because she was so ugly. No, she thought, there was no reason to think that badly of herself. She knew she was not attractive, but she saw the desire in John's eyes. It warmed her heart to think that this man found her attractive. She thought that John cared for her beyond just his physical desire. She had been moved to tears when he had caressed her repulsively deformed finger. How cruel life could be, to dangle such a man in front of her when she was unavailable.

After a few moments she felt John's body relax as he fell asleep. One of the thoughts she had when she first saw the town of Same was that they would sleep in a bed that night. A humorless smile crept on her face as she stared absently at the night sky. Once again she had a beautiful view of the stars under the clear Tibetan sky. Once again the hard earth floor yielded no comfort for her tired muscles. Shigatse was still a long way off, but she promised herself to find a bed once they arrived there.

Sherab's disappointment with Regra's rejection had sucked the last energy out of her. For one of the first times, John woke up before she did. When she awoke from her deep sleep, she found him sitting next to her, and watching her. After wiping the sleep from her eyes, she gratefully accepted the bowl of grains he offered. She still could not get past the thrill of having a man prepare her a meal. Even before her captivity, men in her culture did not prepare breakfast for their wives. She felt her cheeks flush to a crimson red, thinking of the husband and wife analogy that had naturally popped into her head. John and her were indeed living like husband and wife, in all aspects but one.

Breakfast was such a small gesture, but with such a deep meaning for her. This trait of his character continuously melted her heart. Even if they could share a conversation, she would not ask anything of him. She had been raised this way. Yet he came forth and served her breakfast without being asked. John always seemed to know what she needed, and would unhesitatingly provide it for her. She shook her head in amazement, wondering how he did this without ever being able to communicate with her.

Throughout the day the river led them in a slow ascent westward. The valley floor between the mountains narrowed gradually as they made their way to higher elevations. Even for the untrained eye, it soon became obvious how the river had cut this valley through the mountains during the past thousands of years.

Because of the river, the vegetation remained quite lush for a mountainous region. However, the higher altitude gradually diminished the diversity and quantity of plant life. Sherab began to notice that their barley plants were getting scarcer. She hoped the road to Shigatse would eventually head back down, or they may have trouble maintaining an adequate food supply.

They must have traveled close to ten miles that day. Her legs told her it felt more like fifteen miles because of the constant climb.

As the sun began to lower in the evening sky, a cold wind swept through the narrow valley. Sherab worried about the colder temperature they would experience that night. It would be safe to light a fire, but the area lacked any suitable firewood.

John tried stopping for their evening meal, but she would not let him. She felt annoyed at their lack of communication, for it prevented her from arguing with him. This thought made her smile, because perhaps she had discovered the secret to a more peaceful marriage. If you could not speak the same language, it would be harder to have disagreements. She kept walking, ignoring John's unintelligible words. With a shrug of defeat, he trudged after her.

Darkness had almost fallen when she spotted the smoke in the distance. They were approaching the town! She grabbed John's arm and pointed to the smoke.

"Thon," she said, smiling hopefully at him. Same had been a bitter disappointment to her. She thought that she would be able to seek refuge at any temple. But Regra had turned out to be a frightened rabbit. She saw the fear in his eyes as she told her story. To cover up his cowardice, he had even pretended to disbelieve the more outrageous parts of her story. But his nervous and jittery movements betrayed his fear, and she knew that he believed her.

How would John react when he eventually heard the truth about her? He seemed to have a much stronger character than Regra. He had shown his moral strength when he had dealt with Yu. But still, she had a bad feeling about telling him everything. He may not be afraid like Regra, but he would never look at her the same way again. The desire would leave him instantly, and his warm, tender feelings would not be far behind in their departure. This hurt her far more than she would have thought. Perhaps it was a blessing, for the temptation to give herself to John would no longer be an issue. He would feel revulsion for Sherab now.

Sherab had pressed on that night in order to reach this next town. Her plan to arrive at night had worked out perfectly. Now they would be able to get to Thon's temple under the cover of darkness. Their daylight movements in Same had been far too risky, especially now that she had seen John's bad temper. She had been stunned when he had started pounding on the temple door. John had seemed so reliable and rock-steady before then. Seeing him lose control made him more human and unpredictable in her eyes. She thought that she might never fully know this man, even if she had a lifetime to try.

The semi-darkness made it almost impossible to find the few remaining grain plants. They soon gave up, and shared the half-bowl they had gathered. Sherab did not feel as worried about dipping into their food supply tonight, for the town would surely have a market.

Fortunately, she did run into some pretty flowers while hunting for the grains. She felt guilty for having failed to leave an offering to Buddha at the Same temple. But circumstances had prevented her from returning to the temple after they had left in such a hurry. She prayed for forgiveness, and hoped that these flowers would appease Buddha at the Thon temple.

After dinner, John immediately began unpacking the bedroll. Sherab's hands caught him by surprise when she prevented him from releasing the bedroll from the backpack. He looked up at her questioningly.

"Thon" she said, indicating that they had to move on. She was not surprised by his reaction, because normally they slept away from towns. But she was unable to explain her reasons to him, and had to simply point to the town.

Sherab saw the exhaustion in his movements as he sat down wearily. "No," he said tiredly, followed by a stream of incomprehensible foreign words.

"John! I don't know what you're saying! Does this make you understand how it feels to be spoken to in a language you don't understand? Get up! We're sleeping in a temple tonight." She was tired, and did not like losing her patience like this. But he could be so stubborn!

John looked at her determined face, and sighed. He mumbled a few more words to her before standing up painfully. He donned the backpack, and once again followed her towards Thon.

They traveled the last mile to Thon in total darkness. Each step posed a risk of twisting an ankle in an unseen hole or over an unseen rock. At least the slow pace suited their tired legs. They slowed down even more when they reached the outlying huts of the town.

In these rural towns, Tibetans went to sleep when the sun went down, and got up with the morning dawn. The village seemed deserted as they quietly made their way through the darkened street. Sherab tried to pierce the darkness around her, looking for a building with the silhouette of an elegant Tibetan temple.

As the street narrowed, she recognized the empty stalls of Thon's market area. The houses after the market were noticeably sturdier than the huts earlier on. She knew she was approaching the town center. Up ahead she saw a small light bulb shining a dim light over a building's door. It was too far away to see any details of the building, but she hoped it might be the temple.

John soon spotted the light as well, and froze. She nearly bumped into him after he suddenly stopped. The lit up building was on the right side of the street. John went to the far left side of the street and slowly continued walking towards the light. When they were within just a few houses from the light, John crouched behind a small livestock fence nearby. He got Sherab's attention, and pointed to the light. Staring in that direction, she now made out the faint glow of a cigarette. The smoker was just outside the range of the bulb's illumination. Her thoughts turned back to Same, and the smoking soldier in front of the Chinese office.

This was probably the Thon administrative office, and she understood John's increased caution. But she also felt excited because the temple must be nearby. She could now see the buildings on this side of the office. While they were above the local average in wealth, they did not have the splendor of a temple. The temple must have been on the other side of the office.

She signaled to John that they should go behind the house beside them, and pass the office through alleys away from the main street. He nodded and began making his way behind the house. Unlike Same, they did not have to worry about people seeing them, the whole town seemed to be sleeping. Sherab hoped that John now understood why she had wanted to reach Thon that night.

Soon they could see the office between two of the houses they were passing. They were now directly across from the smoker. Sherab could not see the cigarette glow from this distance, but the light bulb marked the position clearly. They passed two more houses before turning and heading back towards the street. As they rounded the last corner, she saw the unmistakable outline of the temple.

"The temple," John whispered to her, pointing his finger at it in the darkness. She nodded, mentally registering this new word in his language. "Lhakang", she answered, giving him the Tibetan equivalent. They had to begin learning each other's language slowly, she thought as she smiled in the darkness. They quietly crossed the street, and ran along the side of the temple. Her heart beat wildly, while she kept imagining sounds of pursuit from the Chinese soldier stationed at the office. They followed the temple's wall and went around to the rear of the building.

After walking the length of the rear wall without encountering a door, her pulse began to quicken once more. They would have to enter through the front door. She cautiously peered around the front of the temple. The next building's light bulb seemed impossibly bright now that they were this close. The faint glow of the cigarette momentarily brightened as the soldier took a puff.

The temple's semi circular front wall would take them out of the soldier's line of sight when they reached the doors. A set of double doors at the center of the circular arc broke the otherwise smooth wall. Each end of the arc was punctuated with a pillar rising up to the top of the wall. Hugging the wall, Sherab began creeping into the arc. Each step brought her closer to the point where the opposing end of the arc would hide her from the soldier's view. She did not so much hear John as feel his presence behind her as they approached the central doors.

The ornately carved doors stood before them at a height of perhaps eight or nine feet. She had no doubt that they were made of thick and very solid hardwood. They had reached the door, but did not know what to do now. A quick pull on the handle confirmed their suspicion that the door was locked. Tibetan temples were not usually wired with doorbells either. Pounding at the door would surely bring the soldier to them more quickly than someone inside. Sherab knocked timidly, barely making a sound. She was not sure that someone standing immediately inside could have heard that knock through the solid door. She tried knocking a little bit louder, but it still sounded too muted to draw anyone's attention inside.

They looked at each other helplessly. Sherab stomped her foot in frustration. Here was the flaw in the plan of a nighttime entry into a town. They had made it safely to the temple, but had no way of getting behind its doors. She finally sat down in front of the doors, trying to collect her thoughts. Her tired mind only thought of going back out of town to sleep, she could not think of any clever tricks for breaking into the temple.

Sherab jumped when she heard the latch being worked behind her. Before she could move out of the way, the door was swinging open. The door struck her back when it had opened two feet outwards. A startled cry came from inside when the door stopped suddenly against her back. The woman inside could probably see her legs, as well as John standing next to the door. The door began to close again. John quickly stuck his foot between the door and the wall. His boot absorbed most of the impact, but he still winced with pain when the weight of the door crushed his foot against the wall.

He kept his foot in the door, while the three of them stared at each other silently. As Sherab had feared, their scuffle had made enough noise to alert the nearby soldier.

"Who is there?" he called out in Chinese.

Sherab spoke quietly to the woman inside the door.

"Please, we mean you no harm. I am Tibetan, and I need shelter just for tonight." She did not mind lying, she only had a precious few seconds to convince this woman to let her in. The woman hesitated, shifting her eyes between Sherab and the dirty, western foreigner blocking her temple's door. "Regra from Same sent me to see you," Sherab lied again. They were still out of sight from the soldier, but then she heard the unmistakable sound of approaching footsteps.

"Please," Sherab told the woman, "we won't hurt you. We have done nothing wrong, at least hear our story before giving us to the Chinese. This western man is simply trying to help me."

Sherab's back tingled in expectation of a bullet piercing through her robe. The soldier shouted another question as he approached. The woman inside finally shouted a response.

"It's just me, Lobsang. I tripped on my own robe while going for my evening walk."

She grabbed John's shoulder with surprising strength and pulled him inside the door. Sherab needed no help, she jumped in right behind John. The woman stepped outside and left the door open just an inch. Sherab could just make out the soldier's footsteps as he climbed the stairs to the temple wall. Sherab took small shallow breaths, too afraid of making the slightest noise. The two outside talked for what seemed like an hour, but realistically was no more than three minutes.

Sherab released a long breath when she finally heard the soldier's footsteps returning towards the administrative office. After his retreating footsteps could no longer be heard, the door swung open once more, and their benefactor came inside. Her head was shaved, like Sherab's had been not long ago. Her long orange robe gave her an almost regal appearance. The unassuming nun's eyes contrasted with the colorful robe. The brown eyes seemed sad and humbled by life itself. Despite the defeat in her eyes, a spark of intelligence flashed behind them as she quickly assessed her two intrusive guests in much the same way they were currently sizing her up.

"Thank you so much for letting us in," Sherab said, finally breaking the silence in the dark temple.

"You're welcome," she replied, "I am Lobsang Yangkyi. Who are you, and why were you standing outside this temple?"

"My name is Sherab Choezom, and this is John Pearson. I can't thank you enough for protecting us. I know you took a risk for us. We didn't think anyone would hear our knocks on the door."

"I heard no knocks on the door. I like to take a short walk in the evening, it's very peaceful."

John asked her a question then, and to Sherab's surprise Lobsang answered him is his own language. Visible relief spread over John's face, someone finally understood him. He smiled charmingly as he spoke to her again. Sherab felt an irrational twinge of jealousy as the two of them held a private conversation.

"What language does he speak? English?" Sherab had guessed the most obvious choice.

"Yes, he's Canadian," Lobsang informed her. Sherab felt saddened that this woman could learn so much about John in such a short time, just from speaking his language. "Now I think we had better go into my office to discuss your situation."

Lobsang then led them down the darkened hallway. They turned into another hallway, and soon stopped in front of an office door. It was unlocked, and Lobsang motioned them to enter as she opened it. Unlike the Same office, this one was bigger, and did not adjoin into a bedroom. The long hallway and this office told Sherab that Thon had a more prestigious temple than Same. This town was either larger, or was lucky to have wealthier citizens.

John surprised Sherab when he immediately took control of the conversation. Although she felt excluded, Sherab decided to let them talk as much as they wanted. She began to understand how frustrated John must have been in the Same temple.

"May I ask what you've been talking about?" Sherab asked Lobsang politely when she detected a break in the conversation.

"Certainly. John has asked me to be a translator between the two of you. He told me about your problems with his tour guide. I already explained to him that these 'guides' are all government employees. They're usually ex-military, and Communist party members.

I also explained to him that nuns do not enjoy a lot of freedom in Tibet. Therefore, beyond translation services, I may not have much to offer the two of you. But John seems determined to help you. His main frustration is that he doesn't know what you are running from, and what help you need. All he knows is that you want to go to Shigatse."

"I'm also frustrated by our lack of communication," Sherab answered. "I told my story to Regra, but he didn't seem to believe me. I actually told you a small lie at the front door. I'm sorry, but Regra did not send me to you."

Lobsang smiled at her gently. "That's why I decided to let you in. If you were desperate enough to lie, I knew you really needed my help."

This puzzled Sherab. "How did you know I lied?"

"I know Regra. He has a kind heart, but he fears his own shadow. He would never send someone in trouble to me or to anyone else."

"He just forced us out of the temple," Sherab confessed.

"Don't think badly of him. He and his family have suffered much at the hands of the government. He's a broken man now."

Lobsang studied Sherab for a moment. "From the look of your apparent abuse, I would assume you spent some time as a political prisoner in Lhasa. This would explain the guide's interest in returning you to prison."

"I would like to explain everything to you, and to John. Are you ready to translate for me?"

Sherab felt eager to finally 'talk' to John. Lobsang turned her chair so that she sat between Sherab and John, facing both of them. John settled into his own chair, and listened to Sherab through Lobsang's voice.

"My name is Sherab Choezom, as you already know. My brother, Jhampa, was a monk. I have not seen him in six years, I don't know if he is still alive. Jhampa was always frustrated by the Chinese presence in Tibet. One day he let out his frustration, and joined a protest march in Lhasa. I didn't go of course, but I can still imagine his proud face chanting 'Free Tibet!'

My brother was arrested when the soldiers broke up the demonstration. My parents and I did not hear anything about him for almost one year after his arrest. I was nineteen when the Chinese soldiers arrived at our door. We were informed that my brother had escaped, and now his family was under arrest. My father tried to shut the door on the soldiers, but they beat him with their rifles. My mother was also hit in the head when she screamed and refused to let me go."

John looked at Sherab while she spoke. Neither her voice nor her expression revealed any of the emotions that were boiling inside her. She kept her tone very formal, like she had practiced in her head so many times. She did not want John to pity her, nor to feel disgust for her. She would reveal the facts as plainly as she could, knowing that she would probably lose him anyway. She had been arrested five years ago now, only because her brother had escaped prison. Logically she knew she was not at fault, but emotionally she could not deny the self-hate she felt. John seemed to study her deformed finger, and the scars on her head. Her self-consciousness increased dramatically under his gaze. She lowered her eyes away from him.

"The soldiers used me in the truck, in front of my parents. The pain and shame were the smallest part of my sorrow. I wanted to become a nun like you," Sherab said, looking in Lobsang's direction.

"I had saved myself until that day. They took away my purity. That was the last time I saw my parents, and I still don't know whether they're alive or not.

For the first week they tortured me every day. They kept asking me where my brother was. I don't know if they believed me or not when I repeated that I had not seen him since his arrest a year earlier. They smiled when they touched me with the electric stick. I would try to avoid it as much as I could, but they would corner me, touch my face, my arms, and my ears. Once they tied me on top of the table and put the stick between my legs. I don't know how long they left it there, but I remember screaming alone in the room. I thought I had died and was sent to hell for my brother's crime. I could not believe I could be alive with this amount of pain."

Sherab tried to keep her face expressionless as she recalled her captivity. Twin streams of tears now ran down each eye, defying her attempts to remain emotionless.

"One day they stopped torturing me earlier than usual. In trying to avoid the electric stick, I had spun around quickly and smashed my head against the corner of a metal cabinet. I bled a lot, and fell unconscious after a few minutes." Her hand reached up and rubbed the white scar on her head as she told them about her injury. "The next day they resumed their interrogation, but tied me to a chair so that I would not re-injure my head.

After the first week, a high-ranking officer came into the room while the regular guards began to torture me. He looked at me for a while before doing anything. Then he stopped them, and said that I was to be transferred to another location. I didn't care then where he took me, as long as it was out of the torture room. How could I know how evil the officer would be?"

Sherab broke down sobbing then. Lobsang took her and had her lean against her while she cried. She hid her face in the older nun's robe, not daring to look towards John. If she were to finish her story, she could not face the look in his eyes. When Sherab regained her composure, she continued speaking to Lobsang.

"They tied a bandana over my eyes, and put me in a truck. They drove me to my new location, where I stayed for the next five years. For the first few days they let me recover from my first prison. They fed me, gave me fresh clothes, let me sleep, and above all, did not beat me.

The officer returned to see me after a few days and informed me that I was to be part of a great plan for the good of China and Tibet. I was to follow all orders given to me without question, or I would be beaten. If I continued to resist I would be killed. There were no other options, obey or suffer and die. He told me that I was going to meet a boy, and that I must not speak to him except to directly answer his questions. Others were going to be with me, and I could use them as guidance for what was proper and what was not. He smiled then, and said the guards would be happy to help me learn appropriate behavior.

The officer led me through several hallways, and then down an elevator. We descended a long time, my final destination was deep underground. I never went back up those elevators until my escape several weeks ago. From the elevator, we went down a short hall where two armed soldiers guarded a metal door. They recognized the officer, and immediately let us pass. When I entered the room, I saw the boy sitting in a big, soft, red chair. That was the first time I saw our Panchen Lama."

Lobsang's jaw literally dropped open after she translated this last sentence. Sherab continued to speak, but Lobsang was unable to go on. Sherab noticed, and politely stopped talking until she could get Lobsang's attention once more.

The supreme leader of the Tibetans is the Dalai Lama. After the 1959 conflicts between China and Tibet, the Dalai Lama escaped to India. He has been holding together a government in exile in India since that time. The second highest-ranking Tibetan is the Panchen Lama, or 'Great Scholar'. The Dalai Lama announced the reincarnation of the eleventh Panchen Lama in 1995. Sherab knew that the Chinese did not want to allow the Dalai Lama to have any influence in Tibet. Even though they had no authority in such matters, they rejected his choice of Panchen Lama. The government arrested the Panchen Lama, who was then just a six-year-old boy. The boy and his family had not been seen since.

In order to support their claim that the Dalai Lama's choice of Panchen Lama was invalid, the Chinese declared that they had found the true reincarnation of the Panchen Lama. Then they escorted him from Beijing to Shigatse, the traditional home of Panchen Lamas.

"You do mean the real Panchen Lama?" Lobsang asked, when she recovered from the shock. Sherab could tell that Lobsang already knew the answer to the question, but felt compelled to ask it anyway.

"Yes, Lobsang. The Panchen Lama as discovered by His Holiness the Dalai Lama."

"You are the first person to have seen our real Panchen Lama. Part of me is overjoyed to find out that he's alive. But part of me is so angry that he is being kept as a prisoner." Sherab remained silent, giving time for Lobsang to adjust to the startling news.

"I suspect that your desire to go to Shigatse has something to do with the Panchen Lama," Lobsang added thoughtfully.

John spoke up then, asking Lobsang a question. Sherab avoided his eyes, and looked down at the floor in front of her chair. Lobsang spoke with John for a few minutes.

"He wanted to know the significance of your story," Lobsang explained. "I briefed him on our Panchen Lama's troubled history."

"May I continue now?" Sherab asked. She felt her resolve to continue begin to weaken, and she desperately wanted to finish the story. Lobsang merely nodded, and waited for her to resume her narrative.

"The boy was nine years old then, he had been in captivity for three years. The first thing I noticed about him was how fat he had become. I had never seen a child with a double chin. His arms and legs looked like they were overstuffed furniture. His yellow robe was dirty with food stains.

His face had a look of concentration when I entered the room. He never looked towards us to acknowledge our presence, despite the loud noise made by the metal door. I turned to see what he was staring at, and almost fainted with disbelief. A Tibetan monk had lifted up his orange robe above his stomach, and was mounted behind a nun. The nun was on her hands and knees, and was moaning in lust as the monk entered her."

Lobsang began to shout at Sherab then. Such outrageous accusations were not to be taken lightly by a member of the order of Tibetan nuns.

"No nun would take part in this kind of perverted behavior! How dare you try to tell me these lies?"

Sherab replied with just as much anger, feeling the defeat at Same returning.

"I am telling you what I saw! Do you want me to finish the story or do you want to hide in your temple like Regra?"

After everything she had been through, the last thing Sherab needed now was for the outside world not to believe her. The sting of Lobsang's words cut into

her heart with the same deadly efficiency of a pointed dagger. Lobsang calmed
down somewhat after Sherab's harsh words.

"I'm sorry," she said without real feeling, "please continue."

"Later I found out that they were not true Tibetan monks and nuns. They were
simply prisoners like me, given a choice to obey or die. The Chinese dressed
them in holy robes simply to help destroy the young Panchen Lama's mind."

Lobsang's face softened noticeably. She looked guiltily towards Sherab as the
truth dawned on her.

"That was their great plan you see. They were going to totally corrupt the
Dalai Lama's chosen boy. At some point when he is old enough, they'll release
him to the public. Then Tibetans will think that the Dalai Lama has chosen
incorrectly when they see such a terrible young man. The Tibetans will embrace
the Chinese Panchen Lama. The Chinese will have achieved a great victory over
the Dalai Lama. His influence in Tibet will diminish as people lose confidence in
his abilities to manage Tibetan affairs from India."

"This explains many things, Sherab," Lobsang said. "For the last two weeks
the Chinese have been conducting far more searches than usual. I've heard the
same from other monasteries, it's not just in Thon. Until now I've had no
explanation for this. But it seems obvious that they're searching for you. They
can't let you tell what you've seen."

Sherab was eager to continue her story. It felt like she had been cleansing her
mind by getting it all out.

"Before I could react to such a disgusting sight, I felt someone trip and push
me to the floor. I turned over and saw the officer removing his pants. I turned my
head in panic, and noticed that I had the boy's attention now. He smiled at me
and turned his body to watch me more comfortably.

I was still too stupid to realize I was helpless. When the officer began to come
down on me, I swung my hand to scratch out his eyes. How could I participate in
hurting this innocent boy's mind? The officer reacted quickly, and almost
avoided my fingernails. Only my smallest finger scratched him. I cut a small
mark on his cheek."

She held up her deformed small finger then. Lobsang took a deep breath
before continuing. Hearing the story was hard enough, but repeating it to John
was also taking its toll on her nerves.

"The officer looked at me with his cold brown eyes, and told me I would pay for that. He then called three men over to come help him with me. Two men held down each of my legs, spread out. The third man held one of my arms over my head, while the officer held the last arm. They let me struggle for a while, until I tired out. Then the officer called the boy over.

I looked up in shock when I saw him eagerly bounce out of his chair and run towards us. He looked at the officer with what seemed like worship. The officer nodded at my arm, and told the boy to hold it down. The boy was so excited to help the officer. He kneeled on my arm, and also used his hands to steady it. The whole time he smiled with excitement at his officer's adventure. I gave up then, and cried while the officer used me, and Tibet's great Panchen Lama held me down."

Sherab noticed the great tears running down Lobsang's face. She thought that Lobsang might have preferred hearing that the Chinese had killed the boy, rather than corrupting him in such an evil way. These were not the first tears shed for Tibet, Sherab thought sadly.

Lobsang fought for control of her voice as Sherab continued.

"When the officer was done, he got up and used my robe to wipe himself. He then got dressed, came around, and took my arm from the boy. 'Look what she did to me with her finger!' he said to the boy. He then grabbed my finger and bent in backwards until it snapped. I screamed in agony and a woman quickly silenced me by stuffing a cloth into my mouth. The woman was another Chinese officer in this new prison. The boy asked the male officer if he had broken the finger. The officer said yes, and held my hand to the boy. 'Move it around, you'll see it's broken.' My body convulsed as the boy played with my finger, easily bending it in directions it could not normally have gone. I screamed and screamed into the cloth held against my mouth, but no one seemed to notice.

That's when I realized just how effective was the Chinese plan. They were completely stripping the boy of any morals, of any care for people's suffering.

For the next month, once a week the officer would re-break my finger. On the last week he held my hand down and gave the boy a hammer. After that, the finger became so swollen and purple, that they left it alone for fear that I would lose it.

The boy had a name for all the prisoners in his jail. He enjoyed giving people silly names like 'Potato', or 'Chair'. For the girl named Chair, he often sat on her back while watching the entertainment around him. My new name was 'Claw'."

Sherab held up her deformed finger to show how appropriately she had been named.

"They spent several hours per day educating the boy. They did not want a stupid young man, just an immoral young man. They taught him the history of China, and adjusted the facts to show that Tibet indeed was part of China. They taught him to read and write Chinese as well as Tibetan. He proved to be a good student. He learned very quickly, and paid careful attention to his teachers. I'm sure he would have made a great Panchen Lama."

Sherab ended her sentence with a sob. She felt such deep sorrow for the innocent boy, and for the Tibetan people. Politics and religion have caused far too much suffering in human history, she thought angrily.

"They also taught him how to hate. They fed him hatred for all foreign countries, hatred for Tibetans seeking independence, hatred for the poor, hatred for women. They taught him how to behave like an immoral God. He learned these lessons just as well as the more academic studies.

When the Panchen Lama was old enough to..." Lobsang paused as Sherab sought her words, "old enough to perform like a man, he also began to use the women in the jail. That was the worst part for me. He was still a boy, and supposed to be a great Panchen Lama. The Chinese tried to interest him in using the men too, but thankfully he was not curious enough to try. Perhaps with time he'll get bored with women and start experimenting, I don't know.

The first years were almost impossible to endure for us. But when the Panchen Lama began to take part in the activities, we all pretty much lost our sanity. It wasn't much longer before I had an opportunity to escape.

Two of the male prisoners had planned to kill the Panchen Lama. It was a great sacrifice for them, they would be punished in their next life for committing such a terrible murder. But they chose to pay this price in order to save the Dalai Lama's reputation.

None of us knew of their plan until they tried to execute it. One day when the Panchen Lama went into the restroom area, they jumped on him. This was the time when he was furthest away from the guards. One man used his hands to strangle him, while the other kicked his head. When the guards approached, the second man stopped kicking. He tried to hold off the guards while the first continued to strangle the boy.

I was near the metal door when it crashed open. The armed soldiers had heard the commotion and were coming to help. One soldier ran towards the fighting, while the other continued to guard the door. By the time the first soldier arrived at the fighting, the prison guards had already knocked down the blocking prisoner, and were beating the strangling prisoner off the boy. I had time to see the boy roll away in pain, but still alive, when another fight broke out near me.

A man and woman took advantage of the situation and attacked the soldier at the door. As they advanced he swung his rifle and struck the man down. The woman reached him and began clawing and biting at his face. Remember that I said we had all lost our sanity, we were almost animals by then. The soldier began overpowering the crazed woman. I noticed that his head was close to the opened metal door. I went to him, and with all my strength smashed my elbow into the side of his head. His head snapped against the edge of the door, and he lost consciousness.

By then the other soldier spotted this new trouble. From across the room he simply raised his rifle and fired at us. The woman's chest seemed to explode all over the wall. I took a single step, and was out in the hallway. I heard another shot ping loudly against the door now protecting me. Alarms began ringing throughout the building. I ran to the elevator just as the doors were closing.

When I reached the top, there was even more confusion there than in the jail. The soldiers getting ready to enter the elevator looked at me uncertainly. I shouted at them hysterically that the Panchen Lama was in danger, and that the officer had sent me to get help. The mention of the boy was enough to panic them and send them down the elevator without bothering about me. Soon I was outside, using the confusion around me as cover."

Sherab relaxed visibly after ending her story. It was like a great burden had been lifted off her shoulders. Lobsang stared straight ahead of her, lost in her own thoughts. Sherab still could not face John. She accepted that their close relationship had to be over, but that did not make it any easier to look into his eyes. Sherab felt ashamed for having John near her for so long without his knowing her ugly secrets. Neither John, nor any other man, would ever want her now. She thought about her coming ordainment as a nun, hoping to fill the newly formed void in her heart.

\*\*\*

John's mind was reeling with all the implications of what Sherab had told them. He first looked at Lobsang, but she simple stared into space now that the translation was over. All in all, Sherab seemed to be in the best mental condition among the three of them at that time. Although she frustrated John by avoiding his eyes, she seemed relieved to have finally told her remarkable story.

So Yu was probably a Chinese soldier then. That explained some of his rough behavior. John broke the silence first.

"Well this explains Yu's eagerness to arrest her. Even if he didn't know about Sherab, as a soldier he felt committed to returning her to prison."

In his own mind he also thought how her story explained Regra's warning about John's life being in danger. "I think we are all in great danger, aren't we?" he asked needlessly.

"Yes, John, we are." Lobsang answered. "But more importantly, Tibet is in great danger. If the Chinese succeed with their plan, our hope for freedom is lost." She paused a moment before adding a thought that chilled him to the bone. "You have to get her to India, John. You must take her to His Holiness the Dalai Lama, he must hear her story."

Well at least that fit in well with his plans to get out of the country. But he had no idea that such a political bomb would accompany him. In retrospect, he felt lucky that Yu had not killed him. If Yu had not had so much confidence in his ability to arrest them both, he might have simply done away with John in the remote countryside.

John felt like Sherab had awakened him and exposed him to real life. He thought about the reckless life he had led, and suddenly felt so immature next to Sherab. He had never taken life seriously. Her story made him appreciate what he had always taken for granted. Suddenly he was overcome with a need to show her what it felt like to have a good life. He wanted to care for her, and give her the life she deserved. He had never before felt such strong emotions for a woman. The feeling was strange and exhilarating. He committed himself to getting her through this. If she would allow him, he would devote his life to bringing her happiness.

He had to suppress the happy smile that came from this thought. The mood in the room was somber after Sherab's revelations. Lobsang would think him callous if he started grinning like a mischievous schoolboy. With a flash of insight he realized that he was hopelessly in love with Sherab Choezom.

Lobsang interrupted his thoughts. "John, we must get her out of Tibet, or she will be killed. You must get her to the Dalai Lama before she is captured!"

His nerves were already raw from their journey across the Tibetan countryside. He did not take well to Lobsang's added pressure.

"You've already told me that," he retorted. "But you haven't told me how I'm supposed to magically fly her off to India. I'm just a backpacking tourist visiting your country. Apparently my life is in danger too, so believe me, I'm very interested in leaving as quickly as possible. Now if you can stop telling me what I need to do, and start telling me how I'm supposed to do it, I will be very appreciative."

"I'm sorry" Lobsang replied, "I know this is difficult for you. I am still shocked by what is happening to our Panchen Lama. Forgive me, I am not thinking clearly."

Perhaps he had overreacted with her, he thought. He was worried about his own skin, and Lobsang was worried about her entire country. He tried to soften the blow. "Besides, you need to convince Sherab to leave the country. She's been trying to get us to Shigatse for a long time."

Lobsang turned to Sherab, and began speaking to her in Tibetan. He heard his name mentioned a few times, as well as "Shigatse". Soon Sherab lost her calm demeanor, and began to argue with Lobsang. Sherab seemed very opposed to Lobsang's views, which he assumed were the plans for India. It became almost comical to watch the two of them babbling away in a foreign tongue, hands and arms waiving frantically as they tried to persuade each other. Finally Sherab stood up in anger, and stomped her foot. She shouted something to Lobsang, and clearly ended her sentence with emphasis on "Shigatse". She then walked off to the other side of the room, and stood facing the shuttered window.

"Care to fill me in?" he asked Lobsang, with a barely suppressed grin.

Lobsang did not miss his humor. "How can you find any of this funny?" she asked. Before he could answer, she told him of their argument.

"Sherab wants to go to Shigatse to expose the Chinese plan. Since that is the Panchen Lama's traditional home, she sees it as fitting that the plan is made public there. Each month there is a small press conference at the Panchen Lama's home. The Chinese use this opportunity to show how peaceful life is in Chinese occupied Tibet. The conference is carefully controlled, but a few foreign journalists are invited to attend. That's where Sherab wants to tell her story, in front of the foreign journalists."

"But why in Tibet?" John asked. "She can talk to as many foreign journalists as she wants once we leave the country."

"I do agree with you John," Lobsang answered him. "But Sherab does have some valid points. First, leaving the country will not be easy. You mentioned flying, but that is completely out of the question. The only illegal way out of Tibet is to cross the mountains into Nepal or India. Many people try to do this. Some succeed, but many are forced to turn back because of the difficult conditions. Many also die, and many are captured.

Second, you are a white man. This will help her a lot with the journalists. It will add to her credibility, and it will prevent the Chinese from stepping in before she has a chance to talk.

Her third point is more emotional, and should not have any weight on our decision. This is her country, and she does not want to run away. She wants to stand up here and tell her story to Tibetans. She wants our people to know that the Panchen Lama is alive, and being abused by the Chinese."

John's head ached with all the information that flooded it that night. Perhaps Sherab was right, his only safe way out of the country was with public exposure. He could stand up in downtown Lhasa with this story, and still be arrested. But in front of international journalists, the Chinese would have to be much more careful.

Especially in his tired state, this option was sounding much better than getting a crash course in mountain climbing. He had enjoyed looking at the snow capped Himalayas from a distance. John did not think he would enjoy hiking through them.

"I think this is Sherab's game more than ours," he told Lobsang tiredly. "I have followed her this far, I think I can follow her to Shigatse. Like you said, she has valid points. I personally don't really see an option here. India sounds great, but also impossible."

"Very well," Lobsang said, resigned to their decision. "But there is not much I can do to help you. It would be foolish for me to endanger myself now. If you two should get caught, I am the only one left who can bring this story to the Dalai Lama's ears."

"I was not asking you to take risks, Lobsang. Sherab and I are already in danger, there's no need to put more people at risk."

Lobsang nodded, accepting his excusal of her reluctance to be put in danger. "But there are some things I can do to help you. Of course you may take as much food as you need for your travel. But I will also arrange for a truck to pick you up tomorrow morning. You will need to get off near the Chinese checkpoint, and then meet the truck again after the checkpoint. But at least you will be able to drive most of the way. I'm sure you've had enough walking."

"Yes," he nodded vigorously, "a ride to Shigatse is the best thing you could do for us. But also, look at how Sherab is dressed. Could someone go into the town tomorrow and buy her some more suitable traveling clothes? She needs decent boots, pants, and a warm shirt. I have money to pay for all this."

"That will not be a problem," Lobsang replied. "I will send someone as soon as the markets open in the morning. Is there anything else you need?"

He smiled at her. "Right now what I want most is a hot bath and a soft bed."

She smiled back at him then, "I'm sure that can be arranged too. You are a brave man John, it is fate that Sherab found you. Tibet can never thank you enough for what you are about to do."

He felt uncomfortable under her sincere gaze. It was not bravery that kept him going, it was the danger to his life. He looked down and his feet, and then over at Sherab's back. Lobsang reached over and took his face in her hands. She gently turned his head so that he had to look directly at her. "No matter what happens John, you must understand that you will be greatly rewarded for this in your next life."

John was taken back by the sureness of her voice. He did not believe in reincarnation, yet hearing her say these words so naturally, raised doubts in his mind. He certainly wanted to believe her.

"Thank you Lobsang, your words are a comfort to me." It was not a lie. Even though they did not share the same beliefs, the care in her words comforted him.

He glanced at his watch, which showed the time to be just past midnight. Lobsang noticed his gesture and began preparations for their night in the temple. "I will get someone to help you with your bath, and then I will help Sherab," she said as she left the room.

There was an awkward silence when Sherab and John were left alone in the room. They were both a little embarrassed by the intimacy of the details she had shared earlier. He felt selfish for letting his embarrassment keep him away from her when she needed someone so badly. He walked over to her, and took her hands as they faced each other. When her eyes began to water, John released her hands and quickly wiped the tears away with his thumbs. She grabbed him then and they embraced in silence. He tried unsuccessfully to prevent his own tears from spilling out when he thought of all that she had been through. He hoped to wipe them away before she could notice. Some behaviors are learned, he was taught not to cry in public. However, before he could pull away, she felt his wetness on her face, and turned to look at him.

Despite the dirt and the streaking tears, she was so beautiful. Their bodies were still touching in their embrace. John could not resist her face so close to his. He closed the few inches of space between them and kissed her lips. For a brief second he felt her body stiffen, but then she relaxed. Her lips moved against his, and her hand reached up behind his head to press their lips together harder. His hands began to explore her back, then her hips. The passion was mounting between them at a frightening speed. Both her hands were on his head and neck now. He reached down and pulled her waist firmly against his, wanting her to feel him.

A second before the door opened, they both heard the approaching footsteps. Like children caught stealing cookies before dinner, they quickly separated and faced the door. Lobsang paused for a moment, seeing their expectant, guilty faces. A sideways glance showed him that Sherab was blushing as much as he must be. He prayed that Lobsang attributed the redness to crying.

Before she could say anything, a young man, barely past being a boy, entered the room behind Lobsang. "This is Gyatrul," she told John. "He is studying with us to become a monk. Unfortunately he doesn't know very much English yet. But I have instructed him to prepare a bath for you, and to show you to your sleeping quarters for tonight."

Gyatrul looked at Sherab briefly, and then concentrated his attention on this foreigner in his temple. The boy's eyes were red, Lobsang must have woken him up to come help them. His eyes shone brightly as he studied every detail before him, with the natural curiosity of the young.

Lobsang spoke a few words to him. He nodded, and motioned John to follow him. John gave a quick, guilty nod to Sherab as he picked up the backpack and followed Gyatrul. The boy led John down a flight of stairs. The layout of the temple seemed like a maze for his tired mind. John lost count of how many turns and hallways they walked. He almost bumped into Gyatrul's back when he stopped suddenly in front of a door. John followed him into a tiny bedroom, like a college dorm room.

Holding up his hands like two stop signs, Gyatrul proudly said, "wait," in English. John gladly dropped the backpack, and sat heavily onto the edge of the bed. He bent to unlace his boots, and kicked them off. Never had a bed felt so comfortable as when he gratefully lay back, his feet still dangling over the edge.

Gyatrul could not have been gone more than five minutes, yet he still startled John out of a light sleep when he returned in the room.

The bath no longer sounded as interesting, sleep was now John's primary desire. He shuffled after Gyatrul in his socks, thankfully only a short distance away. Gyatrul showed him into a small bathroom where a steaming bath awaited him. A towel and a large white robe sat on a bench by the tub. On the rim of the old steel tub, a rough chunk of handmade soap lay ready for use.

"Thank you," he said to Gyatrul, with a weak smile on his face. The boy nodded happily, almost bowing. He shut the door behind him as he left. After undressing, John lowered himself into the bath, and smiled with the immense comfort the hot water gave his tired body. He remembered the times in his life where stress or fatigue had made him pour a hot bath. Each time the bath brought deliciously soothing sensations. As the Tibetan dirt washed off his body, he thought how this bath made all the others pale in comparison. The rough soap invigorated him. John scrubbed until his skin turned pink.

If he had not dirtied the bath water so much, he might have just stayed there and slept for the night. The thought of the clean white sheets waiting for him supplied the energy required to haul himself out of the bath. After quickly wiping himself dry, he slipped the clean robe over his head and carried his bundle of clothes to the bedroom.

His thoughts strayed back to his home in Toronto. He used to train somewhat regularly on his Nordic-Trac exercise machine. After this adventure, he would probably beat the poor machine into the ground with his newfound fitness. If he ever got back home, he thought darkly.

John's watch read a few minutes past one when he finally slipped into the sheets. He wanted to stay in bed until noon, he thought dreamily as sleep began to numb his mind. He felt completely at peace under the cool linen. He drifted off to sleep with a smile on his face. Of course he did not know that a frantic Gyatrul would come bursting through the door in an incredibly short two and a half hours.

## Chapter 9

"There is one more service I can offer you," Lobsang told Sherab after John had left the room.

Sherab tried to concentrate on Lobsang's words, but her lips would not stop tingling from John's kiss. She had been sure John would reject her after hearing the horrors of the last five years. Instead he had wiped the tears from her eyes and passionately kissed her lips. She could no longer deny her love for him. This truth increased her pain until it became unbearable. She loved a man, and he loved her in return. And once he brought her to Shigatse, she would leave him to become a nun. Fate seemed determined to crush her already broken heart.

"Sherab?" Lobsang said. Sherab shook her head and focused on Lobsang once again.

"I'm sorry, I must be tired. What did you say?"

"I said we have a very well-respected astrologer in our temple. I'm sure he would be interested in giving you a reading. He might be able to provide some information to help you on your mission to Shigatse."

A Tibetan astrologer here in this temple! This great news was the best thing to happen to Sherab in a long time. Well, not counting John.

"Oh Lobsang, that would be wonderful! I'm in need of some counseling for my future, not just for this Shigatse trip. My inner self is in such turmoil after those years in jail. Yes, please, let me consult your astrologer."

"I thought you would want to. I already sent someone to let him prepare for your visit. I hope you have enough energy left to see him tonight."

Sherab's pulse was beating quickly in anticipation. "Of course! I'm wide awake, this is so exciting."

Lobsang led Sherab down several narrow hallways before stopping in front of a set of double doors.

"I wish you well," Lobsang told Sherab, as she opened a door to let her in. Sherab entered the brightly lit room alone, and Lobsang shut the door behind her. She felt scared to find out her future. Logically she knew that she could better prepare for difficult situations with the knowledge that the astrologer would give her. Yet there was a certain security in not knowing what was ahead.

Several dozens of candles illuminated the astrologer's room. Candles were lit on the floor, on shelves, and on the desk tucked into the corner of the room. A large black and white board marked the center of the small room. Sherab recognized the nine magic numbers that would be used to help the astrologist read her future. He would arrange the numbers according to the date and time of her birth. Like most good Tibetan parents, Sherab's parents had made her memorize these critical statistics of her birth.

Symbols for the twelve astrological animal signs were carefully arranged in orderly positions beside the board. Sherab also recognized carvings for the five elements: wood, fire, earth, metal and water. The concept of the eight parkhas originated from ancient Chinese astrology. Tibet's unique astrological science was a blend of teachings from neighboring countries, mixed in with Tibetan Buddhist beliefs. The parkhas were formed as three sided figures. Each of the eight parkhas, arranged in a circle around the central board, represented a spirit, or deity. These spirits would each exert a different influence on an individual. An astrologer had to interpret the combinations of magic numbers, animals, elements, and parkhas to help guide a person's life.

"Welcome Sherab Choezom, I'm pleased that you were brought here tonight. My name is Yeshi, won't you please sit down."

The old man who spoke sat in front of the numbers board. His hand gesture invited Sherab to sit across from him. His gentle, smiling face helped Sherab overcome her nervousness. The astrologer's eyes twinkled in the candle glow, like small celestial systems within his wizened face. A long fold of yellow cloth hung beneath his outstretched arm. The rest of his robe hung loosely over his bony frame. Sherab felt exposed under his penetrating gaze, yet unafraid. She wanted him to see into her, and to share the wisdom of his years.

"Thank you for seeing me Your Holiness," Sherab spoke in an awed whisper.

He smiled demurely at her formal speech. "We're alone within these walls Sherab, please call me Yeshi."

"Thank you Yeshi."

He stared at her in silence for a few minutes, his eyes roaming over her entire body, and then resting on her face. She then gave him her birth information, and he began working on the astrological objects in front of him.

After several minutes, he looked up at Sherab with a sad expression. "You have suffered much my child. I see both the astrological and physical signs of this." Yeshi glanced at Sherab's hand as he spoke. "But I'm afraid your suffering is not yet at an end."

Sherab fought back tears of despair at his words. She had hoped to find comfort in his predictions, not fear.

"I have an important mission in Shigatse. Is there anything I can do to improve my chances of success?"

He studied his symbols carefully before replying.

"You would be best served by waiting at least three weeks before undertaking a major project. You are currently under the influence of Mars, a violent planet. Soon you will transition to Jupiter, which will greatly improve your chances of success in all your endeavors."

He paused a moment, and then added another piece of advice.

"I also think you should avoid meat for the next few weeks, fruits and vegetables will bring you better luck."

"That shouldn't be a problem!" Sherab laughed. "We have very little opportunity to have meals with meat lately."

"I think that will change soon," Yeshi told her with a hint of a smile. "No matter the size of the banquet, stay clear of the heavy foods like fresh meat."

She did not know how John and her would get access to such food, but she took note of his advice anyway. Astrologers frequently recommended which foods to eat and which foods to avoid during certain periods. She was happy that he had not told her to stay away from grains, their staple food along the road to Shigatse.

Sherab cleared her throat before asking her next, burning question.

"What about my next life? How can I improve my standing from my current realm?"

Yeshi smiled again before answering. "You need not ask questions for which you already know the answer. I don't think you came here for lessons in Buddhism."

"I'm sorry Yeshi," she replied quickly. Of course she knew how to improve. She had just wanted to indulge in her insecurities, and let this man tell her that everything would be OK. "I've been suffering from self-doubt for a long time now."

"You are young Sherab. You will have many years to improve your karma. Believe me, you will have lost your self-doubts by the time your child returns you to your people."

"My child?" Sherab replied in a startled voice.

"Yes, your child. Being an excellent mother will help you in your future lives as well. Help your child to grow strong and proud, and he will return you to where you belong."

"Yeshi, I'm confused! I am not leaving Tibet, and I will not have a child. I will remain here and become a nun." Sherab's mind was whirling. It was as if the old astrologer spoke of a stranger's life, not her own.

"The calling of the nun is a noble one indeed, but it is not your calling, Sherab."

"But Your Holiness, the astrologer who read my future years ago encouraged me to become a nun."

Yeshi looked at Sherab with great pity in his eyes. He made her feel like sitting on his lap, and having him rock her like a child.

"Sherab, what did you think about during your worst years of suffering?"

She thought carefully before answering. "Well, I often dreamed of finding peace in a temple. I dreamed of providing comfort to the suffering, as a nun in my temple."

"And how would you have survived all that time without your conviction of becoming a nun?"

Sherab saw where he was leading. "I, I don't know," she stammered. She felt deceived and saved at the same time. Her previous astrologer had lied to make her survive the hardships of captivity. Yeshi interrupted her confused thoughts.

"You are stronger now Sherab, never forget that. You have the strength to achieve your goals. Have faith, and you will make it."

"Thank you, Yeshi," she said weakly. Sherab certainly did not feel strong, for this man had just turned her world upside down. All through her life she had worked towards a single goal: ordainment as a nun.

"Like I told you before, you have some very trying times ahead of you." Yeshi reached around his neck and pulled on a leather necklace. "I would like you to wear this amulet. It can't save you, but it will help you receive some good luck."

Sherab looked in awe as Yeshi removed the intricately carved amulet from his neck. The wooden amulet had a dull sheen from years of being worn next to the skin. She hesitated to reach for such a gift. Yeshi leaned forward, took her hand in his rough and aged palm, and dropped the amulet to her. She felt a tingle of electricity as the amulet rested in her open palm. She slowly curled her fingers around it, drawing a miraculous strength from its aura. She could not remove her eyes from the beautiful designs on the ancient amulet.

Sherab looked up, not knowing how to express the depth of her gratitude to this man. He was gone. The door had been left ajar as he left, and she could see Lobsang waiting expectantly in the hallway.

"I hope His Holiness was of help to you."

"Yes," Sherab replied in a daze, "he certainly gave me a lot of new information."

"We can discuss it in the morning if you like. I am tired, and you must be exhausted. Let me bring you to your room for the night."

Sherab followed Lobsang through the temple's hallways. She felt totally disoriented with her life's goal taken away from her. Becoming a nun had been her life's compass, steering her in the right direction when she had doubts. Now what would she do? Then she thought of John.

\*\*\*

The avalanche roared in his ears. John stood at the foot of a mountain that seemed to touch the sky at its peak. The wall of snow fell towards him, gathering speed and mass. He had trouble staying on his feet as the earth shook underneath. He was frozen with fear, for there was no way to escape the collapsing mountain.

John jerked awake just before the snow buried him. His head almost bashed into Gyatrul's face as the boy tried to shake John out of his sleep. The backpack was slung over Gyatrul's shoulder, and John's clothes were bundled under the boy's arm. The undeniable fear in the boy's eyes jolted John awake more than the nightmare or his shaking. Once Gyatrul had succeeded in waking him up, he pulled his arm and literally dragged John out of the bed.

"Get your god-damned hands off me!" John cursed him loudly. "What the hell are you doing?" he asked uselessly. He was physically and emotionally exhausted. It was not a good time for him to be on his best behavior. He cursed again when he remembered that Gyatrul knew almost no English.

It was as if the boy could not hear him. John was still trying to regain his balance when they were halfway out of the door, his arm still caught in Gyatrul's grip. On his way out, John grabbed the doorframe, and used it to jerk himself out of the boy's grip. Gyatrul almost fell backwards from the force of the movement. His eyes were pleading with John when he turned around. He took a chance, and hoped John would follow him on his own will. He was right, John quickly chased after him in his bare feet as the boy ran down the hall.

They dashed up the stairs and down a long corridor to their right. At the head of the stairs John heard a commotion to the left, which he thought was the front of the temple.

"Where is Sherab?" he asked Gyatrul. Again Gyatrul ignored John, either out of fear or lack of understanding, or both. After a few more turns, he led them up yet another staircase. The narrow stairs ended at a small door, which he quickly opened and raced into.

Gyatrul stood in the center of a darkened room, panting and trying to catch his breath. John jumped when someone shut the door quickly behind him. He breathed an enormous sigh of relief when he recognized Lobsang. John's relief was short-lived when he saw her panic stricken face.

"You must leave now John. The Chinese are searching the temple as we speak. I haven't spoken to them yet. I have no idea why they're here in the middle of the night. This is very unusual, I pray that they haven't heard of your presence here."

"Where is Sherab?" he asked her. The words had barely left his mouth when he saw Sherab approach him from the dim rear of the room. She wore a robe similar to the one she had before, but this one was clean. There would be no market shopping trips for them in the morning, he realized with regret. Gyatrul handed John his clothes, and he quickly began putting them on, over the robe he had slept in. As he clumsily tucked the long robe into his pants, he asked Lobsang a question.

"There's only one door into this temple," he told her. "Sherab and I walked around the building looking for a way in last night. How can we leave without the Chinese seeing us?"

"That's why Gyatrul brought you here. You won't leave by a door, but by a window." John stopped tucking the robe in then. He noticed it was bunched up in his pants just beneath his belt. He looked like he had drunk too many beers in his life. His potbelly looked ridiculous with tuffs of white robe sticking out of his zipper. He impatiently shoved in the tuffs and zipped up while talking to Lobsang.

"You expect us to jump out a second story window?" he asked incredulously.

"There is an awning that slopes downward from this window. If you hang your legs over the bottom edge, it should be no more than a ten foot drop. There's no other way out of here John. The Chinese are quite thorough, they'll find you if you stay."

She continued on without pausing to see if he agreed or not. He had to admire her confidence, even if it was born out of panic and a lack of options. He had noticed Sherab shared the same decisiveness as Lobsang. John wished that he could learn to act with the same determination that these two people had shown him.

"When you get on the ground, you'll be at the back of the temple. Continue walking in a straight line until you're well past the last of the houses. Keep going until you reach the highway. Walk west from there until you reach the intersection of the highway with the Thon main road. You'll see a dark blue truck parked there. The driver will be in regular clothes, but he lives here at this temple. It's easier for us to travel without our orange robes. He'll get you to Shigatse, if you just do as you're told. He knows the dangers of travel much more than you or Sherab. He only speaks Tibetan and Chinese, so he'll instruct the both of you through Sherab. Do you understand everything so far?" she asked.

John nodded his understanding. He hoped that he would not forget any of these details.

"Once in Shigatse there is a man who will help you. I have given his name and location to Sherab. I also gave her a note from me, to authenticate your identity."

Lobsang had planned well. She gave John all the details for immediate action without burdening him with Shigatse information. Similarly Sherab simply had to follow John for the next few hours without worrying about any immediate details.

"Thank you for everything, Lobsang. I know you took great risks is letting us stay, and for arranging transportation. I promise you that if we get away from here tonight, we'll never mention your name or this temple. I know there would be repercussions."

"Be careful of what you promise John. If you're caught at any time, I don't think you'll be able to keep my name from them." Lobsang spoke with that same matter of fact confidence. But John saw the fear in her eyes, as he was sure she saw his. He shuddered at the implications of her words.

John remembered the gun in his backpack then, and made a decision that he was not sure he could follow through on. The Chinese would never catch Sherab and him alive. Now he had heard what went on in these prisons. He was far too great a coward to ever face that kind of imprisonment. If the time came, he would offer Sherab a bullet in her head if she wanted it. Whether she did or not, he would then turn the gun on himself.

After those grim thoughts, the ten-foot leap out the window seemed trivial. Without hesitation John climbed through the window and carefully made his way down the steep awning. He dropped the backpack off the edge, and heard it thump below. On either side of the temple, long eerie shadows moved back and forth. The Chinese must have had trucks or jeeps parked in the front of the temple with their headlights on. Each soldier that walked across the headlight beams threw long grotesque shadows that reached all the way to the back of the temple. The shadows seemed to leap hungrily towards John, trapped by the edge of the temple wall.

He swallowed hard, turned on his stomach, and swung his legs into the darkness below. A second before letting go, he looked up and saw Sherab anxiously watching him as she came down the awning. The skin on the back of his neck prickled with fear as he released the awning. He shut his eyes as his body plunged towards the ground. His legs could not support his weight when he landed. He sat down heavily, sure that he would develop a bruise of interesting shades of purple in the next day or so.

Sherab made scrambling noises above him. Ignoring his sore bottom, John hurried to grab the backpack and get out of her way. A dark shadow flew down and landed with a thump before he could recognize it as Sherab's body. By the time he reached her, she was already getting up, a bit awkwardly. He took her arm to help her regain her balance. With a small tug he indicated the direction that they needed to go.

Sherab resisted his pull. She turned John around and reached into the backpack. Did she understand the danger they were in? Before he could guess what she was after, she pulled out the flowers she had inexplicably picked earlier that evening. John felt an urgent need to put distance between them and the soldiers in the temple. He watched in dumbstruck fascination as Sherab approached the temple, and carefully laid down the flowers at the base of the wall. She knelt before the flowers, and began to pray. John did not pretend to understand the ritual. He quickly walked up to Sherab, put his hands under her arms, and hoisted her to her feet. He held her arm tightly, and began trotting away from the temple.

They quickly made their way through the rows of silent houses. Soon they left even the smallest huts behind, and reached an area well beyond the town. Belatedly, John regretted not getting some idea of distances from Lobsang. Sherab began to look as worried as he felt inside. He turned to check if they had stayed on a fairly straight line away from the temple. A faint flicker of light in the distance marked the jeep headlight locations, and therefore the temple as well. Putting his trust in Lobsang's hurried instructions, he continued walking into the darkness.

John was getting ready to turn around to get his bearings again when he almost stumbled on the suddenly smooth surface of the road. By now the night's excitement had given way to the exhaustion of too few hours of sleep. Sherab's feet were dragging when she caught up to him. She did not look up at him or question their location. She saw that John had stopped and then passively stopped next to him.

Lobsang had told John to go west along the highway. He looked towards the invisible asphalt below him, and wondered which direction was west. They were traveling west when they entered the town. He remembered the temple was on their right. With the temple behind him now, west had to be on his left. His brain felt so fuzzy, he was not quite sure if he had followed his logic correctly. Too tired to start over, he gave a slight tug on Sherab's arm and started walking on the road, hopefully in a western direction.

Distance became impossible to measure between the darkness, the featureless road under their feet, and the overpowering fatigue. At one point, they were both startled by the sound of an opening car door. They spun around to face the sound that had come from behind them, slightly to the left. The dome light revealed enough of the vehicle to show that it was not a car, but a truck. The dark shadow of the man standing in front of the light reminded John of the villains in cheap horror movies.

Forcing his pulse to slow down, John noticed that the light also illuminated some asphalt under the truck. Although he could not see the intersection from where he stood, John knew then that they had simply passed it by. If the driver had not been watching for them, they would have missed the truck entirely.

"Wait here," he told Sherab, using his hands to hold her in place. He wanted to verify that this really was their ride before bringing her closer.

"Are you from the temple?" he asked the driver when he arrived at the truck. The driver looked at John for a moment, and then looked over his shoulder and spoke in Tibetan. Just great, John thought, remembering now that Lobsang had told him that the driver spoke no English. John turned to get Sherab, and bumped into her directly behind him. She had not stayed behind, and was already answering the driver. Feeling like a useless third wheel, John stepped over to the truck and leaned back against it to rest.

Sherab tugged on his arm as the man led her to the back of the truck. The back of the pickup was filled with gardening equipment and supplies. A stack of rakes, shovels, and pruning shears occupied the right side of the truck bed. Near the tailgate, a large mound of topsoil was loosely covered by a tarp. The left corner, directly behind the driver's seat, had a stack of tarps held down by branches and shrub cuttings.

The driver jumped into the truck bed, and began moving the branches off of the tarps. He then lifted up a few of the stacked tarps and spoke to Sherab. She motioned John to follow her into the truck. Sherab lay down on some tarps where the driver pointed. He threw a tarp on top of her, and motioned John to a spot about two feet away from her. John felt the driver cover him with a tarp. A slightly heavy weight fell on them then, the rest of the stack of tarps. Finally John heard the rustling noise of the branches as the driver finished covering them up.

The muffled sound of a slamming car door broke through the silence of the tarps. The truck rumbled to life, and John soon felt that he was moving. He tried reaching for Sherab, but there were too many tarps and branches between them. He contented himself with bunching the tarp underneath him into some semblance of a pillow.

Based on his calculations, they were perhaps one hundred miles from Shigatse. The driver would not be able to maintain a speed much above forty-five miles per hour along this winding mountain highway. So not counting the Chinese checkpoint Lobsang had mentioned, they had at least two hours of driving time. Ignoring the rattle of the truck as it traveled into the night, John soon drifted into a light, fitful sleep.

John slid and bumped his head on the cab of the truck as it came to a sudden stop. Groggy from sleep, he started to struggle out of the tarps to see where they were. The truck did not move when he heard a door slam. He froze, realizing that another vehicle was nearby. Fortunately he had not had time to untangle himself from the tarps. He made a quick check with his hands and feet, to make sure that he was still covered everywhere.

Two voices spoke to each other. The voices were too muffled by the tarps for John to make out which was the driver's and which belonged to the new arrival. His heart began to race as the voices approached the rear of the truck. Soon he heard the clanging of metal tools as someone went through the stack of shovels. The truck lowered from a man's weight as he climbed into the back. At first John could not determine the new sound he heard. The regular rhythm of the shovel digging in eventually told him that someone was shoveling the topsoil mound he had seen in the truck.

At that moment John desperately longed for the gun in his backpack. These must be soldiers conducting a very thorough search of the truck, he thought. Each dip of the truck as the shovel bit into the dirt increased the tension in his body. When they were done, the branches and tarps would be next. John tried to calm down and think of a plan. The darkness and the weight of the tarps pressing down drove him crazy. His mind frantically fought for control of the urge to throw the tarps off and run.

Just as suddenly as the digging had started, it stopped. John waited expectantly for the weight of the branches to be removed from his back. He was puzzled, and hopeful, when he felt the truck rise up again as the man stepped back onto the ground. He heard the voices terrifyingly close as the two men walked around John's side of the truck. They spoke a few more words, and then the truck driver sat back into his seat. John's heart resumed beating when he heard the engine start, and the truck begin to roll back onto the road. He did not dare raise his head out of the tarps for fear that the soldiers might be following close behind them.

Sleep was no longer a possibility. John shifted onto his side when his chest became too sore from being hammered by the constant bumps in the road. Perhaps twenty or thirty minutes passed before he felt the truck slow down. It came to a stop much more smoothly than the previous stop that had jolted him awake. This time he only heard their driver get out of the truck. He did not panic when he felt the branches being lifted off. All John felt was the relief of being able to get out of there. He struggled out of the tarps and sat up in the truck.

\*\*\*

The sky was a light, pre-dawn gray. Thankfully, the road seemed deserted. John's head popped out of the tarps a few feet away from Sherab. Sherab smiled at him, glad to see John again. She gave him a brief, pre-occupied smile before launching into a discussion with the driver.

"What happened before, on the highway? Was it an inspection?"

The driver snorted at Sherab's question. "Not an inspection. Just a soldier whose wife needs some topsoil in her garden."

Sherab shook her head in disgust. Some things had not changed during her captivity. Corruption and abuse were still rampant.

While Sherab spoke to the driver, she noticed John hop over the side of the truck to stretch his legs. Sherab also climbed out of the truck, stretching her cramped muscles. The driver pointed at some nearby hills on their right.

"The checkpoint is in the valley between those two hills. You'll need to walk over the nearest hill from here. On the other side, you'll run into a dirt road. Turn left on the road, and keep walking until you see my truck. I'll wait for you near the highway, to make sure I don't overshoot your position."

"How long do you think it will take for us to get there?"

"Oh, at least three or four hours I think," the driver answered, as he dug out the backpack and handed it to John.

"Thank you for getting us this far," Sherab answered. "We'll see you on the other side then."

"Good luck!" he called out after her.

Sherab watched John give an awkward, and slightly embarrassed wave, bidding the driver goodbye. Her heart went out to him as he followed her into a narrow trail. The poor man had no idea where they were going at this point.

The sun was just poking its eye above the horizon when the truck disappeared around the next bend in the road. They started their climb up what could either be called a small mountain or a large hill. After about an hour they were midway up the hill. Sherab stopped and asked John with hand motions if he wanted to eat. He nodded to her, and unloaded his backpack.

They did not bother trying to find food around them. Instead they simply ate the supplies they carried in the pack. In Thon they had not even had time to refresh their water supply. Yu's canteen was empty, but John's gourd was still about half full. The water tasted old and stale. She swallowed some quickly, her thirst after the dried food rations did not allow for any other option.

Without realizing it, she was smiling contently at John. This is how she knew him best, traveling dirt trails by themselves. She could not be sure if he understood why she smiled, but he smiled back at her with a very peaceful look on his face. After the hectic activities around Thon, they both drew comfort from the solitude on this remote hillside. She remembered their kiss the day before, when Lobsang had left them alone for a moment. Looking at John smiling at her, she wanted him immediately then, right there on the hill where they stopped to eat. John's gaze became too intense, making her lower her eyes in embarrassment and stare at the ground between them. The smile never left her lips.

Sherab still had difficulty getting used to the idea that she would not become a nun. She should have felt destroyed by the news. But all she could think about were the possibilities the news gave her with John. In hindsight, she should have discussed John with the astrologer. Would Yeshi have thought less of her for wanting a western man? Could Yeshi or anyone else ever change her mind about wanting John? She did not think so.

With one last quick glance in John's direction, Sherab stood and began closing up the backpack. It was time for them to move out again. He helped her with the last few items, and then swung the backpack over his shoulder. She started up the hill, and he followed a few feet behind her.

When they crested the hill, they could see the highway snaking through the valley for several miles. Sherab pointed out a small set of buildings straddling the highway in the distance. A few cars and trucks came to a stop on the far side of the buildings. Ant-like people came out of the buildings to meet the new arrivals. This was the feared checkpoint that they were circumventing.

The long hike ahead of them seemed discouraging. Even though the checkpoint was no more than two miles away, they had no easy trail to follow for that distance. Sherab carefully started picking her way down the slope, keeping them in a direction well away from the road. John partially slid down the slope behind her, leaving a cloud of dust in their wake. The terrain consisted mostly of loose rocks. While they lacked any serious obstacles as they walked, they had to contend with the constantly shifting ground underneath their feet. Additionally, it seemed that they were never on level ground. The rolling hills were beautiful to look at for passing drivers, but they made for a difficult hike.

In the early afternoon, a barbed wire fence indicated that they were level with the checkpoint. The Chinese had built this fence to prevent people like John and Sherab from avoiding inspection. The fence stood perhaps eight feet in height, with an additional three strands of barbed wire along the top.

John's quick slap at the fence confirmed their doubt that it could be electrified. They had not seen any signs of a power station able to carry that kind of current to this remote area. The fence went on to their right as far as they could see. Sherab assumed it was built far enough to discourage travelers from simply walking around it. Their only advantage was that they were traveling light. Once at the top they simply had a backpack to throw over. Of course tearing their bodies on the barbed wire was not a prospect to look forward to.

John unhooked one arm of the backpack, and began climbing the chain-link fence. When he reached the top, he faced the three looping strands of barbed wire. All together, the three sets of loops added perhaps four feet to the top of the fence. John snuck his arm under the lowest strand, and hooked it over the top of the fence. With his other arm he began swinging the backpack into an increasingly high arc. When it was swinging high enough, he let it go at the upper apex of the arc. The backpack easily cleared the four feet of barbed wire, and landed heavily on the other side of the fence.

Smiling, he bent his arm into a classic body builder pose for Sherab. She laughed and clapped at his small victory. Now they had to address getting their bodies over the wire. Sticking both feet firmly into the fence, he leaned forward so that he could have both hands free. He gingerly pinched the two closest loops, and tried pulling them apart to make room to pass. The loops looked far flimsier that they actually were. He had to pull very hard to get them to move only a little bit.

It seemed impossible to pull the strands apart enough for him to slip through. Instead, John pulled them apart and signaled Sherab to come through. On the other side, she would be able to do the same for him. John hooked one arm around the fence again, and this time used his boot to push the two lower loops as far away as he could. With his other arm he pulled on the closer loop. The closer loop moved, but much less than the loops under his boot. Sherab saw the strain on his face and lost no time in beginning to climb over him. Up close, the barbs looked far bigger than they did from ground level. For one frightening moment her entire body was within the space he had created for her in the barbed wire loops. The bottom hem of her robe caught on a strand. She used her right arms to tear the robe away. Soon she had both legs swung onto the other side of the fence.

As she moved her stomach over the fence, two barbs caught the back of her robe, and held. John's hands and legs began to tremble from the exertion of holding the loops apart. She tried frantically to remove the barbs with her left arm. She swung her right arm around when it became obvious the left one could not reach. The right one could not help her either. Sweat began to pour into John's eyes as he helplessly watched her struggle against the unrelenting wire.

With her right arm tugging the back of her robe, she began to heave her body backwards in hopes of tearing the barbs out. John shouted a warning to her. Her movements shook all the strands into a rocking motion. Before she could stop, his boots lost their grip on the swaying wire. Two loops whipped back onto her. The lower loop embedded itself into the top of her left shoulder. She screamed as John tried to maintain his balance. The wire continued swaying, making the embedded barbs fire a continuous, stabbing pain into her shoulder. John's boots found no hold, and were soon falling off the fence. His hand was forced to let go of the other strands. As he fell, the loop he was holding pushed against his hand, tearing it in long cuts on his way down. Sherab screamed a second time as soon as he landed.

"Sherab!" she heard him call out. The loop he had released with his hand had closed in on her right arm, which was bent around her back to dislodge her robe. For a brief instant she seemed suspended in mid-air, crucified by the barbs. Her body was off of the fence, only the barbed wire on her right arm and left shoulder supported her weight. She felt the pointed metal tearing into her flesh. Sherab's feet were kicking wildly, and soon the barb in the left shoulder tore free. Her body swung like a pendulum until all her weight was on her right arm. For one terrifying moment she thought she would remain hanging, with the barbed wire pulling the skin of her arm. Then the downward pressure pulled it free and sent her crashing to the ground.

"Sherab!" she heard John shout again, along with other words she could not understand. She could not move from her position. Her body was in shock from the pain in both her arms. The sound of John's insistent voice made her begin to pick herself up off the ground. Thankfully she did not seem hurt from the fall itself. A huge hole was torn out of the back of her robe. She fought back panic as she noticed that both arms of the robe were torn and bloody. It was hard to tell apart the flesh from the robe, both were torn and red. She winced from the pain, but stood up and began walking back towards the fence.

John was sitting down, rubbing his ankle with a pained expression on his face. She hoped he had not broken anything in his fall.

Sherab tentatively put her hands on the fence, wanting to climb up and spread the wires for John.

"Sherab," John called gently to her. Their faces were less than a foot apart on either side of the fence. She looked at him with a dazed expression, fighting back the pain in her arms. John pointed to the backpack, and mimed laying out the bedroll. She wasn't sure what he meant until he made throwing motions over the fence. Her eyes lit up briefly when she understood. John wanted to cover the wires with the bedroll. She felt stupid that they had not tried that in the first place. She walked over to the backpack and removed the bedroll.

She did not think she would be able to throw it over with her injured arms. John must have thought the same thing, for he signaled her to hang on to it. He began climbing the fence again. He kept most of his weight on his left, uninjured foot, which seemed to make climbing all the more difficult. He reached over the top of the fence and quickly opened and closed his hand, signaling her to pass up the bedroll. Her first throw was too weak, and peaked about a foot under his clutching hand. Fresh blood poured out of her wound from the tearing induced by the throw. She bit down on her lip, squeezed her eyes shut, and threw again. This time the bedroll hit his hand so hard that he almost failed to hang on to it. She collapsed into a numbed sitting position after that throw.

She watched John carefully sneak the bedroll under the bottom loop of wire. Folding it lengthwise, he stretched it out over the loops on his left side. He leaned against the bedroll and tested its ability to protect him from the barbs. The barbs did not seem to protrude from the bedroll's padding. John leaned all his weight against the loops as he swung his injured leg over the fence. Using his arm to support part of his weight, he managed to get his second leg over the fence.

John then began untangling the bedroll. The first few barbs pulled out easily. As he progressed towards the middle of the wire loop, the difficulty increased rapidly. Towards the second half of the loop she heard him utter words that could not be anything but curses in his native language. He began jerking violently on the bedroll. The last few barbs were impossible to shake loose, he would have to tear the bedroll out. He let the bedroll hang over the edge of the fence and then climbed down. Standing on the ground below he reached up, grabbed the bedroll, and tried to pull himself up. With a loud tearing sound, and a miniature snowfall of stuffing, the bedroll fell around his shoulders.

Letting the bedroll fall around him, he limped over to sit by Sherab. That's when she noticed the long tear in his hand. She grabbed his bleeding hand just as he reached to examine her shoulder. He shook her off impatiently, wanting to get a look at her shoulder. She grudgingly admitted to herself that her injury was more severe than his, and decided to let him examine her. As gently as he could, he moved the torn cloth away from the main puncture. A sideways glance told her that is was not only deep, but it was also long from the tearing motion as she hung from the barbed wire. From the backpack John took out his knife, and began cutting her sleeve off.

Sherab braced herself when John showed her the water he was going to use to clean the wound. A sharp intake of breath was the only outward sign she gave of the pain he caused. She tried calmly reciting a mantra in her head, but it came out in the equivalent of a mental scream. The blood continued to flow freely out of the cleaned puncture wound. He sliced the sleeve he had cut off her robe, and used it as a bandage. He tightly wrapped it over the hole in her shoulder. Her eyes watered, but she said nothing as he tightened the knot. Her main concern was to put pressure on the wound to slow the bleeding. The bandage soon turned bright red, making her wonder how effective it was.

With his knife, John repeated the ritual of cutting off her other sleeve. Her right arm had several punctures, but none as serious as her left shoulder. After washing her arm, he loosely wrapped the sleeve over the wounds. They were barely oozing blood by then, but the bandage would protect them from dirt.

Sherab looked at John questioningly when he took his shirt off. He smiled at her and pointed to the bunched up robe he was still wearing from the Thon temple. She smiled in return, seeing how silly he looked with a robe underneath his regular clothes. Then she realized why he was removing it. She felt very grateful and overjoyed to replace her torn and bloody robe with his clean white robe. There were no bushes to provide privacy as he undressed. He smiled at Sherab and held her face pointed towards the fence. Despite her pain, she had to hold back laughter as his modesty.

After dressing, he handed her the robe, and took his turn staring at the fence. She tried lifting the robe over her head, but was unable to. The tear in her shoulder pulled terribly when she tried raising her arms. What could she do? She would either stay in the torn and bloody robe, or get help.

"John," she called out, almost in a whimper. Her face flushed with embarrassment at what was about to happen. John turned to her, and saw her caught in the old robe. She saw his eyes briefly light up as he realized that she wanted him to undress her. His look of desire made her shiver imperceptibly. Behaving like a proper gentleman, he went behind her to remove the robe. She noticed how he carefully avoided contact with her more personal body parts. She tried to control her breathing, as she felt his hands working the old robe up over her head.

She stood before him, completely naked. She handed John the new robe, which he began by slipping over her left arm. Her breasts betrayed her own desire, but if he noticed, he refrained from showing any sign. John then lifted the robe over her head. Holding out the last sleeve, he carefully guided her right arm into it. His mouth was near her ear, and she heard his irregular breathing. She shut her eyes, caught in a burning flame of desire. Then he turned away, and let her finish pulling the robe down over her body.

How many men would be this good to her? None that she had met up to now, she realized. She sat in front of John and, ignoring her pain, reached over to cup his cheek in her hand. She smiled to show her gratitude. He had not only tended to her wounds, but he respected her privacy. He took her hand away from the painful position and held it gently on her lap. This time Sherab would not be stopped from examining his bloody hand when she noticed it again. Before she could get up, he rose to his feet to retrieve her discarded robe. John used his knife to cut another strip from it, which she then used to bandage his hand.

She decided to pack the torn robe in case they needed more bandages. With some difficulty, they rolled up the shredded bedding. It had lost a lot of stuffing, which would greatly reduce both its comfort and warmth. They would have to buy another in Shigatse, she thought.

Then she realized that they would not need to buy a bedroll if her plan succeeded. If she announced her story in front of the journalists, all of them would be more than happy to fly John out to their respective countries for exclusive interviews. Her upcoming separation from John hit her like a giant fist to the stomach. She had not really thought about it until now. Success meant John leaving Tibet and Sherab behind him forever. Her fondness for him had grown considerably, she was surprised how strongly attached she had become to John. Sherab would be reasonably safe after he left. Once the story was out, she became unimportant in the scandal. The Chinese would have no reason to risk further scandal by harming her. No, the only thing bothering her was that she would not see him again.

John studied her, trying to understand her suddenly sad expression. She forced a smile in his direction, and motioned him to follow her. John had no clue where she had agreed to meet the driver, so he had to content himself with following her wherever she went. That was not such a bad thing, she thought, with a real smile this time.

They were soon out of sight of the hated fence. Perhaps two hours later they ran into the dirt road. It was more like a pair of worn tire tracks than a road. No doubt its only customers were off road vehicles, no ordinary car would survive its deeply rutted surface. With a pleased smile she unhesitatingly turned left and began walking along the track.

Twenty minutes later an anxious driver questioned Sherab insistently when he spotted his two bloodied, limping passengers.

"What happened to the two of you? You're so late, and now you're bandaged like car accident victims!"

Sherab answered all his questions in a calm but tired voice. "You didn't warn us about the barbed wire fence. We both were injured trying to climb over it."

"I'm sorry, I didn't even know about the fence. Are you alright?"

"I think so. My shoulder has a deep cut, but it will heal. John's hand has a scratch too, and he is limping. I think he twisted his right ankle. But he made it this far, so it can't be too serious."

The driver climbed into the back of the truck, and began the ritual of moving some tarps aside for Sherab. Before he could cover her, John stepped in front of him and moved the pile of tarps that had separated them before. He lay down next to Sherab, ignoring the driver's raised eyebrows. Sherab's heart beat wildly at this unexpected gesture.

The driver knew better than to interfere, and decided to ignore their impropriety. As the tarps and branches pressed on them, she felt John's hand find her hand. Before he could get a good grip on it she grabbed it with all her strength and squeezed tightly. How she wished she could properly convey the passion she felt for this man.

As the truck began to move, each bump in the road gave Sherab a jolt of pain in her shoulder. John released her hand, and began burrowing under the tarps to get closer to her. He was on her left side, and had to be careful not to touch her shoulder when he brought his face next to hers. It was too dark to see anything, but she felt his breath against her mouth. She timed her own breath to inhale when he exhaled, wanting to breath in his discarded air. She moved a little, and soon their foreheads were touching. The sounds of the road all but disappeared as they lay in their dark and private world.

Time slipped by unnoticed. They were jolted out of their reverie by an unexpected horn blast. Sherab tensed, wondering what new danger awaited them. The truck came to a sudden stop. She braced herself for the worst. Unexpectedly, the truck accelerated once more, and in the distance she heard another horn blowing. Their driver blew his own horn, and soon stopped again. She could make out other car or truck engines nearby. She smiled to herself then. They were in the same kind of danger millions of people faced every day. They were driving in city traffic. She stared at the darkness in John's direction and said "Shigatse!" A hand squeezed hers in response.

## Chapter 10

Every stop, twist, and turn along the busy city streets increased John's anxiety under the oppressing tarps in the truck. After half an hour, the driver finally stopped the engine. The first clue to their new location was the resounding echo of the slamming truck door. The driver had brought them into a garage, John thought.

The truck dipped as the driver climbed into the back to dig them out. They were indeed in a garage, as John had thought. However it was not a private garage like he had imagined, but a large underground parking garage. The driver had wisely chosen a remote parking spot far from other cars. They soon brushed themselves off and began to examine their new surroundings. The driver spoke a few words to Sherab and they began walking towards the elevator doors on the far side of the garage.

As the elevator doors shut, John noticed that the building had ten floors. The Chinese had poured an enormous amount of money to modernize Tibetan cities and roads. They enticed Chinese citizens to settle in Tibet, and promote Chinese culture. These large apartment buildings were one of the results of this effort. Large housing projects like this one has sprung in every Tibetan city.

Sherab pressed '6', and the elevator shot upwards. They stepped out onto the sixth floor. After a brief false start down the right hallway, they retraced their steps towards the left of the elevators. Sherab and the driver kept their eyes on the apartment numbers and finally stopped in front of one of the doors.

John's legs turned to jello when a Chinese man opened the door. John considered kicking out at him versus simply running back towards the elevator. Before he could take any sort of action, their driver calmly spoke to the man. John's pulse began to slow down when Sherab handed Lobsang's letter of introduction to the man. He quickly read through it, and then asked the driver a few questions. The driver and the man spoke for a few moments, while John impatiently scanned up and down the hallway.

They shook hands, and the driver backed away. He gently shook Sherab's hand, not wanting to shake her injured shoulder. Sherab spoke a few words of gratitude to him. He then shook John's uninjured hand.

"Thank you," John said, hoping he understood the meaning, if not the words.

"You may come in now, Sir," the man at the door told John. After hearing so much Tibetan and Chinese, his English startled John.

"You speak English!" he said unnecessarily. John was overjoyed to have this luck once again. The man smiled without answering, and held the door open for John. Sherab had already entered, so John quickly stepped into this stranger's home.

The apartment was not spacious, but neither was it cramped like the Same and Thon temple living quarters. On their right, a half-height wall separated a clean, white kitchen from the entrance they stood in. The small fridge and gas stove still had the brilliance of newly bought appliances. Beside the stainless steel sink a dish rack held clean, drying lunch dishes. The counter was bare except for a small toaster in the corner.

John took a few steps into the apartment and looked at the living area just beyond the kitchen. The dining area consisted of a square table with four wooden chairs. On the other side of the room was a sofa facing a small TV. A side chair sat under an overhanging lamp. The bookcase next to the chair was filled with Chinese books. Getting up from the chair as he entered was a stunning Chinese woman.

She gracefully stood up and walked towards them. She wore a black skirt that showed enough of her black-stockinged legs to take John's concentration away from the rest of the room. With effort he looked up and saw her full, smiling red lips. Even her large brown eyes seemed to smile at him. Her styled black hair formed smooth flowing curves that fell along each side of her head. Rather than hiding her eyes, the small wire frame glasses she wore seemed to showcase the eyes as her face's prize possession.

"This is my wife, Luhping Lee." The man's words jolted John out of his rude staring session. He turned to look at his host but was frozen midway by Sherab's burning glare. John's admiration for Luhping's beauty had not gone unnoticed. He could not suppress the smile from his lips. He was overcome with such happiness by Sherab's angry stare. The fact that she had noticed, and that it had made her angry, selfishly brought him great satisfaction. She cares, he thought wildly. John's untamed emotions reinforced his belief that he had fallen in love with her.

His smile did not soften Sherab's deadly eyes. He shook himself out of the flood of overwhelming emotions. Regretfully turning away from her, John faced the Chinese man who he realized was still speaking to him.

"I'm very sorry," John said to him, "We've had an exhausting journey, and my concentration isn't very good right now. Could you please repeat what you just told me?"

An almost imperceptible frown in his eyes betrayed the annoyance that the man felt at John's rudeness.

"I am Muyih Su," he repeated, "and this is my wife Luhping Lee." Very conscious of Sherab looking at him, John shook Luhping's hand in a formally stiff fashion.

"My name is John Pearson," he told her. "Do you also speak an excellent English like your husband?"

She smiled at his attempt to win back Muyih's favor. "I don't think I have as much ease with the language as he does Mr. Pearson, but I know enough to carry a conversation."

"You are obviously as modest about your talents as you are beautiful Ms. Lee," he answered her. He was proud of the charm oozing out of him at the moment, and relieved that Sherab did not speak English.

"And you are too easily impressed Mr. Pearson," she replied smartly. "I don't always dress this way, I just came home from work."

"Please, both of you may call me John," he told their new hosts. "I can't thank you enough for taking in two strangers like this simply based on Lobsang's letter."

"We occasionally help Ms. Yangkyi when she is in need," Muyih explained. "The driver told us about your encounter with soldiers along the way here," he added.

"Sherab and I were buried under a lot of tarps and branches. I know the truck was stopped, but I have no idea why."

"Unfortunately some of my countrymen enjoy their positions of power in Tibet. One of the soldiers on patrol needed soil for his wife's garden. When he saw the truck filled with gardening supplies, he stopped it and took what he needed. It's people like these soldiers that bring shame to the rest of us."

Muyih sounded defensive about himself, John realized. Surely most Chinese citizens knew that the outside world thought poorly of the Tibet situation.

"I wonder how his wife will feel about the stolen soil?" he asked Muyih, trying to take the focus away from the more global issues.

"I doubt she will even know or ask," Muyih replied, shaking his head sadly. "Please don't judge all of China by what you see here in Tibet Mr. Pearson."

"John," he corrected. "What about you, Muyih, what brings you to Tibet?" John regretted the question the moment it left his lips. He was afraid of backing Muyih into a corner with such a probing question. His regret was short-lived, however, Muyih seemed relieved that he had asked the question.

"Luhping and I are school teachers," he answered proudly. "Tibet's education system is far below China's average level. We are doing our part to help overcome this problem in one Shigatse school." He smiled with pride and love at his wife as he spoke of her. "Luhping mainly teaches mathematics and science to adolescent Tibetan children. Unfortunately the material they can grasp is more at the primary school level, but they are catching up to their grade level quickly with her care and devotion."

Luhping smiled and looked away in embarrassment. Muyih continued without worrying about her, evidently accustomed to embarrassing her with compliments.

"I teach mainly the languages, and some geography. The children know only a small amount of Chinese, because they don't practice it at home. I spend some time advancing their Tibetan skills, but I'm forced to concentrate on Chinese because of their reluctance to learn it."

An awkward silence fell over the four of them as the small talk ran out. Finally Luhping broke the silence.

"John, you must realize that our work is very important to us here. Though they resent our presence here, the Tibetans do need Muyih and I. We are trying to prepare these children for a tomorrow that they must face whether they like it or not."

"I understand," he interrupted her before she could continue her defense. "I'm not here to judge China-Tibet politics. And I know what you and Muyih are doing can only be beneficial for these children. I admire you for settling here under such negative conditions. Please don't feel you need to defend or justify your work to me."

Muyih cleared his throat awkwardly, and looked like he wished to be any place but there with them. John looked nervously from Muyih to Luhping, wondering what was wrong. Luhping's eyes seemed to have doubled in size as she stared at John in silence.

"Mr. Pearson," she began with barely controlled fury, "I was not 'defending' our work to you. I wasn't aware that you felt I had a need to defend teaching children how to deal with mathematics. Nor do I feel I have to justify our presence in Tibet to a foreigner!"

"Luhping!" Muyih shouted at her. "Please, these are our guests! I'm very sorry Mr. Pearson, Luhping has strong opinions on political matters."

"You don't need to apologize for me Muyih," Luhping cut in.

John began to feel like a spectator at a tennis match as his head bounced back and forth between these two. He noticed Sherab looked both curious and concerned with the tension John seemed to be creating between their benevolent hosts.

"Of course Muyih is correct Mr. Pearson," Luhping continued, her attention once again focused on John. "You are indeed our guest and I have been rude. I apologize for my outburst."

"No, please, I'm the one who was out of line with my comments." He was anxious to make peace with Luhping. John truly had not meant any harm with his careless words. "Please accept my apology, I didn't mean to imply anything about you, your husband, or China itself."

Another awkward silence fell over them.

"Can we start over? Please call me John again, I noticed you slipped back to 'Mr. Pearson'." He held his hands up in supplication while he said this. Her small smile encouraged him.

"And I promise to watch my rude foreign tongue!" Both laughed at this last comment. Sherab smiled as she saw the tension melt away from the group.

"What I was trying to tell you, John," Luhping hesitated a split second before using his first name, "is that Muyih and I like to help Ms. Yangkyi when we can, but we do have severe limits. Our first priority is to the children at the school. Whatever we can do to help abuse or injustice can only be done as long as there is no risk to our work here."

John nodded, about to speak, when Muyih added his thoughts. "We really do hope we can help you. At the moment however, we have no idea why you're here. You're welcome to stay with us as long as you need. Beyond that, you must tell us what else we can do. As Luhping said, we will try to accommodate your requests if we can."

"Muyih, Luhping, you're both very kind people," John told them honestly. "But before I can begin to tell you what we need, I think you have to ask Sherab to tell you her story."

Muyih hesitated before answering him. He seemed to be considering his words carefully. "Of course we will speak with Sherab. However, the less we know about both you and her, the safer it is for all of us. We have worked with Ms. Yangkyi long enough to trust the nature of your motivations. All that we need to know is in which way we can assist you."

As if on cue, Luhping broke away from them, leading Sherab by the arm. Although they may have trusted Lobsang, they wisely interviewed John and Sherab separately to see if their stories matched up. John wondered what motivated these two teachers to risk their lives for Lobsang, and for Tibet.

Muyih walked John to the dinner table, where they sat for their discussion. Sherab and Luhping were speaking softly on the sofa in the adjoining room. Distance was not a factor in keeping each interview separate, language differences sufficed.

"Muyih," he began, "you mentioned that you have helped Lobsang before. What kind of help do you give her?"

"Like I told you John, Tibet has more than its share of abuse by Chinese citizens. Sometimes Ms. Yangkyi will ask us to hide a monk or nun who is wanted by the police. Eventually someone comes to take them away, we never hear if they escaped successfully. We are very sensitive about getting too closely involved, we must never endanger our work.

Other times we get simpler requests from Ms. Yangkyi. We may act as messengers between her and other temples or monasteries in the area. We know even less about these situations, for the messages are always sealed shut."

Muyih paused in his discussion, with a far away look in eyes. John imagined that he and his wife must have often questioned their decision to be involved with Lobsang.

"You see John," he continued, "this proves my point about education. The majority of abusers are poorly educated brutes. They are the ones who prey on the defenseless Tibetans. That's why Luhping and I will not risk our work. Education truly can solve most of this country's injustices."

"But then why does the Chinese government send such people to Tibet? Surely they've heard of the abuse as much or more than the rest of the outside world."

"That's another problem we have in China, John. Education is not a requirement for rising to power in the communist party. In fact sometimes it may limit your opportunities. All that is promoted is the unquestioning devotion to communist China. These same brutes that beat on Tibetans today may manage entire cities tomorrow."

Muyih's voice was filled with bitterness. How frustrating his life must be, trying to teach unwilling students in a society governed by intimidation and abuse.

"Have you ever considered leaving China?" John asked him. In his situation, he certainly would want to live in a freer environment.

"No John, I have not." Muyih smiled wistfully as he spoke. "And I suggest that you don't ask the same question to Luhping!"

John smiled at Muyih's joke. He had no intention of approaching such topics with the fiery Luhping.

"I am Chinese, John. I love China. Our current government has many problems. Governments come and go in history, but the Chinese people remain. If we abandoned our country every time we had problems with our leaders, we would not be the powerful and cultured people that we are today. Thousands of years of history cannot be wiped out by the government of a few generations."

"You're an interesting man to talk to Muyih," John told him with respect. "I admire your values and determination."

Muyih smiled at the compliment, John had obviously touched a point of pride within him. "Thank you John. I think you and I could discuss Chinese issues all night. But we really should discuss you and Sherab's requirements right now."

John sat back, thinking about where to start and how much to tell him. He decided to follow Muyih's advice to the letter, and tell him just what they needed from him.

"There are really two things we need. First, as you can see, we need new clothes. Money is not a problem, I can pay for our clothes as well as the food we eat while we're staying with you."

Muyih interrupted him with an upraised hand. "Please don't concern yourself about money, Luhping and I can buy you the supplies you need. And of course we can go shopping for you."

"Thank you for your generosity," John told him. "But I intend to leave China soon, and I really have no use for the money after that. Please, let me pay our way."

John pressed on before Muyih could raise more objections. "You mentioned that you will go buy the clothes for us, don't you think it's safe for us to go to the market? Shigatse seems to be a big enough city that people must be used to seeing foreigners shopping for souvenirs."

"Remember John, foreigners must always be escorted by a Chinese guide," Muyih replied. "You would not raise suspicion if I went with you. However, I'm very sorry to say that this is an unacceptable risk for me. I don't know what you are hiding from, but I don't want to be seen in public with you."

John tried to hide his disappointment. This man was already doing so much for them. But he could not help feel some resentment at being forced to stay within the apartment.

"Now Sherab is Tibetan," Muyih continued, "she can wander through the city by herself with much less danger. But I have to wonder why you would consider exposing her to any risk at all. Luhping and I can buy what you need without risk to any of us."

"I understand Muyih. I won't go outside until it's necessary. As for Sherab, that's her decision. But you're right about unnecessary risk, and I'll certainly not encourage her to leave your home."

Muyih nodded with satisfaction at John's response. Now that the easy issue was out of the way, John had to broach the trickier issue of the press conference.

"It's my understanding that there are regular international press conferences at the Panchen Lama's residence."

"Yes, that's true. They are held on the first Monday of every month. This coming Monday there will be a press conference."

John looked at Muyih with some embarrassment. Traveling along back roads for weeks at a time had made him forget simple things like daily calendars.

"I'm sorry if this sounds stupid, but can you tell me what day this is?"

Muyih seemed surprised and amused at the same time. "Today is Wednesday. The next press conference is in five days. May I ask why you're interested in the conference?"

Five days, John thought. That was closer than he had expected. But it still gave them enough time to prepare for an unauthorized entry into the conference.

"Sherab and I must attend that conference," he said, rather vaguely. He did not need to explain how he and Sherab would actually steal the show with their unplanned storytelling.

"We need you to find a way to get us into the conference. I have no idea how securely guarded are the entrances to the Panchen Lama's home."

Muyih's eyes opened wide when he heard John's request. "That's not possible John! Even if I had access to a forged reporter id badge, there is no way to get Sherab, a Tibetan woman, into such a conference."

"But what if I told you that you only had to get us into the conference, and not back out? If we make it in, then I can tell you we'll have safe passage out of the conference. So perhaps we don't need id badges, if there's a less traditional way of getting into the conference." John smiled at Muyih as he said this, hoping to disarm the man's fright as well as his own.

"Don't get me wrong, I still think it's not possible." Muyih seemed thoughtful. John could almost hear his brain working out the possibilities. "The one advantage you have is that it's summertime. In this warmer weather the Panchen Lama conference is often held outside, in the back of his residence. Security is still tight, but you have much more opportunities than if the meeting was held inside the home."

John began to get excited then. "Is there a fence we can climb over, or cut our way through? Are there side gates that might be less well guarded? What about tourist attractions? Are there any tours through the estate where we could sneak away and spend the night before outside?"

Muyih shook his head at John's last suggestion. "No, tourists aren't admitted on these grounds. I've been to a few of these conferences, and I am trying to remember the layout. A fence of solid concrete surrounds the Panchen Lama's home. To get inside you will have to climb over it. But I'm sure that soldiers patrol these walls. I don't know if there are any other gates. I can investigate the outside perimeter tomorrow."

"That would be very useful to us," John told Muyih. "But are you sure you can do this without risk to yourself?"

"The Panchen Lama's home is located in a beautiful area of Shigatse, John. Many people walk in the area to relax and enjoy the scenery. I'll stop there after work tomorrow. There's absolutely no risk."

Muyih turned in his chair to look towards the two women. Luhping was facing his direction and gave a slight nod.

"Bring your chair John, let's go join Luhping and Sherab."

Sherab cleared her throat as Muyih and John settled down near them. With a nervous glance towards Luhping, she spoke to John with an embarrassed but determined face. "Thank you for help John," she said in halting English.

John broke into an astonished grin as he stared at Sherab. "As soon as we were done, she asked me to translate this sentence into English for her," Luhping added.

"Same, Thon, Shigatse," Sherab continued, enumerating their travel progression. "John help Sherab," she ended.

A lump formed in John's throat when he heard her thanking him in his language. "Please tell Sherab she is more than welcome," he told Luhping, with a slightly cracking voice. Sherab smiled warmly at him as Luhping translated his overly simple response. How could he truly explain to Sherab the love and affection growing in him with each passing day that he spent with her? He only had five days left with Sherab. He could not afford to get any more deeply involved with this woman.

"You must be getting hungry after all your travels," Muyih said to break the growing silence between Sherab and John. "It's well past dinner time."

"I don't know about Sherab, but I'm starving!" John answered eagerly. "We've had nothing but nuts, dried meat, and dried fruit for weeks."

Luhping and Muyih rose as one in response to his enthusiastic reply. "We'll go prepare some dinner for you," Muyih told him.

"I don't want to impose on you, is there anything I can do to help?" John asked.

"No," replied Luhping, "but please excuse us if we serve a simple meal. We weren't expecting guests for dinner."

John understood then that they wanted to be alone in the kitchen to compare notes from the interviews. With Muyih and Luhping busying themselves in the kitchen, John got up and sat next to Sherab. They looked contently at each other, only able to communicate with their eyes. He reached over to cup her cheek in his hand. She leaned her face into his hand, seeming to enjoy the touch.

Rather than simply wishing that they could speak, John decided to take advantage of her interest in learning English. While waiting for dinner, they went through several related words. He rubbed his stomach to explain 'hungry', he pointed to Luhping and Muyih to explain 'cook', and he finally used eating motions to explain 'eat'. They both enjoyed themselves at this game. Sherab seemed happy to be using her mind after weeks of survival outdoors.

"Please, will you come join us for dinner now?" Luhping asked them, when supper was ready. By now John's stomach was growling and his mouth was salivating because of the wonderful smells coming from the kitchen. Sherab must have felt the same, for she clapped her hands once and said, "eat!" Luhping and John laughed at Sherab's outburst in her newfound language. Luhping spoke a few words to her in Chinese, John guessed to congratulate her for learning some English.

As they brought the chairs back to the dining room table, Muyih came out of the kitchen with the first dish. He placed the steaming pan of scrambled eggs with fried tomatoes onto the table. John tore his hungry eyes away from the hot food and followed Muyih into the kitchen to help carry out more food. Muyih handed John a pot with some cooked cabbage and what seemed to be small shrimp. He followed Muyih, who carried yet another dish of beef with green onions, back to the table. John did not notice Muyih slip away to the kitchen. The royal feast awaiting them entranced him. He decided to sit down when Muyih returned with some fried meatballs. Finally Luhping returned to the table with the ever-present bowl of white rice.

"Luhping," John exclaimed, "you said this would be a simple meal!"

She smiled, and handed him the meatballs. "One day we should prepare you a formal Chinese dinner, John. Then you will also call this a simple meal."

Muyih handed John a small bowl of clear, thick sauce. "This is for you John, a sweet sauce for the pork balls. Westerners like sweet sauces, right?"

"Yes, that's true Muyih," John smiled to him. "In Chinese restaurants back home they have sweet red sauces for chicken balls, and sweet plum sauce for egg rolls. And the list goes on!"

"The saying in China is that if you can make something taste sweet or sour, then you can open a successful restaurant in North America." Luhping's comment brought a round of laughter from three of them, and a puzzled stare from Sherab. Muyih leaned towards her to translate the joke. She laughed politely, as one usually does when getting a joke after everyone else.

John eagerly served himself healthy portions of the hot dishes. The only one he avoided was the rice. He did not want to embarrass himself with his poor chopstick skills on such a small food item. He noticed that Sherab seemed to be picking only vegetable items.

"Is Sherab vegetarian?" he asked Muyih and Luhping. He had seen her eat dried meat during their hike. Her abstinence during this meal puzzled him. Luhping asked John's question to Sherab.

"No, she is not vegetarian. She consulted with an astrologer in Thon, and he suggested avoiding meats for the next few weeks."

John looked up at Luhping, not sure if she was playing a joke on him or not. He broke into a nervous smile when he could not read her expression.

"Are you serious?"

"Yes. You don't believe in astrologers?" Luhping seemed surprised by John's reaction.

"Well not really. But even if I did, I never heard of an astrologer making recommendations on your diet."

"Oh, yes," Muyih broke in, "that's quite common in our culture. At certain times in your life, some foods are conducive to good luck, and others to bad luck. The astrologer might also recommend colors of clothing to wear, for instance."

John tried to hide his surprise that these people believed in such superstitions. "Wow, we certainly come from different worlds!" he answered.

"I guess that's your way of saying you think we are crazy?" Luhping asked with a smile.

John laughed, his face reddening with embarrassment. "No, not crazy. Different, but not crazy!"

Later, when John felt positively gorged with food, he thanked their hosts. "Luhping, Muyih, that was the most wonderful meal I've had in all my travels. Thank you so much."

"You're welcome John, but I hope you still have room for the soup," Muyih replied. John had forgotten the curious Chinese custom of serving soup at the end of the meal. He truly had no room to eat more, but he still nodded back, indicating that he wanted the soup.

"Hungry?" he asked Sherab jokingly, as he rubbed his stomach to remind her of the word's meaning. After releasing a genuine laugh this time, she loudly returned a "No!" to all of them. He managed to finish about half of the vegetable broth served to him before giving up.

"I'm so full," he said, putting down his spoon. "Sherab and I are not used to such big meals anymore." He looked at Sherab and was glad that she had not understood his mistake. Sherab must never have been used to big meals, he realized sadly.

A yawn escaped his open mouth before he could suppress it. Muyih caught it and asked if John was tired.

"Excuse me," John said, "but we only had two or three hours of sleep last night."

"We don't have a big apartment," Luhping told him. "There is a small guest room that Sherab may use. But I'm afraid we only have the sofa to offer you as a bed John."

"Believe me Luhping," he told her, "that sofa will be extremely comfortable after sleeping outside for a month."

When their hosts stood up, John tried clearing dishes from the table. He barely resisted when Muyih pulled him away and led him to the sofa.

"You sleep John, Luhping and I will wash the dishes." John gave in when he saw Luhping leading Sherab into a back room. "Thank you so much Muyih, you can't understand how much you're helping us."

"If we can help you go home with a better feeling towards China and Tibet, then our help to you has been rewarded ten times over," Muyih told John sincerely. "That's how you can thank us John. Let others like you know that not all Chinese are devout communists trying to squash Tibetan culture."

"I see that, and I'll tell others, Muyih. You and Luhping are far better people than most westerners I know."

Muyih shut the living room light as John stretched out on the sofa. John soon heard the soft clinking of dishes from the kitchen area as Muyih and Luhping cleaned up. Their soft Chinese murmurings soothed him as he fell into a deep and untroubled sleep.

\*\*\*

Sherab woke up early, despite her lack of sleep the previous night. She stretched luxuriously, enjoying the feeling of the sheets hugging her body. This had been her first full night's sleep in a real bed ever since she had been taken from her parent's home several years ago. The jail had some thin, lumpy mattresses on a wire frame. To call those 'beds' seemed ridiculous when compared to the soft guest bed she now rested in.

She heard faint noises emanating from the kitchen. Muyih and Luhping were undoubtedly preparing their breakfast before leaving for work. Sherab did not know what to think of her hosts. They were Chinese, which made her want to hate them. Yet they seemed genuinely interested in helping her out. Not just Sherab, but helping other Tibetans as well. Sherab would have to make an effort to get over her racist feelings towards the Chinese. Logically, she should hate the government, not the individuals. Emotionally, she had difficulty distinguishing the two. It was individuals who had tortured her, not some abstract government entity.

Muyih seemed to be the nicer of the two. She had never met such a gentle Chinese man. Maybe he has some Tibetan blood in him, she thought with a mischievous smile. His wife seemed more typical in her superior attitude. Luhping probably had a harder time being humble since she was so beautiful. Sherab had not missed John's reaction to Luhping's beauty, and Luhping had certainly not missed it either. It still made Sherab's face flush with anger when she thought of how that woman almost purred under John's attention.

Sherab felt a stab of guilt as she realized how many negative thoughts she had towards these people who were helping her. Why was she so bitter? Chinese jailers had taken away Sherab's beauty. Luhping still enjoyed her innocence and her beauty. That had to be part of Sherab's resentment. But the way Luhping had captured John's eye hurt Sherab deeply. She would never see him look towards her that way.

Sherab swung her legs out of the bed before her indulgence in self-pity could bring tears. She knelt on the floor and began her morning prayers. She asked for forgiveness of her negative thoughts towards Luhping in particular. After several minutes of meditation, Sherab felt ready to go face her hosts.

"Good morning, Sherab. Did you sleep well?" Luhping spotted her first, coming towards the kitchen.

"Yes, I did. The bed was so comfortable, I slept like a baby."

"There's another one sleeping like a baby," Luhping added, pointing towards the living room sofa. Sherab walked towards John's sleeping form, and watched his slow, even breathing. He slept peacefully, like he did not have a care in the world. She smiled at him, enjoying his innocence.

"Would you care for some tea?" Muyih asked, offering her a cup.

"Thank you, Muyih." Sherab felt guilty once again about her earlier thoughts as she took the cup from his hand.

"Come join us for breakfast," Luhping called out softly, "you're up just in time."

Sherab sat at the table with Muyih and Luhping. Her eyes hungrily took in the prepared breakfast. A cold glass of soymilk dripped with condensation in front of her plate. Muyih brought a pan heaped with delicious-smelling scrambled eggs. She felt a child's wonderment at the luxuries she enjoyed in this apartment.

"We advise both of you to stay in the apartment today," Muyih said as they ate their morning meal. "After work, Luhping will pick up the clothes you requested. I will go take a closer look at the Panchen Lama's house."

"When is the press conference?"

"On Monday, four days away. Well, five if you count today."

"When is the next one after that?"

Muyih gave her a curious look. "One month later, why?"

"The astrologer in Thon warned me about undertaking any major projects for the next three weeks. Maybe this press conference is not such a good idea."

Muyih swallowed hard, thinking over what Sherab had just announced.

"Don't worry, John and I will not stay with you for a month! We'll need your help to find a place to stay of course, but we'll definitely just stay a few days in here."

"You can stay with us the whole time if you like," Luhping said, with only a trace of hesitation in her voice. "But are you sure it's wise to wait a full month for whatever it is you need at the conference?"

"No, it's not wise. Neither is it wise to go against the sound advice of an astrologer. I really don't know what to do."

"What does John think?" Muyih asked.

"John doesn't know about the astrologer's prediction. But you saw his reaction last night, he obviously doesn't believe any of it."

"Well if you're considering waiting for a month, we need to discuss it with him tonight!"

"I know," Sherab answered miserably. "But the truth is that it's very unfair to him. He's now in danger because of me, and has to leave our country as soon as possible. But I need him at the conference. I think I have to go to this Monday's conference."

Her mind seemed made up now. Following her thread of logic, she owed it to John to try the upcoming conference. She fingered the amulet under her robe, wondering how powerful it would be during this time of Mars influence.

"Well," Luhping concluded, "ultimately the decision is yours and John's. Muyih and I will respect your choice."

"Thank you, but I think the decision is made. I can't keep John locked up for another month."

"Maybe it's his lucky time," Muyih added with a hopeful smile. "Perhaps his good luck will cancel your bad luck!"

Sherab smiled weakly at his remark, not really drawing any comfort from it. After a moment, Luhping stood up to clear the morning dishes. Sherab had to admit that the woman was indeed beautiful. For a Chinese woman, she certainly did not dress conservatively either. She wore skirts that would capture any man's attention.

"You look beautiful again this morning, Luhping," Sherab forced herself to say. She was determined to get past her resentment for Luhping. The woman had shown nothing but support for Sherab.

"Thank you Sherab," Luhping answered, glancing at Sherab in surprise. "Oh, that reminds me. I'll buy some clothes for you tonight. But for today, let's go in my room and pick something for you to wear. That will also give me a better idea of your size."

Luhping quickly walked Sherab towards her bedroom, while Muyih finished clearing up the breakfast table.

"We're in a bit of a hurry now, we might be late for work." Luhping briskly opened the closet door to reveal more clothes than Sherab had ever owned.

"What would you like, a dress, a skirt? My pants might look funny on you, since you're taller and have a much smaller waist."

Sherab tried to hide her awe at all the expensive looking clothes. "With my shoulder, I think it might be nice to have something with short sleeves."

"I have something you might like," Luhping said as she searched through her closet. "Here, this dress is sleeveless. It should be quite comfortable."

Sherab blushed when she accepted the slender black dress. She had never worn something so daring. Luhping must have noted her reaction.

"That ought to get John's attention," she smiled teasingly.

"I," Sherab stopped in mid sentence. She had planned to say she was becoming a nun, but that idea had vanished. "I am not trying to get John's attention." She felt flustered, and somewhat annoyed by Luhping's teasing.

"I'm just kidding, Sherab, don't take everything so seriously." Luhping's face seemed genuine. Sherab saw that she did not mean any harm with her comments.

"Now my shoes won't fit you, but you're staying in the apartment all day anyway. Here's a pair of nylons for you." Luhping still faced the closet as she blindly handed a pair of pantyhose to Sherab.

"I really have to go now," Luhping told Sherab hurriedly. "In that dresser you will find underwear and some bras, please take whatever fits you best." Luhping shut the door behind her as she left the room.

Sherab felt like she was in another world, as she stood alone in the room holding nylons and the black dress. She could hear Muyih and Luhping preparing their last minute affairs before leaving for work. She had never worn nylons in her life, and did not really want to start putting them on now. Besides, they looked so thin and small, that she would probably rip them while trying to put them on.

She managed to take off her robe, though with some difficulty. Her shoulder wound still hurt quite a bit, but it did not have the same intense pain as yesterday. She slipped on the dress, thankful that it was sleeveless. She gasped in surprise when the dress's hem fell well above her knee. No doubt it was meant to be somewhat short, but Sherab was taller than Luhping. She debated whether or not to change back into her long robe. No, it would be too embarrassing to admit her discomfort to Luhping.

Her small breasts had no need for a bra. Years ago she had worn bras, but her wasted body no longer needed one. She went to Luhping's drawer, and looked at the pretty assortment of underwear. The prisoners had not been allowed to wear such garments while in captivity. Sherab longed to feel the luxury of having underwear again. She picked up a pair, and felt its silky softness. While she admired the personal garments in Luhping's drawer, she could not bring herself to actually borrow a pair. Instead Sherab decided to be careful how she sat during the day, and discarded the underwear back into the drawer.

Sherab left the room quickly in order to bid Muyih and Luhping farewell.

"You look great, Sherab," Muyih said as she entered the room.

"Thank you," she muttered, feeling her face turn red again. She walked over to the window, where she was able to observe John sleeping.

"We're leaving for work now. I'm going to wake up John to let him know, since you two can't understand each other. I'll let him know about breakfast."

"When do you and Luhping expect to be home?"

"We should be back around 6:30 or 7:00 this evening," Muyih replied, heading for the sofa.

Sherab watched in amusement as Muyih slowly shook John awake. She was in a position to see his face, but was behind him, out of his line of sight. John opened one eye sleepily, as Muyih spoke to him. He mumbled something to Muyih, making him laugh. Sherab wished that she could understand his humor, and laugh with him.

John sat up, wiping the sleep from his eyes. Sherab was reminded of the little boy in him again. He called out a farewell to Luhping, who was ready to leave at the front door. Luhping replied cheerfully, and then she and Muyih were gone.

A silence fell over the room as John turned to look over at Sherab. She felt a stab of self-conscious fear when he saw her. Her dress suddenly seemed impossibly small. He drew in a sharp breath as his eyes opened wider. Her pulse quickened when she recognized that look, she had seen it directed towards Luhping last night.

John's eyes lowered to her bare legs below the dress's hem. Then his legs began to move on their own. He almost ran to her as he crossed the room. She felt a mixture of fright and excitement as he rapidly closed the distance between them. Her arms already began to open up as he encircled her in his arms and kissed her hard.

She had no hesitation like the last time. She immediately kissed him back hungrily, not believing that he could still feel desire for her. Their hands pawed at each other's head and back as they continued their passionate embrace. John reached down, put an arm behind her knees, and picked her up. Her head spun with the sensation of being carried so tenderly. They continued kissing as he limped to the guest bedroom on his sprained ankle. Her arms clamped tightly around his neck as he carried her. Her lips and tongue worked feverishly against his mouth. She had never felt this sexually excited.

They tumbled onto the bed when he finally made his way into the bedroom. Without ever breaking from their kiss, his hand crept up her leg and under her dress. Her breath became irregular, sharp gasps as his hand slowly caressed her stomach. In her mind she willed him to go more slowly, to make the moment last. His hand did not listen, it quickly moved up and began to squeeze and caress her small round breasts. She felt like she could hardly breathe as the sensations enveloped her. She brought her leg up between John's legs and rubbed it against him.

John suddenly tore himself away from her kiss, and from her arousing leg. His shirt was off in record time. Sherab was suddenly afraid. His hunger brought back too many memories of the jail. She wanted to make love to him, but could not stand the wild look in his eyes. She wanted their lovemaking to be perfect, not ruined by her own fears. Before she could stop herself, she spoke the words:

"No, John."

His hands had been working on his belt when she spoke. The hands did not leave his belt, but hung there motionless as he looked up at her in disbelief. Her dress was lifted up to her thighs, where his roaming hand had left it. His eyes stared between her legs, seeming to notice for the first time that she wore no underwear.

Sherab quickly pulled down her dress, and crossed her arms over her breasts defensively. A small tear was forming in her left eye as she looked at him. "No John," she repeated, shaking her head. It was as if he had not heard her the first time, the hungry, predatory look remained in his eyes.

A single tear running down her cheek seemed to break through the hypnotizing effect of his desire. John's hands dropped to his side, the belt still securely around his waist. Sherab could see the bulge in his pants continue to press firmly outwards. She felt horribly guilty. Against all odds, he still felt desire for her, and now she had rejected him. How could she ever again have a normal relationship with a man?

He bent over her, with her eyes following his every move. His hand wiped away her tear, and he lay down beside her. How many times would he wipe tears from her face before tiring of her weakness? He lay on his side, and with his arm he rolled her towards him. His chin was just above her head as he held her tightly against him. His bare chest filled her senses and she looked at him, and breathed on him. She began to sob softly in his arms. Sherab tried not to feel sorry for herself, but it was hard to be strong when he held her like this. She wanted to cry, and to be comforted. He used his hand to gently stroke her hair. She felt emotionally as well as physically exhausted. Under his affection, she felt herself drifting to sleep, and welcomed the escape.

Sherab woke up slowly, feeling John's fingers playing with her short hair. At first she did not recognize her surroundings. Then the embarrassment of the situation returned with full force. She did not know how long she had slept in his arms. She leaned on her elbow and looked up at him. He smiled when he saw her, and seemed grateful to shift his position slightly. She looked at his bare chest, and reached out to stroke it. She loved the comforting sensation of lying there while he looked at her and she touched him tenderly. She began to feel she had made such a mistake by rejecting him.

John spoke to her softly. She looked at him quizzically, wanting to understand what he said to her. He took her hand and put it over his heart. Holding it there, he put his other hand over her heart. He spoke a single word then. She repeated the strange sound: "love". John nodded enthusiastically.

"John loves Sherab," he said, with an intense stare into her eyes. She felt her eyes begin to moisten, as she understood his meaning. She was overwhelmed with her feelings for him.

"Sherab love John," she said to him, trying not to let her voice break. His eyes began to water as he listened to her speak. She made a decision then.

Sherab bent over him and kissed him on the lips. The earlier uncontrolled hunger was replaced by tenderness as they simply enjoyed the closeness. Inevitably, the kissing became more passionate. His tongue tentatively entered her mouth. She sucked it in deeper and caressed it with her own swirling tongue. She shifted her weight so that all of her body was on top of him, pressing him into the bed.

She soon broke from the kiss, and looked hard into his eyes. Her face stayed close, hovering an inch above his. She felt powerful staring at him like this, for he seemed defenseless. His eyes seemed disappointed like the last time that she had interrupted their mounting passion. Without using her hands, she bent until their faces touched, and she nudged his sideways. Her mouth blew warm and softly into his ear. Once again she felt his arousal, this time it pressed against her leg. He began to shudder with every breath she blew into his ear. His eyes blinked with disbelief when she finally whispered into his ear: "Yes, John."

After their lovemaking, they lay contentedly in each other's arms. John squeezed her tightly against him as she enjoyed the afterglow of their amazing union. Sherab stroked his chest, playing with the hair. He turned to her and again placed his hand on her heart.

"I love you Sherab", he told her once again.

"No", she replied sadly, using what little English she had learned. "No love. Sherab Shigatse, John Canada" She waved her arm in a sweeping arc, showing how far apart they were going to be. She had chosen to give herself to him out of love, but she did not want him to feel any obligations towards her. Why should he be forced to repeat that he loved her when they were about to separate?

John spoke to her again, but she could not make out his words. He used the new word 'love' several times, which brought her warmth. She stared intently as he spoke these words to her, trying to read his facial expressions. Her curious eyes followed him as he leaned and kissed her on the lips.

His growling stomach comically broke the intimate moment.

"Eat," he said to her, as she laughed. She smiled, nodded, and began to dress. In the dining room she sat beside him, simply to watch him eat. Since she had eaten with Muyih and Luhping, he had to eat alone. John seemed both amused and uncomfortable by having her stare at his every bite. She enjoyed the feeling of making him bashful, but she also enjoyed just watching him move. After a while he pulled his chair back, and, smiling, had her stand up. She let out a surprised squeal of laughter as he pulled her down onto his lap. With one arm around her waist, and her arm around his neck, he finished his breakfast. She resisted the urge to nibble on his ear while he ate, not wanting to be too forward with him. Overall, this was the best breakfast she had ever been part of.

The next few days in Luhping and Muyih's apartment turned out to be one of the happiest times in her life. Sherab and John made love every day, they ate, they laughed, and they lay in each other's arms for hours at a time. Their communication level slowly increased with the English lessons he gave her during those days. While she had no grammar to speak of, her vocabulary increased daily. These heavenly days truly were the calm before the storm. The coming storm would prove to be fiercer and longer than either of them could ever have imagined.

# Chapter 11

"I want to go over these plans one more time," John told everyone around the table. Muyih and Luhping tried to be attentive, but they were obviously bored with the repetition. Sherab concentrated on every word, trying to grasp any meaning that she could.

The rough hand sketches of the Panchen Lama's residence were spread out over the dining room table. Tomorrow morning Sherab and John would make their dangerous attempt to infiltrate the press conference, and reveal Sherab's story. He felt more confident than at any other time in their trip. They were well fed and rested, they had fresh new clothes, and above all, he knew the plan. More than just knew it, he had conceived most of it, and would be leading its execution. Sherab seemed content to concentrate on what to say once he got her to the front stage. Muyih and Luhping played the role of data providers, not planners. Any questions John had, they would find the answer for him as he formed the conference plan.

"The conference begins at 10:00 tomorrow," he began, "but journalists are admitted starting at 9:30. At 9:40, Muyih will drop Sherab and I off one block south of the Panchen Lama's residence. We will go to the stand of trees near the southeast wall. As soon as Muyih sees us there, he will start honking his horn across the street to get attention. The few people who are around will hopefully look his way, while Sherab and I climb the trees.

During the press conference, the guard dogs are not on the loose, so that should not be a concern. However, the two or three patrolling soldiers may see us. Along the inside south wall lies the main garden. Hopefully if we stay low and make our way through the garden we will have reasonable cover."

John stopped at this point, in order to make sure everyone was still listening to him. He stared at Luhping expectantly. With a sigh she turned to Sherab and translated what must have been a much shorter version of what he had just said.

"Now, if all goes well, the garden should get us to within fifty yards of the press conference itself. We'll be behind the Panchen Lama. Unfortunately this means that most of the audience will see us the moment we begin to approach. The good news is that the guards are likely to be standing next to the Panchen Lama's chair, facing the audience.

When we get close, I'll go to the right of the chair, and attract attention with my voice. Sherab will slip to the left and use the microphone for as long as they are busy with me. Hopefully she will have time to tell the audience that I am a western journalist, and that we have news to share. I think the lie about being a fellow journalist will win over the audience. Their support is absolutely critical in the few seconds after we make our entrance."

Luhping dutifully repeated to Sherab what he had just said. By this time Sherab herself looked bored, and he decided to give it a rest. The repetition had a calming effect on John's nerves. However, he thought it had become unfair to the others who did not need him to explain the well-known plan once more. Part of him wished the plan was not so well known. The fact that they learned it so quickly emphasized how simple a plan he had. John was not a spy, and he never claimed that he could plan the infiltration of a guarded compound.

"Perhaps you and Sherab should get some rest for tomorrow," Muyih said politely, with drooping eyelids. It was past 10:00 in the evening, and they all felt tired from the stress of the coming day. John never wanted this night to end, for it could be the last night that he ever saw Sherab. He tried not to dwell on that fact. Instead he drilled the plan into everyone's head until they were about ready to kick him out of the apartment.

"You're right Muyih," John sighed. "I'm sorry if I'm exaggerating with the amount of times I'm repeating tomorrow's plan."

With a few words of goodnight they all retreated to their beds for the night. Sherab and John had kept their affair a secret from Muyih and Luhping. On this last night he wanted to risk it all and go to her bed. But wisdom dictated that they have a good night's sleep before tomorrow's final step in their adventure. His eyes were struggling to stay open and he knew that he would be asleep within minutes.

John thought back to the first time he had made love to Sherab. He ruefully remembered that the night before he had promised himself not to get involved more deeply with her. But he had no regrets. He loved her deeply, and had been amazed at how good a lover she proved to be. Her body seemed to know just how to drive him wild with lustful desire. He still remembered the overwhelming emotions he felt when she said that she loved him. Even though she could not understand him, he had promised to return to her. Once this whole mess had blown over, he would come back and find her. She had been reluctant to discuss love because of their upcoming separation. But John knew that they would discuss love again, when he returned to Tibet.

At first John thought he was dreaming on the sofa when he saw her angelic face hovering above his. When Sherab's lips touched his, John knew that he was fortunate enough not to be dreaming. Her hand reached down hungrily while she crushed his lips with her kiss. They soon made love with the hurried passion of their first time, combined with the desperation of knowing it was their last time. More accurately, John felt that she made love to him, for she never allowed him to move from his near sleeping position on the sofa. When it was over, she gave him one last lingering kiss before silently disappearing to her room. He lay on the sofa for a long time, enjoying the afterglow. John could not believe how blessed he was to have her, and how cursed he was to lose her tomorrow. Eventually he fell asleep, with these conflicting emotions swirling through his head.

John's first glimpse of Shigatse brought him no thrill of discovery. The tension in Muyih's car was unbearable. He tried not to think of the danger they would face in the next hour. In vain, he focused on the curious mix of modern and ancient architecture in the city. Modern Chinese multi-level buildings were intermixed with stone houses and temples. The skyline of the downtown core reminded him of a long roller coaster, filled with sharp ups & downs.

Far too soon for John's taste, Muyih pulled up to a curb.

"This is where you get off John," Muyih announced. He turned to face Sherab and John in the back seat. "Good luck to you my friend," he told John as he reached to shake his hand. John was touched by Muyih's use of the word 'friend'. Every night he and Muyih had shared long conversations. They were pleasantly surprised to find that their views on most things, from politics to economics, differed very little. They had indeed become friends in a very short time.

John shook his hand firmly as he spoke. "Thank you, for all you have done Muyih. I'll always remember your kindness and treasure your friendship. I hope to return to Tibet one day, under more pleasant conditions. Perhaps we can meet again and renew our long evening discussions."

Muyih smiled at him and said: "That would give me much pleasure John, I hope you do come back."

Muyih turned to Sherab and they exchanged farewells in Chinese. She surprised them both when she leaned forward and gave him a small kiss on the cheek. This was not the same Sherab John had seen running through the Tibetan plains like a stalked creature. He wondered sadly how sweet and trusting this woman might have been if she had grown up in a peaceful setting.

They stepped out of the car, instantly realizing that the danger would be immediate and continuous until the outcome of the press conference was known. A white man and a Tibetan woman walking together down the street was very conspicuous. If any soldiers spotted them, they could be arrested before arriving at the Panchen Lama's home.

John had to fight back the urge to run as they made their way down the block. They drew a few curious stares from the local residents, but none questioned their presence. There were enough people on the street that they had sufficient cover simply mixing in with pedestrians. They soon reached the Panchen Lama's residence without any interruptions.

It seemed ludicrous to call this a home. It was more like a small, golden village. The estate was nestled against a large, barren hill. Two main structures stood out among the rest. Both were tall, three-story buildings. The lower two floors were made of red brick, while the upper floor was painted black. The rooftop was painted gold, with a balcony for the resident to walk along. A second, slanted golden roof covered the balcony. Each building seemed to have golden spires along their roofs. Luxurious curtains in white, black, or gold decorated every window in sight. Multi-colored banners fluttered lazily in the morning breeze.

Despite the splendor, John felt pity for the occupant. Trapped forever in this small kingdom, the Panchen Lamas throughout history never tasted the freedom of life out of the limelight.

The concrete wall surrounding the compound added to John's perception of the estate as a glorified prison. The walls jaggedly stepped up the hill along both sides of the residence. They met behind the compound, at an enormous concrete monolith. The rectangular monument measured approximately sixty feet high, and fifty feet wide. An immense, colorful tapestry draped over the entire surface of the monolith. John recognized the central figure of a meditating Buddha, as well as other characters involved in prayer or meditation. A large platform at the base of the monolith formed a stage of sorts, where John imagined public ceremonies must be held.

Sherab tugged on his sleeve, interrupting his examination of the estate. She pointed his attention to their right. Perhaps thirty yards away, John spotted the grove of trees Muyih had described. The crowds were thinner on this street. His legs trembled slightly as they tried to appear casual in their approach to the trees. Even though John anticipated Muyih's arrival, the car pulling up on the opposite side of the street still startled him. Muyih came to a screeching halt behind a parked car. The driver of the car was apparently waiting for someone inside, for he sat with the engine running. Muyih began honking his horn a little ahead of time. He played the part of an angry motorist annoyed by the car in front blocking his way. Enough heads began to turn his way that Sherab and John sprinted the last short distance to the trees. John snuck one last peek at Muyih's situation, and saw the other driver frantically trying to wave Muyih around his parked car.

Anyone looking for them could have seen their bodies making their way up the tree. However, with the general activity on the street, plus Muyih's obnoxious honking, they were pretty much invisible.

When he reached a sufficient height, John looked beyond the garden wall. He breathed a sigh of relief, for no patrols could be seen. Choosing the sturdiest branch that crossed over the wall, he began to creep away from the safety of the tree trunk. He had gone perhaps two feet before the branch bent over and rested on the top of the wall. The branch had no trouble holding his weight after this point. He sat on top of the wall, holding the branch down while Sherab clambered across.

Like they had discussed many times before, they both turned and swung their legs over the wall. They lowered their bodies until they hung from their hands, and then dropped the rest of the distance. Part way down, John's legs got caught in some vines growing along the face of the wall. He fell backwards and landed hard on his back. The soft garden soil broke his fall so that he only had the wind knocked out of him for a moment.

John rolled onto his stomach and rested against the wall. Sherab similarly rested just a few feet in front of him. He lifted his head slightly and was relieved to see only vegetation around them. The garden was sufficiently wide and thick to completely hide them from the buildings he could no longer see.

They began the arduous crawl along the garden floor. John expected someone to begin shouting with every movement they made. Soon his knees and elbows began to feel raw as they decreased the distance to the edge of the garden. He had not thought about the sight they would be when they emerged from the garden to meet the journalists. Both their fronts would be covered in garden dirt.

John kept crawling along, keeping his head low to the ground. He stopped short when Sherab's feet suddenly appeared under his face. He looked up to see why she had stopped so unexpectedly. The west wall of the compound loomed ahead of them. This was their destination. They should now be directly behind the conference. Sherab's eyes were opened wide with fright. All of their travels had led them to this moment. He crawled up to her and held her hand. They kissed each other in one last fierce embrace.

When they finally separated, John began to crawl through the garden to get a glimpse of where they had to run. Just ahead of him, he began to see the well-maintained lawn beyond the garden. He slowly raised his head until he had a clear view of the area beyond the garden. His heart began to thump loudly in his chest as his panic stricken eyes searched for some sign of the press conference. The lawn was completely empty. Not a person, not a podium, not a chair could be seen. Had they gone in the wrong direction?

Sherab let out a stifled scream a split second after the guard dog began to bark. The dog had seen John stick his head above the garden's vegetation.

"Muyih said there were no guard dogs on the day of the press conference!" he repeated to himself dumbly. No, they had not gone in the wrong direction. For some reason, there was no press conference today.

The running dog hypnotized John. Sherab nearly strangled him when she yanked on his shirt, trying to pull him to his feet. All thoughts of press conferences and stealthy approaches were lost when he saw how quickly the mad dog closed the distance between them. John knew that the dog was just one of their problems. No doubt the angry yelps would attract the soldiers that had to be patrolling the yard.

Sherab and John ran headlong back towards the treed area. He could hear the dog's bark getting closer and closer to them. It soon became obvious that they would not make it to the trees. Up ahead, John saw some climbing vines supported by stout poles. Without saying a word to Sherab he stopped and began tearing one of the poles free. No sooner was he done that the dog leapt the final distance between them. John saw the dog's body lifting off the ground from the corner of his eye. Swinging the pole like a baseball bat he spun around to meet the animal.

The dog's front paws scratched at John's chest, but the pole knocked its jaw away from his throat. They both fell to the ground. Momentum carried the animal through a few rolls before it regained its feet. This time John was ready and facing the dog with the pole outstretched before him. The dog's lips were curled back as it growled threateningly and began to stalk its prey. John kept the pole in front of him, jabbing in the dog's direction. He realized that he was simply forcing a stalemate. He still had not found a way to get past the dog.

With a swift, fluid motion, he backed the pole away and swung it in an arc towards the dog's head. The pole thudded hard against the earth, spitting up a small handful of dirt. The dog had easily sidestepped his swing and was now lunging at his right side. John had no time to swing the pole between them. The short end of the pole stuck out perhaps a foot from his hands. He used this end to once again block the beast's hungry teeth. The dog pawed at him in frustration as it chewed on the short end of the stick, its angry snout mere inches from John's face.

The dog began shaking its head up and down, trying to wrench the stick out of his hands. John fell backwards, and the dog followed with its jaws still clamped on the stick. A shadow loomed over them and before John knew it, Sherab had delivered a sharp kick to the dog's throat. With a strangled yelp it released the stick and rolled over once. Now with a new enemy, it tried to run past John to attack the unarmed Sherab. Still lying on his side, John jabbed with all his force at the dog's running body. He felt a satisfying jerk as the stick dug into the dog's side, almost tearing the pole from his hands. The dog's yelp was cut short as its jaw slammed into the earth in front of Sherab. Before John could get up Sherab pulled the pole out of his hands and drove it into the dog's body with determined savageness.

The dog's dying howl hurt John's ears and chilled his bones. They hardly had time to pick themselves up before they heard barking in the distance. Across the lawn they saw a pair of dogs racing to help their fallen comrade. Sherab, armed with the bloody pole, and John sprinted once more towards the trees. Although they arrived ahead of the dogs, John was still surprised by how much distance the beasts had covered.

The overhanging branches were out of their reach. John quickly laced his fingers together and motioned Sherab to put her foot in his hands. As she jumped upwards, he heaved on her foot. She grasped a stout branch and hung from the tree for a moment. He quickly put his hand up under her feet and supported her weight until she pulled her body up onto the wall. Without wasting a moment she lay flat on her stomach and extended her hand down to him.

A quick sideways glance showed two frightening dogs less than thirty yards from John. He tried jumping twice, but her hand was not within his reach. Fifteen yards. He saw the pole lying on the ground near the wall where Sherab had dropped it. He quickly picked it up and leaned it against the wall at roughly a forty-five degree angle. Ten yards. John put his weight on the top end of the pole, praying the bottom end would not simply slide out under him. Five yards. The pole dug into the ground, and for a fearful second he thought it was sliding along the ground's surface. The closest dog leapt at the same time that John used the pole to jump up to Sherab's waiting arm. Sherab caught one of his arms, while his other hand barely hung onto the edge of the wall.

The first dog had not anticipated his jump, and John heard it crash harmlessly into the wall well beneath his hanging legs. The second dog had time to adjust its course for John's new position. It leapt up and managed to catch his boot in its massive jaws. The sudden additional weight made John loose his grip from the wall. Sherab herself nearly tumbled down from the downward jerk on the arm she was holding.

A sharp kick to the dog's snout did not break its hold on his foot. He felt his arm slipping out of Sherab's grip. Using his free leg, John scrambled up enough to put his other arm back onto the wall. By now the first dog had recovered and was snapping at him as well. It alternated between jumping for his free leg, and trying to compete with the second dog on the captured leg. With the added support of both arms on the wall, John was able to kick down much harder. The kicks were timed to hit while the first dog was heading downwards from its jumps. John did not want to risk having both legs caught by the dogs.

Eventually the dog was forced to release his foot, after repeated blows to the snout and head. Both dogs did not stop barking and jumping ferociously against the wall even when John and Sherab shakily fell to the ground on the other side. The only good, though unexplainable, fortune on their side was the absence of patrolling soldiers.

A quick survey of the street told John what he had feared: Muyih was long gone. How long could they wander these streets before being arrested? Then he noticed the small satellite dish mounted on the faraway van.

"A news crew!" he told Sherab excitedly. He knew that she did not understand him, but his enthusiasm gave her the hope she desperately needed.

Throwing caution aside, they ran down the street towards the parked van. The van idled near the corner of the estate. John assumed the front entrance to the Panchen Lama's estate must have been just around the corner. They could see a technician through the open back door of the van. He looked up as they approached, his eyes opening wide in surprise at these two running figures.

His Caucasian skin gave John hope, someone who could sympathize and understand him. The man put his headphones down next to the rest of his monitoring equipment and stepped out of the van defensively. Like a mother protecting her young, John thought. They stopped in front of him, but John was too breathless to say anything. He noticed that the man had a badge identifying him as Franz Schmidt from some TV station John had never heard of. The overweight technician simply stared at them in surprise as they puffed air in giant, dry gulps.

"What happened to the press conference?" John managed to gasp between breath intakes.

John thought his question surprised Franz even more than their original appearance.

"The conference is nearly over," he answered in heavily accented, halting English. His German accent sounded almost comically identical to the ones John had heard in war movies when he grew up.

"Where is it being held?" John asked him. "It's not outside like it was supposed to be."

"The boy is not feeling very well today. He did not want to go outside. The meeting is inside, they told us this morning." He paused a moment before continuing. "You do not look like you belong in this meeting. Who are you?"

There was no time to explain anything to this man. In fact Franz might become trouble as he overcame his surprise. How could John get into the house? And the conference only had a few minutes remaining, he realized.

John's eyes stared enviously at the technician's badge. If only they had tried getting forged press badges, he thought. John's logical mind went blank, and instinct took over. He turned as if to walk away from Franz. As John hoped, Franz did not take kindly to strangers asking questions and then ignoring his. Franz took two steps towards John's back, and put a hand on his shoulder.

"Sir, kindly tell me what business you ..." He never finished his sentence. Sensing the distance between them, John spun around on his heel and lifted his elbow. His whole arm felt numb from shock when his elbow drove into the technician's mouth. John heard a sickening noise as some of the man's teeth were knocked out of his mouth. His hands flew to his bleeding mouth as he fell backwards, his back slamming on the edge of the van door.

For once it was Sherab's turn to stare in shocked silence. John knew that he would soon go into his own shock from this unexpected violence. While the animal in him remained in control, he bent over Franz who now leaned limply against the back of the van. The man's eyes filled with fear as John grabbed his shoulders, and bent him over forward. With one hand on his forehead, John whipped Franz back, slamming his head on the unforgiving metal of the van's doorframe. This time his body slumped into unconsciousness.

The only way to get Sherab's attention at this time was to physically grab her arms and bring her down to the technician with him. Together they managed to roll Franz back into the van. John ripped the photo id badge, his prize possession, from the man's shirt before slamming the van door shut.

Franz and John looked alike about as much as Sherab and John did. It was a desperate plan, but he hoped the guards at the entrance only gave a superficial glance at the badge. After hurriedly pinning it on his chest, John took a look at the two of them and realized that they did not stand a chance. He jerked the van door open once again, half expecting Franz to leap out at him. With relief he saw Franz was still out cold on the van floor. By rummaging through the van he found a loose floppy hat for Sherab. He snapped a pair of earphones over her head, and plugged them into a video camera to complete her outfit.

For himself, John found a clipboard for journalistic note taking. Although he had nothing to plug it into, he grabbed a microphone and stuck the dangling cable into his pocket. They were still disguised horribly, but at least a guard at the door would have to spend more than a second to notice something wrong with them. Once again they shut the van door and hid the downed German from view.

John motioned Sherab to follow close behind him. He wanted the guards to mostly see her camera and the hat on her head. They walked briskly to the end of the street, and rounded the corner of the estate. A public notice board was mounted on the wall to their right. The lettering was in Chinese, so John did not pay attention to the various papers pinned on the board.

The entrance gate was slightly ajar, with four guards protecting it. Three of the guards leaned against the wall leisurely, their guns held loosely in their hands. The fourth guard examined a journalist's badge before waving her through. They stood perhaps twenty yards from the gate. With a trembling heart, and a still throbbing elbow, John began walking towards the gate.

Up ahead an army jeep headed in their direction. The jeep carried four soldiers in addition to the driver. The passenger soldiers seemed bored and busied themselves by looking at the passing scenery. John did not want them staring at Sherab and him, nor did he want to reach the gate while they were still nearby. He quickly turned around and spun Sherab to face the notice board.

John felt the microphone slip out of his hand as he stared at his face on the wall. Sherab's gasp of surprise confirmed that he was not hallucinating. There among the rest of the public notices, his grim face stared out in grainy black and white. His head pulsated with fear. He could not understand why his picture hung there, but John knew it could only spell disaster.

"Yu," Sherab whispered in a shocked hush. John looked at her dumbly. "Yu!" she repeated, this time using her finger to draw a line across her throat. The fear centered in the pit of his stomach as realization dawned on him. Yu had died in the wilderness, and now the Chinese had found his body.

The repercussions continued to pound mercilessly at his defenseless brain. John was on record as the tourist Yu escorted. The Chinese had plenty of real circumstantial evidence to prove he had killed Yu. They would have no problems planting any more phony evidence if they needed it. John was a wanted murderer. All the credibility he might have had at the press conference disappeared. Now they presented themselves as a murderer and an escaped political prisoner. No foreigner, journalist or not, would lift a finger to defend them. The press conference plan had to be aborted!

He was incapable of thinking of any strategy at this moment. His only thoughts were to find their way back to the safety of Muyih and Luhping's apartment.

"We must go to Muyih and Luhping," he told Sherab. She nodded her understanding. The defeat in her eyes seemed unbearable for John to see. He looked away from her and began walking back in the direction they had come. They had not gone more than ten steps when he heard one of the Chinese guards calling out to them. They both froze for a brief second before stiffly continuing to walk towards the corner of the wall.

When the soldier cried out once more, John looked at Sherab questioningly. "Stop," she whispered to him, nodding back towards the soldier.

"Keep going!" John told her, picking up the pace a little. The soldier shouted again and this time John heard the unmistakable sound of boots beginning to pound the pavement in a run. "Run!" he told Sherab as he began to race the remaining distance to the street corner. Other soldiers began to run as John and Sherab tried to make their escape.

John's eyes settled on the van the moment they turned the corner. A quick peek through the window showed the technician's keys on the dashboard.

"Get in!" he told Sherab as he raced around to the driver's side. They both instinctively looked into the rear of the van, and were relieved to see Franz still lying motionless.

The well-tuned engine roared to life immediately. John turned the van around in a tight arc just as the first soldier rounded the corner of the wall. With squealing tires he took off down the south wall, praying that the soldiers would not start shooting at them. As far as the soldiers knew, John and Sherab had not committed any crime other than refusing to stop. Two blocks later John knew they were safe from the soldiers until they found a jeep to give pursuit.

This morning it had taken them about twenty minutes to get from the apartment to their drop-off point one block south of the Panchen Lama's home. Although he could not read the street signs, John knew that they had to head roughly southwest of their present location. Besides, he did not want to park the stolen van too close to Muyih's apartment. John smiled when he realized that he could now add auto-theft to his rapidly growing criminal record.

They drove the van through many of the smaller streets. John thought the risk of discovery diminished in the less populated areas. He focused on driving through the unknown streets and failed to notice the approaching German in the rearview mirror. As the thick hairy arm wrapped around John's neck clumsily, he saw the furious and bleeding face frighteningly close in the mirror. Without thinking, John slammed on the brakes. The technician's head whipped forward as he flew between the seats and landed hard against the dash and windshield. John slammed into the steering wheel and fought to remain conscious.

A dazed and bruised Sherab picked herself up off the dash. The injured German began to stir, trying to find the strength to get up. Sherab ended his struggles by slamming the heavy camera into his head. John had seen her smack a man on the head for the third time, he thought with a sick humor. First John, then Yu, and now this innocent Franz had all felt her fury on their poor skulls.

John had been planning to abandon the van very soon anyway. Now seemed like the appropriate moment. They left Franz between the front seats and climbed out of the van.

"Do you know how to get to the apartment?" John asked Sherab. She looked at him with the puzzled look of incomprehension. He pointed at her and said: "Muyih and Luhping?" She nodded tiredly then, and pointed to their right.

"Come Sherab," she said to him. He was so thankful that she seemed to know her way around. Even without his pounding headache, John doubted he could find the apartment.

Sherab had blood on her clothes from Franz. John wondered how far they could possibly get before drawing one too many curious stares. Sherab must have thought the same thing, for she soon led them into a narrow alley between two stone houses. The alley appeared deserted, strewn garbage testified to its lack of maintenance. The alley ended forty feet later against the back wall of another building. Sherab motioned John to sit down. She looked at him and pointed at the sun.

"Sun sleep," she said. John nodded his understanding.

"We'll wait until night comes," he told her.

Sherab sat beside him as they waited for the hours to go by. They huddled together in the protective semi darkness of the alley. The stone pavement underneath dug into their weary bodies. Each passing car or distant shout made them tense up like frightened rabbits. By afternoon, John felt the familiar hunger and thirst they had grown accustomed to in their travels. It seemed like an eternity had passed before darkness finally fell over them.

Sherab stood up stiffly and shook the numbness out of her legs. John followed suit and then headed cautiously out of the alley. Sherab led them through several streets, always hugging closely against the walls where she could. At times she hesitated, looking in various directions. Helplessly, John stayed by her side and prayed she could find her way.

Hope filled his spirit when she breathed a sigh of relief at a particular street sign. John had no idea what the sign said, but he knew she had found the way to the apartment. The streets were almost deserted at this time of night. Only once did they have to duck into another alley when they saw someone approaching in the distance. John never saw if it was a soldier or not, nor did he care to know. He only wanted to reach their destination without further confrontation.

Before he knew what was happening, Sherab ducked into the familiar parking garage they had left earlier this morning. What a welcome sight, John thought, as relief flooded his entire being. Within minutes they were knocking at Muyih and Luhping's door. A very frightened and surprised Muyih pulled them quickly into his apartment before slamming his door shut. Without saying a word, John stumbled to the sofa and fell, rather than sat, in it.

"What has happened to you two?" Luhping asked, finally breaking the stunned silence.

"Muyih, Luhping," John began tiredly, "we need your help again."

# Chapter 12

"We never meant to kill him," John assured Muyih and Luhping when he had finished describing their day. He tried to block out of his mind Sherab's vengeful face as she struck the unconscious Yu with a rock. "We only knocked him out so that we could escape imprisonment. He was still breathing when we left him. Perhaps he never regained consciousness, and died of exposure."

"But why did Yu want to arrest you John?" Luhping asked.

"Because one night I helped Sherab escape. That man was brutal to her, I couldn't let her go through more of the same torture she had been subjected to before."

"Well it certainly explains the night raid on the Thon temple," Muyih added. "They must have found Yu's body on that day, and immediately started searches in the nearby towns."

"That's a good point Muyih!" John exclaimed as more pieces of the puzzle came into place. "Lobsang had told us that in the previous weeks they had already been conducting searches, presumably for Sherab. Now when they found Yu's body, I'm sure they saw signs that I wasn't alone with him. If Yu kept two prisoners tied up, would it be that much of a leap in logic to think that perhaps he had caught Sherab? I know we westerners have a reputation for disregarding your laws when it comes to human rights. They may have guessed the whole scene! The beaten woman shows up, Yu mistreats her, westerner tries to help her, and then Yu has two prisoners."

John paused a moment before adding: "They must really want to find us badly now."

"After the affair at the Panchen Lama's home, you can be sure they'll be especially vigilant in Shigatse," Luhping added.

Muyih seemed uncomfortable before he spoke. "Do you think you killed the German journalist as well?"

"I really don't think so. Sherab struck him with a video camera. That's not quite as bad as a jagged rock. He was pretty beat up though, he may need a short hospital stay."

"Have you thought about where you'll go now?" Luhping asked.

His hosts' rapid fire questioning barely left John a moment to think of any plan beyond that evening.

"Well," he said thoughtfully, "Lobsang had told me that we really had two choices. Expose Sherab's story at the press conference in Shigatse, or escape out of Tibet over the mountains." Finally uttering the words he had tried to avoid throughout the day brought a chill in his spine. John could not imagine how he and Sherab could possibly cross the Himalayas.

Muyih's eyes opened wide as he sucked in his breath. Luhping on the other hand seemed to take it in stride, and merely nodded her head thoughtfully. John guessed that she had already reached this conclusion herself.

"That will be a long and difficult journey," Luhping stated. "I don't mean just the mountains themselves. But the most logical crossover point is about two hundred miles from Shigatse. That journey in itself will be extremely dangerous and difficult. The police and soldiers will be looking for you at every checkpoint along the way."

John looked at Luhping in exasperation. "Well what do you suggest then?"

Luhping shook her head. "I'm not suggesting anything. I agree that you don't have many options. I just want you to make an informed decision."

Sherab began asking questions in Chinese. John felt grateful to have some time to gather his thoughts. It was impossible to make it across the mountains alone. He did not think Muyih or Luhping were experienced mountain climbers either. John would have to find a guide willing to take them across. He had heard stories of escaped political prisoners making their way across these terrible mountains with the help of guides. These guides actually specialized in smuggling Tibetans out of the country. Sometimes a parent might even smuggle their child out of the country in hopes of getting them a better education in neighboring India.

Sherab's rising voice pushed John's thoughts aside. She and Luhping seemed to be arguing loudly about something. Muyih occasionally interjected, seemingly to placate both of them. A final outburst from Luhping pushed a defeated Sherab into angry tears.

"What's going on?" John asked during the pause in the argument.

"Sherab is having difficulty in accepting that she can't reveal her story in Shigatse," Muyih answered diplomatically.

"What he means is that she's being stubborn and won't accept reality!" Luhping added hotly. "How can she expect to speak publicly after all you two have done?"

Luhping's voice brought another string of angry Chinese from Sherab.

"It's OK, hold on a minute," John told Luhping as she braced herself for a scathing reply. Only by holding his hands out in front of her did she bite her tongue.

"Sherab," John called softly. She looked up at him with a tear-streaked face. He stood in front of her and motioned her to stand up. His hand pulled her head until it rested on his shoulder. He held her close and said "No Shigatse, Sherab."

Her strength seemed to melt then, and her doll's body hung limply in his arms as she wept in her defeat. John's arm stroked her back as he tried to rock her gently while she released years of sorrow and pain.

Eventually she raised her head slightly, and looked at him in embarrassed silence. He leaned his forehead against hers.

"We'll go to India, Sherab. You can tell the Dalai Lama your story directly." He was not sure how much of that she understood, but at least he knew she caught the words 'Dalai Lama'. With that he kissed her softly and sat her back down on the chair. She let herself be led into the chair in a childlike manner.

Muyih and Luhping gawked at them with twin, open-mouth stares. John flushed when he suddenly realized that what had been a most natural kiss to Sherab and him had shocked the unsuspecting couple. A look of understanding came over Luhping's eyes as she digested the scene she had just witnessed, and undoubtedly thought of the days they had spent alone in the apartment.

A short cough failed to hide John's embarrassment. "We really need to discuss this mountain crossing idea," he said, trying to divert attention away from the revealed intimacy between him and Sherab.

"Yes," Muyih answered enthusiastically. John thought Muyih also felt relieved to dive into a discussion. "I'll tell you what I know, which is really not that much."

John sat down and listened attentively to Muyih's words.

"In eastern Tibet there are mountain passes that you can cross. They are about two hundred miles from here. These passes will lead you into Nepal. The altitude is more than fifteen thousand feet in some areas. But the cold and the altitude are not your only enemies. All along the trail, nomads will try to turn you in to the local police for money. They're paid for each refuge that they capture. The same is true for the Nepalese police, if you do get across the border. Many, many people have tried and failed this escape route."

"Both you and Luhping are equally encouraging with your remarks," John noted sarcastically.

"You're asking me for what I know John. Don't be angry because I can't tell you that there is an easy way out of Tibet."

"I'm sorry Muyih. I'm getting very sick of this whole thing. Sherab and I have been running for almost a month now. Don't lie to me, but help with ideas instead of trying to frighten or discourage me."

"We're not trying to do either of those things," Luhping interjected. "You need to make these difficult decisions with your eyes wide open. This isn't a playful adventure, you really are putting your life at great risk."

"What decisions are there for me to make? What choices do I have? I can't hide in your apartment forever."

Luhping looked down at her feet while she spoke her next sentences. "There is one other option you must consider, John. If you turn yourself in, your government will raise enough diplomatic protests that there is a very good chance you'll be returned to your country."

She held her hand up to silence his protest. "Let me finish, please. There is no definitive proof that you murdered Yu. The murder of one man is insignificant in China, especially in light of the world coverage of a jailed Canadian.

Now you can leave Sherab completely out of your story. We'll keep her here for a while, and then communicate with Lobsang. I'm sure she has arranged for the escape of many Tibetans before."

"Are you finished?" John asked Luhping coldly. She nodded meekly, intimidated by his tone of voice.

"No," he told her quietly, and firmly.

"John," Muyih began, "put aside your romantic western ideas for a moment. Have you considered that perhaps Sherab has a better chance of escape with a group of Tibetan refugees than with a white man?"

John refused to believe his argument. Still, a small, logical part of John, buried deep inside his brain, suggested that perhaps Muyih was right. John hoped that he was not being selfish by refusing to leave her.

"If that's the decision you two were talking about, then consider it made. The answer is an absolute no. I would prefer not wasting valuable time discussing this option any further. Sherab and I are going together."

A few moments of wordless silence, accompanied by the careful study of shuffling feet, followed his declaration.

"This is where you're supposed to say 'as you wish John', or 'we accept your decision'," John told them.

Muyih managed a wan smile. "We accept your decision John."

"And I just hope your foolishness will not lead both you and Sherab to your deaths," Luhping added bitterly.

"Thank you for your concern Luhping," he answered her. They stared at each other in open confrontation, until she finally looked away, shaking her head.

"Now, is there a way for you to find out much more details about escaping Tibet through the mountains?" John asked them both.

Muyih shook his head slowly. "I can make some inquiries, but we really have never been involved this deeply with escaping fugitives."

Luhping surprised them both when she spoke up. "I know someone," she said. "One of the teachers at the school has a brother who is close to ..." She hesitated, searching for the right words. "Close to those who help Tibetans escape. If I speak with her, perhaps she can arrange a meeting with someone experienced in this area."

Muyih looked puzzled. "Why didn't I know this?" he asked his wife.

Luhping smiled at his question. "You don't know everything I talk to my friends about, my husband." Her tone was mischievous and insinuating.

Muyih did not miss her suggestive humor, and grinned openly at her. "It seems there are always new things I can learn about you, Luhping."

"Luhping," John said, interrupting their semi-private intimate moment, "I would be very grateful if you could arrange this. Otherwise I have no idea where to begin."

"I can't promise anything John, but I'll speak to her tomorrow."

There was nothing more to say. Luhping and John had reached an uneasy truce that he did not want to shatter. His growling stomach reminded him that he had far more simple needs to take care of at the moment.

"It seems that we're destined to rudely arrive at your apartment at night without food or shelter," John told them with a smile.

"Think nothing of it John," Muyih replied. "We're glad to be able to offer what little help we can. You and Sherab must be hungry, let me go see what I can find in the kitchen."

"No Muyih, let me go." Luhping held him down as she stood up. "I think it would do Sherab some good to busy herself with me." She spoke to Sherab, who nodded briefly before following Luhping into the kitchen.

Muyih looked at John solemnly. "Please don't think badly of Luhping. She has strong opinions, and does not hesitate to speak her mind. But her intentions are always good. She really does fear for both your lives."

"I know Muyih, and I'm sorry that I had disagreements with her. This is a difficult time for all of us. Sherab and I are trying to survive, and you and Luhping are trying to accommodate a pair of strangers wanted by the police. Although I don't like it, I think it's normal for the stress to cause some friction between us. I truly believe that both you and Luhping are wonderful people. Don't lose site of that just because of a little disagreement."

"You're also a wonderful man John," Muyih told him warmly. "I don't know if you're making a wise decision by staying with Sherab, but it's certainly an honorable decision that I respect."

They sat in silence for a few minutes, enjoying the understanding and friendship that they shared.

"Oh, Muyih, I forgot to tell you." John sat up with a smile. "You were such an obnoxious driver at the Panchen Lama's house this morning! Do you always make such a fuss when a driver blocks your way?"

Muyih laughed at this. "No, I'm a very patient and tolerant driver. But I have to admit that I enjoyed releasing all the frustrations of years of driving in this city!"

They both laughed at this remark, and John felt the stress drain from his mind. The rest of the evening retained this peaceful atmosphere. Until Luhping spoke with her friend the next day, there was very little they could do in the way of planning their escape. A stranger walking in among them could not have known just how desperate a situation Sherab and John were in.

That night John dreamed of Sherab's eyes again. He was shivering outside in a blinding blizzard. The swirling snow blotted out all traces of his surroundings. Her eyes shone like beacons through the blustering snowfall. He felt frozen in place. Then slowly he lifted one leg out of the snow and stepped towards her bright eyes. The next step was easier, and the one after easier again. Soon he ran in long sinking strides, hopping at each step to get above the snow. Her eyes began to fade, no matter how hard he tried to run faster. Soon he was alone again, in a featureless world of snow. In despair he let himself fall into the snow. A warmth spread over his body as the snow buried him in its cold caress. Before the dream ended John remembered thinking that he should not have let Sherab get so far away in the first place. If he had stayed closer, he would not be dying alone in the snow.

***

Sherab sat by the small window, staring outside and lost deep in her thoughts. Both Muyih and Luhping had already left for work. John slept soundlessly on the sofa. Yesterday morning she had thought she would lose him forever. She smiled and turned to him, enjoying the sight of his softly breathing body.

The astrologer had been right of course, Sherab thought. She should not have gone to this press conference. She was thankful that she and John had escaped the soldiers. Perhaps Yeshi's amulet had helped their luck and allowed them to get away unhurt. And now John wanted to cross the mountains on foot.

She turned away then, unable to bear the thought of him dying in the frozen mountains. How could she stop him? She loved him for wanting to take her to India, but she had already risked his life too many times. Now all she wanted to do was find a way to get him to safety. But the weight of her responsibility pressed hard on her shoulders. His Holiness the Dalai Lama had to know about the captured Panchen Lama, and it was up to Sherab to get him that information. She could not have made it this far without John's support, and without his love. In the darkest moments of despair she thought about his love for her, and how they might have a good life after India. It was pure fantasy of course, but it did help her get by moments like this morning. She looked outside sadly, realizing that in all probability she would fail her mission, die, and kill the man she loved in the process.

So much of this situation was her fault. She had killed Yu, and now John was accused of murder. No matter how hard she tried to follow Buddha's teachings, she seemed destined to stray further and further from the path to enlightenment. She had let anger make her strike Yu again, this time delivering a fatal blow. She would never escape this downward spiral in her behavior.

"Good morning Sherab," John croaked in his early morning voice.

She broke into a smile and turned to him. "Good morning John," she answered.

They both stood at the same time and drew close together. He put his arms around her and hugged her tightly against him.

"I love you Sherab," he told her once more. She squeezed him harder. There was no point in rejecting his statement for silly reasons like before, when they were going to separate after the conference. She squeezed him out of love, but also out of sadness. No, they were not going to separate, but they were going to die together.

"Did you eat?" he asked when they finally released each other. She appreciated so much the ability to have some communication with him.

"Eat," she nodded her reply. She smiled in confusion, not knowing if he wanted her to eat or if he was asking if she already ate. He smiled back, perhaps sensing her hesitation, and tried again.

"I did not eat," he said pointing to himself and shaking his head. "Did you eat?" he asked, pointing to her.

"Sherab eat," she told him slowly, "John not eat."

"Well John is hungry!" he declared as he headed towards the kitchen.

Muyih and Luhping had left him a breakfast plate, which she took out for him. She returned to the sofa while he ate hungrily. The sofa still held on to the warmth of his sleeping body, which brought her a mixture of comfort and desire. John rejoined Sherab on the sofa to finish his breakfast with an orange from the fruit bowl. She watched him peel it slowly and methodically. Sherab liked the way he could put all of his concentration on such a simple task. He tore off a segment and offered it to her. The way these small, caring acts came naturally out of John always moved her deeply. She could have asked for a piece, or she could have peeled the orange for him. But John's way was to peel the orange and offer her the first piece. Instead of reaching for it she just stared into his eyes. Would John ever understand how much she cared for him? She eventually reached for his hand, but instead of taking the orange segment she just held his outstretched hand.

"I love you John," she said simply. He blinked a few times, as if he had not understood correctly. His wet, brightly twinkling eyes rendered her helpless. Then he calmly put the orange down on the side table. Without releasing her hand he stood up and led her into the guest bedroom of the apartment.

Sherab greeted Muyih and Luhping at the door as they arrived home that evening. "Well I'm afraid neither John nor I are skilled cooks like yourselves! We've prepared supper, but it didn't turn out as well as we hoped."

"There was no need to do that Sherab," Luhping replied politely.

"It certainly smells good in here!" Muyih added.

"Did you talk to your friend?" Sherab asked Luhping immediately.

"Yes I did. She'll call me tonight with an answer."

Sherab looked at Luhping expectantly, not quite satisfied with such a simple answer after waiting all day.

"She said she can probably arrange it, but we'll know for sure when she calls." Luhping shrugged her shoulders, there was nothing else she could tell Sherab.

Neither of them spoke very much during dinner. Sherab barely tasted any of the food John and her had prepared. The tension of waiting for the phone became more unbearable as the evening wore on.

After dinner they sat in the living room and tried to pass the time engaged in idle chatter. The shrill ring of the phone was a welcomed interruption. Luhping answered, giving them one side of a Chinese conversation.

"Tomorrow night at seven? That's perfect, thank you very much!" When Sherab heard Luhping's words she squeezed John's hand and nodded at him with a big smile. Now he was the one left out of the conversation. She wanted to let him know that Luhping's friend had indeed arranged some sort of meeting.

Luhping spoke to John, after hanging up. John seemed relieved to have her confirm Sherab's interpretation.

"This is great news, Luhping," Sherab added. "Now what do we know about this man. Who is he?"

"We hardly know anything about him, nor are we likely to learn anything. We won't even learn his name. All we know is that he has information regarding mountain escapes out of Tibet."

"I guess that's all we need to know then," Sherab replied. "As long as he knows what he's talking about, that's good enough for me."

"Does he himself take people across the mountains?" Muyih asked his wife.

"I don't know anything more about this man. We'll meet him tomorrow and hopefully he'll answer all our questions."

The next day proved to be another waiting game. Fortunately, spending a day alone with John made the time go by much quicker than Sherab thought possible. By the time the knock came at the door, all of the previous two days of waiting were forgotten.

An old Tibetan man shuffled into the apartment in front of Muyih. Muyih had gone to open the door for him, and was now staring at the man's back in confused wonder. About the only thing that appeared to have life in this ancient body were the man's eyes. His crystal clear gaze seemed to examine each of them with piercing accuracy.  He walked a little unsteadily as he went from Luhping, to Sherab, and finally to John. When he stood close to John, Sherab could make out the deep crevices throughout his face. She had never seen more wrinkled and weather-beaten skin in her life. His hands were partly clutched into fists of gnarled hardwood. The paper-thin skin pulled tightly against his bony arms, a sharp contrast to the folds on his face.

The old man's strong voice belied the frailty of his aged body. "I may be old now boy, but I brought countless people through the Nangpa La before you were even born."

Even as he ended his sentence, his voice began to rasp out of his throat like an unused door rusted at the hinges. He cleared his throat, waiting for a reply.

John stared in confusion, even as Muyih translated the man's Tibetan to English. Sherab wondered why the old man had singled out John so quickly. Perhaps he felt disdain for foreigners.

"What is the Nangpa La?" John asked him through Muyih.

A derisive snort escaped the old man's dry, flaking lips. "You will get to know the Nangpa La very well, boy. From the looks of you, you may have an eternity to get acquainted with it." He laughed at his own morbid humor. A few throaty chuckles brought on a fit of coughing as he made his way to the sofa. The rest of them were too thunderstruck by his imposing presence to follow him into the living room.

"500 Yuan," he called out from the sofa. The talk of money brought John out of his stunned reverie.

"You can get us across the mountains for 500 Yuan?" John asked him incredulously. Muyih had no difficulty in using John's tone as he translated, for he seemed as surprised by the price as John.

This produced another peal of laughter from the old man, followed by deep chest coughs. Through his laughing mouth Sherab could make out the few remaining yellow teeth sticking out of his gums like ancient monoliths.

"No boy," he said when he recovered from John's unintended humor. "500 Yuan to talk to me tonight. My days of trekking through that frozen hell are long over."

"You want money to talk?" John asked, again surprised by this strange character.

"Of course!" he answered with disdain. "Where else do you expect to get this kind of information? Did you check your travel brochures for more directions?" His near toothless grin threatened to break into that haunting laugh again.

"Well I just assumed that you were the friend of Luhping's friend. I mean, how do I know I'm getting information worth that much?" John had not yet adjusted to the idea of paying the old man to talk to him.

"Then good luck to you, boy." He struggled out of the sofa and began limping past John.

"Wait!" Sherab said suddenly. "We will pay you your money. Please sit back down." She felt annoyed by both John and the old man. John's stubbornness over the money made her feel angry. And why the old man chose to deal with John instead of her made her resent both men. She hated the way they excluded her just because she was female.

"Well at least one of you has some sense!" the old man said gruffly and pushed his way back to the sofa.

"I'm sorry," she said, placating him. "John just wasn't prepared for paying for the information. Let me get the money now."

She retrieved his money out of John's dwindling reserve of cash in the backpack. John looked at her as she returned with the money. She glared at him, trying to show that she would handle the old Tibetan man. The guide did not bother counting the money. With an experienced, fluid motion he slipped the money into his shirt as smoothly as a birthday party magician.

The old man seemed to regain some of his lost youth as he began to retell what must have been his life's work. The rest of them faced him in a loose semicircle, and listened with rapt attention.

"The Nangpa La is an eighteen thousand foot monster that will do its best to suck the life out of you. It is the highest mountain pass that you will have to cross. But first, let me start you at the beginning of your journey."

The guide paused while Muyih quickly translated an abridged version of his words for John.

"The safest way to avoid the most dangerous checkpoints is to drive to Shekar, about 180 miles from here. But then you have more traveling to do on foot, including the 16,000 foot Pang La."

'La' was the Tibetan word for 'pass'. The guide named the various mountain passes like they were his old friends.

"If you can make it by the soldiers, then you should drive all the way to Dingri. It's only twenty miles past Shekar, but it will feel like one hundred miles on foot.

There is a bridge you'll have to cross between Shekar and Dingri. The Chinese have a permanent checkpoint on this bridge. If you're lucky, the guards are sometimes asleep in the middle of the night. If not, then you'll need to find a shallow crossing and go on foot through the water. Bring an extra pair of socks, or your feet will freeze against your boots after crossing the river."

His face seemed tortured with a distant memory when he made this last remark. It frightened Sherab to think that most of what he told them came from his own personal experience. What courage a man must have to make this trek across the mountains countless times.

"From Dingri you will cut south towards the mountains. You will see Nangpa La from far away. The Himalayas hide the sky from your view when you're that close. The local nomads call Nangpa La the 'great notch in the sky'.

Oh, that reminds me, be careful of the nomads. While some will gladly share what little food they have with you, others are bounty hunters. They can get about 200 Yuan per head from the local authorities.

There are many checkpoints between Nangpa La and Dingri. If you get past them all, then you are clear of Chinese patrols for good. On the other side of Nangpa La lies the Nepal border. Now Nepal has no obligation to return you to China. In fact, if you get far enough into the country, they will help you get to India. But you must be careful of the border police. They, like the nomads in Tibet, get paid for each Tibetan that they capture and return to the Chinese.

Once in Nepal you have a few options. You could go to the Chailsa refugee center, and rest there until you can make your way to India. Or, if you make it to one of the nearby villages, like Namche Bazaar, you can probably get a ride to Katmandu. From Katmandu there are buses that can take you to India. The choice depends a lot on the situation you're in when you cross. I would recommend that you let your guide decide for you. He'll have a good sense of the recent treatment of refugees in the area."

"That brings up a good point," Sherab interrupted for the first time. "Where can we find a guide that will take us across?"

The old man seemed to hesitate for the first time since arriving among them. "I can give you names of guides and places where you can find them. But I have to warn you of something. If I were still a guide, I would refuse you. It will be too difficult to smuggle a white man through the many checkpoints. All along the trail, every passerby will notice you. If anyone is chasing you, and trying to stop you, you will leave a very visible trail of witnesses. The risk is simply too great."

With a sinking heart she digested this new information. "Do you think we could make it on our own?" she asked lamely.

"Don't even think of it. That's certain death for you and the white man." He nodded towards John as he said this. "A guide crosses the mountains many times with a more experienced guide before ever attempting it alone. Even then, guides often perish along with their refugees while crossing the mountains. For someone who has never been there, there is no chance at all of making it."

"Then I'll have to find a way to convince a guide to bring us," Sherab said grimly.

The old man smiled, and said with new respect: "Maybe you will, but I doubt it."

They talked with him for perhaps one more hour before he got up to leave. As they walked towards the door, he stopped and looked at John sincerely for the first time.

"I do hope you make it. But I think you're too soft, you won't have the determination it takes." He turned his attention to Sherab. "You can make it. He'll have to learn to rely on you to get him through his moments of despair."

His analysis of their characters stunned Sherab. He seemed so sure of his judgment. John also looked surprised, and a little embarrassed, after Muyih's translation.

"You look like you have money," the guide continued with Sherab. "That's one advantage that you have over most refugees. Many people cross these frozen mountains in cheap running shoes and thin sweaters. At least you and the white man can buy appropriate clothing for winter conditions.

Also, the guide, if you find one, will not be cheap. Under normal circumstances, he may charge two thousand Yuan per person. But for a group of just two people, and one of them white, he would be a fool to charge less than four thousand Yuan for each of you."

With one last sweeping survey of the room with his sharp eyes, he slipped out of the apartment, and out of their lives.

No one spoke for a minute or two after the old man's departure. The first to speak was Muyih. Sherab was grateful to him, for he spoke in a low voice to John, summarizing the last words from the old man.

***

After collecting his thoughts for a few moments, John began to speak to Muyih about the trip.

"There are so many things to discuss," he began. "One of the first that comes to mind is money. I don't have nearly enough cash for this trip. Do you think we can safely get to a bank in Shigatse? I could have all the money I need wired to me from my home branch."

"No John, you know very well that's not possible," Muyih replied. "I'm sure the banks have been alerted with your identification. The moment you identified yourself, they would notify the police. You don't need to worry about the money. Luhping and I have enough savings to cover your costs."

"Muyih, I really hate having to do that. Please accept my promise that I'll find a way to repay you. If it's not safe to wire you the money directly, then I'll mail you some US dollars, in small amounts at a time. I will get you this money."

"I won't lie to you John, this is a very large sum of money for a pair of Chinese teachers. While I would like to tell you not to worry about it, the truth is that you will drain most of our savings. So yes, I really do appreciate your efforts at returning at least some of the money, at your convenience."

"There is one more thing regarding the money," John said quietly. "I have a lawyer who handles all my personal legal matters, including my will. I will write a letter to him, and give it to you. Should something happen to me, you can still get repaid by …"

"Stop right there, John!" Muyih interrupted him quickly. "I don't want us to discuss this possibility. It's not always a good idea to discuss death, I believe it's bad luck. Our money is nothing compared to your life. If something happens to you, I don't care about the money."

"That's not very practical," John answered Muyih with an amused smile. "But I'll respect your wish." Actually, he had no plans to respect Muyih's wish. He would find the time to write that letter and leave it behind in the apartment.

"The next issue is the timing of our departure. Logically, it makes sense for us to leave Friday night. Like the old man said, checkpoint guards are likely to be less vigilant during the night. Also, you and Luhping will not be missed at your work the next day, Saturday. Now I hope we can make it all the way to Dingri, instead of stopping at Shekar like he said. Do you have a map so that we can ..."

John let his sentence drift off when he noticed three pairs of eyes staring at him. Sherab simply looked puzzled because she did not understand what was being said. Luhping was staring at him with a surprised look. Muyih seemed the most uncomfortable, almost afraid of something.

"What is it?" John asked them. "What's wrong?"

"We're not bringing you there," Luhping said quietly, but firmly.

"What? You're not serious!" John looked at Muyih pleadingly.

"Luhping!" Muyih cried out. "Please!"

"So it's not true then?" John asked Muyih.

The look in Muyih's eyes told John what he needed to know before Muyih could summon the courage to speak.

"I'm afraid it is John. The risk of being seen or caught is far too great. Like we told you from the very beginning, Luhping and I cannot risk our work here."

"Risk your work?" John shouted at him. "Sherab and I are risking our lives!"

"That's your choice John, you made it!" Luhping shot back.

He looked back and forth between Muyih and Luhping, unable to believe the situation. "Just how do you expect us to get anywhere near Dingri then?"

"John, please, calm down," Muyih said.

"How can I calm down with two hundred miles to cover before I even start crossing the mountains?"

Muyih looked at him helplessly. "Damn!" John cried out in frustration and stalked off into the kitchen to be alone. Sherab's voice could barely be heard as she caught up on the events with Muyih and Luhping. John's mind was reeling from the terrible news they had just delivered to him. He remembered how difficult it had been for he and Sherab to travel alone in the remote areas of Tibet. Another two hundred miles would sap the strength out of them, leaving nothing for the most difficult part of the journey.

Logically he understood Muyih and Luhping's position. Sherab and John were just one more pair of strangers in need of help. If Muyih and Luhping risked everything for them, they would certainly endanger their careers. But more importantly, they may also fail to help the countless others that would come after John and Sherab.

John sensed, more than heard, someone standing behind him. Muyih's eyes were downcast when John turned to look at him. "Your situation represents everything in your world right now, John. Please, try to look at it from our perspective. We cannot permit ourselves to face such a great danger."

John's mind still seethed with the anger of feeling abandoned in this time of need. The logical part of him understood and accepted their standpoint. But the emotional side of him could not find enough kindness to let Muyih off the hook easily.

"Does your offer of getting us proper equipment still hold, or have you decided that losing the money is too risky?" He felt ashamed the moment the words left his lips. Ashamed that he had cut Muyih down, and even more ashamed that it had felt good.

"Make a list and we'll pick it up tomorrow," Muyih said with a trace of anger mixed in with the sadness. He left John alone in the kitchen before he could utter a word of apology.

Still the anger would not leave him. He realized that it was not directed at Muyih and Luhping directly, but more at the situation he and Sherab now faced. So many problems had compounded themselves to bring them to this near hopeless situation. He thought of Sherab's suffering and his possible death. These in themselves were motivation enough to carry on. But above their lives, Sherab's story held a greater importance. Without over dramatizing it, the fate of a nation literally hung on this story being made public.

A renewed determination entered John's spirit as he felt the burden of her message press down on his shoulders. He had to get her out. He had to find a way to get Muyih to drive them as far as possible. Just like Sherab's story held an importance above their lives, so did it hold an importance above Muyih and Luhping's wishes.

Some semblance of confidence had returned by the time John reentered the living room. He ignored the three sets of eyes trying to gauge his reaction. Speaking directly to Muyih, he tried to convey a sense of moving on from their current impasse.

"Leaving this city will be very difficult on foot. Do you think you can drive us outside the city limits?"

"Yes, of course, that's not a problem." Muyih seemed relieved to reply positively to at least one of John's requests.

"I'm sorry about my comment in the kitchen," John finally told him. "It was unfair and unjustified."

"Forget it John, I already have," Muyih answered graciously.

"Can we work together to come up with a shopping list?" John asked him. "You have a better idea of what's available in this city."

"Certainly, John. We should work on it right now, so that Luhping and I can pick up the supplies tomorrow."

Luhping joined them at the table with some notepaper. "Muyih rarely goes anywhere, I'm the one who knows the shops in the area."

"She's right on this point, that's for sure," Muyih answered with a brief smile.

"I think we could use all of our brain power for this," John told Luhping. "In fact, Sherab may know the terrain more than any of us. If you two can translate for her, I think she should be part of this too."

When they all sat at the table, the others looked at John to begin their brain storming session. "I think the most obvious thing we need is proper clothing. Warm hiking boots are essential. A winter coat, a wool hat, warm gloves, I assume you can get all these?"

"This is summer John, and Shigatse is not a big city. These items may not be available," Luhping told him. "We can certainly get the boots. We can get a light coat, with perhaps a wool sweater to wear underneath. Two pairs of gardening gloves may have to do for winter gloves. A sunhat will be the best we can do for your woolen hat."

"Well, you know what I need, find the best replacements that you can. Now my bedroll was torn when we climbed a barbed wire fence, I need a new, and preferably warmer one."

"One or two?" Luhping asked shyly.

"One," I told her. "Sherab showed me how to ignore social niceties for survival purposes. We will need the extra warmth of sharing a bedroll." He tried to keep a straight face as he logically explained his decision.

"Next, I ditched my lean-to a long time ago. If we're going to face snowstorms, I think we should have some kind of portable shelter from the freezing winds and snow."

"I think we can find that in some of the outdoor stores." Luhping answered. "But again, it will be made of light summer material. If your only purpose is to find shelter from the wind, it should be fine."

"I've done some mountain skiing before. I know enough about snow blindness to tell you that we really need some kind of ski goggles," John continued.

"No, we won't have that. This is not a resort, no one can afford professional ski equipment," Luhping countered.

"Then sunglasses, anything tinted that will protect us from the sun's glare off the snow."

"What will you eat?" Muyih asked.

"Right, that's a big problem. We need to carry a lot of the most nutritious and high-energy food that we can find. My guess is to continue with dried food since it is so much lighter. Meat, fruits, grains, that kind of stuff.

Oh, and that reminds me, we need a second backpack for Sherab to carry." John smiled ruefully. "I'm sorry, I know the price tag for all this must be skyrocketing in your head. Let's just continue with a wish-list, and then remove the less important things when we're done."

Sherab spoke up then, and exchanged a few words with Luhping. "Some kind of heating device, she said." Luhping translated. "To warm yourselves on the really cold nights, but also to melt snow for drinking water."

"Yes, that's a great idea. Do you think your stores would have a small propane bottle, like those used on camp-stoves?"

"Maybe," she said uncertainly. "I'll have to go look around. I'll at least get you matches."

They shot back several more ideas, from scaling ropes to flares, to spikes and hammers for rock climbing. In the end they settled on a fairly simple list of the initial essentials they had discussed. There was a practical limit of how much weight he and Sherab could carry. In reality, without mountain climbing experience they were unlikely to successfully use some of the more advanced equipment anyway.

The next day passed by quickly. Most of the day John racked his brains going over the trip, trying to find anything obvious that he had missed. He also thought deeply of how he could make Muyih take them further than he wanted to. John didn't like where his thoughts were leading, and purposely strayed from that topic whenever he lingered on it too long.

John and Sherab exchanged some thoughts on the trip. But each idea had to be explained several times with hand motions and drawings on paper for them to be able to communicate. By the end of the day they both kept more to themselves and wrote notes for Luhping or Muyih to translate for them later that evening.

Muyih and Luhping's arrival almost gave John a Christmas morning feeling. Their arms were full of bags of goods they had purchased. Muyih and John even had to return to the car to finish unloading everything.

Although the hiking boots were not particularly warm, they had bought an extra pair of socks to provide the added warmth. For once Sherab would be hiking along in decent clothes. Instead of a robe and sandals, she would have pants and boots.

Luhping proudly displayed two pairs of pants made of thin, stretchy material. "These are meant for exercising," she said. "They will fit nicely under your pants as a second layer of clothes over your legs."

"What a great idea!" John told her. "It's like the long underwear we have in the northern regions of Canada."

"Here John," Muyih said, handing him a bundle of papers. John found it amusing how they were eager to show all the things they had bought for the trip. "These are maps of the area you will be traveling."

"Thank you Muyih, these are invaluable. I'd like to go over them with you tonight."

Luhping then unrolled a warm, down-filled sleeping bag.

"What a prize!" John told her admirably. "This is far superior to the cheap bedroll I had before."

Muyih then solemnly handed him a letter-sized envelope. "This should be enough to pay for a guide, as well as some extra food or supplies that you may need."

John quickly counted nine thousand Yuan in the envelope, a small fortune for these people. "Oh Muyih, Luhping, how can I ever thank you enough for this?"

"It's the least we can do to get you and Sherab to safety." Muyih answered.

John looked at Luhping. "Like I told your husband, as soon as I get back home I will arrange to pay all of this money back to you."

She nodded briefly to him, accepting the offer. John wondered how much faith either of them had in ever seeing that money again. They may not have risked their lives, but they risked their financial future without hesitation.

Barely a word was spoken during dinnertime. Tomorrow, Friday, they would be leaving under the cover of darkness. John thought about the dangers ahead, and the risks they were all taking. And he still wondered how he could get Muyih to drive them all the way to Dingri.

The next morning, Sherab and John spent a few hours packing and repacking their backpacks, until they found the right load balance between them. It felt strangely comforting to feel the weight of his pack again, with Yu's canteen dangling at his side. Yet he was more afraid now than at any other time since meeting Sherab.

Today they would begin their trek into the highest mountain range in the world. There were no rescue teams waiting to come and whisk them away in helicopters if they ran into trouble. They were fugitives from the law, having to survive on their own and battle both seen and unseen enemies. They had prepared themselves as much as possible for the coming severe climate. But nothing could prepare them for the unknown dangers lurking in the form of human beings. How many soldiers would they encounter? How many hostile nomads? Would they find a guide? So many unanswered questions tore at John's already frayed nerves.

Luhping had to force John to eat some dinner that night. He was so nervous that he did not think he could keep any food down. Luhping seemed like an anxious mother sending her children off to school. The rest of them were silent in their own thoughts, but she managed to keep up a stream of small talk throughout dinner. John marveled at how different people dealt with high tension in different ways. The ever-calm Sherab now seemed unable to stop tapping her fingers on the table or her foot on the floor. Muyih checked the clock on the wall every thirty seconds. And John watched all their little quirks to keep his mind off a dark and slowly forming decision.

The time had come to leave. Sherab and John had gathered their belongings by the door. Muyih would drive them outside the city and drop them off on the highway. Luhping would stay in the apartment. John tried to tell himself that this was how it was meant to be, and that he should leave the plan alone. As he began to speak, he knew he could not stop himself from engaging a far more cold and dangerous change to everyone's plans.

"Muyih," John said, putting down his backpack, "one last time, I'm begging you to bring us to Dingri."

"John, please, you know it's not possible." Muyih looked at him with pleading eyes, begging John to stop the guilty torture.

"It's more than our lives we may lose," John continued. "There is so much more at stake here. If you didn't refuse to listen to Sherab's story, you might change your mind. Please! We need you so much. Don't let it end like this."

Luhping stared hard at her husband, ready to jump in if he showed any signs of weakening.

"John, we've done all we can for you. Please accept what we gave and ask no more. We simply cannot bring you, I'm very sorry." Muyih seemed genuinely sad at not being able to help more, which made John's next move even more difficult.

He bent down to his backpack, but instead of lifting it up, he reached inside. Standing up, gun in hand, he heard a collective intake of breath from those around him. He pointed Yu's gun at Muyih, the man who had called him his friend. "I'm very sorry that we had to get to this point Muyih. But you will bring us to Dingri." Glancing over to Luhping, he added "And you're coming too Luhping."

# Chapter 13

Muyih's face turned white from shock. "After all we have done…" his voice trailed off, the disbelief in his eyes growing stronger with every passing second.

"You can't be serious," Luhping finally spoke, in a hushed voice.

"I'm very serious. You may never forgive me for this, but one day you'll understand my motivation."

"You can't be serious!" she screamed at John. "We have given you everything you asked for. You hold our entire future in an envelope in your pockets! We let you stay with us as long as you needed, we fed you, we shopped for you, everything! And this is our reward? What kind of an animal are you? What kind of …"

Only by swinging the gun in her direction could John silence her hysterical shouts. Without addressing any of her painful truths, he fished out an envelope from his pocket. It was not the envelope of money that Luhping had referred to.

"As I promised you, here is a letter I wrote to my lawyer in Toronto. As soon as you return home you may begin working with him. I have authorized him to transfer twenty thousand Yuan to your account. This should cover the nine thousand in cash plus all of the things you have bought, including food during our stay with you."

Neither of them made a move to take the envelope from him, so he let it fall onto the floor behind him.

Sherab came to him and gently put her hand on his gun arm. "No John," she whispered softly.

He shook her hand off. "It's the only way Sherab. John will help you." He wished he could make her understand more clearly.

Luhping began speaking in a low urgent voice to Sherab, in Chinese.

"Stop that right now!" John raised his voice for the first time. Even Sherab cringed at the sound of an angry man holding a gun. "There will be no Chinese communication from now on. I don't want you twisting her mind."

Luhping summoned enough courage to tell him: "I think it's your mind that has become twisted."

"It's obvious I have to take you John, but please leave Luhping out of this," Muyih pleaded. "You don't need both of us to come with you."

"I'm sorry Muyih, but she is coming. I know there will be times where you have to drive through a checkpoint alone, while Sherab and I walk around it. Luhping is my guarantee that you'll wait for us on the other side. She'll walk whenever Sherab and I walk."

"It seems you've spent a lot of time thinking out the details of your treacherous plan," Luhping noted.

"Believe it or not, I haven't Luhping," John said sadly. "I never intended something like this, believe me. I value your friendship, I hate destroying it like this."

"It's not too late John," Muyih added quickly. "You're under stress right now. Put the gun away and all is forgotten. Please! Be reasonable, I know this is not like you."

"No, it's not like me Muyih. But then I've never had such an important mission in my life before. This is bigger than you or I. Now let's stop wasting time, let's just go."

A wave of the gun prompted them to gather the things at the door. Then John noticed how Luhping again wore nylons and high heels. "Wait, hang on a minute. Luhping, you'll be walking over rough ground, you need to get changed into more suitable clothes."

She looked down at her dress, and nodded silently. None of them spoke while she went to her bedroom. She returned a few minutes later in snugly fitting pants and running shoes. John could not help but notice once more how she was beautiful, she even made ordinary clothes look attractive. Still not the best choice for hiking, he thought, but then she was not going into the mountains with them.

When the car was packed, John slipped into the back seat with Luhping. He did not want anyone sitting behind him, and having Luhping in the back gave him a psychological advantage over Muyih. As Muyih pulled out of the parking garage, John tried to ease the tension in the car.

"Alright folks, we can relax for a while now. According to this map, we have about one hundred miles to get to Lhatse, directly west of here. I doubt we'll have any trouble, and there are no checkpoints. From Lhatse, we have to go sixty miles south to Shekar, and the first checkpoint. So that gives us about three hours of easy driving."

"And do you have a plan to get us from Shekar to Dingri?" Luhping asked immediately, already knowing the answer.

"Not really," he told her. "We'll have to make up a plan as we go, and as we evaluate the situation."

With each passing mile John felt relief that they were making progress towards their destination. Yet the fear of the coming checkpoints, followed by the search for a guide, and then the mountain crossing itself, also increased as they drove on. This is the calm before the storm, he thought to himself.

John jerked nervously when Luhping reached over to touch him. Her eyes were the softest he had ever seen them, she truly seemed vulnerable for the first time. Her hard exterior had finally begun to crack under the stress.

"Please John," she said, "we're bringing you so far tonight. Can you not let us go at Shekar? Maybe you could get a lift from someone else, a passing truck maybe, for the last small part of your journey."

"I promise you Luhping, if I see that it will be impossible for us to drive that most dangerous section, I'll let you go. But I'm the one who will decide if we go on or not. You have to trust me that I won't have us all captured to save a few miles of walking for Sherab and I."

She slumped back into her seat. John wasn't sure if she did so out of defeat or relief. Either way, he was glad to have ended her plea. These two people were his friends, and he hated himself for what he was doing to them.

"That's the turnoff for Lhatse," Muyih announced from the front a while later. A small sign with Chinese lettering lit up under the headlights. The universal arrow pointing off to the right indicated the side road to nearby Lhatse. The highway began to veer left as they passed the exit and began their southward travel towards Shekar.

After an hour had passed, John noticed the first few signs of an approaching city. A shack here, an abandoned truck there, each sat in its isolated space, an outcast of nearby civilization.

"Slow down, we should be approaching the Shekar checkpoint soon," he told Muyih.

Ten minutes later they could see a brightly lit area ahead of them. From this distance all they could make out were a set of spotlights illuminating a few buildings that seemed to block the road.

"Shut your headlights, we don't want to attract any attention yet." Muyih killed the headlights as the car rolled to a stop. "Now," John continued, "what are you going to tell them when you cross through?"

"They usually won't question Chinese citizens," Muyih answered. "But if they do, I can just say that I'm a teacher and I need to visit some of the outlying schools in the area.

"OK, whatever you think is best," John replied unnecessarily. "Drive far enough so that your taillights are out of sight after you cross through. Hopefully it will take an hour, or at most an hour and a half for us to reach you on foot."

John glanced at his watch, which read 12:30 AM. "We should be back on our way at two o'clock. The old man gave us an address of one guide in Shekar, and two in Dingri. I think we should go to the Shekar guide's house tonight. I don't want to be seen in that city during daylight."

A bleary eyed Muyih nodded wearily at John through the rear view mirror.

"Come Luhping, let's walk," John said as he climbed out of the car. Muyih drove on as Luhping, Sherab and John began marching into the black night, away from the road.

\*\*\*

Fortunately the terrain consisted of low scrub grass and small stones, a far easier night walking surface than they could have had. Sherab still felt in shock from John's unpredictable, and desperate action. She had felt guilty for having some negative thoughts about Muyih and Luhping. How would John feel now after forcing them at gunpoint to drive him and Sherab to Dingri?

Sherab had briefly considered stopping John's plan. She had made a half-hearted attempt back in the apartment, but really, she knew it was the only chance they had. In that sense she shared the same guilt that John must feel. Sherab knew she could talk John out of his betrayal of Muyih and Luhping. But she chose to remain silent and let him commit them to the drive. Perhaps she was guiltier than John, in that she reaped the benefits of the plan without even having to appear ruthless like John.

"You know what John's doing isn't right. Why are you letting him do this to us?"

Sherab wondered if Luhping had read her mind. She could not let Luhping see any signs of weakness. She did not trust Luhping anymore. Luhping was a smart and powerful woman. Sherab feared that Luhping could be a dangerous enemy now that John had backed her into a corner.

"John said not to speak Chinese anymore, you should be quiet Luhping."

John walked perhaps twenty feet behind the two women. In his tired and stressed state of mind, Sherab doubted that he would care if Luhping spoke to her or not. Sherab's hopes that her statement would quiet Luhping were quickly dashed.

"Come on Sherab, only you can stop this madness. Don't let yourself get into deeper trouble than you already are. He's a foreigner, he has no idea what he's getting into."

"There's no other way to get to Dingri. I don't like what John's doing, but you left him no choice."

"Going on foot is a lot safer than trying to drive. And if they catch you kidnapping Chinese citizens, they won't be very kind to you or John. I don't think even his government will be able to save him."

Sherab knew that Luhping tried to rattle her resolve to stick by John. She used the oldest trick in the world, divide and conquer. But her words had a ring of truth to them. Maybe it was safer, if slower, to go on foot. Sherab shook her head. It was too late for doubts.

"I know what you're trying to do Luhping, and it won't work. I've trusted John this far, and I still trust him. He will get me to India."

"Only a fool continues to follow a mistaken path."

Sherab did not bother answering Luhping's last barb. Perhaps if she ignored her, Luhping would stop sharing her disturbing thoughts.

John spoke to Luhping with a commanding tone. Sherab feared that he might be upset about the conversation she had with Luhping. But her fear was short-lived.

"He says we don't need to go too far from the road until we get closer to the checkpoint buildings," Luhping translated for Sherab. Sherab led their small group in a path parallel to the road for a while. As they drew nearer to the checkpoint, she noticed that it was nestled against a large hill. To avoid the checkpoint, they would have to climb the hill. A sheer wall of rock presented itself near the checkpoint, as well as part way around the face nearest to them.

"Stop for a minute," she told Luhping. "Look ahead, we can't go over those rocks. We're going to have to go further away from the road to be able to climb an easier face of the hill."

Luhping glanced to the other side of the road, and noted the higher, and more jagged, peaks of the hills over there.

"We won't make it back to Muyih by two o'clock," Luhping said matter-of-factly.

"I know," Sherab answered glumly, "but he'll wait for us. We have no choice." Luhping spoke to John, and they changed course again, heading for the other side of the hill.

They reached the summit of the hill near two o'clock. The late hour combined with a strenuous climb in the darkness left them breathless. John called a halt to their march, so that they could rest before attempting the equally dangerous route down the hill.

Sherab found herself a flat rock slightly ahead of the rest of the group and sat down with a tired grunt. Luhping decided to join her and sat on one of the few small patches of grass on the rocky hill. Sherab was not surprised to see Luhping keep well away from John.

"You know, I envy you," Luhping said in the darkness near Sherab. Sherab turned and found Luhping looking at her intensely.

"How can you envy me after what I've been through, and what remains ahead of me?"

Luhping continued to stare silently at Sherab, as if she had not heard her question. Just when Sherab decided that Luhping was not going to answer, the woman spoke again.

"You have a man who loves you so much that he will risk his life for you." Sherab stared at Luhping in astonished silence. "I know Muyih loves me, but he always plays it safe, and would never take such a risk. Everything is for our career, our work for Tibetans."

Sherab reflected on how sleep deprivation and danger worked together to loosen a person's tongue. Luhping would never have admitted these things to her under normal circumstances. Not a day ago when they were friendly, and certainly not now while John forced Muyih and Luhping to drive them at gunpoint.

"Muyih is out there risking his life for you right now," Sherab told her, trying to comfort her.

Luhping smiled sadly. "No, he's not doing it out of love for me. If he left now it would be just as disastrous to our work," she paused, "to 'his' work. He would have to explain my disappearance. It's much better for him to follow your instructions and then bring me back safely to our apartment."

"I think you're wrong Luhping. I've seen how Muyih looks at you, and how he speaks of you when you're not there. He really does love you, more than you think."

"You don't know us," she answered coldly. The old Luhping had returned. "Don't ever pretend to know anything about us as long as you and that foreigner wave your gun in our direction." She quickly got up, brushing a hand against her moist eye. "Let's go, I'm tired and I want to get to the car."

Without another word, Sherab got up and they all started to walk. John asked Luhping a question, but Luhping just waved him off and continued walking, in the lead this time. John turned questioningly to Sherab. She simply shrugged and put her arm around his waist to walk with him down the path. Although she felt sad for Luhping, the woman's words had nevertheless warmed Sherab's heart.

A very worried Muyih spotted them ten minutes past three o'clock as they trudged up the road. He crossed the road and ran to his wife.

"Are you alright? Is everything OK?"

Luhping simply nodded and rested her head on his shoulder as he held her.

"What took so long?" he asked Sherab in an irritated voice.

"Didn't see the hill when you stopped the car," she answered him tiredly. "What about you, any trouble getting through the checkpoint?"

"No, they took one look at me and waved me through. But they were definitely not sleeping as the old man suggested they might be."

"Well this is one of the biggest checkpoints, maybe the security isn't as tight in the smaller checkpoints. Come on, let's get into Shekar before we run out of night."

The turnoff into Shekar was another mile down the highway. Muyih turned the car smoothly onto the exit road and they drove a silent five minutes before entering the small town.

Sherab took out her notes from the old man's instructions, and began to navigate for Muyih. "He said that we'll easily see the town temple, his instructions are oriented around that."

The old guide must have assumed that they would enter Shekar in daylight, for the temple was not easy to find. It was only on their third drive through the main road that Luhping finally spotted it tucked away on a small dead-end street off the main road.

"Now," Sherab said, looking again at her instructions under the car's interior dome light, "turn right on the second street past the temple." Muyih almost missed the small street, but was driving slow enough to sharply turn into it at the last second.

"At the end of the street there is supposed to be a dirt road that will lead to this guide's house."

When they reached the end of the road, Muyih had to circle around with the car to sweep the ground with the headlights. Only then were they able to spot the pitted dirt road that seemed to lead nowhere. They drove perhaps a quarter mile before reaching a small cluster of homes, no more than tiny shacks.

"Which one?" Muyih asked from the front.

"He said it was the only house with a fenced backyard. Apparently our guide likes to keep a dog with an attitude problem."

As they drove close to the homes, a dog started barking ferociously.

"I think we found it," Muyih said humorlessly.

All four of them approached the man's house, conscious of the late hour. Sherab knew the others waited for her to do something, for she was the only Tibetan among them. She approached the door and gave it a solid knock. She felt foolish knocking on the door when the crazed dog in the back had long ago announced their presence. When no one came to the door, she knocked harder, and harder still a few seconds later.

The dog's barking masked any sounds of the man's approach behind them. His close voice made them all jump with startled fright. As one they turned to see a middle-aged man staring at them with mistrust in his eyes. His hair had the tousled look of an interrupted night's sleep.

"Are you the one who lives here?" Sherab asked him, pointing to the house.

"The man who lives here left three days ago, and no one knows where he's gone, or when he'll be back. He often leaves for weeks at a time."

The tired man waved at them as if his sweeping hand could magically make them disappear. He then shuffled back towards his own house, the door still ajar from his nocturnal exit.

"Damn," Muyih said. "He might be crossing the mountains right now for all we know."

Sherab kicked at some dirt in dejection before heading back to the car with Luhping. Muyih held back, explaining the situation to John.

***

"When can we stop John?" Muyih asked tiredly as he climbed into the driver's seat.

"Dingri is not far from here," John answered. "Let's cross the big mountain pass, and then you can drop us off outside Dingri." He checked his notes briefly. "The guide mentioned a 16,000 foot Peng La between here and Dingri, I want to get over that first. You're free to go then, Sherab and I will continue on foot."

The road's condition deteriorated rapidly as they left Shekar. Bumps and potholes rattled their bones continuously. Muyih sometimes had to slam on the brakes as the headlights illuminated particularly deep holes in the road. With morning approaching after a sleepless night, all of them were in a terrible mood. Each jolt of the car, each time Muyih stopped, seemed to make John angrier and more fed up with the trip. He had to resist simply calling a stop so that they could catch a few hours of sleep.

The engine slowly began to labor as they started to gain altitude. "This might be the Peng La," John told his fellow uninterested passengers. Soon enough the road headed upwards sharply in a set of tightly snaking switchbacks. The constant twisting and turning of the car made his eyes droop with sleepiness.

He was jolted out of his semi-sleep when Muyih brought the car to a sudden stop. They had just rounded a sharp curve, and now faced a manned roadblock. John's stomach instantly tied itself into knots when he saw one of the soldiers clumsily approach the car.

"What do we do now?" Muyih asked in panic.

John's mind screamed with fear as the reality of this unexpected inspection sank in. His travel permits would simply identify him as the wanted man. Sherab looked quite suspicious in her hiking clothes, native Tibetans did not have that kind of money. All of that, combined with the fact that they were traveling so close to the border in the middle of the night, just begged for them to be detained by these soldiers.

Muyih looked back at him anxiously. John inserted the gun back into his pack, but kept his hand on it.

"Listen Muyih, just stay calm. Your face right now will surely give us away. Remember that I still have the gun. If you do anything to give us away, I will use it."

Muyih looked at John with a mixture of fear and hate.

"I won't lie Muyih, I care too much about you and Luhping. I could never shoot either of you. But I will shoot the soldier rather than be captured." He let this sink in for a second before continuing. "That will certainly ruin your career here in Tibet. And of course the soldiers will fire back at us."

The soldier continued his zigzag approach to the car. It was the first time that his odd behavior registered in John's mind.

"Look!" he said. "He's drunk out of his mind. We can make it out of here if you stay calm. Be smart with your words Muyih, I think you can convince this guy of anything."

Sitting in the back seat, on the passenger side, John still could smell the alcohol on the soldier's breath as he slurred some questions to Muyih through the window. Muyih seemed to answer in a calm, friendly tone. Sherab stared straight ahead, not wanting to catch the inquisitive soldier's attention.

To John's dismay, a second soldier began weaving towards the car. He came along the passenger side and brought his face close to Sherab's window. His eyes blinked a few times as if he tried to get his drunken mind to focus his reddened eyes. His face slowly disappeared as his breath fogged up the window.

Sherab had begun to tremble in her seat, yet she still remained like a statue, staring straight ahead. The second soldier finally straightened his crouched body, much to the relief of a terrified Sherab.

Muyih must have been earning academy awards for his improvised story, for he kept babbling on to the first soldier on the driver's side.

The second soldier leaned over to John's window now. John saw his eyes open wider as he recognized John's western features. He tried tapping on the window with his gun barrel, but the result was a sharp blow that threatened to shatter the window. John felt the car rock as Luhping jumped in her seat, but thankfully remained quiet. Muyih only briefly interrupted his story with the first guard when he whipped his head around to discover the source of the sudden noise.

John hurriedly rolled down the window to avoid another dangerous blow from the obviously drunk soldier. The smell of alcohol swept into the car with renewed force as the man leaned into the car. His face was obnoxiously close to John's as he loudly slurred his words in an almost unrecognizable English.

"You American? American?" he asked.

"No, I'm Canadian," John informed him.

Either he did not hear John, or chose to ignore him. He lifted his head out of the car and shouted a few words to his buddy on the other side of the car. The only word John recognized was "American".

John almost lost control of his bladder when the soldier quickly lowered down and painfully pressed the muzzle of his rifle against John's head.

"American!" he said triumphantly. "Bam-bam!" he shouted. Involuntarily, John jumped when the soldier made the shooting noises, and he felt the muzzle scrape against his temple. John's eyes stung from a cold sweat dripping down his face. The muzzle continued to jiggle against him as the soldier laughed hysterically at his own joke.

The soldier abruptly cut off his laughter, and John felt the gun move away from his face. John turned to see what the soldier was doing, and found him staring past John with an open mouth. John shifted his head around to see what had caught the soldier's attention. A frightened, and beautiful, Luhping stared back at the soldier. She reminded John of a prey caught in a snake's deadly eyes. The soldier murmured some appreciative words in her direction. John did not need to understand Chinese to know he was speaking lustfully about her. That is when John realized that these men were not just feeling tipsy from a few too many drinks. They were dangerously and recklessly drunk.

The soldier ducked his head out of the window one more time and spoke with a slightly hoarse, throaty voice to his friend near Muyih. The first soldier immediately left Muyih in mid-sentence and went to tap at Luhping's window. The second soldier was back in John's face, grinning in Luhping's direction. A second insistent tap forced Luhping to slowly roll down her window with a look of dread on her face.

The soldier on her side looked at her appreciatively and made some remarks to the soldier near John. They both laughed then, and John saw Muyih's knuckles whiten on the steering wheel.

Luhping's soldier stepped back and motioned her with his gun to step out of the car. Muyih spoke in an angry tone for the first time. John looked longingly at the backpack down at his feet. There was no point in reaching for the gun now. Even if he was quick enough, the third soldier popping out of the hastily erected inspection office ahead killed any hopes of a successful shootout.

The soldier spoke low and invitingly to Luhping this time. Her entire body began to tremble. Muyih shouted at the soldiers and began to step out of the car. With barely a glance in his direction, the soldier kicked the opening door so that it crushed Muyih's legs as he tried to step out. An anguished cry escaped his lips and he bent over his injured legs.

The third soldier cautiously remained near the office, and called out inquisitively to his companions. They both began speaking at once, and pointing into the car at Luhping. He barked back an order to them, which they received without question. Soon all four doors were opened, and the soldiers were having everyone climb out of the car. John grabbed his backpack on the way out, hoping that he would not have a need to use the gun inside. He briefly wondered if he would be able to use the gun against another human being, even if the need arose.

They marched at gunpoint into the small office. The four of them naturally lined up against the far wall. The soldier that had stayed near the office behaved like the superior officer. These were the only three people manning the tiny inspection station. The officer came to inspect his detainees while the other two stood back expectantly.

He drew near John first, with a cloud of alcohol fumes enveloping him like a shroud. The officer's eyes were clear, however, he was not in the same wasted state as his subordinates.

"American!" one of the soldiers behind him proudly declared. John began to feel like a prize turkey at Thanksgiving.

"Canadian," John corrected for the benefit of the officer.

The officer's eyes did not register that John had spoken. He moved on to Muyih briefly, and then stopped in front of Luhping. John felt Muyih stiffen, and he prayed the protective husband would not make any rash moves. Luhping stared down at the floor, not wanting to meet the officer's eyes. The officer reached for her chin and lifted her face to meet his own. John grabbed Muyih's arm to restrain him, he could feel Muyih was near the point of springing into action.

Without unlocking his eyes from Luhping, the officer spoke a few curt words to the other soldiers. They immediately came on each side of him, raising their rifles. One of them stood in front of Muyih with his gun aimed directly at his head. The other stood one step back and covered Sherab and John. The officer reached down, grasped Luhping's wrist, and walked her into the center of the office.

Muyih began to shout questions at the officer. A brief command from the officer and the soldier approached Muyih until his rifle almost touched Muyih's forehead. Rage, fear, and helplessness painted Muyih's face. None of them could tear their eyes away as the officer slowly backed Luhping into a corner, murmuring continuously to her in a soft voice.

The officer must have drunk more alcohol than John thought earlier. Treating a Chinese civilian like this in front of witnesses was foolish beyond words. John looked outside, hoping someone else would drive up to the roadblock. By the maintenance state of the road leading up to there, John knew that it must not be a well-traveled highway. Also, the odds of someone coming through there were further diminished by the fact it was just past four o'clock in the morning.

The officer finally crossed the line when he felt Luhping's breast. Until that point John had clung to the hope that these men would come to their senses despite the fog of booze clouding their minds. Now he understood how deeply they were in trouble. The reality of the situation washed over him like an icy shower. If the officer went further with Luhping, what would become of the witnesses when he was done?

Muyih lunged forward, literally pushing the gun barrel aside with his head. John grabbed him with both arms before the soldier could panic and shoot. Muyih screamed at John in Chinese as John used all his strength to hold him back. The soldier recovered from the surprise move, flipped his gun around, and slammed the butt into Muyih's exposed abdomen. The force of the blow cut off his air supply, and he fell to his knees, dragging John down with him.

When John looked up, the soldier appeared more nervous and frightened at the escalated situation. The gun wavered as he now pointed it at them once again. Perspiration began to bead on his forehead, and John new the soldier's drugged mind was beginning to panic.

Luhping was shaking her head, as the officer seemed to shout some orders at her. Her eyes sought out her companions wildly like those of a trapped animal. Tiring of his game, the officer reached forward and quickly tried to lift the sweater over her head. Luhping screamed, and forced her elbows down against her body before he could clear the sweater over her head. They danced a tangled step together, with her sweater half off and his hands caught in its material.

Luhping saw the opportunity, and brought her knee up. The officer reacted quickly. Twisting his body, he took the blow on his thigh. He became angry then, and quickly worked his right hand free of the sweater, while retaining his clutch on her with his left hand. He jerked her towards him with his left arm, while his right fist punched her on the side of the mouth. Blood spurted from her split lip as she cried out in pain.

Still unable to breathe, Muyih lifted his head at the sound of his wife's cry. His eyes were wet from tears, both from his own pain, and from the sight of his wife's bloody face.

Luhping remained stunned by the punch for just a second, but it was long enough for the officer to lift the sweater over her head. He did not remove it completely, instead he left her arms tangled in it above her head. He lost no time before beginning to tear at her bra while she was in this exposed position. Luhping struggled wildly, shaking her body from side to side as he clutched at her bra. She finally tore loose of the sweater, and immediately brought her raking fingers towards the officer's face. Her face a mask of wild terror, she attacked him with the violence of an unleashed rabid dog. The officer backed off a few steps under the assault of gouging and scratching fingers.

When she stepped forward to press her attack, he took the opportunity to swing his left arm into her outstretched arms. Her balance was lost in mid step, and she spun sideways from his pushing blow. The experienced combat officer stepped in quickly and delivered a terrific punch into her midsection. She doubled over without a sound escaping her open mouth. With one leg behind her, he pushed her easily onto the floor.

While she lay in helpless agony at his feet, the officer began to untie his belt. He even took the luxury of flashing a bright smile to his subordinates who cheered him on with grunts and laughs. One of the soldiers asked a question, and the officer nodded in return before kneeling down hard on Luhping's unprepared stomach.

"LUHPING!" Muyih wailed as he caught his breath, and watched the officer go down on her. This time John threw his entire body weight on Muyih to prevent him from getting up. He knew the soldier would greet Muyih with a bullet if he escaped John's desperate clutches.

"Get off me!" Muyih managed to gain enough control to yell in English. "You bastard, this is your fault! Why are you helping them?"

"Muyih, they'll kill you if you don't stop!" John tried to reason with him, but it was no use. Muyih remained in a state of uncontrollable rage. Just when John felt he was losing his grip on Muyih, the soldier stepped forward and snapped a sharp kick to the side of Muyih's head. John felt his body relax as he slumped down from the force of the stunning kick.

Luhping began to yell and struggle once more. From his position on the floor, John could not see her. But he could see the hateful officer sitting on her, as he swung his mighty fist down on her face, once, twice, three times. His fist was red with blood as he took a break, breathing heavily. Luhping was silent. The officer bent down and began working her pants off, and then his own. John looked away, but could not shut out the sounds of his grunts as he used her unconscious body.

"Luhping…" Muyih sobbed, lying helpless on the floor underneath John. John looked over at Sherab, and was surprised at her expression. He had expected tears, but instead she stared at the officer with cold, calculating eyes. From her standing position, John knew that she could see everything that was happening to Luhping. Yet she did not look away. Her eyes winced slightly in rhythm with the officer's grunts. But other then that almost imperceptible movement, she could have been a stone statue.

After a minute or two of this hell, Luhping began to moan and scream in pain, though without any of the previous ferocity. The officer did not strike her again, he just kept moving and grunting. Less than five minutes passed before the officer's rapid breathing reached a climax. He disappeared from John's line of sight as he lay down on her, his breath slowly returning to normal. John saw his sweaty face when he sat back up, and then finally stood. John felt sick to his stomach when he saw the blood below the officer's stomach, as well as on his fists.

The officer called the soldier who had been keeping watch on Muyih. The officer smiled, and invited him to come over to him. They were going to gang rape her, John realized with growing horror. He had been ashamed for feeling some relief when the officer had finished with Luhping, each of his grunts ripped into John's heart. His mind began to numb with the knowledge that the horror had only just begun.

The soldier watching Sherab and John gave an envious and encouraging pat on his friend's back. Any doubt that the chosen man had in his eye quickly left with his friend's encouragement. As he lowered his rifle to go over to Luhping, John saw a blur of movement to his right. While both soldiers were looking away, and one soldier's rifle was lowered, Sherab leapt like a crazed animal. Before the drunken soldier could react, Sherab had already kneed him in the groin and was in the process of removing flesh from his face with her nails.

With a mighty heave Muyih threw John's stunned body off his back and lunged at the nearest soldier. John immediately rolled over to the backpack, and began fishing out Yu's pistol. With gun in hand he looked up, and saw Muyih entangled with one soldier, while Sherab began to lose her battle. The soldier she attacked had raised his rifle with both hands to fend off her clawing hands. With her main attack becoming useless, he lifted his boot to kick her in the stomach.

"Squeeze the trigger, don't pull it." A dozen pieces of disjointed firearms advice coursed through John's brain in random order. While he took aim, part of his brain recognized the actors who had spoken these bits of information in countless westerns and action movies. "Squeeze two rounds into each target, just to be sure." Yu's pistol sights found the chest of the soldier that Sherab was fighting with. "Take your time, aim carefully." John pulled the trigger hard, and did not aim carefully. Yet the soldier's chest suddenly had a red hole in it, and he almost lost his footing as he was pushed backwards. Without moving or taking the time to register what he had just done, John shot again. Part of him felt surprised to see a second hole sprout a few inches from the first, much redder hole.

"When you've hit your target, don't wait for it to go down, find the next one."
The movie clips provided John with a detached feeling as he swung towards
Muyih and his soldier. Here again, the experience of the fighting man began to
overwhelm the crazed civilian. The world stopped for John, all he could see was
Muyih and the soldier, in slow motion. John patiently waited for what must have
been one or two seconds, but seemed like a few hours. Finally Muyih shoved
against the soldier, separating them for a moment.

"Wait until you have a clear shot, then don't hesitate." He aimed a little more
carefully this time, and fired at the exposed soldier. John nearly dropped his gun
when Muyih's chest seemed to explode before his eyes. "I hit him!" screamed
through his brain. Before Muyih could fall to the floor, a second explosion of
flesh and blood erupted from his stomach. John had forgotten about the officer!

He swung his pistol towards the officer, and saw the smoking rifle begin to
turn towards John. Their eyes locked before the rifle had completed its arc. John
was amazed by the knowing look in the officer's eyes when John squeezed the
trigger. The officer knew John had the first shot, yet without panic he continued
to bring the rifle around towards him. John's bullet tore into the officer's
shoulder, causing him to spin around further than he had planned. The rifle barrel
moved upwards involuntarily, as he fired a few rounds into the ceiling. The room
turned into a storm of falling debris from his devastating bullets tearing into the
ceiling above them. John fired his second shot. It hit the officer in the side of his
chest, knocking him over. John's third shot flew harmlessly over his fallen body.
John stood up, arms still extended with the pistol. Pointing downwards, he fired a
fourth time into the officer's body. The fallen man twitched slightly, and then
was still.

John's last bullet had gone into the officer's naked thigh. It must have been
the second bullet that killed him. There was something incredibly grotesque
about a dead man with his pants down around his ankles. Thunderstruck, John
suddenly realized that if the officer had not been drinking, John probably would
have been killed. Why would an experienced soldier first shoot at the unarmed
Muyih? It made no sense. If the officer had been thinking clearly, it would be
John's insides that would be spread all over the floor, not Muyih's. No, that was
not quite right. Undoubtedly, both of them would have been killed.

John's hands began to tremble violently now. Still, he forced himself to turn
back to the second soldier to see if the single shot had killed the man or not. The
soldier was lying on his back, perfectly still. One could have thought he was
sleeping, if not for the hole in his chest with the rapidly spreading red stain
around it.

John stumbled over to Muyih, his mind nearing a state of complete shock. Two gaping holes pierced his still body. "Muyih," John whispered. The gun clattered loudly onto the floor where he dropped it. He turned Muyih's body over to see his face, and almost vomited when he saw the exit wounds of the bullets. His entire front seemed to have been torn apart. His lifeless eyes remained open, and accusing. "Murderer!" they seemed to cry out to John.

John fell back into a sitting position, and sobbed uncontrollably. "I'm so sorry Muyih," he blubbered through a distorted veil of tears.

Sherab's legs appeared in John's view. She hesitated in front of Muyih, and then bent down to shut his dead eyes. She stepped over his body, and continued on towards where Luhping's body lay.

# Chapter 14

Luhping's sweater stuck out obscenely from under the dead man's partially naked body. Sherab unceremoniously twisted the corpse over with her foot, and retrieved the sweater. She paused a moment, and turned the officer's body again. She leaned in close and stared into his lifeless eyes. She had dreamed of seeing each of her captors this way. No matter how hard she focused on the Buddhist teachings, she could not rid herself of the burning hatred that consumed her. She spat violently into the silent face before returning to Luhping.

Luhping was curled up on the floor, her swollen, vacant eyes staring at the space in front of her. Her lips were cut open in two places, and still trickled blood. The blood had been smeared all over her face, and looked like a horrible mess. Even as Sherab watched, a fresh drop of blood formed under Luhping's left nostril. Sherab knew exactly how Luhping felt right now, and her heart went out to her.

She gently removed the torn bra from each of Luhping's arm. The semi-catatonic woman offered no resistance. Sherab fetched the canteen out of John's backpack, and moistened the right half of the severed bra. Using it as a facecloth, she lightly patted Luhping's face, washing away the worst of the blood. Then Sherab struggled to get the sweater over Luhping's head, and put her arms through it. She pulled up the woman's pants, and buttoned them around her violated body. Luhping returned to her fetal position the moment Sherab released her.

Sherab approached John cautiously. His bravery had saved their lives a few moments ago, yet now he sat on the floor, crying like a young child. She hoped his mind had not broken under the extreme violence they had just witnessed. Not just witnessed, he had killed three soldiers! She shook his shoulders, but he ignored her, like he wanted to be left alone in his misery.

"John, come!" Sherab told him. He looked up at her with a tear-streaked face, not really seeming to understanding what she wanted. "Come!" she said more insistently. "Luhping!"

That broke through his shock. John had perhaps been mourning the dead Muyih. But poor Luhping was still alive, and desperately needed their help. Avoiding Muyih's body, John walked over to where Luhping lay.

"Luhping?" he croaked through his dry throat. No response. He bent closer down and shook her gently. "Luhping?" he repeated. Still no response, she had fallen into a deep state of shock. Sherab came up behind Luhping, and lifted her into a sitting position. Sherab sat behind her, and let Luhping fall into her arms, cradling her like a child. She began to whisper soothing words into Luhping's ear.

"Beautiful Luhping, I know your world has been shattered today. Trust me, time will diminish the pain. I've been where you are, we're sisters now. Now please, come with us to the car."

Sherab might as well have kept silent. The unresponsive Luhping leaned heavily into Sherab, not acknowledging any of Sherab's words.

"John, help." Sherab called out, reverting to English once again. She was trying to bring a limp Luhping to her feet. They both pulled Luhping up, but her rubbery legs refused to support her weight.

"Car," Sherab said, indicating Luhping and the car outside. John nodded dumbly, and put Luhping's arm around his neck. They walked a few steps with Luhping dangling between them. There was no use, she might as well have been a dead body. Sherab cringed at the unlucky comparison, after seeing so much carnage in the last few minutes.

John stopped, causing Sherab to stumble a few steps. He bent down and hooked one arm behind Luhping's knees. Picking her up like an oversized rag doll, he walked the rest of the distance to the car. Sherab ran ahead of them, and opened the rear door. He awkwardly slid the broken Luhping into the back seat, unable to avoid knocking her head lightly against the too small door opening. As if he did not know what to do next, he took a step back.

Sherab leaned over Luhping, and wisely buckled her into place. With each turn of the car Luhping would likely roll lifelessly. Sherab saw Luhping's lips move for the first time, though silently. She leaned over Luhping and brought her ear close to the woman's mouth. Waiting anxiously for Luhping to repeat her whispers, Sherab finally heard in the loneliest, heart wrenching voice, a tiny word: "Muyih."

Sherab's throat constricted with the pain of her sorrow. How easy it would be to let the tears come out in great racking sobs. She pulled herself out of the car, feeling that she might simply collapse on top of Luhping. Sherab ran back to the office, leaving a numbed John alone by the car with Luhping.

The need for weapons became clear in Sherab's mind now. She realized that she was destroying her life with such thoughts. But she was not thinking of killing to save her own life. More exactly, she was sacrificing her future lives in order to get her story to the Dalai Lama's ears. She could not be sure if this made sense or not with regards to Buddha's teachings. Let others wiser than her contemplate such moral dilemmas. Sherab decided to let her survival instincts take over from her confused mind.

She tried to avoid looking at Muyih. His ravaged body tore at the fabric of her fragile state of mind. She picked up John's discarded pistol, and also his backpack. She briefly scanned around the office to see if there was anything else they might need. Either there was nothing, or her brain was too rushed to really analyze the things she saw. Deciding that it was time to leave, she went to the soldier that she had attacked. She slung his rifle over her shoulder, and headed out the door.

At the sound of her running footsteps, John turned to face her. His eyes seemed to disapprove of the pistol as she handed it back to him. He glared warily at the rifle muzzle sticking up over Sherab's shoulder.

Sherab threw the backpack into the car beside Luhping. "Car, John!" she said urgently. She began pushing him towards the driver's seat.

"No!" he said, followed by a stream of unintelligible English. He in turn began to pull Sherab towards the driver's seat.

"Sherab no car!" she said. She looked at him in frustration. How could she explain to him that she had never driven a car? She then pretended to put her hands on a steering wheel, while shrugging her shoulders.

John cursed when he understood her meaning. He sat shakily into the driver's seat, and stared at the dashboard as if he had never seen one before. It was as if his brain took a moment to accustom itself to such an ordinary task, after such an extraordinary night.

When Sherab shut her door, he fumbled with the keys trying to start the engine. "What about Muyih?" he asked Sherab. She did not need to understand the rest of his sentence to know that he felt guilty leaving their friend's body behind.

"No Muyih!" she told him impatiently. "Dingri. Go!"

Dawn approached rapidly, and she knew they had to go quickly. Part of Sherab resented John for asking about Muyih. It relieved John's guilt of leaving Muyih with the dead soldiers, while Sherab assumed the cold-blooded responsibility of moving on. Why was she suddenly the one who had to be strong? She wondered how long before the bloodbath would be discovered. They had to pass Dingri before this roadblock was discovered. Not only pass through

Dingri, but also stop and convince a guide to bring them across the mountains! Why did John not understand the urgency? She wished that she knew when their prospects would stop looking so bleak and hopeless.

On John's third try, the engine came to life. He drove up to the flimsy wooden barriers across the road, and tried to circle around them. The car scraped noisily against the wood, and finally knocked them out of the way. Before they rounded the next bend in the road, Sherab took a last look behind them, a last look for Muyih. She was unable to focus past Luhping's lolling head. Each bump in the road bounced her unresponsive head like a basketball. Sherab forced her eyes back onto the road, and concentrated on getting them to Dingri.

She was thankful for the continuous hairpin turns as they climbed up the mountain pass. The monotony of a straight highway would have given her too much time to think of what had just happened at the roadblock. The barren landscape soon began to whiten as they reached the permanent snowline. Still the road climbed further and further. The predawn sky had lightened enough to show the frozen world surrounding them as they crested the Peng La.

They were lucky not to have any precipitation as they began their steep descent. Muyih's car was not equipped for winter driving. Even a light snowfall could have them skidding down these curves, and perhaps not making one of them. The car's heater warmed them against the frigid outside air, a luxury they would not have when they continued on foot.

The road only descended a few thousand feet before leveling off at a much higher altitude than the other side of the Peng La. The tight switchback curves gave way to smoother, gentler turns. This allowed them to see a greater distance ahead of them, so that they had a bit more warning for the second roadblock.

John immediately shut the headlights when he stopped at the sight of the familiar shack by the road. Sherab had already swung the rifle onto her lap in preparation. The car came to a stop perhaps fifty feet from the roadblock. No soldiers came out of the tiny office. The wooden structures used to block the road were neatly stacked outside the office. A faint glimmer of hope rose in Sherab, for the roadblock appeared abandoned. They must not man every roadblock during the night, she thought.

"Go, slow," she told John quietly.

He edged the car forward slowly, his eyes scanning in every direction. They drew up next to the office. With a pounding heart, Sherab stole a glance inside the building. Empty. With a wave of relief washing over her, she relaxed into her seat. John pressed on the gas pedal, and the car surged forward. They soon left the closed inspection office behind. Luck had finally swung in their favor. First they had a clear night to drive through the pass, and now an unmanned roadblock.

The road began to twist and turn again, although not to gain or lose altitude. A deep precipice snaked along the left side of the road. The bottom of the canyon remained invisible due to the weak morning light and poor viewing angle of the car. No doubt a river had carved this deep gash in the mountainous terrain over countless millenniums. Eventually the ravine became shallower. As Sherab had suspected, a swift flowing river bathed the bottom of the precipice with what must have been near freezing cold water. It could have been a very peaceful and scenic drive under better circumstances.

John stopped the car about half a mile before the bridge that the old guide had warned them about. The road disappeared ahead, as it curved into another set of switchbacks towards the bridge below. Sherab studied the swift current rushing beneath the bridge and wondered how on earth the guide thought they could ford the river.

The bridge itself was quite narrow, allowing a single car to pass at a time. Its heavy wooden beams were discolored with age, but appeared as solid as ever. Huge wooden posts set at equal intervals held the entire structure above the rushing water. The water surrounded each post with angry swirls, trying in vain to bring the bridge down. In contrast to the massiveness of the main bridge structure, a rather flimsy guardrail sat primly on each side of the bridge. The guardrail offered a psychological protection more than a real safeguard. The bridge designers must have assumed a very low traffic movement through this area.

The guardhouse, or office, had been erected on their side of the bridge. The Chinese were obviously more concerned about outgoing traffic rather than incoming traffic. The office had been built much more recently than the old bridge. The structure was made of a light aluminum, which gave it a military appearance.

One soldier stood outside the guardhouse, smoking a cigarette. He was the only visible person in the area. Based on the size of the office, Sherab guessed that there could not be more than a total of four or five soldiers on duty. Still, that was four or five more than she cared for.

John could not drive through that bridge, Luhping was their only hope. As she climbed into the back seat, Sherab tried not to think of how slim a hope they had with Luhping.

"Luhping?" she said to the expressionless woman. "Can you hear me? It's Sherab." Sherab only received a blink of Luhping's eyes in response. John stepped out of the car, opened the rear door and squatted on the other side of Luhping.

"Please Luhping, none of us will make it without your help," Sherab continued. "We need you to drive us across the bridge. We need someone that is Chinese."

Luhping shut her eyes, as if to shut Sherab out of her world. Sherab decided to gamble bringing down the woman's wrath upon her.

"Don't let Muyih's death be for nothing. He died trying to save you. If you let us all die on this road, you're betraying him and dishonoring his death."

Luhping's eyes dripped with venom when she finally turned to Sherab. Then she turned her head, and before John could react she spat into his face.

Sherab felt grateful that he did not react violently to the offense.

"You can spit on him all you want," Sherab told Luhping as John wiped his face. "But that doesn't change the fact that I'm telling you the truth. Only you can get us out of this."

"We will meet again in our next lives, and both of you will pay for this." Her soft voice belied the hatred and force behind her words. John looked questioningly at Sherab, for Luhping had inadvertently slipped into Chinese. Sherab was thankful for Luhping's confused mind, she did not want John to worry over such a curse.

"Can you drive?" Sherab asked her, deliberately ignoring the threats.

Without answering, Luhping listlessly opened the car door and dragged herself out. She winced perceptibly as she limped over to the driver's seat. Before she climbed into the car she made the mistake of glancing at the bridge below. Her body froze like a statue. Sherab stepped out of the car and raced to Luhping's now trembling body. The woman's eyes were opened wide in fear as she stared at the soldiers below.

"It's OK Luhping, they won't harm you," Sherab lied. "You are Chinese, they won't even question you. Remember how easily Muyih got through the Shekar checkpoint when he was alone in the car?"

The mention of her husband's name made her head twitch as if she had been slapped. This time Sherab had not deliberately used Muyih's memory to shock her, yet it worked just as well as the first time. Luhping forcefully shut her eyes for a second, and then sat behind the steering wheel.

Sherab knew that once again they were taking advantage of Luhping. Luhping did not have the presence of mind to wonder where she would go after the bridge, or what would become of her after this trip.

"Come John," Sherab said, motioning him to the trunk. They had to empty their hiking supplies into the back seat to make room for their two bodies. The now visible hiking supplies added one more risk of curious soldiers asking Luhping too many questions. Sherab and John kept their weapons as they scrunched into the small trunk. John pulled the trunk lid down, cutting out what little light the dawn had given them.

Luhping slowly started down the road. Each bump now produced painful jabs to their bodies jammed into the unforgiving trunk. Sherab tried not to think of the hundred things that could go wrong at the bridge. How would the soldiers react to Luhping's bruised face? If they questioned her, they would notice her broken spirit. If they were aggressive in any way, how long before she panicked from her recent horrible experiences? That is when Sherab started to question the wisdom of locking themselves into the trunk. Luhping had no support from them whatsoever.

Too soon, the car came to a stop at the sound of a man's Chinese voice. Luhping's voice responded weakly to the hard edge of the soldier's question. Sherab began to fear for Luhping, as well as for John and herself. Could Luhping pull this off?

A few more rounds of questions and answers were exchanged, and then Sherab felt the car move. She felt a surge of joy as Luhping rolled the car forward. The joy was short lived when Luhping stopped the car again just a few feet away. They were pulling her over, off the road! Sherab's sweating hand instinctively gripped the rifle tightly, hoping to draw some comfort from the weapon. She thought John was trembling against her before she realized that she was the one trembling against him.

The car door opened, and Luhping stepped out. Her receding footsteps sunk Sherab's hopes as the soldier led her away. Her interrogator began to raise his voice, and Sherab knew the game was over. There would be no peaceful crossing over this bridge. Her mind raced, trying to find a plan. She could shoot the trunk latch and then come out firing. But what chance did she and John have against several armed and experienced soldiers? The soldiers would mow them down before she had untangled herself out of the trunk.

The car rocked as someone began examining the hiking equipment in the back seat. Sherab heard two muffled voices chattering to each other as the men rummaged through the gear. The antagonistic interrogation continued further away, which brought the soldier count to at least three. Soon the two searchers climbed back out of the car. Sherab waited anxiously for the next move, unable to initiate anything on her own. Part of Sherab clung to the hope that the soldiers would just let Luhping go.

A car door slammed, and footsteps approached the rear of the vehicle. Every inch of her body pricked with fear when she heard a key being inserted into the trunk's lid. The same two men were talking casually no more than two feet away from the trunk. The quarter inch sheet of metal that separated her from these men was about to be lifted away.

John grabbed Sherab's rifle barrel, and pointed it to the left. He too was ready to fight it out then. She felt sadder about the coming unnecessary deaths than she felt scared about the danger. They did not have to wait long before the morning sun flooded their private world as the soldier raised the trunk. The soldier who opened the trunk formed a surprised 'O' with his mouth. His friend on the left continued talking, without looking into the trunk.

Sherab's bullet threw the unsuspecting young man off his feet. In quick response, the soldier in front of John moved to slam the trunk shut again. John shot low, below the lid. The soldier fell backwards, clutching his stomach. Sherab's arm stopped the trunk lid that descended lazily from the man's interrupted attempt at shutting it.

John immediately rolled out of the trunk, almost loosing his footing. Another soldier stood a few feet away from the car, staring at the scene in front of him. It took less than a second for Sherab to notice that he carried no rifle, and his sidearm was securely fastened on his belt.

John shouted an instruction to the surprised soldier. The guard did not need to understand English to send his arms into the air with a gun pointed in his direction. The coffee cup he had been holding clattered onto the ground, spilling its steaming contents at his feet. Two guns pointed at him now, Sherab stood beside John.

A movement from within the office caught Sherab's attention. The soldier inside smoothly struck down Luhping with the butt of his rifle and fell to a crouching position. Before he could fire in their direction, John stepped up to the soldier near them, spun him around, and held his pistol at the base of the man's neck.

John cried frantic orders to the kneeling soldier just inside the office door. The only word Sherab understood was 'kill'. She ran behind the car for cover, and pointed her rifle at the office. The armed soldier noticed her, and must have realized that she could take him out at any time. Unless he was willing to lose his friend, he had to give up. With a sullen look he dropped his rifle and stood up.

John called out to him. The soldier looked at him with a puzzled expression, and raised his hands.

John shouted again. Sherab felt he was dangerously close to hysteria. She already guessed the soldier could not understand John.

"I'm unarmed! I don't know what you want!" he shouted back at John in Chinese. Then he kicked his rifle a little further away.

John slowly backed away from the unarmed soldier without ever letting the gun's aim stray from his body. Sherab came around the car and stood next to John. He motioned her to keep the nearby soldier covered with her rifle. John walked around him, and used his hands to show the two soldiers that he wanted them to lie on the ground. Sherab nervously kept her gun trained on them while John retrieved the office soldier's rifle. He threw it into the back seat, and then entered the office to get Luhping.

Keeping her rifle trained on the soldiers, Sherab moved towards the office to see Luhping. She lay slumped on the floor, her back bent against the legs of a chair. An ugly gash on the upper forehead added another wound to her already traumatized face. John gently picked her up, and hurriedly walked her to the car. There was no time for seatbelts. He simply laid her out on the back seat after pushing onto the floor all the hiking equipment they had recently stacked in there.

John then proceeded to completely disarm the soldiers. For each man still alive, he pressed his pistol painfully into their necks while he removed their sidearms. These he simply threw into the river below. Similarly, he disposed of the dead men's pistols and all but one of their rifles. He threw the extra rifle into the car.

"Come Sherab," he said, beckoning her to the car.

"Wait!" she replied.

The guards had parked their jeep behind the office. It would have a radio that she had to disable, as well as disabling the jeep itself. From behind the jeep she took aim at the radio, and pulled on the rifle's trigger. Her finger could not move it. She fumbled around the strange weapon's barrel until she found the safety switch. She had been so lucky not to have needed the weapon in front of the soldiers!

The dashboard exploded into fragments when she fired into the radio. She had prepared herself for a huge kick from the rifle, but was pleasantly surprised by how smoothly it fired. She proceeded to shoot out all four tires, and added a few more into the engine compartment for good measure.

As she returned to John, she wondered how much better off they might have been to keep the jeep and trash Muyih's car instead. But they would soon arrive in Dingri, where they would then have to walk. Arriving in a military jeep would also draw a lot of attention. All in all, her lack of forward thinking had not damaged them. Muyih's car remained the best vehicle for the short trip into Dingri.

Sherab kept watching the soldiers while John backed up the car, and brought it to the mouth of the bridge. With the engine running, he climbed out of the car and covered the soldiers while Sherab ran back to the car. The entire scene seemed unreal to her, especially with the absence of any spoken words. When Sherab shut her door, John jumped into the driver's seat and pressed hard on the gas pedal. The tires briefly spun in the gravel before biting in and hurtling the car across the bridge.

How much time did they have before someone discovered their trail of blood? For all she knew, a squad of soldiers might be waiting for them by the time they got to Dingri. Even if they arrived safely in Dingri, it would not be long before they would be hunted down. If they could not get a guide in the first hour, Sherab decided that they would try to cross the mountains on their own.

Luhping began to moan in the back seat. John slowed down when Sherab instantly climbed over the seat to attend Luhping. She had to come with them, Sherab realized. Neither China nor Tibet would be safe for Luhping now. As an accomplice to murder, she would likely spend the rest of her life in jail. How ironic that she had equipped John and Sherab so well for the cross-mountain trip. Now she had to go, but totally unequipped for it.

They drove less than thirty minutes over the beat-up highway before reaching the Dingri turnoff. Just before turning into the exit, John spotted the checkpoint a few hundred yards down the road. With a slight swerve he straightened the car out and whisked by the exit. They could not handle another checkpoint, Sherab thought with relief. Although Sherab did not get a clear picture of the situation, she had seen some movement at the checkpoint. Even though it was still early, morning had arrived, and all checkpoints would be manned now.

After making certain than the soldiers at the Dingri checkpoint were not pursuing them, John brought the car to a stop. The rocky terrain on their left would barely be passable with an off road vehicle. Muyih's car could not get very far. But Sherab thought it would be foolish to abandon the car on the side of the road.

"Sherab!" John called from the front of the car. When she looked he buckled his seat belt. "Do Luhping," he said, pulling at his seatbelt. Sherab looked at the rough terrain, and wondered if John had been going through the same thought processes that she had been. She nodded, and proceeded to put Luhping into a seated position. With Luhping securely buckled in, Sherab returned to the front seat and buckled herself in.

"Yeehaaa!" John shouted like a cowboy, as he gunned the engine and pointed the car off the road. Sherab braced herself with one hand on the dashboard and the other on the door. She could not help smiling broadly at his exaggerated recklessness. The car performed remarkably well. The fenders frequently hit the ground with a jolt as they dipped into depressions. The car bottomed out numerous times when John ran over large stones. Sherab's entire body rattled, they were bounced off the seat with almost comical intensity.

Just a few minutes later the oil warning light came on, and Sherab knew they had ruptured the oil pan on some pointed rock. John's joyride came to an end. The agonized engine screeched to a sudden stop as the oil ran out. Like its owner, this car was dead, Sherab thought sadly.

John tossed the keys back into the front seat after instinctively having removed them from the ignition.

"Luhping, how are you?" John asked as he opened the rear door.

"My head," she replied with difficulty, not even opening her eyes. Sherab felt a pang of guilt for the rough ride they had just given her. It surely had not helped what must have been a crippling headache. She reached over Luhping, and pulled John's backpack out of the car. After a moment of fishing through it she pulled out the precious supply of painkillers.

"Here, swallow these. They will take some of the pain away." Sherab pressed four of the pills into Luhping's palm, and passed her Yu's canteen. She swallowed them without too much difficulty, and took extra gulps of water.

Sherab took the canteen from her and poured a bit of water into her own palm. As gently as she could, Sherab washed some of the blood off Luhping's forehead. She winced and jerked back when Sherab touched too close to the wound. Good enough, Sherab thought to herself. They could clean the wound some more after the analgesics had kicked in.

"We have to walk now. Dingri is not far." Sherab noticed that John had already started to unload the car.

"Luhping, can you walk?"

Luhping's head rested against her seat as if she had not heard Sherab.

"I'm sorry Luhping, but we can't leave you here and I can't carry you." With that Sherab reached in and pulled Luhping out of the car. She did not resist, nor did she help. Sherab put her arms around Luhping's waist and flopped the woman's head onto her shoulder. Sherab leaned Luhping against the car, and gingerly backed away. Luhping stumbled, but did not fall.

For now, Sherab and John would carry all the gear. They had originally planned it that way, so the burden was not overly tiresome. But Sherab hoped that when Luhping started to recuperate, she could take some of their load as well.

Although they had taken an extra rifle from the soldiers, Sherab decided to leave it behind in the car. Luhping could not carry it, much less use it. Neither Sherab nor John could afford the extra weight, and John seemed more comfortable with Yu's pistol.

"Luhping, come, we're ready to go."

"Leave me alone" she whispered sorrowfully.

"No, I will not leave you alone!" Sherab retorted, beginning to lose patience. "You will die out here." She grabbed Luhping's elbow and began marching her away from the car.

"I don't care," Luhping answered weakly. With Sherab's pull, Luhping took a few clumsy steps, and then slowly began to walk a straight line.

They headed in the general direction of the small town, based on the exit they had driven by. The difference in climate became apparent after a few minutes of walking. The cold, crisp air blew into their faces with a chilling caress. The absence of any significant vegetation also contrasted to the relatively lush valleys

Sherab and John had walked through weeks before. Sherab knew that Luhping's thin indoor clothing must not have offered her much protection from the wind. For now, she preferred that Luhping be cold, it would keep her alert. Sherab worried more about Luhping's listless behavior than for her actual physical wounds. With everything that had happened to Luhping, she threatened to give up on life.

The midday sun had almost reached its highest point in the sky when they spotted Dingri in the distance. It seemed that all directions in Tibet were given based on a town temple. The old guide had given them directions to two contacts in Dingri, again centered on the temple. As they drew nearer to the town, Sherab could make out both the main road leading into Dingri, as well as its brightly painted temple. She took out the old man's instructions, and got a bearing on the two potential guides. One of their contacts appeared to be on the opposite side of the town. The other, however, was closer to their rear entry point into the town. Both locations were well away from the temple itself, with its accompanying Chinese administrative office.

They skirted around the town to approach it more from its south side. Sherab worried about their very conspicuous appearance: a white man, a beat-up Chinese woman, and an armed Tibetan woman. The only positive side of their imposing presence was that people would go out of their way to avoid them. Whether they were dangerous or not did not matter, their appearance alone attracted trouble from the authorities.

The first farmer they saw confirmed Sherab's suspicion. One look at the approaching party, and he darted inside his house. The houses, mostly huts, were scattered randomly along the town's limits. The old man had not given Sherab precise instructions. They approached another farmer, who did not seem to be close enough to his home to go hide.

The farmer backed away a few steps when he realized they were coming to see him. His eyes darted from side to side, as if looking for an escape. Sherab decided to approach him alone, and have John stay behind with Luhping.

"Excuse me sir, can you tell me where we can find..." she looked at the instructions again, "Jigme Tashi," she finished.

"I don't know anyone by that name," the farmer replied furtively. The suspicious look in the farmer's eyes put doubt into his words.

"Please, I'm a nun." Sherab found that people reacted more favorably towards her when she used this wishful title. "I need his help, he was recommended by someone in Shigatse."

The farmer seemed to size up the truthfulness of her statement before answering.

"What do you want with Jigme?"

Sherab smiled inwardly. The farmer admitted that he knew the guide, and now was simply being curious.

"I'm sorry, but that's between me and Jigme. All I ask is that you please point out where he lives."

The farmer grunted his disappointment at her refusal to provide him with interesting gossip.

"See the three houses over there?" He pointed to a small cluster of shacks about one quarter of a mile away. "It's the house behind that group."

"Thank you very much sir," Sherab told him warmly. The farmer quickly retreated once he had satisfied her question.

Sherab led the way to the nearest house, and approached the one they wanted behind it. As they drew near, a man came around the opposite side of the house. Both he and their group froze as they faced each other. His dark brown eyes never showed fear, they simply analyzed the situation before him. The muscles on his right arm bulged and quivered as he tightened his grip on the hammer he carried. His short, powerful legs spread themselves apart ever so slightly, putting his body into a defensive stance. Despite the cold morning air, some perspiration glistened on his short, cropped black hair. He had been working hard at some repairs before they came upon him, Sherab concluded.

"Jigme Tashi?" she inquired.

"Maybe. Who are you?" he asked Sherab, glancing over at her companions.

"I'm Sherab," she answered. "We would like to hire you to bring us into India."

His eyes widened in surprise, displaying the first emotion from his passive face.

"Why do you think I can take you there?" he shot back.

"An old guide in Shigatse gave me your name. He didn't want to tell us his, however. So I can't tell you who sent me here. But we do have money with us, we can pay you."

He thought about her words for a few seconds, while he approached them. "All three?" he asked, sweeping his hammer in front of all of them.

"Yes, all three," she answered, instinctively taking a step away from him.

"No way," he told Sherab with a smile. "A white man and a Chinese? Too dangerous."

"I can pay you six thousand Yuan in cash," she told him. She low-balled the expected price, thinking he would try to bargain for more.

He looked at her carefully before speaking again. "It's not the money," he said. "I'm not bringing you to India. Too dangerous."

"Eight thousand Yuan," she tried again. "Please, we need you desperately."

"Why do you need to go? Why does a white man need to cross the mountains?" Sherab felt encouraged by his curiosity.

"He helped me escape, I was being tortured." Sherab bent the truth a little to improve their chances of gaining his sympathy.

"Tortured where?" he asked her.

"In Lhasa." She scrambled for her thoughts, not expecting him to interrogate her. "I got out of the city and he met up with me and helped me get to here. Get to you," she added hopefully.

"What about Chinese?" He almost spat the word 'Chinese' when he nodded his head towards Luhping.

"She also helped get us here. If not for her, we wouldn't have made it this far." Sherab spoke truthfully, in Luhping's defense.

"Why is she hurt?" he asked, waving his hand in front of his own face.

Sherab had already rehearsed the answer to this question. "There are many hills along the way, she lost her footing and fell down a rocky slope."

Sherab glanced nervously at Luhping, but the woman was too lost in her own world to hear the lies. The guide noted Sherab's nervousness, and looked very skeptical.

"Will you take us?" she asked again, hoping to detract his questioning. "I can go as high as nine thousand Yuan, but that is really all I have."

He examined them again before shaking his head with finality. "I can't take you. Too dangerous."

Sherab felt like sitting down, the despair weighed heavily on her shoulders. Perhaps they should try the other contact, and come back here if they were stuck.

"Fine," she told him with defeat in her voice. "Can you tell us where I can find Yeshe Jetar? That's the other guide I was told about in this area."

Jigme's eyes narrowed into small slits when she asked him this question. "Yeshe disappeared almost a year ago. He died in the same mountains you want to cross."

That news hit Sherab like an iron fist to the stomach. She looked at the sheer wall of snow and rock that the Himalayas presented to them. The odds kept getting worse. How could the three of them find their way across those mountains by themselves?

"Please!" Sherab pleaded with him when she overcame the initial shock. "Our lives depend on you. We will die without your help."

"Death in Tibet happens all the time," he told her coldly. "How many more will die because I take you to the mountains and I die too?"

How strangely similar were his arguments to those of Muyih and Luhping when they refused to drive them to Dingri. In both cases these people felt that they were helping others. John and Sherab posed too great a risk for them and for the countless others they would help after they had gone.

Sherab turned helplessly to John. She shook her head as she spoke, handing him the names of the two last guides. "No guide, John. No Jigme, no Yeshi."

She walked past John, tiredly leading the way back towards the car. She turned back, not hearing the sound of his footsteps following her. John had half turned to follow her, but was now staring at her with the same cold eyes she had last seen in Muyih and Luhping's apartment. Before she fully comprehended the meaning of those eyes, John reached into the backpack. Her heart began to

hammer wildly even before she saw his hand emerge with a tight grip on Yu's
pistol.

# Chapter 15

The hammer flew towards John's head at an incredible speed. He ducked wildly to the left, and felt the handle glance lightly off his head. Jigme kicked hard on John's wrist. The gun flew out of his hands before the pain shot up his arm. A fist struck John just below his throat, causing him to choke. His whole body seemed on fire as he strangled from the blow to his chest. A knife appeared out of nowhere, and pressed into his neck as Jigme spun him around and locked a powerful arm around John's already enflamed throat.

Choking and gasping for air, John could do nothing while Jigme barked orders to Sherab. John's bulging eyes noticed Luhping watching them with no more interest than a midweek TV program. Sherab quickly dropped her rifle and spoke urgently to the man in the process of killing John. They seemed to speak forever. John's eyes began to lose their sight, and his world of pain darkened around him.

He finally took in a painful gulp of air as Jigme released his throat. The wind was knocked out of him again as Jigme spun John around and tossed him against the side of the house like a broken toy. Before he could collapse, Jigme had a hand under his arm, and the knife pricking his throat once again.

"If ever you point that gun at me again, I'll kill you," Jigme whispered fiercely into John's ear through gritted teeth. John felt too much pain to be pleasantly surprised by the guide's English. "Girlfriend there will not be able to help you next time." Jigme let him go then, and John promptly fell to the ground.

The next few minutes passed by without John's knowledge of what happened around him. The pain in his wrist and throat were almost as intense as the chest pains he suffered from lack of air. He kept his eyes shut to blank out the spinning earth. He tried to control his breathing. His starved lungs demanded large mouthfuls of air while his throat protested each swallow.

"John?" Sherab's hand squeezed his shoulder. He looked up into her concerned face. "Come" she said, as she started to pull him up.

"Come where?" he asked. His voice reminded him of 'The Godfather'. It did not even have the strength to croak out the words, instead they rasped out in whispery, squeaking tones.

Just as John made it to his feet, Jigme came out of the house. Without a single glance in John's direction, he spoke with Sherab. Jigme had securely tucked Yu's pistol into his belt, and had a backpack slung over his shoulder. Sherab pointed to

John's backpack during their conversation. Without hesitating, Jigme bent over it, and began rummaging through the contents. John felt outraged that he dared go through their belongings, but he did not have the strength to even utter a protest. Jigme found the spare ammo clips for Yu's pistol, and tucked them into his pocket. He kept searching until he found the money Muyih had given them. After counting out the bills, he pocketed all of it.

Jigme asked both Sherab and Luhping a question, to which they nodded a "yes". He nodded back and began walking away.

"Come John." Sherab told him, as she bent to close up the backpack Jigme had carelessly left open.

He ignored her outstretched hand and stumbled a few feet towards Jigme.

"Where are you going?" he tried to shout at the guide, but John barely got above a harsh whisper.

Jigme turned to him with a snarl on his face. "I'm taking the women across the mountains. You may try to keep up with us, but stay out of my way. If you do anything I don't like, I will leave you in the snow."

He spun on his heel and continued marching quickly out of the town. Sherab caught up to John, and took his hand. In addition to her own backpack, John's was also slung over her shoulder now. Her back bent with the effort, while she tried to encourage John to come along. The pain prevented him from smiling at her courage. He reached over to take his backpack, and let her help him put his arms through the straps.

Sherab became the sheepherder as their new guide continued to march further ahead of them, oblivious to their delayed start. Sherab gave John a gentle push towards the guide's path before she went to help Luhping. He took a few steps and looked back to see a passive Luhping being led by the arm. He resolved to later ask Jigme what Sherab had done to change his mind. For now, he enjoyed the comfort of being led by an experienced guide as they headed for the towering wall of mountains nearby.

It did not take John long to learn to work with Jigme. The man hated all Chinese, which crossed Luhping off his list of people to be civil to. Perhaps westerners were the only people he hated worse than Chinese. John's stunt with Yu's pistol had definitely moved him to the bottom of Jigme's list. That left only Sherab, for whom Jigme seemed to have taken a liking to. If John wanted to ask the guide anything, he gave his request to Luhping, who translated it for Sherab. Coming from her mouth, the request had far greater chances of being granted.

Their group had not slept all night, nor had they eaten any lunch. After the first hour of following Jigme at his grueling pace, John felt ready to faint from exhaustion and hunger. Luhping and Sherab seemed in no better shape. He passed the word up the chain through Luhping and Sherab. Jigme seemed impatient with Sherab for the first time. He looked them over, and decided to let them rest. All three of them ate hungrily, and then lay down under the afternoon sun. John took a moment to fish out the warmer jacket in his backpack, and handed it to the underdressed Luhping. She wrapped it around herself gratefully, making the first positive face he had seen since they left Shigatse.

The guide let them rest for a mere twenty minutes before he called them to their feet.

"We have to get further from Dingri," Luhping informed John, after Jigme spoke to her. The thin, cold air at this altitude did not help their fatigue. John felt lightheaded as they continued to climb. He never seemed to get enough oxygen into his aching lungs. Jigme kept pulling ahead of them, and having to wait for them to catch up. The guide made no effort to hide his irritation at their slow, shuffling march.

By the time they had their evening meal, Dingri was no longer within sight. Jigme had stopped them early, knowing that he could not push their exhausted bodies much further. The lowering sun no longer protected them from the frigid mountain air. John's hands began to feel numb from cold as he ate his supper.

As soon as they had finished eating, Sherab and John began to setup the thin nylon lean-to. It would not shelter all four of them from the wind, but it was better than nothing. The guide seemed to find their efforts amusing. John guessed that Jigme did not see much point in a lean-to. He could not help but feel embarrassed. They were so new to this environment, that anything they did might seem foolish and unnecessary before this imposing man.

John stared dumbly at the sleeping bag attached to his backpack. They had a warm, well-insulated sleeping bag that would fit two people quite nicely. Luhping's presence began to pose some serious problems to their planning.

"Luhping, you and Sherab sleep in this tonight." He handed over the sleeping bag and its promised warmth with considerable regret. He looked expectantly at their guide, as Jigme unrolled a very narrow sleeping bag. Jigme stopped what he was doing when he noticed John watching him. His eyes flared with anger when he noted the lack of sleeping bags.

"Where are you going to sleep White Man?" he growled at John. John looked helplessly at him, feeling more of a fool with each passing second.

"We weren't expecting Luhping to come with us," he told him lamely. "I'll sleep against them, I'll be warm enough."

Jigme grumbled something at him in Tibetan, and stood up. John jumped to his feet in fear when Jigme pulled his ugly knife out again.

"What are you doing?" he cried out as the guide began to slash their brand new lean-to. He ignored both John's question and Sherab's as she jumped to her feet also. The guide cut the thin nylon off of the aluminum frame of the lean-to and threw it to John.

"Wrap yourself in that, and maybe you will survive tonight. I doubt you will make it when we reach the Nangpa La."

The guide did not exaggerate. The temperature dropped dramatically when the sun disappeared. Despite his exhaustion, John spent much of the night awake and shivering. His face felt frozen as he continued to breathe in the ice-cold air. The nylon wrap, turned brittle from the cold, crinkled loudly with every move he made. His feet suffered the most, despite the extra socks and boots. At least he could keep his hands against his body, but his feet had to remain exposed.

The next morning, John had trouble getting out of the lean-to nylon covering. His limbs were extremely stiff from the cold. He shivered continuously, as Sherab passed him some breakfast.

"Still with us, White Man? I'm surprised." Jigme chuckled as he helped himself to some of their food.

"My n-n-n-ame is J-J-John," he said through chattering teeth. "Now get the h-h-hell away from our food."

Jigme burst into laughter for the first time. John could not help but smile as Jigme slapped him on the back. He felt like a dumb child who had finally pleased his father.

"Don't worry John White Man, we all share the food now. I think you need to eat less, it doesn't look like you brought much food with you."

More logistical problems with Luhping's presence, John realized. They had brought plenty of food for two people. Of course there would not be enough for three. They would have to start rationing out the food.

"How long do we need to make the food last?" he asked Jigme. The strength had not fully returned to his voice yet, but at least he was not croaking like a frog anymore.

Jigme thought about the question for a moment before answering. "Chinese there doesn't look strong," he indicated Luhping with a nod of his head. "I think two days to get to Nangpa La, maybe three days to go over it. Then two days to cross Nepal and into India."

The old guide had prepared them well. With his help they had also estimated seven days of travel. Just in case, they brought nine days of food for two people. Dividing that food three ways, they had enough for six days. Cutting back just a little bit each day should make up for that seventh day. All this made perfect sense, assuming they kept on schedule.

"I'm sorry about the gun," John told Jigme meekly. "I was desperate, you were our only hope for survival."

Jigme merely grunted, neither accepting nor rejecting the apology.

"What changed your mind about bringing us through?" John finally asked him.

"Sherab told me that you risked your life many times for her. She's a headstrong woman." He smiled towards her. "She said that if a white man saved a Tibetan, then a Tibetan is obliged to save the white man in return."

"So you're doing it to return a favor to me?" John asked incredulously.

"No" he said, "I don't take other people's debts. But she said that she's a nun going to work for the Dalai Lama. She will ask His Holiness to pray for me."

What a clever woman. Where money and obligation had not budged the man, she found yet another way: religion. She should have warned John about her small lie though. He might have inadvertently let it slip out that she had changed her mind about becoming a nun. It still amazed John that a person could change their dream based on an astrologer's predictions. John could not object, for Sherab and he had been able to become much closer because of her change of plans.

They broke camp and continued on the trail to the Nangpa La. A brisk wind blew across their path, sending tiny fragments of crystallized snow into their side.

The left side of John's face grew numb from the stinging pellets, and he instinctively kept his head turned towards the right as they walked.

As usual, Jigme stayed well ahead of them, trying to motivate them to move faster. Just when John began thinking about lunch, Jigme suddenly turned around and ran towards them.

"Go!" he shouted, pointing to the right of the trail. "Get off the trail. Go!" John's confused mind hesitated a few seconds before obeying the frantic guide's instructions. Luhping stood closest to John, so he took her arm and herded her away from the trail. Sherab saw that he had Luhping, and hurried off the trail herself.

Jigme kept them running through the snow for about two hundred yards.

"What's going on?" John puffed, when he caught up to Jigme and Sherab behind a snow covered outcropping.

"People coming."

It took John several seconds to spot the tiny dots moving along the trail far ahead of them.

"Who do you think they are?" he asked, fearing Chinese soldiers.

Jigme shrugged his shoulders. "They're coming this way, so they're not runaways like you. If they're not runaways, they're enemies."

"Soldiers?"

"Maybe. Probably just nomads. Nomads we can deal with," Jigme said, patting the revolver in his belt. "But nomads can talk to Chinese later on. We don't want anybody to see us."

They waited interminably for the distant specs to shape into recognizable people. Four shabbily dressed men leaned against the wind as they made their way down the trail. They seemed to be wrapped in several layers of rag-like clothing, which all but covered their faces. They walked without a glance in the hidden group's direction, oblivious to the four sets of eyes watchfully monitoring their progress.

These were the nomads that lived off the land in Tibet. Moving with the seasons, they traveled the most remote areas of the country. They, more than anyone else, enjoyed true freedom. Neither the communist regime, nor the previous theocratic rule affected their life to a significant degree. This kind of freedom came with a price: poverty. As a result John and the others hid behind the rock, for the nomads would be eager to get the cash reward for bringing in escaping Tibetans.

When the nomads were a safe distance past them, Jigme led the way back onto the trail. They encountered one more such group before they stopped for supper and a night's rest.

"We were lucky today, the trail wasn't busy," Jigme announced between mouthfuls of John and Sherab's food.

"Lucky?" John asked. "I thought we wouldn't run into anyone at all out here."

"Nomads use these trails a lot. They could use shorter trails, but these trails can bring them money." He smiled devilishly with these words, daring John not to be afraid.

"'Dead or alive' I suppose you're going to tell me now?" John asked with a grin.

"No, only alive," he answered. "But can be broken." John didn't like the sound of that. If the prisoners would be tortured in jail, the nomads probably did not worry about being too careful not to harm them. An injured prisoner was far easier to return to the authorities than a healthy one trying to escape.

"Besides," Jigme continued his cynical dialogue, "it helps control overpopulation. Jailing and killing enough of us Tibetans helps control world population!" The guide's mouth smiled, but the eyes held no mirth.

"There are far easier ways to control overpopulation," John answered humorlessly. "Just legalize assisted suicide, and soon drug companies will have handy one hundred percent guaranteed painless suicide kits. Within the first year, we'll lose twenty-five percent of our population."

"You have a dark heart White Man."

"Maybe I've seen enough shit to darken it."

Jigme continued to eat in silence, ignoring John's remark.

John's teeth were already beginning to chatter from the evening air. Between the constant walking, and the sun, they did not feel the cold as much during the day. But after having sat down to eat, the cold lost no time in getting inside their clothing. He was the most poorly dressed in the group. He had an undershirt, a cotton sweater, and a heavy woolen sweater. But Luhping wore his winter coat. Jigme must have seen him shiver before addressing him.

"Tonight you sleep between us White Man." John nodded to him, not wanting to think about another bitterly cold night. "While you sleep, give the sweater to Chinese, and take your coat back."

Luhping made no indication of having heard Jigme's words. John worried more and more about her. She barely ate, and looked paler with each passing hour. Sometimes he had to call out to her three times before she lazily brought her eyes up to meet his.

The temperature plunged that night. They had gained a few thousand feet in altitude during the day, which contributed to the increased cold. John wore his coat now, and wrapped himself again in the thin nylon. Jigme slept on one side of him, while the two women slept on the other side. Since Luhping now only had the warm sweater, she slept on the inner side of her sleeping bag, next to John. Sherab slept on the outer side of the sleeping bag with her full winter coat. John felt terribly lonely being separated from her on a night like this.

Once again John slept poorly. He stole what warmth he could from the bodies laying next to him, but it was still insufficient to beat off the intense cold. The long hours in the dark gave him time to react to the loss of Muyih and the assault on Luhping. His sorrow for them intensified as he remembered all that they had done for he and Sherab. The dinners they shared brought warm memories of their friendship. The only other emotion that could dominate his sadness was the guilt he felt. If he had not forced them out of Shigatse at gunpoint, they would still be enjoying their lives within their little apartment. He examined his guilt with a certain morbid fascination, like a wounded man might study his amputated arm. Their loss would remain with him forever. The guilt became a new, permanent part of his soul.

Mercifully, he fell asleep for a few hours near the end of the night. His eyes opened once again as soon as the sky had begun to lighten. He had to blink some snow out of his stinging eyes. A light wind had dusted a thin film of snow over them.

Luhping's face had a deadly white pallor. The snow accumulating on her eyebrows and the crook of her nose added realistic details to her corpse-like appearance. Her lips were slightly separated, allowing a very faint vapor to escape as she took sickeningly shallow breaths.

John's hands and feet were numb. The cold seemed to sap the strength out of him to the point where apathy began to reign. So what if he froze? So what if he already had succumbed to frostbite? So what if he just lay there forever? Only an act of focused concentration allowed him to push these defeatist thoughts aside. He tried to summon enough courage to get up and restore circulation to his frozen limbs.

That's when the distant wup-wup sound of the helicopter first reached his ears. At first he thought he might be dreaming. Why would a helicopter be flying in this remote region? He lifted his head to try to spot the aircraft. It approached from the north, much along the same trail they had been following for the last two days. The distant dot on the horizon began to grow as the helicopter continued to fly in their direction. Jigme's head suddenly snapped up when the mechanical sounds became more insistent. His eyes widened with surprise, and then scanned around them.

"Head back down!" he shouted at John.

By now, Sherab also awakened, and propped herself up on her elbow. Jigme screamed at her as well, and she flattened herself back into the snow.

"Stay down. Don't move." Jigme gave his final instructions before the deafening noise drowned out his voice.

The helicopter roared over them, creating its own miniature snowstorm as it traveled. Even if John wanted to look up at it, the swirling snow tossed by its huge rotating blades forced him to keep his eyes shut. For one panicky moment the noise was so loud that he thought the helicopter might be landing on top of them. Then he felt it gradually move away. The artificial windstorm died off, and the noise slowly diminished.

Jigme looked like a snowman when he sat up. Too preoccupied with the retreating helicopter, he did not bother to wipe the snow off his face. Sherab dusted herself off and asked Jigme a question. Without taking his eyes off the helicopter, he answered her. Luhping continued to lie in the sleeping bag as if nothing had happened.

John understood now why Jigme had told them to remain still. The night's little snowfall had made them all but invisible from an overhead perspective. The entire landscape was made up of rocks covered in snow. From a distance, they were just another set of lumps under the snow.

Sherab put her hand under Luhping's head and tilted it upwards to wipe the snow off. Luhping's eyes fluttered open, but she neither spoke nor acknowledged their presence. John felt sick to his stomach seeing her like this.

Before John could untangle himself from the nylon wrap, Jigme's face appeared a few inches in front of his. The guide's eyes appeared furious as he stared at John.

"Who are you White Man?" he asked through gritted teeth.

His question confused John. "I told you who I am, what do you mean?"

Jigme's fist struck the ground next to John, disappearing into the snow.

"The Chinese don't send out search helicopters for a runaway prisoner. It must be you they're after. Now answer me! I need to know what I'm up against if I'm supposed to get you across the mountains."

"How do you know the helicopter was looking for us?" John asked him.

"Only nomads and runaways go on this trail. From the start I knew there was something wrong with you. Why are a white man and a Chinese running with Sherab? I was stupid to come. Now start talking!"

His tone had increased in intensity. John decided to tell him a partial truth. The full truth might make him turn around and abandon them.

"We killed a soldier." John felt relieved telling him this. He had answered Jigme's question without giving too many details.

"Not good enough!" Jigme almost spat the words out. "Chinese don't send a helicopter because of one dead soldier. Soldiers die all the time. Tell me the truth or I'll kill you and leave you in the snow. That will just make it easier for me to get across the mountains. I don't like having a white man with us."

Jigme's face looked at John quite seriously, daring him not to believe the threat. "I killed five soldiers, at two different checkpoints." It was a gamble, but John really did not want to get into Sherab's story.

Jigme raised his eyebrows at him in surprise. "You killed five soldiers?" he asked again. John simply nodded.

Jigme thought about this for a few seconds before continuing.

"OK, listen John, that's still not enough reason to send out a big helicopter." His first use of John's name was just one sign of Jigme's renewed respect for John. His tone had also calmed down, making him John's peer instead of his inquisitor. It was a subtle change, but suddenly they were working together to analyze the mess they were in. This new bond convinced John more than the guide's earlier threats to share the truth with him.

"It's Sherab they want, not me," John finally admitted. Jigme just looked at him, waiting for an explanation.

"She has seen the true Panchen Lama. The Chinese are keeping him prisoner, and they are …" he tried to find a quick summary of the boy's treatment. "They are destroying the young boy's mind with lies."

Jigme eyes seemed to light up with a rainbow of emotions. John saw rage, surprise, and fear.

"What do you mean by destroying his mind?" Luhping's voice broke through their conversation like a brick through glass. She had not spoken since early yesterday. Her voice broke up from disuse and from the cold, but the new strength in it could not be ignored.

John swallowed hard, not sure of how much details she or Jigme wanted to know. "They teach him incorrect history. But they also teach him how to behave without any morals. He is exposed to suffering every day. Sherab tells me that he is not affected by it. He can watch another person's pain without feeling anything. They also are perverting him with abnormal sexual experiences." The last sentence John spoke out rapidly, almost hoping that they would not hear it.

"The Chinese are doing this to our holy scholar?" Jigme gasped. It was a rhetorical question, spoken in disbelief.

"That's what all this has been about?" Luhping asked John. He nodded. "My husband died because of what my people are doing to their religious leader? My own people killed him." She stared at John with a horrified expression.

"No Luhping. A few crazed animals killed your husband. Not your people." John felt the tears beginning to form in his eyes as he prepared to say what he had kept inside. "I killed him more than your own people did, Luhping. I killed him, and I beat you." Having spoken the words did not relieve any of the oppressing guilt that crushed down on him. Luhping simply accepted his words, as the life drained out of her. She flopped back down into the sleeping bag with her ghostly white face as expressionless as before.

"I can't believe they would do that." Jigme said to himself. "Those ..." he lapsed into Tibetan to curse the Chinese holding his boy-leader a prisoner. Then he turned to John. "I should kill you for not telling me this when you asked me to guide you. The only reason I'll let you live is because in your own stupid way you're trying to help this woman."

John nodded eagerly at Jigme's last thought. "Her plan is to reach the Dalai Lama, to tell him what she has seen."

Jigme still shook his head in disbelief. "They are such fools, how do they think they can keep this a secret?" He paused, and then asked John: "How did she see him?"

"They kept other prisoners with him. They taught him how to use slaves."

Unable to speak, Jigme just growled his anger and held his fists tightly at his side.

"I don't know how, but we're going to get her there," Jigme announced to John. "That helicopter will be back, and it has a good chance of finding us."

"Maybe we should stay off the trail," John offered.

"We might have to, but that will add days to the crossing. We don't have enough food." The guide spoke thoughtfully, searching for alternatives that only his experience could come up with.

After a moment of thinking, he simply shook his head. "We have to risk the trail. The sooner we're over the Nangpa La, the better chance we have of getting away. If you see or hear the helicopter coming, you go flat on the ground. Don't move. From up there they will mostly notice movements, not shapes."

He fished out some food from his own backpack for once, and began eating a quick breakfast. Sherab and John followed suit, and tried to get Luhping to eat a decent amount of food.

"I'm not waiting for Chinese," Jigme announced. "Look in her eyes, she's already dead. You should leave her behind."

"We are NOT leaving anyone behind," John shouted. He could not believe what Jigme had just suggested. Perhaps his own guilt at what had happened to Luhping fueled his rage at the guide's inhuman coldness. "You can go wherever the hell you want, but we're not separating. We are not leaving anyone behind, even if we have to carry her. Is that clear?"

Jigme smiled at him a little too forcefully. The determination in John's voice did not leave any room for arguments. "Calm down White Man. Save your strength for climbing."

Still angry, John shook Luhping by the shoulders. "Eat, Luhping! We're going now, and we won't stop until lunch time."

Her eyes fluttered opened and she looked at John disinterestedly. John forced some dried meat into her hands and waited until she brought it to her mouth. She chewed it slowly, more to get rid of his attention than to satisfy the hunger she must have felt by now.

Jigme had already finished packing by the time Luhping began to eat some food. Without a word he walked away from them, following the trail ahead. Sherab had been busily packing their backpacks while John attended to Luhping. After Luhping ate, John took his sweater back from her, and dressed her with his winter coat.

"Come on Luhping, we have to go now." He stood behind her, put his arms under hers, and lifted her to her feet. Absurdly, she refused to support her weight, leaving him with an oversized doll in his arms.

"Luhping, enough!" he cried into her ear. Her legs stiffened, and clumsily held her weight like a newborn foal.

He let her go when he felt she could stand on her own. He went around and faced her. "Can you make it for me?" John coaxed her. "Please, our guide is already far ahead of us. We need to catch up to him."

Her eyes lit up with life for the first time since they left Shigatse. She grabbed at his coat and brought her face close to his. "Please John, have some mercy. Leave me here, please! Muyih is waiting for me."

John's mouth hung open in shock. "You can't mean that Luhping. Get a hold of yourself! We'll live through this, I promise you. Dying is not what Muyih would have wanted you to do."

The spark of life began to seep out of her as quickly as it had come. Her eyes welled up with tears at the mention of her husband's name. "Muyih left me, he can't tell me what to do now. I want to go see him. I want to be with him. Don't you understand?" Her voice had taken on a child-like quality. She was the misunderstood child trying to explain her world to an uncomprehending adult.

"Let's go Luhping. You have to walk now." Dealing with this kind of psychological problem was far out of John's reach. All he could do was push her along and hope to keep her going until they reached India. He put a hand on her lower back, and gently pushed her towards the trail. She followed his guidance without resistance, again reminding him of a young child. After a few minutes he let his hand drop, and felt relief when she kept moving on her own accord.

The Nangpa La loomed ahead of them. When faced with its daunting presence, one easily understood why the nomads referred to it as the notch in the sky. The great peaks of the Himalayas seemed to touch the sky above John in a solid wall of rock and snow. The Nangpa La truly did look like the 'V' cut of an axe on a fallen log.

"The helicopter won't be able to follow us into the pass." Jigme informed him during lunch. "The cold air and low oxygen that high up stalls their engines. By tomorrow we should have one less worry."

"So if we escape the helicopter, that should be the last of the Chinese, right?"

"Two more checkpoints to cross first," Jigme answered casually. "There's one at the base of the pass, and another near the top of the pass."

John had not expected this news, but his mind was too tired and numb from the cold to react very much. Jigme seemed to be telling him a story rather than what he would actually have to live through.

"How do we get past those checkpoints?"

"The first one is tricky. We'll go through it at night, and hope that the guards are sleeping. The second one is easier. The Chinese are stupid to put a checkpoint up there. It's so cold that the soldiers stay inside their tent, they don't want the trouble of having to come out and freeze. As long as we're quiet, we can get by them."

"And if the guards at the first checkpoint are not sleeping?"

"They picked a spot where the trail narrows between two cliffs. You can't go around it. Either we wait for another night, or we kill them." Jigme stared hard at John, trying to gauge whether he was up to another violent confrontation.

"Will you let me carry my pistol?" John's question served as his answer as well.

"We'll see about that White Man," Jigme answered with a small smile. "I'm not sure I want you waving that gun around me again."

Sherab took her turn to feed Luhping. She spoke to her in a gentle, soothing Chinese voice. John desperately wished Luhping would recover from her horrors. They had another several days of travel, under increasingly worse conditions. Having to force feed her, lift her onto her feet, and keep pressing her along added an enormous burden to their already strained minds and bodies.

Without warning, the helicopter swooped over a nearby ridge, and headed straight for them. The ridge had acted as a sound barrier, completely masking the helicopter's approach. Sherab immediately pushed Luhping down and lay flat on top of her. Jigme dove into the snow from his standing position. It was impossible to tell if the pilot had spotted them before they merged into the ground around them. John's heart seemed to pound in rhythm with the beating rotors of the aircraft. He fought to control the terror as the mechanical monster hovered above them in its storm of sound, wind, and snow.

For a horrifying moment, it seemed to stop directly overhead. The maelstrom became their only world, even time seemed to have no meaning. Then it retreated as suddenly as it had enveloped them. John could not be sure whether it had actually stopped over them or if it was just an illusion caused by the overwhelming sensations the overhead helicopter produced. Regardless, relief swept over him as the aircraft slowly receded in the distance.

"That was too close!" he said to Jigme, when the noise level had dropped sufficiently for speech.

"Hard to say if he saw us," Jigme added. He stared at the retreating helicopter, looking for any sign that it might be coming around for another pass.

"Let's get out of here," Jigme said, as he quickly gathered his belongings. Sherab and John needed no further encouragement. John didn't bother trying to convince Luhping to hurry. Instead he just hauled her onto her feet and pulled her along.

The rest of the afternoon consisted of simply plodding along in the snow. The unchanging white landscape numbed the mind. Eventually John just kept his head down and concentrated on placing one frozen foot in front of the other. Sometimes Luhping would slow down in front of him, and he would nearly bump into her. A few words of encouragement, a little push on her back, and she was moving again.

"There's the checkpoint," Jigme announced suddenly. He always walked far ahead of them. John had not even noticed when he stopped and they had caught up to him. Ahead of them, the trail passed through a narrow gorge leading up to the Nangpa La. A small wooden structure could be seen at the narrowest part of the gorge. As Jigme had described earlier, no one could pass around the checkpoint without considerable mountain climbing. Certainly they were not prepared for that level of difficulty. They would have to follow Jigme's plan, and hope the guards slept during the night.

"They won't see us from this far away, but I don't want to get any closer. When the sun goes down, we'll try to make it across." Jigme looked around them after having spoken. "Let's get off the trail, there's a good set of rocks over there."

They headed away from the trail, towards a cluster of large rocks on their right. The moment they left the trail, their feet sank into the snow up to their knees. The snow found its way under John's pant legs and into his boots as he fought his way to their resting place. Luhping fell once, and half her body disappeared into the snow. She just lay there until John caught up with her and pulled her out of the deep snow. Her head hung in wet, freezing strands across her face and the side of her head. Even as he tried to brush her off, the snow on her neck melted and ran under her coat. Her eyes never changed expressions, as if she did not feel the cold. More accurately, she seemed to welcome the cold, for it matched her dying spirit more than the warmth of the coat ever could.

Sherab helped John settle Luhping down as comfortably as possible. They shoved the sleeping bag behind her, and leaned her against a rock. John needed to hold Sherab, but felt uncomfortable showing any affection in front of Luhping's loss. He tugged on Sherab's sleeve, and walked her a few yards away, slightly behind Luhping's rock. Jigme, ever the practical guide, used these moments to rest well. His eyes were already shut and he seemed to be asleep in his sitting position.

John leaned into Sherab, and they held each other tightly. They had not had a moment of privacy in so long. Like a drained battery he sucked new life into himself from her closeness. She pulled away, and looked into his eyes. Did she know how helpless he became when she did that? All he could do was stare back at her until she decided to release him from her loving eyes. She leaned closer to him, and released him with a kiss. She shut her eyes as he pressed her cold lips against his own. As her face moved against his, her frozen nose traced a path of coldness wherever she touched him. How he longed to be back in Muyih and Luhping's apartment again.

They separated once again, and just leaned their foreheads together, enjoying the closeness of their bodies. Her red cheeks contrasted with the pallor of the snow all around them. She reminded him of childhood fairy tales, a beautiful woman living in a permanent winter setting. She could be his own fairy tale, if he ignored the soldiers waiting for them at the checkpoint, and the destruction he had brought down on Muyih and Luhping.

"You are my very own snow queen," he told her softly.

Her familiar puzzled expression replaced her peaceful look.

"I love you," he said by way of explanation.

She pulled him towards her into another hug. His head went onto her left shoulder, allowing him to look into Luhping's cold, lifeless eyes. Sherab felt his body stiffen as he stared guiltily at Luhping. Luhping stood next to the rock where they had left her. She leaned on her arm, using the rock to prop herself onto her feet. John would have preferred to see anger or sadness in her eyes than the look she gave them now. Sherab turned around to see what had made him react so strongly. She sucked in her breath when she noticed Luhping staring at them. The silence seemed to stretch forever as the three of them looked at each other. Shame and guilt threatened to drown John's senses.

"Luhping, I ..." John tried to stammer some kind of excuse, or soothing words. His sentence fell flat, and Luhping silently turned away from them. She slipped back down into her seated position, her back towards them.

"Oh God," John said sorrowfully, not knowing how to right the wrongs he had done. Without a word, both Sherab and John quickly headed back into Luhping's view. They sat apart, not wanting to show any more signs of affection in front of Luhping. It did not seem to matter what they did, for Luhping kept her eyes shut the rest of the late afternoon.

Jigme's eyes flew open when they heard the distant sound of the helicopter. The sun sat low on the horizon, ready to release the sky to the incoming darkness. The helicopter came in from the opposite side of the trail. It headed for the checkpoint, which left them out of its path this time. They watched it land next to the checkpoint.

"Damn!" John exclaimed. "They're not going to sleep now. How are we supposed to get by a helicopter too?"

"Can you fly helicopters, White Man?" Jigme asked him with a smile.

"No!" he answered emphatically. John did not want Jigme to think in any way that he might be able to get that bird into the sky. Jigme looked away from John, and continued staring at the checkpoint activity.

"Can you?" John asked after a moment.

"No," Jigme answered without diverting his attention from the checkpoint. "But maybe I should learn." A reckless smile formed on his lips as he said this.

"You're not serious! You'll get us killed quicker than the soldiers." Jigme merely smiled at John's remark, and continued studying the scene ahead of them. This man definitely made John nervous.

The situation quieted down near the checkpoint. "Let's eat supper now," Jigme announced. "We're going to have a long night."

They ate silently, each of them lost in their thoughts of what lay ahead. When they finished eating, they packed up their bags and waited for the cover of darkness.

"Wake up Chinese there, and let's go," Jigme said later on with a nod towards Luhping. Plodding through the snow proved to be much more difficult in pitch darkness. John lost all sense of direction, and relied on Jigme's sounds of struggle ahead of him for guidance. All four of them gathered on the trail, and then continued towards the checkpoint.

John lost track of time as they marched into the evening. Walking on the slippery and rocky trail was doubly difficult in the dark. Only the sounds of their heavy breathing and shuffling feet broke the dead silence of the night.

The sudden blinding light finally told John just how close they had come to the checkpoint.

"Down!" Jigme whispered harshly at them before John could locate the source of the light. John tackled Luhping on his way down, trying to protect her head as best as he could when they fell. The whine of the helicopter's engine began to fill the night, adding to the confusion of the spotlight that blinded them. The rotating blades began to make their own noise as they sliced through the air, adding to the ever-increasing pitch of the engine.

The light rose into the air as the helicopter lifted off. Its powerful searchlight threw a bright, circular beam of light on the ground below it. The circle of light approached the motionless group as the helicopter began to fly away from the checkpoint. The edge of the circle narrowly missed them by less than ten yards.

"There's one less person to worry about," John told Jigme when the sound disappeared in the distance.

"Yeah. But now we need to wait a while to let our other friends fall asleep."

The minutes ticked by with agonizing slowness. Jigme slipped into his sleeping bag for warmth. John unzipped their sleeping bag and used it as a blanket over himself, Luhping, and Sherab. They huddled under it, shivering and waiting. After a seemingly endless delay, Jigme finally got them going again.

"Real quiet now. No talking. Let's go see how the soldiers are doing tonight."

They walked as quietly as they could, but it still sounded like a herd of elephants to John's overly sensitive ears. With each breath he took, he feared alerting a Chinese soldier within the tiny office.

A dim light bulb from within the office cast a pale light through the office window. They were within forty feet of the building now. The interior illumination cast just enough light for them to make out the shape of the office exterior. The only door faced the trail, as did the lone window on its right. A sharply angled roof hung over the doorframe, protecting any observers below from the rain and snow. Two stout wooden beams supported the overhang, forming an entrance far too formal for such a rural outpost.

Jigme moved in close to John. "You wait here, I'm going to try to see what they're up to." He pulled Yu's pistol out of his belt, and advanced into the darkness.

They watched him slowly inch his way forward, a darker shadow among shadows. John held his breath when Jigme reached the office. He tread onto the steps leading to the door. Moving ever so slowly, he approached the lit window. Halfway between the door and the window, some ice cracked loudly under his boot. Jigme froze, his back against the wall.

John's heart began to hammer frantically in his chest. He reached over to Sherab and took her rifle. Noise no longer seemed to be their major concern. John crouched down and trotted the short distance to the office. He knelt down, pointing his rifle towards the door. The rifle shook as his body trembled from both the cold and the terror.

Jigme and John remained motionless in their positions for perhaps two minutes. No sounds emanated from within. Slowly, Jigme continued his stealthy approach towards the window. Bending down lower still, he carefully peered passed the edge of the window. After a few seconds, he boldly went forward and fully stared into the window. Jigme turned with a big grin on his face.

"The pilot came to get the guards. Probably having a good time in Dingri tonight!" Jigme's loud voice showed the relief he felt. He also seemed to find satisfaction in having caught the soldiers abandoning their post for a night of entertainment. No doubt they decided that no one would try to cross this late at night.

John's heartbeat began slowing down to its regular rhythm. "Luhping, Sherab, come!" he called out shakily to the two women. A moment later Sherab appeared, dragging a stumbling Luhping by the arm.

"They'll be back before morning." Jigme told them. "We need to be far away, out of sight."

He turned then, and continued marching into the darkness. The elation of having passed through the checkpoint quickly faded as they trudged through the frozen night. The checkpoint must have reduced the traffic considerably, for the trail now became ever harder to follow. The only sure indication that they were on the trail was that their feet only sank ankle deep in snow, instead of knee deep.

After a few hours of this forced marching, John began to stumble more often. The extreme cold sapped what little strength he had. The nights of poor sleep also took their toll on his reserves of energy. He wondered how Jigme kept going so long. They had no choice but to follow the guide or be left behind. Yet Jigme kept pushing forward using nothing but his own determination. Only when Jigme stopped could they tell that he too was near the point of exhaustion.

"Hard to say, but I think we're far enough now," Jigme said between gasps of air. That's when John noticed all of them were having trouble getting enough oxygen at this high altitude.

"Let's sleep now, we only have a couple of hours," Jigme said as he unrolled his own backpack. Luhping and John exchanged a sweater for a coat as she settled into the sleeping bag with Sherab. Jigme and Luhping were pressed on either side of John's nylon wrapped body. For once he had no difficulty falling asleep.

The sky had barely begun to lighten when he woke up. He could not remember the last time he had woken up feeling rested and refreshed. This morning was no different. John did not think he had ever experienced feeling this cold before. He could still feel his right side, tucked against Jigme's sleeping form. But his left side was totally numb. Even his neck seemed frozen stiff as he turned his head towards Luhping's side.

John saw space where there should have been a body. He blinked his eyes in disbelief. Sherab lay sleeping on the other side of the sleeping bag, but Luhping was gone. He sat up quickly, despite the protest from his frozen body. Still unable to believe what his eyes told him, he reached over to where she should have been.

"Luhping?" he said as he pulled back the sleeping bag. His hand felt a soft lump, which he then picked up. In the semi-darkness he recognized the heavy woolen sweater Luhping wore at night.

"Luhping!" he screamed hoarsely, as he struggled to get out of his nylon wrap. Sherab jumped into a sitting position at the sound of his panicked voice. John tossed her the sweater.

"Luhping's gone!" he told her unnecessarily. He limped out of his sleeping area, his right leg not quite responding to his brain's control. John searched the area frantically, wandering in aimless circles.

"Luhping?" he cried out over and over again.

Jigme had joined the search now. Perhaps because of his experience, or simply because he cared less, Jigme had the presence of mind to look for her tracks.

"This way John," he called as he trotted along her footprints in the snow. John raced after him as quickly as he could with his still frozen body. She had not gone far, not without even an outer sweater. Jigme leaned over a dark shape in the snow as John caught up to him breathlessly. As Jigme sat back up, John saw Luhping's face. Her lips were blue, and her skin had an impossible whitish-gray color. Her hair formed frozen heaps around her head. She wore nothing on her upper body but her indoor blouse.

John's mouth hung open in shock, not able to accept what he saw. He looked at Jigme helplessly.

"She's still breathing. Barely," he told John.

John surged towards her, and began to pick her up. Carrying her was nearly impossible, his legs had enough trouble just getting his own body up to this point. As he struggled to lift her, Jigme's hand fell on his arm.

"She won't make it John. Don't stretch it out for her, let her sleep here."

John looked at him, unable to comprehend if Jigme truly meant what he had said. For the first time Jigme looked somewhat embarrassed at his own words.

"She won't make it, trust me," he said again.

John violently shook Jigme's hand loose and lifted Luhping. He took two steps before falling down, and watching Luhping roll into the snow once more. Tears of sadness and frustration formed in his eyes at this pitiful sight. He crawled over to her, and started to lift her again.

Sherab moved in his direction, coming to help him carry her. Then Jigme stepped in front of John, and easily pushed his hands away. He bent down and picked up Luhping like she was no more than a child.

"You're a fool White Man," he said, as he brought her back towards their sleeping area.

"She's going to make it!" John screamed at Jigme's back. Still on his knees, watching the guide go with her limp body, he screamed again. "Do you hear me? She's going to make it!"

John struggled to get on his feet again, and tried following Jigme. Sherab stood by his side and helped him take a few steps.

"She's going to make it," he mumbled to Sherab, looking for someone who would believe him. Sherab's eyes merely looked down at the snow as she guided John back to the others.

# Chapter 16

Some feeling began to return to John's right leg. He hobbled over to Jigme, and threw his coat to the guide.

"Put this on her," John commanded. He then hastily retrieved her woolen sweater for himself. A thousand questions and accusations ran through his mind. Why had she tried to kill herself? Why had he not thought of that possibility? Why did Sherab not wake up when Luhping left the sleeping bag? He looked for someone to blame, when really the blame belonged to none of them, or all of them.

Jigme and John slid Luhping into the double sleeping bag. John crawled in with her, hoping to quickly transfer some of his body heat into her ice-cold body. His arms wrapped up her limp form against him, as his shivering body tried to warm them both. Jigme paced nervously a few feet away from them.

"John, we have to keep moving!" Jigme finally said in a frustrated outburst.

"We're resting here at least until this afternoon. Then we'll see if Luhping can travel or not." John spoke quietly, but firmly. Jigme had to get it into his head that John had no intention of simply leaving Luhping behind.

"We're not all going to get caught because of her!" the guide answered hotly.

"Look, we're in the pass now, you said we were safe from the helicopter. No one has seen us here, so why are you in such a hurry? There's nobody chasing us!"

"When you're trying to get out of Tibet, there's always someone watching, someone chasing. Those who think they're safe, die!" Jigme's frustration was apparent. He was accustomed to being the unquestioned guide, a leader to be followed. John's challenge to his authority flustered him.

The silence after Jigme's last comment told him that John was not buying his argument. The guide thought a moment before continuing.

"And we're not safe from the helicopter yet. We're still low in the pass, they might be able to come this far."

His arguments were running out. The doubt in his voice let John know how lame this last comment really was. Jigme did not expect a helicopter to come searching this far, therefore neither should John.

A stream of Tibetan curses flew out of Jigme's mouth when John would not budge. They must have been colorful curses, for John noticed Sherab trying to suppress a small smile as she looked away.

"White Man, we are leaving after lunch, with or without you!" Jigme stormed off the trail after his proclamation, preferring to be alone than with his strange group of customers.

Sherab took the lean-to's nylon and wrapped it around herself. Then she lay down against Luhping, but outside the sleeping bag. Now Sherab and John simply looked at each other, with Luhping's ghostly face between them.

The morning sun raised itself with brilliance, its promise of warmth already felt on John's exposed face. By midday his body had recovered from the chilling night. Luhping, however, did not regain consciousness. Her lips were no longer blue, but her skin remained ashen. Her chest barely moved, causing John to check frequently near her mouth to ensure that she continued to breathe.

Jigme made a point of eating his lunch at precisely twelve o'clock. Sherab went along with his game to avoid conflicts. She passed some food to John, and then ate her own lunch. Neither of them tried to feed the unconscious Luhping.

"Her skin color is improving," John lied. Before Jigme could announce his departure plans, John took the opportunity to ask for more time. "I really think she will wake up soon. Until then, we can't decide whether to take her or not."

"We're leaving now," Jigme said stubbornly.

"Just give me another two hours Jigme. Come on, be reasonable. This is my friend's life we're talking about."

"And in two hours, you'll ask for another two?"

"I promise I won't," John lied again.

"You're pushing me too hard John. I'm leaving in two hours. If Sherab doesn't want to come with me, then I am going home. If she wants to come, I'll bring her over the mountains. Either way, in two hours I'm leaving this place."

Jigme walked away again, leaving John with his thoughts. Two hours to decide their fate. He removed his thin, frozen glove and touched Luhping's face, praying for her to wake up. The skin felt like cold rubber, devoid of life.

Neither Jigme nor John had to make a difficult decision after two hours. With less than an hour having gone by, the helicopter roared in the distance, heading their way.

"What's it doing this high up?" he shouted to Jigme in an accusing tone.

Jigme shrugged his shoulders, looking both confused and worried. "They must really want you two. Or someone found out that the guards left during the night, and now they're ordered to check if anyone got past the checkpoint. Get down, it's getting closer."

All three of them flattened on the ground. John covered Luhping as best as he could from the coming helicopter's windstorm. It was a sunny day, with no morning snowfall. He worried that they might be easier to see under these conditions.

The familiar deafening noise engulfed their still bodies as the aircraft came over them. He waited expectantly to hear the sound begin to fade away. He smiled when it came, the distinctive change in noise level that signaled the helicopter's departure. The noise did not decrease further, which quickly wiped the smile off his face. He risked turning his head slightly to take a look.

Through the flying snow he could make out the helicopter, a malevolent beast staring down at them. It had passed them only by a few yards, and then had turned to face them again. It hovered in place, observing their location. Fear poured through his veins. He could not be sure if the pilot had seen them or was still trying to determine if he was looking at rocks or people. John could not even see the pilot with all the snow in the air, how could the pilot possibly see them?

The pilot advanced his machine a little closer, until he was over the nearest 'rock', Sherab. With horror John watched the helicopter slowly begin its descent. The aircraft was going to land on her! Sherab remained motionless and unaware, head down into the snow.

John jumped out of the sleeping bag, using his arm to shield his eyes from the snow. He picked up the nearest stone, weighing about two pounds. The helicopter's skids now hovered four feet above Sherab's back. He ran around the side of the helicopter to get on the pilot's side. A sudden shift in the wind jerked the helicopter downwards, until it could almost touch Sherab.

John was somewhat behind the aircraft, but he still had a fair shot at the pilot's window. He hurled his rock. With satisfaction, he saw it strike the pilot's window with a loud enough crack that even he could hear it. The pilot instinctively lifted the helicopter, spinning as he rose into the air. John saw him then. They stared at each other for a brief moment, both of them stunned to see the enemy.

The helicopter surged forward at the same time that John turned and began running down the trail they had climbed with so much difficulty. Twenty yards ahead, he saw an outcropping that would temporarily protect him from the helicopter. A set of large, pointed rocks formed a rough circle, with space inside for him to lie flat.

John left the trail and clumsily made his way through the deeper snow. He dared not look back, despite the helicopter's deafening noise. John thought he would make it, for the rocks appeared almost within his reach. A shadow formed above him. He looked up, and briefly saw the helicopter blades before a metal pole dug into his back.

The pilot used his left skid to throw John onto the ground. The skid did not push him as much as punch into his back, just below the shoulder. He landed hard, face first into the snow. Out of breath, he quickly rolled over onto his good shoulder, only to see the helicopter's belly coming down on him.

John rolled onto his back and lay flat. The metal pushed his body deeper into the snow, but not all the way to the frozen ground. One skid hit a rock, and stopped the helicopter's crushing descent. The pilot quickly brought the helicopter up, and then back down onto the same rock. John's panic stricken mind wondered how many more times the pilot could do this before the skids would miss a rock and crush his chest.

Before the pilot could lift off again, John made a desperate gamble. He rolled towards the nearest skid, and climbed onto it. The helicopter rose a few feet, rotated, and landed hard on the ground where he had lain seconds ago. The sudden drop almost knocked him off the skid that he clung to with dear life.

A shower of glass fell on him immediately after he heard a loud popping noise. He looked behind and saw Sherab standing several yards away with a rifle in hand. Again the pilot surged the aircraft upwards when he detected the danger. The helicopter shot up almost fifteen feet before John had time to release the skid. His body turned as he fell, and landed on his back. The deep snow cushioned his fall, but not enough to prevent the wind being knocked out of him. John lay there trying to suck in air. The helicopter raced away, with a gaping hole where the side window used to be.

By the time Sherab reached him, John was catching his first breath. She spoke to him in rapid Tibetan as she helped him sit up. He smiled at the panic in her voice as she checked him out.

"I'm OK," he told her painfully. The fall had not hurt him, but the skid's jab into his back still had his shoulder and back on fire. She helped him stand, and they made their way back up the trail to Luhping and Jigme.

Jigme sat near Luhping, nursing his ankle.

"What happened to you?" John asked him.

"Stupid, stupid, stupid!" he said angrily. "I ran towards the helicopter, but I couldn't see because of the snow it threw everywhere. I twisted my ankle on a rock."

"How bad is it?"

"Bad, I think. I've crossed the mountains dozens of times and this never happened. Now I go chasing helicopters while trying to bring a Chinese and a white man across the mountains. I am so stupid!"

John did not know what to say. So much had happened in the last few minutes that his brain had temporarily shut down.

"We were lucky that was just a scout helicopter," Jigme added. "If it was a military helicopter we would be dead by now. Instead of running away, he would have shot us with machine guns."

"Is that what they're going to send after us now?" John asked him.

Jigme shook his head. "I don't think they have any attack helicopters near here. They'll fly in some soldiers up to here, that's for sure. But even if they have attack helicopters, we'll be out of reach by then. We're leaving now, John."

"What about your ankle?" John asked, looking for some delay tactics.

"I can walk, but slowly. That's another reason to go right now. They'll have the speed advantage because of my ankle."

"Jigme, be honest. How much chances do we have of making it without being caught?"

He looked up sadly. "Not too good John. They know where we are now."

John knew what had to be done. He was not sure if he had the courage to go through with it, but he forced himself to at least say the words.

"I'm not abandoning Luhping here." Jigme looked up at him with a tired, defeated expression. John pressed on before the guide could interrupt.

"There's a good chance they won't kill me, since I'm a foreigner. My government might be able to get me out with some political pressure. I'm not sure how Luhping will do, but at least she's a Chinese citizen. But Sherab will die. Jigme, I need you to get her out. I'll try to find ways to delay the search for you. But please, explain to her that she must go with you."

Jigme stared at him, struggling to accept John's decision.

"You're making a mistake John. She'll either die or go to jail. That's not worth risking your own life for."

"I've done enough harm to her life, Jigme. I have to stay with her. Maybe they'll go easier on her since I'm here. As long as she has a chance to get her life back, I'm not leaving."

Jigme nodded at him, and they turned to Sherab. John held her hands, and let Jigme speak to her. Partway through his explanation, her eyes opened wide with fright. "No!" she screamed at John, yanking her hands out of his. "John come!" she repeated angrily.

"No, Sherab, I can't come," he told her, taking her into his arms.

"John not come, Sherab not come," she told him, her voice muffled from being pressed into his jacket.

"Sherab, you will die. Jigme, translate for me please. Tell her she will die if she stays." Jigme repeated John's words in Tibetan. "Tell her I will live, they won't kill a foreigner." John waited while Jigme translated. "Tell her I will find her in India, no matter where she is."

Sherab began sobbing against his shoulder. She must have known that he was doing the right thing, but it did not make it easier to accept.

"Tell her I love her." Jigme hesitated, embarrassed to be part of their private lives. Sherab recognized his English words, and squeezed him harder. Jigme spoke to her in a low voice, relaying the message she already understood. John fought against his own tears as she wept against him.

Jigme was already picking up his pack.

"Go Sherab," John said softly.

"I love you John," she said in her muffled voice. Without looking at him she stepped away and spoke to Jigme.

"She says that she'll wait for you in India until her body turns to dust." Jigme translated for John. The guide cleared his throat awkwardly, not being used to speaking about strong emotions. "She says if you don't come by then, she'll wait in her next life, until she turns to dust again. She will wait for eternity, so you must never stop searching for her."

Jigme quickly busied himself after delivering her message. John kissed Sherab once more, wondering if it was for the last time. She held his head against her, unwilling to let go.

"John, I'll leave you my sleeping bag for Luhping," Jigme told him. "Me and Sherab will take the big bag."

John simply nodded at him over Sherab's shoulder. He held back the absurd jealousy he felt at the thought of Jigme and Sherab sharing a sleeping bag on their cross-mountain trek. Jigme opened up his sleeping bag, and transferred Luhping into it. He then rolled up the double bag and fastened it to his backpack.

"Sherab," Jigme said, tugging on her arm. She let John go reluctantly, and took the pack Jigme offered her.

"You're brave," Jigme told John with a small smile. "For a white man," he added.

"Take care of her for me Jigme." John forced himself to return the smile. "I owe you a lot for this."

"Good luck John," he simply answered.

They shook hands awkwardly before Jigme turned and resumed the march up the Nangpa La. Jigme hobbled painfully on his injured ankle as Sherab joined him on the trail. Sherab looked back at John every few minutes, her figure diminishing as she went further. He waved half-heartedly, trying not to let the despair overwhelm him.

At least they won't starve, John thought. They had left him enough food for a day, and took the rest. He took out some food now, and sat beside Luhping eating his snack. He felt exhausted from lack of sleep. After eating, he wrapped himself with the nylon he had learned to hate, and lay down with Luhping to rest. There was nothing for him to do but wait for the soldiers to come find them. How ironic that he and Sherab had evaded them for a month, and now he waited for them as his rescuers.

With all worries of escaping out of his head, John found himself drifting off to sleep. A gnawing fear in the pit of his stomach reminded him of the danger he was in when the Chinese took him into custody. But part of him was at peace. Sherab had a good chance of making it into India now. He had accomplished his goal. This peaceful thought lingered in his mind as he succumbed to the exhaustion and fell into a deep sleep.

The sun had lowered considerably when John woke up. He sat up with a start, surprised to have slept so long. Luhping still lay motionless next to him. He had slept uncomfortably on his side, making his right leg tingle from lack of circulation. He stood up and stretched. Looking up the trail, Sherab and Jigme were now completely out of sight. He turned around, and saw the soldiers.

From this distance they were no more than a handful of dots in the distance. With difficulty, he counted eight separate dots heading towards him. Their steady forward motion brought a chill to his spine. He looked away, and returned to Luhping's side.

"They're almost here Luhping. The soldiers are about an hour away." Her ghostly face remained expressionless when he spoke. A late afternoon breeze blew a steady, light snow around them. He sat next to Luhping, awaiting their fate at the soldiers' hands. He brushed off the snow accumulating in his lap, and then reached over to do the same for Luhping.

His hand stopped in mid-air. His eyes knew immediately that something was wrong, but it took a few seconds for his mind to figure it out. The snow accumulated on Luhping's face. It should have melted away as it landed. He ripped off his glove and tried to feel her breath. No warm breath passed over his fingertips. He hurriedly unbuttoned her coat, and pressed his ear to her chest. He stayed there for almost a minute, desperately hoping to hear the faintest heartbeat.

"Luhping! No!" he screamed through his tears. He grabbed her by the shoulders and shook her. He pounded on her chest, and slapped her face. Her corpse bounced and twitched to the rhythm of his disrespectful attempts at disturbing her eternal rest. She was dead. The thought seared into his brain with horrifying clarity. He collapsed onto her and let his grief flow out in great racking sobs. Both Luhping and Muyih had died because of him.

The thought of the approaching soldiers broke through his grief. He sat up at looked towards them. The dots were larger now, individual arms & legs could be seen. Luhping was dead, so he should run now. His legs felt rubbery, unable to stand. It would be easy to just lie there and wait for the soldiers to come get him. He thought of Sherab then, and her hypnotic eyes. How realistic was it to think the soldiers would not harm him? They could claim to have never found his body. He thought of Sherab's words, of her waiting for him until she turned to dust. For her, he had to try to escape.

His face felt frozen from the tears he had shed. His mind raced with jumbled thoughts. "My backpack. I need my backpack." Muttering out loud helped him get into action. He shouldered the backpack, and bent down to say goodbye to Luhping. Another thought crossed his mind, and he almost fell backwards from the revulsion he felt. "It's OK, it's survival," he muttered to himself.

"Dear Luhping, may you and God forgive me for this." He avoided her dead face as he finished unbuttoning her coat. Her arms already had death's rigidity as he struggled to remove the coat. He sat her up, swung the coat out from behind her, and let her fall back. He failed to reach her body before she flopped back down hard on the snow-covered trail. Her head bounced obscenely when it struck the hard packed snow. Fighting the rising gorge in his mouth, John wrapped the coat around himself. He then spread out the nylon, and wrapped her body in it. Feeling more like a grave robber with each passing second, he rolled up the vacated sleeping bag and attached it to his pack.

"Goodbye Luhping. I'm so sorry." How lame these words sounded. The longer he stayed near her, the more he felt that he was insulting her memory. With a last look towards the soldiers, he began a fast march up the trail.

John stopped to rest when the sun was setting. He took out some dried fruits and munched on them slowly, trying to catch his breath. He felt thankful for his afternoon sleep, it had allowed him to progress far and fast during the evening. He had to be moving faster than Jigme and Sherab, because of Jigme's ankle. He resolved to march through the night, in hopes of catching up before morning. The longer they remained separated, the less likely were his chances of finding them. The trail no longer seemed like a trail. The blowing snow had covered all footsteps that had marked a traveler's passage. The surrounding landscape did not leave much room for doubt at the present. Jumbles of rocks and steep crevices lay on either side of this narrow, relatively smooth path. Doubtless the path would not always be so clear. How long before Jigme's experience brought him to the right where John went left?

Behind John, the soldiers had disappeared from view beneath the encroaching darkness. He was not sure which was more unnerving, watching their moving forms coming, or having them hidden in the darkness below. His lack of progress while he stopped to eat made him nervous. He quickly put on the backpack, and used what little dim light remained to make his way up the path.

It takes a while for a city dweller to get used to the total darkness that comes to rural areas. Before long, John shuffled forward at what seemed a snail's pace. Each step consisted of placing one foot forward, and cautiously feeling the ground below before placing his weight on it. A few times he came close to the edge of a precipice. These occasional adrenaline boosts kept him alert most of the night. Despite his cautious footsteps, he stumbled and lost his balance numerous times. Three times he lost the trail completely. Without realizing it, he would end up surrounded with large rocks. Then he had to trace his steps back until he thought he had found the trail again.

His nerves had a raw edge throughout the entire night's trek. In the end, he fell into a worn out heap. His legs refused to go further. His mind was exhausted from the harrowing experiences and continual high alert status. He thought that perhaps it had now become too dangerous to go on. In this state of exhaustion, he could make a crucial mistake and find himself at the bottom of a ravine.

Using the last of his energy, John unrolled the sleeping bag and slid into it. As he stretched out, a stabbing pain knifed through his shoulder blade. "I've been hit by a helicopter!" he thought with a smile. "There's one for the grandchildren." Soon after his head hit the snow, he slept soundly.

*** 

"He'll be OK, Sherab. They won't kill him."

Jigme's words did not bring her much comfort. They had lost sight of John a few hours ago as they progressed up the trail. There remained only a single checkpoint between her and freedom. Yet she felt more lonely and sad than she had ever felt since escaping from the jail. She could not tell if Jigme believed what he had told her, or if he simply tried to comfort her. She certainly did not believe it. She wanted to, but in reality knew that the Chinese soldiers might easily kill John instead of bringing him back into custody. John and Sherab had killed their fellow soldiers. The angry men would want swift justice for those killings.

Sherab wiped away the freezing tears before speaking with her guide.

"How much longer can you go on that ankle?" She avoided discussing John's plight, for fear that she would break down in front of Jigme. She was embarrassed enough now that he had noticed her tears.

"I'm good until dinner time," he said, with a barely suppressed grimace as he limped along. "After that we'll see."

Since they had met up with Jigme, he had continuously driven them at a hard pace. Now he and Sherab crawled along at a snail's pace because of his injury. She frequently found herself quite a distance ahead of him, and having to stop so that he could catch up. This role reversal brought her a bit of satisfaction, after the way Jigme had mistreated John. She felt ashamed of those feelings, but could not deny them.

"Why don't you transfer more of your load into my backpack?" she asked, hoping to relieve some of her guilt. Not long after having left John, at her insistence Jigme had move items out of his pack and into hers. She found it funny how difficult this was for the guide. His pride had trouble in accepting help from one of his customers. And a woman, on top of it all! She could not hide her smile as he turned down her latest offer.

"Can I ask what's so funny?" Jigme asked with irritation.

"Oh nothing, really," she answered. "You do seem a little bit stubborn."

"Well I'm glad to know my suffering can wipe away those tears from a few moments ago."

"Come on, Jigme! I'm not smiling because of your suffering!"

The guide merely grunted, the effort of talking having become too great. She found it hard to imagine the pain he must be going through. She felt exhausted from all the marching they had been doing in these wintry mountains. Tramping through the snow all this way on an injured ankle sounded impossible.

A cold wind blew through the mountain pass. Sherab kept her head down as they continued trudging forward throughout the afternoon. The sun had lowered on the horizon, reminding her of her hunger. The sting of the cold air on her face numbed her cheeks, making her speak with an awkward, mumbling voice.

"Let's stop for supper now," she called out to Jigme. He looked up at her gratefully, his face having paled to the point of blending in well with the surrounding snow. She knew he was too hurt to continue after supper, he had to rest his ankle for the night.

Sherab took out some food for their dinner while Jigme leaned back against a rock, rubbing his sore ankle. The disadvantage of stopping for supper was that Sherab had time to think of John. What was he doing right now? Had the Chinese picked him up yet? Was he cold, or hungry? Was he being beaten? She shuddered at this last thought and pushed away her speculations. Instead she focused on all the meals they had shared together. Every meal brought back warm memories, from their early crushed barley "tsampa" to the feasts at Muyih and Luhping's apartment.

"Thank you Sherab," Jigme said, as she passed him a handful of nuts. She enjoyed the ease with which she and Jigme could communicate, but missed the awkwardness of trying to share ideas with John. Each exchange of ideas became a small gift between them. There were so many details of John's life that she would never know until they shared a language. But she had learnt so much about his character with the amount of time they had spent together. Tears threatened to break out once more as she wondered if she would ever get a chance to know the little details of his life.

She finished eating quickly, and started unrolling the sleeping bag.

"What are you doing?" Jigme asked. "We've got to keep going!"

"You're not going anywhere on that ankle."

"Yes I am. We have to put more distance between us and the Chinese."

Sherab stopped her preparations and turned to Jigme with her most authoritative glare.

"I need you to get me to India, OK? You're of no use to me if you destroy your ankle in the first night. You have to rest it for tomorrow."

Before he could protest, she walked briskly up to the guide and began unlacing the boot of his injured leg. She slapped away his fingers as he tried to stop her. He gave up quickly, and then Sherab knew he had simply been posturing. He himself must have known it was time to stop for the night.

"Now get in the bag before your foot freezes," she commanded. He crawled over to the sleeping bag, and painfully slipped in his bad foot, along with his other, booted leg.

"Do you think you might get frostbite without your boot?"

"No, not with two of us in the bag. It'll get pretty cold, but that should only help the swelling go down."

Sherab detected the embarrassed tone in Jigme's voice. He had not been thinking about his ankle at all, but about the two of them sharing a sleeping bag at night. Despite the rough exterior he prided himself on displaying, the man obviously had a sensitive nature when it came to sleeping arrangements. Perhaps years of solitude imposed by his line of work had made him uncomfortable around others, especially those of the opposite sex.

"Are you nervous about sleeping next to me?" Sherab could not believe her boldness. No sooner had the thought been in her mind that she teased the poor man with it.

"Of course not!" Jigme retorted, his pale face turning red.

"I would think a guide with your experience must have shared a sleeping bag thousands of times."

"Not really," he answered. "I bring my own bag, and my customers are responsible for their own sleeping arrangements."

His shyness made Sherab begin to feel uncomfortable as she lay down next to him. She had never felt uncomfortable with John, not even the first time she had warmed his sick body near the Tsangpo river. Jigme deliberately left a small gap between their bodies, as she slowly succumbed to a restful sleep.

Jigme's arm lay across her waist when she woke up under the predawn sky. The gap between them was long gone. He huddled next to her, as if seeking the comfort of another human being. She smiled at his uneasiness the night before. She thought of waking him just to see his embarrassed reaction, but decided to let him rest as long as he could.

In the end, Jigme was spared any embarrassment. He woke up slowly, and turned his body as he stretched. When he opened his eyes to the early morning sun, his body no longer leaned on hers.

"Did you sleep well?" she asked with a secretive smile.

"Not bad, considering the circumstances." Jigme nodded to the snow all around them as he spoke. He reached into the sleeping bag, and rubbed his ankle.

"How is it?"

"Not good. Better than last night though. I'm glad we stopped when we did." He acknowledged her part in that decision with a wry smile.

They ate a hurried breakfast, eager to get back onto the trail at their slow walking pace. Sherab thought that John would be off this snow mountain by now. She could not guess where the soldiers had flown him. Lhasa would undoubtedly be the first destination. But she did not know if he would be allowed to go home from there, or if they might bring him to Beijing. She dared not think of darker possibilities.

Less than one hour after having finished breakfast, Jigme suddenly called a halt to their march.

"Nomad," he whispered in Sherab's ear, as he pointed ahead in the trail. At first Sherab only saw the usual snow-covered rocky terrain. Then she noticed that one of the "rocks" was actually a man's sleeping form. The night's light dusting of snow camouflaged most of his body, making him look like another large rock along the trail.

Jigme beckoned Sherab to follow, as he led her off the trail. She kept her silence until they were out of earshot.

"He's alone, why can't we just go by. We're armed, he should not be able to give us trouble."

"Unless you want to kill him, I don't want to go. We have to avoid anyone knowing that we came this way."

Sherab had to agree with Jigme's more cautious logic. It was unnerving to watch the still form from a distance.

"How do we even know he's alive?" Sherab asked. "He doesn't seem to be moving at all."

"I know, I've been wondering about that too. It's unusual for nomads to travel alone. But then they wouldn't leave their dead just lying on the trail like that."

"So now what, we just wait and see if he wakes up?"

"Yes, unless you have a better idea." Jigme looked at her pointedly, letting her know that he did not think she could have a better idea. And he was right of course, she did not have a better plan. The trail was too narrow to go around the sleeping nomad without the risk of waking him up.

They did not have to wait long. The bright morning sun soon had the man showing signs of waking up. As he began to get up, the snow shook off his body. Sherab recognized the sleeping bag an instant before John's face came into view.

"John!" Sherab screamed. Her sudden voice startled him so much that he tripped on the sleeping bag he was trying to climb out of. Her heart raced with joy even as her mind tried to convince her of this impossibility. John kicked away the sleeping bag and faced the direction of her voice.

"How in hell did that white man get ahead of us?" Jigme said with a big grin.

Sherab came bounding out of the snow, racing towards John. She thought she was either dreaming or had died and gone to heaven.

"Sherab?" John shouted, running towards her.

"John!" she cried before leaping into his arms. They both fell, rolling onto the ground. He kissed her hungrily, not even allowing her the luxury of looking at his handsome face for a moment. Her hands brushed the back of his head, as a way of ensuring he really was there with her.

She sat up suddenly, the smile gone from her lips.

"Luhping?" she asked.

The joy of seeing John faded quickly at the mention of Luhping's name. He looked at Sherab and merely shook his head. Jigme limped up to them after John's negative answer.

"Ask him what happened Jigme. Ask him about Luhping." Sherab's voice began to break, as she understood what she did not want to accept.

John and Jigme spoke for a moment before Jigme returned his attention to Sherab.

"Luhping's dead Sherab. John walked most of the night, after she died. He must have passed within just a few feet of us during the night."

John sat up quickly then, and started speaking to Jigme in an urgent tone. Sherab moved aside to give him room.

"John saw the soldiers, they're on their way. Yesterday afternoon, they were about an hour away from him. He doesn't know how far they continued during the night."

"How many?" Sherab asked quickly. Jigme turned to John for the answer.

"He counted a squad of eight men," Jigme told her with an astonished expression. Jigme whistled at that number. "They aren't taking chances this time. Eight men?" he asked rhetorically. "He's lucky they didn't just drop down on him from a helicopter."

"Why didn't they?" Sherab asked him.

"Dunno. Maybe they only had one helicopter close enough. You did some good damage to it," Jigme said with a trace of pride. "Those soldiers won't risk marching at night. They don't know this area, so they'll go by their rulebooks. Now it's going to be a tight race. If we have the strength, we can keep going at night. But with this damn ankle, they'll gain on us during the day. If you two only knew how to get out of here, I would let you go without me."

Jigme seemed genuinely frustrated at his inability to let them go alone. His handicap might get them caught, and yet they were helpless without him.

"The first thing we have to do is lighten your load," Sherab told him. "Let John take some stuff out of your pack."

Jigme had the good sense not to object. After speaking with John, he transferred mostly the heavy food items out of his pack and into John's.

"You and the white man will bring me shame!" Jigme said. He smiled as he pulled his backpack away from John. Jigme spoke with a joke, but he seriously did not seem to want John or Sherab overloaded because of him.

The three of them continued along the trail for the rest of that morning. They seemed to be walking along a gigantic corridor now. The Himalayan peaks towered above them in every direction. Somehow Jigme kept them on course through this one pass that would lead them onto the other side of the breathtaking mountains.

Jigme's ankle kept their walking pace frustratingly slow. Sherab's mind screamed for them to hurry, to push a little harder. She saw the pain in Jigme's permanent grimace. Every step he took must have created his own personal hell. And if John had walked most of the night, perhaps this slow pace was all he could handle as well.

They stopped early for lunch. Sherab assumed Jigme called a stop for the lunch break because of his ankle more than because of hunger. They ate silently, saving their energy for the continual climb ahead of them. Eventually Sherab got them moving again, when it looked like Jigme was prepared to stay seated for a long time.

During the mid-afternoon, Sherab spotted the Chinese behind them.

"Jigme, look!" she said, pointing behind them. Presumably the same eight men John had seen the day before were now in sight. Sherab looked helplessly at Jigme. He seemed miserable as he looked at the advancing Chinese, and then at his own lame ankle.

"Let's keep going," he said hopelessly. "If we can stay ahead for a few more hours, we'll lose them in the night."

Jigme did not look like he could make it for the rest of the afternoon, much less the entire night. Sherab kept these dark thoughts to herself, not wanting to discourage their efforts.

Two hours later, their situation seemed grimmer. The soldiers were gaining on them rapidly. They must have seen their group some time ago, and were pressing their advance.

"Jigme," Sherab said breathlessly. "I don't think we can outrun them."

"No choice!" Jigme spoke through gritted teeth. Even when he was not walking, the pain now tortured him. "What do you want to do Sherab, fight them?"

"Maybe we'll have to Jigme! Come on, look at you! How much further can you go?" Jigme looked away, unable to answer her. "If we have to fight," she continued, "we should prepare now. Find some cover, do something. Not just exhaust ourselves on this open trail."

"I don't know how you and John managed to kill five soldiers before. Maybe it was surprise, maybe it was luck. But these are trained killers. What hope do we have in an open fight against eight of them?" Jigme's logic was equally strong to hers. Neither approach seemed likely to succeed.

"Sherab, Jigme," John said in a soft voice, almost a whimper. They turned towards him, and saw his face drained of color. His eyes were opened wide in horror as he stared at the trail ahead of them.

"Oh, shit," was all Jigme could say. Three soldiers were heading rapidly towards them from above. They were still a good distance away, but would soon be within firing range.

"That's it," Jigme said, as he sat down heavily. "I should have thought of that. They radioed ahead to the last checkpoint. Those soldiers are coming down from there. They've got us trapped."

John turned helplessly back and forth, watching the two groups of soldiers bearing down on them. Sherab's only instinct was to run from there, no matter where they went.

"Your plan's out Jigme. Let's try mine. Let's get off this trail now!" She dragged him to his feet, ignoring his cry of pain. She wanted to shock him, to snap him out of his defeatist thinking.

"Think Jigme. Right or left? Where can we get the farthest out, with maybe some good rock formations to hide behind?"

Jigme leaned on her, and blinked his eyes several times to clear his head. He examined both options before speaking.

"The right side's no good. This pass drops off at a cliff not far from here. The left might get us around back on the trail, but I don't know. I've never gone there before."

"Left then, let's go." She took his arm and started him walking off the trail. The deep snow ended up working in their favor. Jigme's limp did not slow them down much more than the snow already forced them to. All of them had to struggle for each step. The work exhausted each person quickly. Their legs sank up to their knees, and sometimes up to their thighs. Sherab took some comfort in knowing the soldiers would have the same difficulty.

It took just a few minutes for her to realize how wrong she was. Jigme stopped suddenly when he reached an impasse. Canyon walls loomed all around them, up to the cliff's edge where Jigme stood. They had to retrace their steps, and follow another route. The soldiers would see both sets of tracks, and avoid Jigme's mistake. As they retraced their steps, Sherab noticed how much easier it was to walk where three people had already trampled the snow. The soldiers would never have to break new paths like they were.

All eleven soldiers now pursued them in single file. With frightening speed the soldiers kept gaining on them. Jigme did an amazing job of keeping them going in and around canyons, rarely making mistakes. If Sherab had been leading their group, they doubtless would have been caught by now.

With the soldiers no more than fifteen minutes behind them, they reached the forced end of their journey. They came around a set of rocks, and faced a huge semi-circular cliff. The path that they had followed for the last several minutes did not have any alternate branches that they could backtrack and take. If they tried retracing their steps now, they would run headfirst into the soldiers.

Sherab studied their surroundings with a curious detachment. The soldiers could not have asked for a better setting to capture them. The walls on the far side of the canyon stood virtually vertical. Experienced rock climbers might have had a good time there, if not for the sub-zero temperatures. The remarkably flat ground leading to the canyon wall rose with only a slight upward grade as it reached the back wall. More startling was the absence of any large obstructions. Even if they chose to fight the soldiers, they had nothing to hide behind. The entrance they stood in now was too narrow for them to slip out of unnoticed. Just two of the soldiers could cover the entrance perfectly.

"Like lambs to a slaughter," she said quietly. Behind her Sherab could hear the soldiers shouting instructions to each other as they closed the distance between them.

An uncontrolled fury seized Sherab. These soldiers would not catch her.

"They'll kill us eventually," Sherab spoke urgently to Jigme. "So let's fight them now. I would rather die here than be tortured first and then killed."

Jigme shook his head and answered her angrily. "You don't know that they will kill us. We can't just throw our lives away, and kill a few soldiers on the way out."

"You know very well that I will die at their hands Jigme. And if they suspect that you know my story, you'll be killed just as surely."

"What's become of you Sherab? Now you're talking about useless killing. So what if you kill a few soldiers, it won't help you at all. You'll be wasting their lives for no purpose. Is revenge what you're after now?"

Sherab surprised herself and pushed the weakened Jigme. He stumbled, and then his ankle gave way underneath him. He fell backwards in pain while Sherab bent down to him. She quickly took Yu's revolver out of Jigme's belt, kneeled, and took aim at the soldiers.

"Wait Sherab!" John said quickly, putting a hand on her shoulder. She looked up at him, flashing an angry look. Not even John could dissuade her determination to fight. John spoke quickly to Jigme for a translation of what he was saying.

"He says we should head for the canyon wall," Jigme told her. "After you fire your first shot, we'll all be killed in the open like this. Let's try to get to the canyon wall, there might be a little bit of cover at least."

Sherab hesitated a brief second after hearing Jigme's translation. She nodded, and returned the pistol to him. She then headed into the enclosed canyon. John pulled Jigme to his feet, put the guide's arm around his neck, and tried to run with him. Sherab broke a trail ahead of them. Walking side-by-side, Jigme and John could not take advantage of her trail. They made faster progress when John went ahead of Jigme, breaking in the path even more.

They advanced to within twenty feet of the back wall before one of the soldiers spoke from behind. He did not shout, which made the nearness of his voice that much more frightening. Sherab turned warily, and saw the officer approaching them perhaps thirty feet away. His men fanned out in a semi circular line, roughly symmetric to the canyon wall. They were boxed into a circle now, with the canyon on one side, and the soldiers on the other. The officer spoke again.

"There's nowhere to run, give yourselves up peacefully."

Sherab could not take her eyes off the lead soldier. She noticed that the officer's hands were extended towards them in a placating way, as if not to alarm them.

"Why haven't they just shot us Jigme? Why isn't this soldier carrying a gun? John is even holding a rifle!"

Jigme looked puzzled as well by this strange behavior. She studied the officer, and noticed sweat on his brow. He had just finished a long hard march, it would be normal for him to have worked up a sweat. Yet she could not help but feel this was a nervous sweat. Something in his eyes told her that all was not quite right.

The officer's eyes never left them. Sherab looked at the soldiers behind him, and noticed several of them kept glancing upwards, behind her. She did not want the officer to know she was on to something, so she locked her eyes with his.

"Jigme, casually look behind us. The boys back there are nervous every time they look up."

A moment later, Jigme let out a long, low chuckle. He walked up beside Sherab after removing the pistol from his belt. His approach caused another flurry of words from the very nervous officer now.

"You do not have a chance against us. Please don't make us gun you down mercilessly!"

"Take a look yourself Sherab. These soldiers are not going to shoot us." Jigme spoke in a hushed voice, not wanting his words to carry over to the officer.

Sherab risked a look behind her. "There's nothing there, just rock and snow ... oh." She understood then. The peaks of the canyon walls had huge overhanging snowdrifts. The near vertical walls had accumulated blowing snow all the way up to their snow topped peaks.

"Avalanche," she said to Jigme.

"You got it. They shoot their big guns, we all get buried together."

"This is a stalemate then," she said. "We have guns, and we'll use them if they try to take us without their guns. That will kill all of us. This is just like the nuclear showdowns between super-powers."

Jigme relayed their conclusion to John. The officer approached a few more steps. Smiling, John raised his rifle and pointed it directly at the officer. Most of the soldiers behind the officer immediately aimed their guns at John. The officer held his hands up at his men, trying to calm them down.

"Back off," John said, without removing his sights from the officer. Jigme translated in a commanding tone to the officer, who complied immediately. John lowered his rifle then, to the relief of the visibly shaken officer.

"Jigme, there's a shelf about one hundred feet on your left," Sherab whispered urgently. "I think we might be able to hide under it, if there was an avalanche."

"Good idea Sherab," Jigme smiled. "You're crazy but you have guts."

"Nice and slow," she said. "Let's gradually move there. Tell John what we're doing."

They sidestepped to their left. An intricate dance developed between them and the soldiers. With every step left, the line of soldiers behind the officer compressed itself to the left. The far right side slowly opened up as the three fugitives made their way left. The officer followed along with them, not understanding what they were up to.

"How much further, Sherab?" Jigme asked, without turning his eyes away from the surrounding soldiers.

"We're half way," she told him, just as she realized the mistake they had made. The officer followed Sherab's gaze, and saw the protective shelf. Unfortunately for them, the intelligent officer instantly understood the plan. He barked orders to the men on the far left, who immediately broke into a stumbling run towards the shelf.

"Shit!" John yelled. He pointed his gun at the officer and began screaming in English.

"Pull your men back, NOW!" Jigme translated in an urgent tone. The proud officer merely stared at John. Only a slightly quivering lower lip betrayed his intense fear. He stared John down, gambling that he would not shoot. Now the officer knew that John was aware of the danger of a gunshot in this area.

"Go!" John cried to Jigme and Sherab. Before they could understand what he meant, John raised his rifle above the officer's head and fired five rapid shots. In the confusion of running men, several soldiers dove for cover. A rumbling could be heard overhead. Sherab did not dare look up, she simply turned to run to the nearest wall.

"Move!" John shouted to Sherab and Jigme. John grabbed Sherab's arm and pulled her towards the wall as he ran. The three of them raced towards the wall. Sherab found a spot where the wall seemed to bulge out. Far from a protective shelf, but it was the best they had. The low rumble had increased its pitch to thunder as the ground shook underneath their feet. Sherab looked back, and saw Jigme had only covered half the distance to the wall.

"Jigme!" she cried. John turned and instantly stepped out after the guide.

"No John!" Sherab shouted above the deafening noise. She clutched at his arm, but he shook her off. John made one step away from the wall before her arms wrapped around his throat as she jumped on his back. They both fell into the snow. John got onto his hands and knees and looked at Jigme. Sherab saw fear mark the guide's face while he hobbled as quickly as he could through the deep snow.

John scrambled to get up, wanting to try to get him once more. Suddenly a burst of red exploded out of Jigme's chest as his body flew face forward. The officer stood directly in line behind the fallen guide. He seemed oblivious to the men trying to run frantically from the falling wave of snow. Cool and calm, he accepted his fate. With his pistol still in his outstretched hands, he moved slightly to aim in Sherab and John's direction.

Like a great white fist, the first of the snow hit. The officer did not simply get buried, he was struck down and crushed by tons of falling snow. He simply disappeared from view in the blink of an eye.

The main overhang of snow at the top of the wall fell first. Falling through the air without resistance, it reached the ground well ahead of the rest of the snow. It struck the ground approximately twenty feet from the wall, where the officer once stood. Next came the larger mass of snow, which had accumulated along the wall's face. It slid down the wall, starting with the upper, heavily packed snow. As this upper layer descended, it hit the lower, slower moving snow. The result was a gradual snowball effect, with a large, growing mass of snow accelerating down the steep canyon walls.

With a flash, Sherab now understood why the ground around them was so free of obstructions. The spoon-like canyon walls naturally accumulated huge amounts of snow when the wind blew. Periodically, it had to shed its overload of snow in an avalanche. The ground probably did have just as many rocks as other parts of the surrounding terrain. Only, they never saw the bottom. Countless layers of hard packed snow covered any traces of the true ground's rocky nature. Similarly, the ground's slight grade could be attributed to the falling snow being highest near the wall, and gradually rolling off into a slope.

The first of the wall's snow struck John's shoulders and head as he tried to get up. His body was flattened against the ground. Sherab felt instant panic as the snow held him in its vice-like grip. She grabbed his jacket and pulled his body back towards the wall. At first the snow refused to release its grip on his head. John managed to get his hands underneath him and pushed away while Sherab pulled at him with all her strength. John's face tore against the hard packed snow crystals as his head finally pulled free of its frozen prison.

He rolled to the wall, stood, and covered Sherab with his body. The world under the wall's bulge became black. A solid wall of rushing snow surrounded their tiny space as the main mass of snow reached the ground. The falling curtain of snow muffled the thunderous noise of the avalanche. They were no longer part of the outside world, now they had their own universe in this cramped space that they huddled in. The rush of snow seemed to go on forever.

Suddenly the wall of snow around them imploded. With a rush, the snow invaded their private sanctuary. John had covered Sherab's body, in order to protect her. Instead, as the snow rushed in, his body crushed hers against the unforgiving rock wall. His arms pushed against the wall, but he only managed to resist a few seconds before the weight of the snow threw his body against hers. The air escaped from her lungs in a rush.

"This is the end," she thought, thankful to at least have John with her.

# Chapter 17

As suddenly as it had begun, the thundering avalanche ceased. The dead silence could not mask the echoing roar John still heard in his head. He and Sherab took rapid, shallow breaths inside their snow coffin. What little air had been trapped with them instantly grew stale. He could not take in enough air to speak, but only enough to puff out little breaths of air into the snow surrounding his face.

Sherab moved slightly, her body rubbing against his. That small movement made him realize how very much alive they still were. When his arms had failed to hold him up against the snow, they had been thrown upwards. He now stood in the snow, with arms extended towards the sky. He tried moving his arms, but they were too packed in. His fingers began to dig then, like little machines they scratched out the snow around them. He remembered tunneling inside snow forts as a child, digging away at the snow much like he did now. Only then, his entire body was not held captive by an avalanche's remains.

In his childhood, John and his friends would dig snow tunnels towards each other. The surprise of seeing a friend's hand pop into his tunnel as the two of them met always remained a thrill. Much like two tunneling friends, his hands slowly worked their way towards each other. His head began to swim dizzily from lack of oxygen when his hands found each other. Clasping them together, he had much more strength to apply overhead. He began to scrape his linked hands against the snow roof. Each swing of his arms required enormous efforts. His upper body gradually began to have some play as he packed the surrounding snow more tightly. Unfortunately he also applied considerable pressure against Sherab, and felt her squirm each time he crushed her.

The depth of the overhead snow could have been fifty feet for all John knew. He could not believe his luck when he felt his hands break through into loose fluffy snow. He tried to tell Sherab, but only managed to wheeze a little louder. His hands began tossing small fistfuls of snow out of the newly formed hole on the surface of the snow pile. For a while the snow fell back in at the same rate that he tossed it out. But then the hole began to widen, and most of his forearms were free. He jerked and pushed his elbows downwards until his hands could dig at the snow closer to their heads. Never had his own head felt so wonderful as when his right hand finally touched it.

His head shook from side to side now, finally letting precious oxygen into their frozen, would-be grave. He stopped digging, and breathed in the cold, sweet air. John's arms ached from so much overhead work, he longed to bring them down against his body. Sherab worked her head free enough to turn her face upwards, giving her more access to the fresh air.

After he had rested his arms for a while, John resumed clearing the snow around them. When he had worked down to his shoulder level, Sherab managed to free her arms and joined the effort. A few minutes later they were pulling their legs out of the snow. Their backpacks were lodged into the snow, so they slipped their arms out of them before successfully pulling themselves clear. John lost a boot to the clinging snow, and had to dig a little more to retrieve it.

John and Sherab brushed the snow off each other, and stood to survey the scene around them. The avalanche had washed all traces of the human struggle that had taken place there. The new layer of snow blended in perfectly well with the pristine whiteness of the surrounding terrain. Not one soldier could be seen, all of them were lost under the tons of newly fallen snow. The avalanche had struck just a few feet ahead of where they now stood, and had cascaded downward towards the canyon floor. Only near the end had it reached a critical height at the wall itself, and began filling in the spaces against the wall. Miraculously, the snow had only covered them by a couple of feet. Another two feet, and John's hands never would have broken through the surface. He shuddered at the thought of how close they had come to asphyxiation against this canyon wall.

Sherab and John took stock of their situation. His face was still bleeding from the scrapes against the snow when his head had first been trapped. Sherab examined him, but from the look on her face he knew none of the scratches were deep enough to cause her worry. His head felt cold, making him realize that he had lost his hat. That might become a serious problem in this kind of climate. Next came the backpacks. Neither was torn, they still had all their supplies. More than they needed in fact, since John had transferred so much out of Jigme's pack. They had lost Yu's pistol with Jigme, but they still had the Chinese rifle. All in all, they had fared quite well given the magnitude of the disaster.

"Are you ready to go?" he asked Sherab.

"Go," she nodded. She swung her hands around, palms held upwards. She was asking in which direction to go. In their last race against the soldiers, Jigme had led them through many turns, canyons, and rocky patches of ground. Neither of them had any idea where the trail was relative to their current position. To make matters worse, the sun would set soon. Almost every night the wind blew, and tonight it would wipe out any chance they had of retracing their footsteps.

"Let's try to follow our footsteps as long as we can," he told Sherab, indicating the footsteps they had just made as an example.

The newly fallen snow in the canyon sucked at their bodies more than the older, packed snow. Every step they took sunk their legs in deeply. They waded through the snow rather than walking on it. Although the canyon was quite small, it took them almost an hour to fight their way out of it. Cold, wet, and shivering in the evening dusk, they called it quits for the night.

They took out some food, and set it aside. Both of them had the same thoughts of warmth in the sleeping bag. They lay down facing each other. John reached for the food, and brought it between them. He took a piece of dried fruit, and dangled it near her lips. She smiled, and opened her mouth. He put the fruit inside her mouth, but then pulled it out quickly as she tried to shut her mouth around it. Her laughter sounded more beautiful then the greatest symphonies in the world. He played with her again, and this time she bit his hand in her hurry to grab the fruit. Somehow, they managed to ignore all the tragedy behind them, and the danger ahead of them. They stole a few precious moments for themselves on this night, oblivious to the world around them. They laughed and ate for less than half an hour before their exhausted bodies simply clung to each other and fell asleep.

Before falling asleep they had arranged the backpacks near their heads as a partial shelter from the wind. This precaution did not protect John's bare head sufficiently. He woke up during the night with a pounding headache, and a near-frozen ear. He was lying on his right side, curled up against Sherab. That left his other ear exposed to the night's cold winds and subzero temperature.

He tugged on Sherab's shoulder, and managed to turn her around without waking her. When she faced him, he lowered his head against her chest, and felt relief as her arms instinctively covered his head in a hug. He slept that way the rest of the night, with his head nestled in her arms.

The next morning, John kept his eyes shut when he woke up. Sherab's hand brushed through his hair, stroking his head soothingly. He was not ready to face the day, and dared not move for fear of breaking the spell. After a moment, he could not suppress a small smile on his lips.

"John!" she said laughingly, with a small slap on his head.

"Good morning Sherab," he said, and kissed her.

They ate their breakfast quickly, knowing that they had to get going soon. The missing hat problem had to be solved, John had learned that during the night. He rummaged through their packs, looking for some substitute for a hat. The best he came up with was the cotton sacks they used to carry the dried food. He topped off each sack, and managed to empty one of them. The sacks had drawstrings to close them. He could use these to tie the sack over the top of his head. The small opening did not fit over his skull. Once torn, it slipped over his head easily. The result must have looked ludicrous, for Sherab could not stop giggling as he tied the drawstring under his chin. John felt behind his head, and noticed the sack sticking up several inches above his skull. He was glad not to have a mirror, for the sight of his strange chef's hat might have embarrassed him to the point of removing it.

"Stop laughing at me!" he told Sherab in mock anger. He flattened his 'hat' against his head as much as possible.

Dark gray clouds covered the sky that day. The lack of sun added an extra chill to the already frigid morning. As he had feared, the winds during the night had obliterated their tracks. They stood at the mouth of the canyon, trying to get their bearings. No landmarks looked familiar, all of the surroundings melded into a uniform mixture of rock, snow, and mountain peaks. Without Jigme's guidance, they were hopelessly lost.

"I guess we need to try to head uphill as much as we can," he told Sherab. John used his fingers to illustrate a climbing motion. She nodded grimly, understanding how weak a plan they had.

By midmorning, the blizzard foreshadowed by the overcast sky struck with a fury. The air seemed very still throughout the early morning. Then suddenly a strong wind picked up, and blew swirling snow around them. When the actual snowstorm began, their visibility dropped to near zero. They felt their way slowly through the blinding snow, making sure never to let go of each other's hand. Half an hour after it began, they stumbled into a large boulder. John had to shout above the screaming wind to be heard.

"Stop here!" he yelled at Sherab. "No go!" he repeated, shaking his head.

They sat at the base of the rock surrounded by a flickering wall of snow. The boulder offered poor shelter at best, but it had to be better than being fully exposed in the open areas. Sherab pulled out the sleeping bag, and almost had it torn out of her hands by the fierce winds. John held down one edge while she unrolled it and slid into its protection. He followed her in, and placed the backpacks to form a small cove for their heads near the rock. This gave them a small pocket of relatively undisturbed air to weather out the storm.

The storm lasted throughout the day. Occasionally they had to scoop out the accumulated snow from their little alcove. Twice John's body became so cramped that he stood up to stretch. The buffeting winds almost knocked his numbed body to the ground each time. He quickly settled back down with Sherab, and waited impatiently for the weather to clear. Despite the howling wind, they eventually fell asleep that night.

In the morning, a death-like stillness provided a sharp contrast to the previous day's fury. John lifted his head, shaking off the snow that had covered them during the night. The world was now a much more uniform white. Most rock faces were at least temporarily wrapped in smooth white blankets.

"We've got ourselves a real winter wonderland," he mumbled to himself sardonically. The sound of his voice woke Sherab, making her stir in the sleeping bag. She sat up, brushing the snow off herself much like he had done.

"Good morning," he said with a smile.

"Good morning John," Sherab answered automatically, as her eyes scanned the new look of the surroundings. He pulled out Yu's canteen and swallowed some ice-cold water. Each night they stuffed snow into the canteen, and placed it at their feet under the sleeping bag. By morning the snow had melted into slushy, near frozen water. They ate a hurried breakfast, and broke camp as early as possible. After a day of inactivity they were eager to make some progress.

Progress turned out to be slow. The new blanket of snow had covered many of the smaller rocks, causing them to trip and stumble all morning. By lunchtime, their ankles were bruised and battered, but neither of them had any serious injury. They deliberately had kept a slow pace to avoid a potentially lethal injury like a twisted ankle. Jigme's accident near the helicopter had taught them well the value of walking cautiously.

The worst part of their long march was not knowing if they were headed in the right direction or not. For all they knew, the path might end against a wall of rock or at the edge of a deep ravine. To remain in place meant death. To walk meant a slim hope of survival.

Sherab began to tire in the afternoon and John found himself playing Jigme's role of walking ahead of her. Subconsciously she kept plodding on in order not to let the twenty-foot gap between them widen any further. Strangely enough it motivated John also, as he tried to maintain a distance between them. Together, yet separated, they made good progress in the afternoon, despite the rough ground conditions.

John began to think that they should take a short break when the snow fell apart underneath his feet. His heart leapt into his throat as his body went into a freefall. Before he had time to truly panic, he landed hard on his back in a flurry of ice and snow. His back was bent awkwardly over the pack as he fought to regain the wind that had been knocked out of him. His neck had been hurt when his head whipped down over the backpack. The pack might have damaged his neck and back, but it saved his head from slamming on the icy shelf he had landed on.

John's mind still had not figured out what happened when Sherab's panicked face stuck out over the edge of the precipice.

"John!" she shouted. "John OK?"

"I think so," he called out to her weakly. He rolled onto his side to give his back a rest while he caught his breath. Judging by Sherab's face above him, he had dropped about ten feet through the snow. The shelf he landed on measured approximately five feet in width. He crawled the extra foot over to the edge and peered down. His hands instantly clawed at the ice as he dragged himself away from the terrifying view below. The snowstorm had filled up the ledge he was on, but it had no effect on the deep crevasse near him. He lay on the brink of death, several hundred feet below him.

"Sherab!" he called out. "Be careful! This is a really deep hole!" He cursed at their lack of communication as she gave him an inquisitive look.

"Can you see?" he asked, pointing over the edge of the shelf. She looked where he pointed and nodded gravely. He pushed his hands towards her, signaling her to back off.

"No John, Sherab help," she called back to him, unmoving. Fine, he thought, as long as she stayed where she was, she should be OK. John dug his feet into the rocky wall, trying to get a foothold to help him climb upwards. His backpack swung heavily behind him as he tried and failed to climb.

"Sherab! I'm going to throw you my backpack!" His movements made her understand more than his words could. Perhaps if he lost the bulky weight, he had more chance of making it up the near vertical wall.

The next three seconds dragged by in slow motion. As he swung the pack upwards, the rotating movement caused his right leg to slide forward. He threw with his right arm, but the loss of balance made him throw the pack straight up instead of angling it towards Sherab. She grabbed for the pack anyway, for it was just within her reach. He wondered if her mind screamed to let the pack go even as her hand instinctively clutched it. Like a batter going for a sucker pitch, Sherab's outstretched hand found the pack. She was already off balance when the weight of the pack dragged her forward. She bent over, digging her heels into the soft snow to stop her forward motion. Her boots failed to find a grip, and slid out from under her. She fell into a sitting position on the edge of the wall, until the backpack swung down and yanked her into the air.

John watched all of these events with detached fascination. From the moment she reached for the pack, the end was predictable and inevitable. Backpack, snow, and woman all came tumbling down towards the edge of his ice shelf. He jumped forward, trying to tackle her falling body football-style. She spun as she fell, and only his arm managed to wrap around her waist as he threw himself forward. He clutched at her coat as his body mass and momentum struggled to overcome her motion towards the edge of the narrow ice shelf. They fell into a heap near the edge of the shelf. By now Sherab's hand had released the pack, which sailed merrily down the ravine.

"Sherab, are you alright?" he asked her urgently, studying her face for signs of severe pain.

"Ok, John," she answered, still somewhat in shock.

"I thought I might lose you!" he told her, as relief washed over him. He kissed her hungrily, thankful to still have her with him. She must have felt some of the same emotions when he fell, for she fervently responded to his kiss.

Sherab suddenly pulled her head away from his. "No backpack," she said.

The scope of their loss started sinking in then.

"No sleeping bag," he answered. "The food!" John added after a moment of hesitation. His head was reeling with the implications of what had fallen over the cliff. Most of the food had been in his pack. They had about a day's worth of food in Sherab's pack. And now they would spend the nights without the warmth of the sleeping bag. Not to mention they were stuck on a shelf ten feet below ground level, he thought to himself.

"Oh Sherab," he said, pulling her against him, "how are we going to get ourselves out of this mess?" She did not answer, but simply accepted his arms around her and leaned against him limply.

It was Sherab who first broke their gloomy clutches in order to find a way off the shelf. Much like he had done, she searched for footholds in the wall, and tried climbing up in crab-like motions. She was two feet off the ground now, having found jutting stones to support her weight. John came up behind her just as she took another step up. Before she could lose her balance, he awkwardly pushed up on her buttocks. A grin appeared on his face at the thought of how silly this must look. Impulsively he squeezed the buns he was holding in his hands. A surprised squeal escaped her lips as she released her hold on the wall. She fell backwards, landing on him as he went down as well.

John could not help laughing, but Sherab did not find much humor in his antics.

"John!" she said with genuine anger. "No play! Sherab go up!" She slapped hard at his thigh when he could not bring his laughter under control.

"Owww!" he yelped at the sting of her slap on his frozen leg.

"Help Sherab now," she said seriously. Sherab stood near the wall and extended her foot to him.

"OK, fine," he told her, not quite hiding his smile. He laced his fingers together for her to step into. She leaned heavily into his hands as she clambered up the wall. John was holding her foot at chest-height when she could no longer find a place for her other foot.

"My shoulder, Sherab," he called out through gritted teeth. She looked down at him and he nodded his head towards his left shoulder. Her foot pawed at him before finding its place on top of his shoulder.

"Now the other one," he told her, pushing up with his hands. Like some circus act, she now stood on his shoulders while he rested his arms. Sherab's arms could reach over the lip of the wall, but she did not have any handholds to pull herself over. They wobbled unsteadily for about a minute, letting his arms recover from her weight. John's shoulders began to ache, and he knew it was time for the final push.

"OK, Sherab. I'll use my hands on your feet and push up. You try to go up, Sherab."

He braced his legs to ready himself for the extra push. She stepped onto his hands, and he began forcing upwards with all his strength. At first, nothing happened. Then she must have caught some minimal support with her hands, because John managed to push her up over his head. His arms and legs began to tremble with the effort. He was afraid he might let go at any moment, and she was not moving anymore. Suddenly one of her legs left his hand and stretched up over the edge of the wall. If he let go now, she would fall straight down.

Both his hands now worked on the remaining leg, allowing him to push her even higher. With a final kick down into his hands, she jerked herself over the edge. John's arms came down instantly, and he breathlessly fell into a sitting position. His shoulders and arms ached from the effort of holding and lifting her weight.

Before he could start thinking of his own escape from the shelf, Sherab called down to him.

"Take, John," she said as she threw him one end of a rope. John stared at the rope dumbly, wanting to kick himself for not thinking about it before. They would still have his pack if he had thought of Sherab taking the rope out of her backpack and simply pulling up his.

She could pull up a backpack, but he thought he would pull her down if he put his weight on that rope. He stood up, and explained his fear to her by pretending to pull on the rope.

"John pull," he said, with a fake yank, "Sherab come down." He pointed to the shelf he stood on.

She shook her head. "Wait. Wait, Sherab say 'come'." She held her hand out at him, palm extended outward. John was skeptical, yet he had no choice but to wait for her.

John heard her working above him, but had no idea what she was doing. After a few minutes he called up to her.

"Everything OK, Sherab?"

"John wait!" she answered impatiently, and breathlessly, he noticed.

A few more minutes passed before she called to him again.

"Come John," she called from above. The nervousness in her voice did not inspire him to use the rope very much. He cautiously tugged on it, wondering how she planned to hold his weight. Sherab felt his tugs, and called out again.

"Come John. Sherab help!"

John placed his foot into a small recess in the wall, and took the rope with one hand only. His other hand grabbed at the wall until it found a solid place to hold. He wrapped the rope around his hand, taking up the slack, and pulled himself up another step. A few more steps, and he was past halfway up the wall. The rope was the one solid hold he relied on while looking for grips in the wall. He never had to put his full weight on it, but its presence allowed him to always move up in search of new holds.

John could almost reach the top of the wall when a rock crumbled under his foot. He completely lost his grip on the wall. The rope squeezed his hand and wrist painfully as he fell. Only because it was wrapped around his hand so many times did it not slip out when he fell. He heard Sherab cry out in pain when his full weight bounced on the rope. John's hand and shoulder felt enormous pain from the sharp pull. There was no longer any point in trying to avoid using the rope, speed became the main concern. He swung his other hand onto the rope, and began kicking himself upwards off the wall. Hand over hand he pulled himself up and over the edge.

At first he could not even see Sherab. Without bothering to untangle himself from the rope, he ran forward until he saw her in the snow. In preparation, Sherab had dug herself a hole in the snow. From inside the hole, the rope was painfully tied around her waist. He had turned her into a human snowplow when he put his weight on the rope. The rope had dragged her perhaps three feet along the bottom of her enlarged hole, crushing her body into the hard packed snow as she was pulled.

Sherab's body was doubled over at the waist. She looked up at him, her face a mask of pain. John jumped in beside her, and tried to untie the rope from her waist. The knot had tightened too much, his frozen fingers could not budge it. He reached behind her and retrieved the knife from her pack. The knife's blade easily slit through the rope. John sat down, and pulled her bruised body onto his lap.

"Thank you Sherab," he whispered to her, as he gently hugged her body. After a moment, she got to her feet, and looked around them.

"John, look!" she said excitedly.

He quickly got up to see what she pointed at. His eyes could not see anything out of the ordinary. He was about to turn and ask her for clarification when he felt a hard pinch on his bottom.

"Owww!" he said again, in surprised pain.

"Now Sherab play!" she said triumphantly. "Sherab up, John up. Now play!" With that, she slapped his bottom soundly and quickly crawled out of the hole. John was too stunned to move. She stood above him with her arms crossed, smiling proudly.

"Sherab hurt John," he said painfully, limping towards her. Her smile vanished as she bent closer to him.

"John hurt?" she asked with concern.

He lunged for her arms then, wanting to drag her back into the hole. She screamed in delight and fear, and threw herself backwards out of his reach. Lying on her back, she kicked at the snow, showering him with it and not allowing him to come closer.

"Enough!" John called out in defeat, his arms sheltering his face from the snow. "I give up."

She stopped kicking, and looked up at him between her raised knees. She hesitated, her head cocked to the side, trying to search for her words.

"Sherab, yes, John, no?" she asked with a serious, menacing look. She seemed ready to start her kicking on a moment's notice.

John could not help but laugh at her expression. "Yes, you win," he told her. "Sherab wins, John loses."

"Sherab win!" she repeated, this time with a smile on her face.

John jumped out of the hole, and crawled up to her. She stayed on her back, knees up and legs apart. He slowly crawled between her legs, and put his weight down on her. They kissed, and he felt her legs reach up and wrap themselves around his waist. For the first time since they entered this frozen wasteland, John felt the familiar physical desire work its way down his body. They continued kissing feverishly, even though they could not go further.

The sun had begun to lower on the horizon. Regretfully, John tore himself away from Sherab. Without a sleeping bag, they had to find some sort of shelter for the night. Perhaps a closed set of rocks could protect them from the wind, and help prevent their body heat from dissipating too quickly. John helped Sherab to her feet, and they resumed their aimless march in an unknown direction.

An hour later their path ended at the foot of a steep rock wall. They walked along the base of the wall for several minutes before Sherab pointed out their sleeping area for the night. Too small to be considered a cave, the recess in the wall would nonetheless provide them with some sort of shelter for the night.

They settled down to eat some supper in the evening twilight. Sherab's pack contained even less food than he had estimated. When he reached for a second handful of nuts, Sherab put her hand on his wrist.

"Tomorrow."

She was right of course, he needed to conserve their remaining food. With a hungry stomach, John curled up against Sherab for the night. He let her sleep against the wall in the back of the recess, while he covered her from the outside. Sherab may have slept a little bit because of the extra warmth of her position. But John did not think he managed to sleep at all. Each night seemed to grow colder, and that night was no exception. Without their sleeping bag, or even the old nylon wrap he had used several nights ago, the intense cold had no trouble in sapping the warmth out of their immobile bodies.

John's chattering teeth must have woken up Sherab. The sun had not yet risen, but they had to move on just to get warmed up. With a shivering hand, he reached for Yu's canteen. It seemed glued to the wall, John had to pull hard to dislodge it. Ice caked the back of the canteen. He examined it curiously, and then found the split in the thin canteen siding. The water had frozen solid during the night, splitting the canteen open. His gourd had fallen a few hundred feet with his backpack, which meant they would be eating snow from now on.

"One less thing to carry," John said glumly, tossing the canteen aside. Eating snow, when his entire body felt like it could cool down a refrigerator, turned out to be a most unpleasant experience.

They finished the last bag of food that morning. Still hungry, they headed off once more, before the break of dawn. Rather than retracing their steps, they followed the base of the wall in search of a new path. The sun began to rise when a new path rewarded their patience. 'Path' was perhaps too kind a word for the route they took. It was more precisely an area of surmountable obstacles. Countless rocks peppered the ground, in addition to larger boulders that had to be circumvented.

After a few hours, the path's descent became more pronounced. John stopped to try to consult with Sherab.

"We're heading downwards," he began, using hand motions to back up his words. "Are we heading back to Dingri, or Nepal? Which side of the Nangpa La are we on?"

Sherab understood his question, but seemed just as puzzled regarding their whereabouts. Cold, tired, and hungry, he thought, was not the best state to be in for such major decisions. Should they turn around, or continue and hope they had already crested the mountain pass?

"Dingri," Sherab finally decided, pointing ahead of them. She then pointed to the sun, now nearing its midday point in the sky. It rose in the sky from their right, which should mean they were facing north.

"I think you're right, we need to turn around."

They did not bother stopping for a lunch break. Without food, there was no point in sitting down just to get colder and to think about how good a steak would taste. What a strange thought, he realized. John had never been a big beef fan, but freezing up in these mountains without food made him crave a steak like never before. "How long before I would want it raw?" he wondered with dark humor.

By the time evening came, they knew that they had totally lost their bearings. Even though they tried to retrace their path, they never encountered the wall at the path's point of origin. With a start, he realized that they had also changed directions. They wanted the setting sun to be on their right, yet the lowering sun blinded them directly ahead.

Tomorrow morning they would use the sunrise to reorient themselves. Sherab's slow shuffle told him that she also was close to falling apart. John forced a bit of snow between his parched, cracking lips before lying down in the snow. He knew he was not drinking enough, but his teeth and throat resented the cold intrusion of the snow.

To his surprise, Sherab reached into her coat pocket, and pulled out two pieces of dried meat. Like a squirrel, she had stashed away a little bit of emergency supplies. John admired her willpower, to have known about the food's existence and resisted the temptation to eat it.

"Oh, Sherab, you're my savior!" He gleefully reached for a piece of meat, and chewed on it ravenously. She smiled at him, proud of her precious gift.

"Any more?" he asked with dismay when his piece disappeared far too quickly.

"No more." Sherab turned her pocket inside out to prove her point. He declined the remaining bite of her piece, and lay down in exhaustion.

They settled down against a boulder, which provided minimal shelter for part of Sherab's body. The sickening cold invaded John's body with renewed energy. During the night his head began to swim, leaving him with a detached feeling over his body. It was a comforting feeling, for he lost track of the pain and cold. He finally drifted off to sleep, as if he was in the warmest of beds.

John was thirteen years old. Summertime allowed him to stay up as late as he wanted. Thirteen was old enough to recognize and appreciate the liberty he had, but young enough to enjoy it guilt-free. While his parents tried to sleep in the summer heat, he settled down in the living room to watch the late movie every night. Last night he had gone to bed at 2:30 AM. He smiled at the thought that when he woke up around 11:30, his parents would be getting ready for lunch at their work.

His alarm's buzz intruded into his precious teenage sleep. The clock read 5:30 AM. Who had played this dirty trick on him? He buried his head under the pillow, trying to block out the insistent buzz.

"Wake up John!" he heard his mother shouting.

"It's summer, leave me alone!" he answered. She came in his room then, shouting at him to wake up. He tossed the pillow aside, ready to give her a piece of his mind. He recoiled in horror when he saw her. His mother's face was purple with rage as she stampeded to the side of his bed.

"Wake up!" she screamed at him in a monstrous voice. He watched her swing her arm back, palm open. His body seemed frozen in place. He could only watch her hand speed towards him, slapping his cheek hard enough for him to taste blood afterwards.

Before the full burning force of the pain could get its grip on him, the hand swung back again.

"Wake up John!" the purple monster shouted, as the hand shook the side of John's head once more.

"Please Mom, no!" he blubbered, still unable to move from the bed.

On the third swing, the hand held a butcher's knife.

"NO!" he screamed, sitting up in the snow.

"John!" Sherab cried, hugging him. His cheeks felt like they were on fire. Sherab pulled away from him, and he saw she had been crying profusely.

"John sleep, no wake up." Sherab shook his body, showing him how she had tried to wake his unresponsive body. "Sherab hit," she continued, indicating a fake slap with her hand. "Sherab scared."

"It's OK," he croaked in a barely recognizable voice. He lay back down, still frightened by the dream. John felt so tired that he shut his eyes to rest some more.

"No John!" she pulled him back up into a sitting position. "John walk. Now!"

He did not understand her urgency until he tried to get up. His legs no longer worked.

"I can't Sherab," he told her dumbly, still groggy from his unhealthy sleep. A detached part of his brain understood that he had not really been sleeping, but slipping into a deadly, frozen coma. The desire to sleep protected him from any fear of dying. There is no better way to die, he thought, than in your sleep.

"Yes John can!" Her voice had a touch of hysteria in it. She began roughly massaging his legs, while he sat and stared at her sleepily. Soon he grew uncomfortable, she began to hurt him.

"Stop Sherab, it hurts!"

"Hurt?" Sherab asked with her first, hopeful smile. She beat down on his legs even harder then.

John screamed, trying to push her away with his arms. Her hands kept digging into his muscles, firing shots of pain up to his waking brain. He managed to roll over into a crawling position, trying to get away from her. She stood then, and came to drag him onto his feet.

"Walk!" she shouted into his ear. She held his arm around her neck while he tried shuffling along in the snow.

"Please, can we stop?" he begged her when the circulation began to return to his legs with a vengeance. She force-marched him until the pins and needles in his feet made him collapse in pain.

Sherab gave him a few minutes for his feet to calm down, while she herself recovered from the exertion of saving his life one more time. John thought back to the old guide's words in Shigatse. He had said that John did not have the strength to make it across the mountains. The guide told him that he would have to rely on Sherab's strength. How much further could her strength get them, John thought despairingly.

To distract his mind from the pain, he reached over to the backpack and rummaged for possible bits of forgotten food.

Sherab jerked her head up in alarm when she heard his sudden burst of laughter. She could not understand his demented laugh until he handed her his thirty-day traveling permit.

"I'm no longer in Tibet legally!" he managed to gasp out between bursts of laughter.

She smiled when she read the Chinese document. He knew his uncontrolled laughter was not justified by this simple piece of paper, yet he could not stop himself.

"Walk now John," Sherab ordered him when he had mostly recovered from what now seemed like a private joke. She handed him the traveling permit. John simply released it in the wind, watching it flutter away as aimlessly as they walked among the mountains.

The ominously dark sky threatened them with another snowstorm. John searched for the sun behind the dark clouds, but could not make out any bright spot. He should have known, why would anything work in their favor in this godforsaken wilderness? With an uncertain memory of where the sun had set, he led the way towards what he hoped was Nepal.

The blizzard struck less than an hour after they departed. This time they did not have the option of stopping at a shelter to wait out the storm. Without food, time had become their worst enemy. John remembered the hidden crevasse he had fallen into after the last blizzard. That danger seemed insignificant now. The certainty of death by starvation in the coming days overshadowed the risk of falling over an unseen cliff.

The buffeting winds pounded them with snow pellets mercilessly. He gripped Sherab's hand like a vice. If they separated by more than three feet, they might never be able to find each other again. They tried stopping to rest once, but the cold wind had them moving again in less than five minutes.

By late afternoon, the dizziness overwhelmed John. The falling snow warped his sense of direction, and his starving body made him light-headed. He sat down in a heap, bringing Sherab down with him.

"Come John, please." She had to shout to be heard above the howling wind. Yet the pleading tone of her voice got him on his feet once more. She no longer had the strength to force him to go, she could only beg him to continue.

A few minutes later John's foot kicked a metallic object aside. He bent down hopefully, wanting to examine what they had found. His hand hovered an inch above the object. He blinked at few times, not wanting to believe what he saw. Sherab's curiosity overcame her. She pushed his hand aside and picked up Yu's discarded canteen. She stared at it in horror for a brief moment before letting it slide out of her hand.

John could almost see her spirit finally break, right before his eyes. Sherab stared at the canteen they had abandoned two nights ago. They had walked in a huge circle over the past two days. Her shoulders slumped downwards, and she let her arms hang limply at her side. He recognized the dangerous look in her eyes as she let herself fall into a sitting position. He wanted nothing more than to join her, and hold her until the snow buried them.

"Get up Sherab." Summoning all his strength, he began pulling her up to her feet.

"No John. No go."

"Yes go, Sherab, come."

He pulled her to her feet, nearly falling in the process. Instead of holding hands, they linked their arms together in mutual support. They must have managed another half hour of walking before Sherab fell again.

John stood over her, watching her peaceful expression as she lay in the snow. The mountains had beaten him long ago, now they had beaten her as well. He fell to his knees, full of sadness and relief. No more struggles, he thought, just blissful sleep.

Sherab began to shiver, her face no longer at peace. He lay down beside her, not really able to give her warmth.

"It's OK Sherab, the cold will go away. You'll like where we're going."

Soon he felt the familiar numbing sensation that had put him to sleep during the night. He turned his head to Sherab, and saw that her eyes were already closed. While he still had strength, he crawled over her body, and leaned down to kiss her one last time.

Her cracked lips trickled with blood after his kiss. The scarlet red blood began to thin out over her white cheeks as the snow melted and mixed into the blood. The sight of her blood released his tears of failure.

"I'm sorry my love, I did what I could." Her face remained impassive and unaware of his presence.

"Good night Sherab." The wind tore the whisper from his mouth before it could reach her sleeping ears. John put his head down on her chest and surrendered to the cold's soothing caress.

# Chapter 18

"Where do you think they came from?"

"I have no idea. They certainly strayed off all the known trails."

"Do you think she'll recover?"

"The skin damage isn't severe. We can't really know about any internal damage until she wakes up and talks to us. I guess that she'll be OK. At least she has a better chance than the man."

"Why? What's worse about him?"

"You can see more visible skin damage on his hands, for example. They said that when they found these two, he was covering her. So maybe his body heat protected her, I don't know."

"Look! Look at her eyes!"

"I think she's crying! Either she's having a dream or she can hear us. Miss? Can you hear me? Try to open your eyes."

The disembodied voices floated in Sherab's foggy thoughts as she struggled to open her eyes. John was in trouble. She did not completely understand what the two men were talking about. But she caught their reference to a man being in worse condition than her.

"John?" her voice croaked before she could unglue her eyes.

"What is she saying?"

"I don't know. She might be dreaming, or having a vision."

A dark, fuzzy shape appeared in front of her face as one of the men pried her eye open. She shook her head and blinked in pain from the intrusive fingers.

"She's waking up! Can you speak Miss?"

"Where's John?" she said hoarsely.

"That must be the foreigner's name."

"He's nearby Miss. We're taking care of him as best as we can. Can you tell me how you feel?"

"Nyandak, ask her who she is."

"There'll be time for that later. Let's heal her first."

"Sherab," she whispered, trying to fight off the sleep encroaching on her consciousness.

"Welcome Sherab." Nyandak told her softly. "You get all the rest your body needs. We'll be here to take care of both of you. If you need anything, just ask."

Her eyelids felt like they had bricks holding them down. She felt them flutter as she tried in vain to open them once more. She knew she should thank her benefactor, but could not find the strength to move her lips. She relaxed her body, and surrendered to its demand for sleep.

*** 

The fire's crackling reached John's ears before any other sensation registered in his waking mind. He turned his face towards the sound, and felt soothing warmth. Firelight danced and flickered behind his closed eyelids. How appropriate to dream of a warm fire while dying, he thought. Or perhaps he was already dead, in a Himalayan blizzard. The only flaw in the dream was the fire's smell. He would have expected hardwood smoke, but the smoke he inhaled had a faintly unpleasant odor.

His eyes snapped open when he heard a man's voice. John blinked rapidly, trying to adjust to the fire's brightness. A young Tibetan man grinned at him through broken and blackened teeth. He spoke a few sentences before John interrupted him.

"I don't speak Chinese or Tibetan, do you speak English?"

The young man turned his head and called out into the darkness. John began to take in more of the surroundings then. The man's voice echoed off the rock walls that enclosed the dark room. The cave seemed to extend about fifteen feet from where John lay, but he could not see how far it went behind him. The young man sat on a flat rock, one of many that had been arranged around the small fire pit. Now that John's eyes had adjusted to the firelight, he saw how the fire actually gave off a rather dim light. The fuel looked more like coal than wood.

Some sort of straw stuck out from underneath John's body. Although it stank of age and dampness, the bedding felt more comfortable to his abused body than the finest mattress. A heavy blanket, made from animal hide, covered his body warmly. As he reached down to lift the blanket, he noticed the bandages on his fingers. Grimy white linen wrapped each finger individually, on both hands. The first real sign of injury immediately made him think of Sherab.

"Sherab?" he asked the man sitting near him.  The man looked confused, unable to answer John.

"Sherab?" John called out to the room, before the man could find a way to satisfy his question. John tried sitting up, but could not quite manage such a big effort.

"Sherab is sleeping," a male voice told him from behind. A hand pressed down on his shoulder comfortingly, forcing John to relax.

"How is she?" John asked the man as he appeared in front of him.

The man's age successfully hid itself from prying eyes. On the one hand, his wizened face spoke of a full life comprising many decades. On the other hand, his sprightly movements belonged more to a twenty year old body. His piercing brown eyes had the depth and clarity of the old guide in Shigatse. Yet his gentle voice contrasted sharply to the old guide's irascible character.

"She woke up this morning for a little while. I think she's doing better than you, so don't worry."

"Who are you?" John's mind struggled to free itself from the fog of sleepiness that wrapped it like a shroud. He tried in vain to understand his new situation.

"I'm Dorje Gyatso. And you are John, from what I've been told."

"Yes, but who are the rest of you, where am I?"

"We are the Tibetan Freedom Resistance Fighters," Dorje announced proudly.

"Resistance fighters?" John asked rhetorically, "I never heard that Tibet had such a force."

Dorje's eyes clouded over angrily for a moment before returning to their more sedate look. His voice took on a determined, steely tone.

"We're not numerous, but the Chinese regularly feel the sting of our presence."

"What kind of actions does your movement do to the Chinese?"

"We raid their small military outposts mostly. Steal weapons, food. Kill soldiers. Destroy trucks and other equipment. They know we exist," Dorje said with a wide smile, "but they can't find us!"

Another man showed up beside them, with a steaming bowl held in his hand. Young and eager, he threw several questions at John in Tibetan.

"Nyandak thinks you should eat now," Dorje told him. John accepted the bowl of hot tea and the piece of tsampa gratefully. Nyandak pointed at John's hands, and jabbered to Dorje.

"He wants to know how your fingers feel. Nyandak is our doctor. He's not really a doctor, but he studied medicine for a year before being exiled into the mountains with us. We're lucky to have Nyandak with us, he is very smart. He's the one who tended to your frostbite."

"They feel like they've been burned," John admitted. "Just the pressure from this bowl makes them sting."

Nyandak smiled when Dorje translated the symptoms. He spoke encouragingly to Dorje.

"Nyandak says that's a good sign, you probably won't lose your fingers then."

"Lose my fingers?" John asked in alarm.

"They were badly frostbitten. Nyandak was worried about them. If you had felt no pain right now, he says the fingers might have had to come off before they spread infection to your arm."

"Tell him they hurt like crazy then!"

"Don't worry, I think you'll be fine in a few days," Dorje answered with a smile. "Here, let me help you sit up to eat."

Nyandak took the bowl while Dorje put a hand under John's back and pulled him by the arm into a sitting position. When the momentary dizziness left him, John took the hot bowl from Nyandak.

"I want to see Sherab," he said, beginning to stand up.

Nyandak heard her name, and spoke rapidly to Dorje.

"Nyandak doesn't want you to wake her, she needs her rest very badly."

By the time Dorje finished his sentence, John had already walked by him in search of Sherab. The cave's enormous size became clearer as he turned and surveyed the area. Perhaps fifteen or twenty people moved around the cave, busying themselves and trying not to stare at him. While John spotted a fair number of women, the majority of rebels were male. The ages seem to range from little more than teenagers, to adults around forty-five to fifty years old.

"Where is she?" he asked insistently. "I won't wake her, I just want to see her."

Despite Nyandak's protests, Dorje led John deeper into the cave. John saw her angelic face then, sticking out from under a warm hide. She really did seem fine, with her face sleeping peacefully. He awkwardly sat next to her, his stiff body protesting the difficult movements.

Dorje, Nyandak, and the rest of the group disappeared from John's world. All that existed lay before him, sleeping under warm covers. He reached out and cupped her face in his bandaged hand, gently stroking her cheek with his thumb. Like a disobedient child, he felt mildly guilty, but wildly excited, when her eyes fluttered open. Her eyes tried to focus on her surroundings.

"Tsampa," John told her, offering the dough and the steaming bowl in his other hand.

"John!" she gasped, her eyes opening wide in happy surprise. She struggled to her knees and threw her arms around him while John tried not to spill the tea bowl.

"I'm so happy to see you Sherab!" He hugged her with his free arm. She began to kiss him, and then stopped, looking guiltily over his shoulder.

John turned, only to see Nyandak walking away impatiently. The doctor shook his head, giving up on his uncooperative patients. Dorje stayed near them, but looked decidedly uncomfortable in witnessing their reunion.

"You two are lucky to be alive," he said, breaking the awkward silence.

"Can you tell us what happened? How did you find us?"

"One of our raiding parties got caught in the blizzard," Dorje began. "They waited out the storm in a small recess against a mountain wall. After the storm they found you two almost completely buried in snow."

"If that's the same depression in the wall we stopped at once, then we must have passed right by them during the storm!"

"They found you only a hundred feet away. If they had gone in any direction but straight towards you, you would have died out there. When they saw you were alive, they wrapped you in their sleeping hides, and mostly dragged you back here."

"How long did that take?" John asked. He remembered how hard the march in those mountains had been. He could not imagine dragging a pair of bodies through the snow on top of all the other difficulties.

"About a day and a half. They slept with you at night to keep you warm. They were very brave." Dorje's pride in his co-fighters displayed itself shamelessly on his grinning face.

"Not just brave, but incredibly kind," John answered. "I want to meet those people, and thank them for saving our lives."

"Now that you're both up, we'll have a celebration dinner tonight. You'll meet everyone then. And we have one other raiding party that is due back today. With any luck, you'll have the rare chance to see all of us together at once!"

Sherab's fingers rubbed John's palm as they held hands, sitting close to each other. Holding hands became so natural that he had not even noticed when she took his hand. Or had he taken hers? Dorje again seemed uncomfortable with even this simple display of affection.

"John," he began hesitantly, "I will leave you and Sherab to rest now. But I must ask you something. There are many men here, and few women. I know this is not fair, but could you restrain yourselves from being too affectionate?"

He must have seen the surprise on John's face, for he rushed on, trying to explain his request.

"This is a very small community, you have to understand. We are forced to live together all the time. Sherab is a beautiful woman, all the men have noticed that. And you..." He stopped suddenly, his eyes looking away in embarrassment.

"And I'm a white barbarian?" John asked with a smile.

Dorje's embarrassed smile answered his question. "Not a barbarian John, but different. And Sherab is Tibetan. These men …"

"I understand Dorje, you don't need to explain further. This problem exists everywhere in the world, not just in your cave. But I do love Sherab, I won't pretend otherwise. Out of respect for the others, of course we won't make a show out of our affection."

John paused a moment before continuing.

"Did you explain this to Sherab? I certainly can't."

Dorje spoke with Sherab. At first she seemed angry, but then resigned herself to his logic. Her hand slipped out of John's awkwardly as Dorje turned to leave them alone.

John shifted position so that his body hid hers from the rest of the group. His hand found hers again, and held it low and out of site.

"I love you Sherab," he whispered to her.

She pinned him down with her eyes, and whispered back to him. "I love you John."

"Tsampa?" she said with a smile after choosing to release him from her visual grip.

Without releasing her hand, he brought the bowl towards her lips. She tried to take it with her free hand, but he backed it away.

"No, I will feed you."

She smiled shyly, and let him put the bowl to her lips. Her eyes stared at him above the lip of the bowl and she sipped the warm tea. Sherab then tore a small piece of tsampa from his hand, and chewed on it ravenously.

"Now John."

He brought the bowl towards his mouth, but she stopped his arm this time.

"Sherab!" she said, taking the bowl from him.

"Wait!" he told her as she pressed the bowl near his smiling mouth. He could not drink while he was nearly laughing, or he would be wearing tea all over his shirt.

"OK," he said nervously, and accepted the bowl against his lips. The taste amazed him. Starvation could make a man appreciate food and drink like never before. As he drank his second gulp, he made the mistake of looking over at Sherab. John thought he had been the childish one until he saw her cross her eyes and stick her tongue out at him. He spit warm tea all the way up her arm as he burst into laughter. She pulled her arm back quickly in surprise, spilling more tea onto his lap.

Sherab put a hand over her mouth, desperately trying to smother the giggles pouring out of her. John stuck his face against his arm, doing the same. No doubt Dorje would not be impressed with their efforts at concealing their affection thus far.

Between the two of them, they drank three full bowls of tea and two lumps of tsampa. The warmth spread throughout John's body, making him feel more alive than he had been since leaving Shigatse. Tiredness began creeping into him, but he did not want to leave Sherab's side. They sat together for an hour, exchanging what few words they knew in common. But mostly just looking at each other, and touching hands as discretely as possible. When Sherab lay down, John almost surrendered to the fatigue and returned to his own sleeping mat.

A commotion at the cave's mouth disturbed his thoughts of sleeping. Several snow-covered men streamed into the entrance. The rebels near the entrance immediately surrounded the newcomers with shouts of joy and plenty of backslapping.

"The last group has arrived, we'll have our double celebration tonight!" Dorje told John excitedly, as he ran by to greet the new arrivals. One man stood out as the leader of the small raiding party. His voice boomed above the others as he proudly displayed a Chinese rifle and hand grenade. John felt nervous as the grenade was tossed around from one person to the next, each wanting to examine the new acquisition.

The young man seemed to enjoy the crowd of listeners around him as he described the raiding party's adventures. He gestured animatedly to enhance the appeal of his tale. His taller stature also helped him deliver his story to those around him. He turned this way and that, exciting the listeners young and old. His eyes captured every pair of eyes around him as he stared briefly at each onlooker without missing a beat in his monologue.

Even though John could not understand him, he could not help but look at the man's display with total attention. John had not even noticed Sherab getting up until she stood slightly in front of his seated body. The speaker's voice cut off abruptly. He stared in their direction, his mouth still open from the last word he had spoken. All the heads in the group turned to look in their direction.

Dorje stepped up to the man and began speaking to him, to explain their presence. The man simply ignored him and stepped forward towards them. Dorje was left with an unfinished sentence dangling in midair.

"Sherab?" the speaker asked. Alarms began ringing in John's head. "Sherab?" he pretty much shouted, an unbelieving smile forming on his lips.

Sherab literally squealed in excitement as she ran to the tall stranger. She threw her arms around his neck and began kissing his head. John stood up quickly, with a watermelon-sized lump forming in his throat. His eyes could not believe what they were witnessing. The now hateful man's arms crushed her body against his own, as his hands stroked Sherab's back. John took a step forward, fury rising into his blood. Then Sherab turned her face sideways, and John saw a look of pure joy in her face. More than seeing her kisses on the man's head, or seeing his hands on her, that joyous look viciously stabbed through John's heart with a twist of the knife. Sherab's look had been reserved for John exclusively up to this point. Seeing her shine with another man hurt more than death ever could.

John backed away a few steps then, stumbling blindly on some loose items as his eyes began to blur. The group had moved more into the center of the cave now, Sherab and the speaker holding hands and talking rapidly. She seemed so at ease to be near him, a fellow Tibetan who could understand her more than John ever could. A fresh pain in his stomach almost collapsed his legs. He fumbled along the wall towards the entrance, wanting to be anywhere but in this cave.

"John!" Sherab's voice sang above the rest. John was near the entrance, and took one more tentative step towards the freedom of the outside air.

"John!" she called again, her voice closer. Quickly wiping his eyes with his sleeve, John composed himself and turned around. She trotted towards him, dragging the smiling party leader by the hand. A gun butt might wipe that smile off his face pretty quick, John thought darkly.

"Jhampa!" she announced proudly, displaying the man at her side. John could not understand if he had been receiving her messages wrong all this time, or if she was hopelessly naïve, or simply cruel beyond words.

Jhampa stuck his hand out to John. John's mind shuffled through a few alternatives, like spitting in his face or kicking him in the nuts, before he took the proffered hand and shook it briefly. Sherab had enough sense to detect something was wrong.

"John?" she asked, extending her arm to him. John stepped back out of her reach, and noticed Jhampa also looking at him warily. Before, John had been nothing in Jhampa's eyes. Now the Tibetan looked at John as a potential enemy to Sherab.

Dorje came to their side then, blustering with excitement. He came between Sherab and Jhampa, and placed a hand on each of their shoulders. He spoke to them quickly and then turned to John.

"Come, the celebration feast will begin now."

Dorje pulled Sherab and Jhampa inside, and then took John by the arm. Sherab gave John a last worried glance over her shoulder as Jhampa led her deep into the cave.

"I'll sit with you during supper John. I'm the only who speaks enough English to keep you company!" Dorje had missed the entire ugly scene, and John felt grateful for it. His ebullience might help John cope with the hateful, hurtful feelings that threatened to drive him insane.

Sherab and Jhampa were already seated together by the fire when Dorje and John arrived. Dorje chose a free spot across the fire pit from Sherab. Through the haze of smoke, flickering flames and sparks, John saw them continue their happy, intimate talks. They seemed unaware that anyone else existed, much like Sherab and he had been moments before Jhampa had arrived.

"Tonight we have a very rare treat, fresh yak meat." Dorje's mouth made a slurping sound in anticipation of the coming banquet. His comment distracted John enough to tear his eyes away from Sherab and Jhampa.

"How do you people survive up here? Getting supplies must be an enormous problem."

"It can get very difficult at times. But mainly we trade with the nomads, and let them bring us the supplies."

"What can you offer them?"

"Guns, ammunition. We get lots of those."

From some of the stories John had heard about nomads, this particular trade did not strike him as especially wise.

"Aren't the nomads often violent? I've heard that many are no more than bands of thieves. Is arming them a good idea?"

"They're Tibetans. The more Tibetans that have weapons, the better off we'll be when our day comes."

"I don't mean to be insulting Dorje, but I just don't understand how the small Tibetan population could ever defeat the Chinese army."

Dorje looked at him pensively, the firelight dancing in his eyes.

"Stranger things have happened in history, John. But yes, you're right. We could never defeat China. But, we may one day have the strength to seize our own borders again. If world opinion continues to sway in our favor, then maybe, just maybe, the Chinese will decide that Tibet is not worth the political price of another invasion."

John had his doubts about such a possibility, but debating it would only lead to insulting his hosts. Before he could think of something to change the topic, a swell of appreciative murmurs rose from the people gathered around the fire. A heavily built, muscular man carried a large black pot towards a cleared area near the fire. A short, middle-aged woman followed closely behind him, giving sharp instructions. With a grunt the young man put down the cauldron. The hot liquid sloshed inside, with a small wave splashing over the edge. The diminutive woman swung her wooden spoon at the young man, catching him on the side of the arm.

The crowd roared at the sight, while the blushing man quickly made his escape to the back of the cave.

"Poor Gyan!" Dorje said when he recovered from his laughter. "He's the strongest warrior among us, but he has the misfortune of having his mother here with him!"

John smiled politely at the humorous situation, but could not muster the will to laugh. He thought he might never laugh again in this lifetime.

"Can you smell it John?" Dorje raised his head, sniffing the air. "Ngawang is a fine cook. We call her the best cook in the Himalayas!" He laughed at his own joke, as if he had just heard it for the first time.

"She may be the only cook, John!" he explained, when John failed to laugh.

"Yes, I got it Dorje. I'm sorry, I think I've not recovered from my exhaustion. That's why I'm having trouble laughing, I guess." John lied, but it seemed to satisfy Dorje.

"Don't worry, you can go to sleep soon. But you must eat with us first, we don't have yak stew very often."

The fire crackled loudly then, throwing a spark near Dorje and John.

"Do the nomads bring you your wood too? Or coal, or whatever it is you're burning, there." John kicked at the red ember near their feet.

"Wood?" Dorje said with a wide grin. "That's dried yak shit!" He laughed at John's ignorance then, and despite his dark gloomy mood, John could not help chuckling a little bit also.

"I thought it smelled funny," John told Dorje, causing him to burst into laughter again. John looked above the fire, and saw Sherab smiling at him. His smile vanished at the sight of her with Jhampa's held hand protectively in her lap.

John turned back to Dorje, and found him also looking across the fire.

"I have never seen Jhampa so happy," he told John with a smile. "Never could anyone have guessed that he would find his Sherab again. And for her to find him here! That's even more improbable." Dorje shook his head in amazement, totally unaware of how he was killing John.

"Jhampa is a great warrior, very smart. He leads teams well. He could end up being one of our great leaders one day."

John was seething by now, and did not want to hear another word about this Jhampa character. Fortunately Ngawang saved him by signaling he and Dorje to come get a serving of stew.

Without a glance in Sherab's direction, John followed Dorje over to the large pot of stew. Ngawang filled his bowl with the same large wooden spoon she had struck her son with.

"Thank you!" John said a little too loudly, not wanting to incur her wrath. She mumbled something to him in return before calling for the next small group to come fill their bowls.

"Oh God, this is delicious!" John told Dorje after his first spoonful.

"Did I tell you?" he beamed at John. "Ngawang is a great cook."

"Ngawang!" Dorje called out. She looked at them above the soup bowl she was in the process of filling. Dorje spoke loudly to her in Tibetan. John heard his name mentioned, which made her eyes briefly look over to him. She replied shortly, maintaining her expected bad humored behavior.

"What did she say?"

"I told her that you liked her stew, it made her happy."

"How can you tell?" John interrupted him.

He smiled, ignoring the comment. "She answered that you can get her a job in an American restaurant."

John smiled at this, and swallowed another spoonful.

"So what happens to us now?" he asked Dorje.

"Well, Nyandak thinks you need to rest here for a few days. But after that, we can escort you out of Tibet. It should take about three days to cross the border from here."

"I owe you so much Dorje. How can I ever hope to repay you?"

"The best thing you can do for us is spread the word about our situation here. Remind the world of Tibet's Chinese occupation."

Muyih flashed into John's memory then. He remembered Muyih's words so well. The one request Muyih had made to John was to let people know how most Chinese in Tibet are good people, trying to help. And now Dorje wanted him to say the opposite. John looked up to both of these great men, and wondered how war and politics could separate good people so easily.

Sherab's high-pitched laughter broke through his thoughts of Muyih. He looked at her through the flames in time to watch her cover her mouth to stifle her laughter. John had trouble swallowing, the lump in his throat had returned. He recognized so many of her mannerisms.

"Sherab seems to be as happy to find Jhampa as he was to find her." Dorje commented.

"Yes," John agreed. "In fact, you may only be escorting me out of Tibet. If things keep going like they are tonight, she may not want to leave."

Dorje chuckled at John's bitter comment. "I don't think so, her brother would never let her stay in these dangerous conditions."

John shakily dropped the spoon into his bowl. It splashed into the stew, spattering hot liquid onto his lap. A tremendous pounding in his temples kept him staring straight down into the bowl. He replayed Dorje's words in his head, not quite believing what he had understood.

"Are you alright?" Dorje asked, seeing his strange behavior.

"Brother?" was all John could get out of his mouth.

"Yes," Dorje answered. "Jhampa thought she was dead. After so many years, I doubt he would let her stay with us, and face death every day. Is there something wrong with that?"

John looked up at him then. "Jhampa is her brother?" he repeated in disbelief.

Dorje frowned in confusion. "Yes, of course he is. What did you think…" He broke his sentence off midway. His eyes suddenly lit up with understanding. A wide smile spread over his face as he now looked at John with disbelief.

"You mean, you thought Jhampa and Sherab were…"

John's reddening face lowered, confirming Dorje's thought before he could even finish his question. This time his laughter erupted loud enough to hurt John's ears. He spilled his stew while clutching his stomach. The rest of the group stopped their conversations and observed Dorje with a mixture of amusement and curiosity.

Dorje wiped the tears from his eyes, as he tried to convey John's mix-up to his attentive audience between his own fits of laughter. When he got the message across, the entire room thundered with laughter. By then John barely heard the others. His mind still struggled to cope with the incredible news he had just heard. He replayed all the scenes between Jhampa and Sherab, looking for any signs that they were indeed lovers and not siblings. Their lips had never touched, he realized. Affectionate kisses on the head, strokes on the back, handholding, and laughter. Really that was the only evidence that had led him to the wrong conclusion.

John's thoughts were interrupted by Sherab's hand under his chin. She raised his face up and locked it in place with her eyes.

"John," she said softly, her hands caressing his face, "Sherab love John. No Jhampa, no Dorje, no Nyandak. No, no, no." She shook her head with an amused smile. "Sherab love John."

She brought his face to hers then, and ignored Dorje's earlier plea. She kissed him hard, and John responded even more passionately. He had lost her, and now he had her again. A dull tinkling sound filled the room as the rebels around the fire encouraged them by knocking their spoons against their wooden bowls. A few whistles and catcalls accompanied their long embrace.

Sherab leaned back, and asked Dorje a question.

"Silly," Dorje answered her in English.

"John silly!" Sherab said with a smile.

"John loves Sherab very much," he answered her, his eyes once again wet with emotion.

"Dorje, can you translate for me, I have something I need to tell Sherab."

Dorje nodded, and relayed the message to Sherab. By now they had the entire group's attention, and John felt embarrassed to have his every word broadcasted by Dorje. He pressed on, determined to continue after having felt what it would be like to lose Sherab.

"Sherab, in a few days you're leaving Tibet. You may never return to your country again." The mood grew somber as John enumerated these realities to Sherab. While the rest of the group technically lived on Tibetan soil, they still lived a life of exile. The separation from their country remained a very painful subject for them.

"You will leave behind your people, your customs, and your culture. You may never see your own brother again." John nodded towards Jhampa while he said this. Sherab no longer smiled as John went over the harsh realities of her coming exile.

"Before you leave all this behind, I think we should use these days wisely. I want to be part of this culture. I want you, and the rest of your group, to teach me all that you can about Tibetan life."

Sherab smiled happily then, and moved to put her arms around his neck. He blocked her arms, and held them in place.

"Wait, I'm not finished. While you still have access to your precious culture, and to your brother, I need to ask you one more thing." He swallowed hard, as fear crept into his shaky voice. John partially stood up, keeping one knee on the ground and taking her hands.

"Sherab, will you marry me under Tibetan customs and religion?" A few hushed gasps of surprise filtered to his ears from the surrounding group. "Tomorrow!" he added quickly. "Will you marry me tomorrow?" The fear had given way to excitement now as he thought of the possibility.

Sherab's mouth trembled, as tears welled in her eyes. He waited expectantly, praying for a positive answer. She lost control then, and brought her hands to her face. Her shoulders shook as she sobbed heavily. John was dumbfounded, and did not know what to say or think. He had prepared himself for either answer, but not this.

"Sherab?" he asked weakly.

She looked up suddenly, and saw the confusion on his face. She must have realized she had not answered, for she began to nod enthusiastically. Her hands still held her face as her entire upper body seemed to nod at him.

A cheer rose all around the fire, followed by loud clapping. Sherab threw her arms around John while still heaving with great sobs. He buried his face in her hair, wanting to hide his own tears from the group now surrounding them and pounding their shoulders in congratulations.

John pressed his mouth to her ear, to make sure she heard him above the din. "I will love you forever Sherab."

# Chapter 19

The group waited impatiently for Sherab and John to release each other from their prolonged embrace. When they did, John took her hand and stood up shakily. Jhampa immediately came to Sherab, and turned her towards him. With a wide smile he hugged her tightly.

"Congratulations, little sister!" he told her happily.

"Thank you Jhampa, I'm so happy today!" She held her brother tightly, letting the last of her tears dry on his shirt. Sherab could not come to grips with all that had happened in the last few hours. She had been reunited with her brother, and the man she loved had asked her to marry him. Before meeting John, Sherab was certain that no man could ever be interested in her again. What a shock to have a wonderful man want to spend the rest of his life with her. Maybe she had finally begun moving on towards some of the higher realms of life.

Sherab released her brother to look at John again. She wanted to confirm that he really was there, that she was not dreaming all of this.

Dorje pumped John's hand in congratulations. They spoke to each other in English. As John answered, Sherab saw him smiling for the first time since Jhampa's arrival into the cave.

Jhampa turned to face John now. John offered his hand to him. Jhampa looked at it with a small smile, pushed it aside and wrapped him into an enormous bear hug. While he squeezed the breath out of John, he called a question to Dorje.

"How do you say 'brother' in English?"

Dorje had to say the word a few times for Jhampa to pick it up.

"Bwadda!" Jhampa declared loudly, squeezing John tighter. He released him then, and held his hands on John's shoulder, smiling at him. John spoke to Dorje, keeping his eyes on Jhampa.

"He would like to apologize for wanting to kill you earlier this evening," Dorje told Jhampa with a wide smile.

Jhampa looked at John in surprise, and then burst into laughter. Another seemingly painful bear hug rewarded John's humor.

Sherab became caught up in the festive mood and decided to tease John.

"Dorje, ask him if he has any brothers."

Jhampa shoved his sister playfully after hearing her remark. He knew what she meant by that question. According to Tibetan laws, a woman may marry several men. After her first husband, the only other men she may choose to marry are his brothers.

"What?" John asked curiously, watching Jhampa and Sherab.

Dorje translated Sherab's question. John looked at her curiously, and she smiled impishly at him.

"He has two brothers," Dorje answered her. John raised two fingers at Sherab, confirming the translation. She giggled, before asking another question.

"Are they handsome?" The others began to laugh at John's confusion then.

Anyone can recognize when they are the butt of a joke. John began to ask pointed questions to Dorje, with a mixture of embarrassment and impatience.

Instead of answering him, Dorje joyfully translated his question.

"He insists on knowing what is going on!"

They all laughed again. Sherab began feeling bad for John, and came to hold his arm protectively.

"Come on Dorje, that's enough," she said. "Explain our customs to him."

When Dorje explained the joke, John pulled his arm out of her grip. "No way Sherab" he told her, shaking his finger at her. John was unable to suppress his smile, as he tried to chastise her.

She gave him her most dazzling smile then, inviting a kiss. Unable to resist, he bent to kiss her. She uttered a few more words just before he reached her lips.

"Tell him that I will consider his request."

John stayed where he was, but cautiously threw Dorje an inquiring look.

Dorje's face positively beamed with pride at her play on John. After hearing the translation, John's eyes widened in mock anger as he looked at Sherab's lips waiting for a kiss mere inches away from his face. She screamed as his hands shot out to her sides and began tickling.

"One husband!" he shouted repeatedly as she squirmed under his tickling and jabbing fingers. She felt so helpless now that he had discovered how ticklish she was. His hands moved quickly on her sides, never staying in one place long enough for her to block them.

A hushed, appreciative murmur arose from the surrounding people. Sherab and John stopped their play to see what new attraction had caused a stir. A somber, graying man approached them slowly but deliberately. The crowd parted, letting him through unhindered. In one hand he carried a small bottle of liquid, much like a beer bottle. His other hand held an aging white scarf. The material seemed to have a fine origin, like silk or satin. But time and use had worn and discolored it so that it resembled little more than a rag. Still, the manner in which the gentleman carried the scarf redeemed some of its lost dignity.

Surprisingly, the older man stopped directly in front of John. The man extended his arms, offering the bottle and scarf. After a moment of hesitation, John accepted the gift with a solemn thank you.

"That is Sonam, our spiritual leader," Jhampa explained to Sherab. With this information, Sherab now understood the purpose of Sonam's gesture. Since John did not live in the area, Sonam was giving him the ceremonial gift that John's family would offer the bride's family in order for the marriage to be accepted. Normally the groom's family would offer the white hada and the bottle of barley beer to Sherab's father or uncle. Sonam's offer was an honor for John. The offer showed the leader's support and acceptance of their marriage to the rest of the group.

John sought out Dorje's help to understand the situation. Dorje immediately came to his side and spoke to him in a low whisper.

"Will you act as my father and uncle?" Sherab asked Jhampa.

"Of course I will. But who will John choose to represent his family?"

"I don't know. I hope Dorje explains all of this to him."

A small murmur of approval sounded out as Dorje translated John's choice.

"John would like Sonam to represent his family."

Sonam smiled at John, and gave a slight bow of his head in acknowledgement.

"That was a wise choice," Jhampa said to Sherab with a smile. "Perhaps there is some Tibetan in him under all that white skin."

Sherab elbowed her brother instead of answering him.

After a few words from Dorje, John returned the beer and hada to Sonam now, so that he could present it to Sherab's family. Sonam took the gifts and looked at him expectantly. The people around John began to back away. Sherab hesitated a moment before backing away, waiting for Dorje to pull John away as well.

Everyone stretched out in a large circle around Sonam and Jhampa. With much formality, Sonam approached Jhampa to within five feet, and stood waiting. In imitation of the Tibetan custom, John's 'father' approached the home of Sherab. Sherab's 'father' could immediately decline the wedding offer, or could tell Sonam that her uncle must decide. Despite knowing the outcome, Sherab could not let her eyes stray from the drama unfolding in the center of the cave.

Jhampa waited less than a minute, and then spoke to Sonam. He gestured towards a flat stone near him, and invited Sonam to sit down. Sonam first stepped closer, and graciously draped the hada around Jhampa's neck. Sonam spoke in a low voice to Jhampa, gesticulating towards Sherab and then John. At this point, Jhampa had to act as the father and uncle. If he approved the wedding, Sonam would open the beer for Jhampa.

Jhampa paused dramatically, allowing the suspense to build in his show. He turned to look at his sister, who smiled happily at him with her fingers laced together. She looked at him pleadingly, wanting him to hurry with the ceremony. With a flare, Jhampa returned to Sonam's attention and gave a long, slow nod. Cheers rose out of the spectators as Sonam uncorked the beer bottle and handed it to Jhampa.

This ceremony had now engaged Sherab and John to be married.

John stepped forward hesitantly, as if unsure of his role in the pre-wedding ceremony. Sherab bounded across the room and jumped into his arms.

"Come Sherab," Jhampa told her as he placed a hand on her shoulder. "Leave your future husband alone, you have many preparations to take care of."

Sherab released John reluctantly.

"What about John? He has to prepare too." Sherab looked at Dorje expectantly.

"The groom's job is easiest," Dorje answered with a smile, as he put an arm around John. "He just has to show up! John and I are going to go have a few beers. We'll continue this celebration the right way."

Sherab caught Sonam's arm as he headed off to prepare for his part of the ceremony.

"Sonam, could I speak to you for a moment?"

Perhaps the tone of her voice, or the look in her eyes, conveyed to him the urgency she felt within herself.

"Of course. Let's go back there," Sonam indicated an isolated area near the back of the cave. "We can't even hear ourselves think with all the preparations going on around here. Our little group rarely sees this much excitement in one day!"

Sherab followed the older man's youthful stride towards the rear, dimly lit section of the cave. Agitated voices echoed off the rock walls, combining and dividing into thousands of broken words that shattered into a confused clutter of noise. Sonam had tried to seek a quieter place, but Sherab realized that quiet did not exist in this enclosed environment. At best, they had achieved some semblance of privacy.

"What would you like to ask me?" Sonam spoke just loud enough for her to hear, as if he had practiced the art of hushed communication in this echoing chamber.

Sherab hesitated, unsure how to begin her private discussion with the spiritual leader, who was nonetheless a stranger to her.

"Is it about your wedding, or your choice of groom?"

"No, no," Sherab smiled. "I have no doubts about that. John is a wonderful man, I never thought I could be this lucky."

She paused a moment, sorting out her thoughts.

"Well maybe it is related to John, in a way. Like I said, he's the best thing that has ever happened to me. That's what puzzles me. Most of my life has been about suffering. And when I look back at my actions, I don't see anything that

I've done to help me move up in the Buddhist realms. In fact, I have violated several of the teachings."

Sherab appreciated Sonam's patience as she tried to put to words the vague thoughts that troubled her.

"So why suddenly would I get a great husband? Is it so that I will eventually suffer a great loss? Is that why he has been given to me, so that he can be taken away?"

Sonam reached forward and took her hands. His dry, rough skin caressed her hands with a firm, comforting grip. She instinctively leaned forward, putting some of her weight into his arms. Her emotional need for support manifested itself into a physical need as well.

"Your worst critic is often your own self." Sonam smiled reassuringly at her. "I haven't known you for long Sherab. I cannot deny or agree with your own assessment of your actions, I won't pretend otherwise. But what I have seen since you arrived here is a surprisingly gentle creature, not the ignoble person you have described.

We all stray from the path of enlightenment during our lifetimes. That doesn't mean that you can't improve your current standing. You must love who you are, Sherab. Try to see yourself through John's eyes, and then decide if you are such a bad person."

Sherab knew that Sonam would say anything to comfort her, but she still welcomed the words.

"I wish I shared the same confidence as you do," she told him. "So you really don't think this is just one more cruel punishment for me?"

"Do you love him very much?" Sonam asked instead of answering her question.

"Yes, I do. Very deeply. I love John with all my heart."

Sonam smiled, as if she had answered what he hoped for.

"Love is one of the purest emotions, Sherab. Don't you think that loving someone will help you on your path to enlightenment? What is true enlightenment but a love of all things? You love someone now, and I believe you are loved in return. How much clearer must the sign be for you to see it? You are back on your path my dear Sherab. Stay on it, and your suffering will be over."

Sherab was stunned by his words. She had never considered her love for John to have anything to do with her spiritual status. John was a gift to her. She had never reflected on the positive affect he could have on her path to enlightenment. That made the gift of his love worth even more than she could have imagined.

"Oh, Sonam, you really do encourage me now! I want to believe you are right. I feel it inside, but I'm just afraid to completely believe it. It's too good to be true!"

"Love always seems too good to be true, Sherab. Not only have you found love, but also the both of you are able to join together. Sometimes one finds love with someone who cannot be joined to them for any number of reasons. Marriage might be impossible because of political reasons, societal traditions, or simply finding love in someone already married. You and John are truly blessed."

"I'm not so sure about John," Sherab answered with a peaceful smile, "but I know I am surely blessed."

"Trust me Sherab, John is blessed by this union as well! But there won't be a union if you and I don't stop talking, and start preparing!"

"Thank you Sonam, I really needed to talk to someone about this. I'm grateful that you shared your wisdom with me."

"Now you're getting too formal with me! Although, I am acting as your father-in-law for this ceremony, so maybe it is appropriate for you to be formal in front of me."

Sherab laughed at his joke as much as she laughed in relief of a great burden being lifted off her shoulders.

"Are you ready to continue, or do you need to discuss anything else with me?"

"No, I'm ready Sonam, thanks again."

"Are you sure? The others can wait, you know. You are the bride, your peace of mind comes before the wedding guests."

"Yes, Sonam, I'm very sure. Even if this turns out to be a cruel punishment, I will enjoy the moments of love and happiness that I'm given. Let's go."

Sonam released her hands and reached to hug her. She held on tightly, drawing a fatherly comfort from him. She felt an acute longing for her real parents at this moment. How she wished that they could witness this amazing moment in her life.

Although Sherab was finished with her spiritual discussion with Sonam, she was not yet completely at ease. Upon returning to the cave's busy area, she sought out her brother. Jhampa came to her when she caught his eye. There was one more burden that she needed to unload before being ready to be wed.

"Are you nervous about tomorrow, sister?" Jhampa asked with a smile and a playful push on her shoulder. His smile vanished when he saw the seriousness of her expression.

"What's wrong?" he asked her gently.

"Why haven't you asked about my life during the years you were gone?"

Sadness filled Jhampa's eyes at her remark.

"I didn't want to push you. I know you must have suffered a lot. I also knew that you would tell me about it when you were ready. You can never understand the guilt that has crushed me these past years. I knew my family would be punished for my crimes."

"No Jhampa, you didn't commit any crime. We were all very proud of you. Believe me, Mother and Father never expressed any anger towards your actions. I was even jealous sometimes," Sherab confessed shyly. "They had a light in their eyes when they talked about your resistance to the Chinese."

Jhampa's eyes glimmered with unshed tears as Sherab spoke of their parents.

"Thank you Sherab, you're very kind to try to relieve my burden. But the fact remains that because of me, our parents are likely dead, and I'm sure you have suffered so much."

Jhampa hesitated a moment before speaking again. "Do you want to talk about your imprisonment?"

Sherab sensed that he seemed almost reluctant to hear about her suffering. She was tempted to spare him from her story. But the importance of the Panchen Lama's imprisonment was too important for Jhampa's delicate conscience.

Sherab began her story, although she glossed over some details of her own suffering. As she spoke, Dorje and a few others sat down to listen to her tale. She tried to focus on the Panchen Lama's abuse, but Jhampa would not allow her to totally skip her own mistreatment. He pointed to her mangled finger, and demanded the story behind it.

Jhampa alternated between red-faced rage and tearful sorrow as Sherab recounted her experiences. The others in the group listened with rapt attention, the horror of her story reflected in their incredulous eyes.

Sherab finished the discussion of her time in prison, and came to the story of her meeting with John and Yu. When she discussed their time with Muyih and Luhping, Jhampa interrupted her angrily.

"You make it sound like these two Chinese were heroes."

"They were good people, Jhampa. They helped me as well as other Tibetans in trouble."

"Maybe helping a few Tibetans relieved their guilt at destroying Tibetan culture for classrooms full of young people. Relieve their guilt for turning a generation of our people into Chinese!"

"You don't know them Jhampa. The Chinese government is trying to eliminate our culture, not Muyih and Luhping. They were thrust into a pre-existing condition, and tried to help where they could."

"If they weren't so eager to help, the government wouldn't have anyone to suppress our culture."

"Come on," Sherab replied hotly, "if they had not come, others much worse than them would gladly fill in their place. There are plenty of Chinese immigrants to fill any vacancies left by people like Muyih and Luhping."

"Still, cooperating with the government policies is an implied support for them."

"Refusing to denounce the government does not make them bad people! Tibetan children need the education these teachers have to offer a lot more than they need your guns! Our future generations will need to gain independence through their intelligence, not through violence."

Jhampa thought about this for a moment, before nodding thoughtfully.

"You might have a point there, little sister. But I still have difficulty thinking of any Chinese as good people."

"I know Jhampa, it was hard for me too. And right now I think our people need your anger and intolerance to keep our culture alive in the eyes of the world. But let's not forget our needs for the future. Anger and violence will not be passed on through many generations. People forget, and adapt. We need to arm our children with the intelligence to remember and care about their past, about their heritage."

"And the will to regain their heritage!" Jhampa added forcefully.

"Yes," Sherab agreed. "Give them the will to take their country back into their own hands. That's one reason that I need to expose the Chinese conspiracy regarding the Panchen Lama. I don't want a corrupted Tibetan leading our children astray."

"You're very brave, Sherab. I'm proud to have a sister who accepts such heavy responsibilities."

"Do I have much choice, Jhampa?"

"Yes, you could go live happily in America with your new husband." Jhampa smiled at her, gently reminding her of the happy occasion awaiting his sister.

"If I don't start getting ready soon, I won't have a husband!"

Jhampa reached for his sister, and they embraced tenderly. She drew comfort from her big brother, happy to have unloaded her story and its burden onto his shoulders.

"Concentrate on your wedding, Sherab. Let us worry about getting you to India."

"Thank you Jhampa, that's what I need the most from you right now."

"Not to worry little sister. We're used to dancing around Chinese soldiers. This is our land, not theirs. We'll get you out without any problems."

As they parted company, Sherab tried to forget the deadly seriousness of her mission. For the next two hours, she was kept busy preparing for her upcoming wedding. Her adopted family helped her organize an area of the cave that would be her home for the purpose of the ceremony. Sonam had disappeared after their talk, to prepare on the groom's side of the wedding.

A musician strode to the center of the cave, and sat near the fire with his pair of drums. He began to pound a slow, marching beat. Sherab, as well as every other person in the cave, stopped what she was doing and focused her attention on the drummer.

A roar of laughter and clapping broke out when Sonam entered into the cave. Six men stretched out a yak hide, and carried the seated Sonam into the cave. Sherab looked at Jhampa curiously.

"The groom's uncle will ride to the home of the parents of the bride on a white horse," her brother reminded her. "It looks like Sonam has compromised on the horse!"

Sherab watched the procession with humor and a touch of anxiety. The uncle was bringing the horse for the bride to ride to the wedding ceremony the following day. She watched Sonam balanced precariously on the yak hide and wondered how she would keep her balance on it the next day.

The men carried Sonam in a circular path for all the spectators to see. Suddenly two women ran to Sonam's side carrying three bowls. Sherab recognized them as representatives from her family, greeting the groom's uncle before he reached the bride's house. They spoke to him loudly, for all to hear.

"We respectfully greet you, Great Uncle. Will you please accept this beer to help you on your journey?"

The women offered Sonam the three traditional bowls of beer before he could continue on his way to the bride's home.

Before he could answer, Sonam almost rolled over backwards as the men put him down. The crowd laughed, and shouted at the men. They returned the laughter, but waved off the crowd. The uncle had to drink the beer without dismounting his horse. Sherab smiled since Sonam's 'horse' needed a rest.

Conversations resumed around the cave as Sonam worked on his three bowls of beer. By the time he finished, Sherab noticed that he was smiling a lot more than earlier in the evening.

The drummer resumed his beat when Sonam finished his beer. The horse-men picked up their load, and continued carrying the smiling Sonam. The procession stopped at the opposite end of the cave from where it had begun. The crowd dispersed before Sonam.

Sherab and Jhampa were seated in a cleared out section near the wall. Scattered about them were various Tibetan household items. Sherab and the others had carefully laid out a grinding bowl for barley grains, a butter churn, some utensils, and a small Buddha statue.

Sonam dismounted ungracefully, with the effects of the beer not helping the difficult situation of the yak hide. Sonam draped yet another white hada around Jhampa's neck, and then presented him with a small bowl of butter. Having presented Sherab's family with gifts, he then went to Sherab, and presented her with a white bundle. Sherab unfurled the long, flowing, woolen dress for the marriage.

"It's beautiful, Sonam, thank you!"

"Not as beautiful as the bride wearing it tomorrow," he replied.

Without a pause in the pre-wedding ceremony, Sonam walked further in to bless all the objects in their house. He knelt before the Buddha statue and began singing in a low voice. He bowed before it, and then moved to the butter churn where he continued his chants. Sonam made his way through the array of objects scattered about Sherab's 'home', chanting a prayer in front of each one. Only when he had sung before each object did he finally leave their area. The audience applauded his efforts as he walked out of Sherab's 'home'. Sonam took a deep bow, acknowledging the applause.

With the evening's ceremony having ended, Sherab sought out her future husband. She spotted John trying to make his way to her. Dorje grabbed his arm, while a few other men stood before him ready to intercept the over-eager groom. Sherab laughed softly, knowing that they would never let John near her on the night before the wedding. But she was very happy to see John trying to get to her.

Sherab felt the fatigue of her not quite fully recovered body reacting to the excitement of the day. She was grateful when Jhampa insisted that she go to bed early, rather than fussing over last minute wedding details. The sounds of preparations drifted to her ears as she contentedly settled into the straw mattress in a darkened nook within the cave.

***

A loud clattering sound woke John up the next morning. He blinked towards the center of the cave, trying to discern the origin of the noise. The cave had become a beehive of activity during his sleep. Everyone seemed terribly busy, yet he had trouble identifying specific activities being performed. He sat up, and stretched lazily. It had been a long time since he had felt this rested.

Ngawang appeared out of nowhere with some harsh Tibetan words, and some breakfast. She tossed a piece tsampa onto his lap, and handed him a bowl of yogurt.

"Thank you Ngawang!" he called to her as she walked away briskly. John wondered if camp cooks had to be bad tempered by some unspoken international law. He began to eat, slowly waking up to all the frenzied activity around him.

The rest of the cave's inhabitants seemed to blur in his vision when John spotted his bride walking towards him. An unfinished piece of tsampa remained unchewed in his mouth as she smiled at him in her approach.

"Good morning husband," Sherab said proudly, handing him a steaming cup of tea.

"Good morning my wife," John answered when he had recovered from the pleasant shock of hearing her words. "Where did Sherab learn 'husband'?" he asked happily.

"Dorje help Sherab."

"Hey! You two are not supposed to be together!" Dorje called out when he saw them, as if on cue. "Sherab!" he continued expressing his disapproval to her in Tibetan. Sherab seemed unable to wipe the smile away from her face, but her eyes had the good grace to appear guilty in front of Dorje's accusations.

For the first time, John noticed that several brightly painted pots had been arranged around the entrance of his 'house'. A white mat had also been laid out as a form of welcome mat. A man and a woman painstakingly placed grains of barley in an intricate pattern on the mat.

"What are these symbols?" he asked Dorje. In part he asked out of curiosity, but he also asked in order to deflect Dorje's irritation at Sherab and John being caught together that morning.

"Those symbols are for good luck. When Sherab arrives here during the ceremony, she will step onto the center of this mat."

Before Dorje could continue, a third man John had not noticed before appeared beside them. He appeared decidedly uncomfortable, as if he wished to be elsewhere. Dorje nodded to him, and introduced him to John and Sherab.

"This is Jigme, he is our finest craftsman. Give him some rope, some wood, a few stones, and he will build you anything you ask!"

John shook hands with the shy man, trying to recover from the shock of hearing their dead guide's name again. Sherab also looked sad when she took Jigme's hand.

The three of them looked at Jigme questioningly, waiting to hear why he had approached them. The man mumbled a few barely audible words and quickly stuck his hand out to John. He held a small ivory colored ring between his large thumb and forefinger.

John accepted the ring, staring in awe at the delicate designs carved around part of the circumference. Jigme immediately started backing away.

"Wait!" John said, taking his arm. Further words failed to come to his mouth, he felt so moved by Jigme's gift.

Dorje and Sherab bent to take a closer look at the ring.

"He must have worked most of the night!" Dorje exclaimed. "This looks like it was carved from yak bone. Look at the details! This symbol here represents a vase filled with treasures. It will bring you a long life and many riches. I believe this flower here is the lotus, which will purify your body and mind. This wheel here is an important symbol in Buddhism, it represents the teachings of our religion. This is a fish, to protect you from fear and suffering. Oh, this is a masterpiece!"

John looked up at their benevolent craftsman with gratitude. Jigme's bloodshot eyes testified to the long hours he must have spent carving the ring during the night. He spoke to John then, or more accurately, he spoke to John through Dorje.

"Jigme is very humble. He apologizes for not having completed all the designs on time. He asks you to return the ring after the ceremony so that he may finish it."

John shook his head in disbelief and grabbed Jigme's hand in a firm handshake. The craftsman grew even more embarrassed when Sherab hugged him and gave him a small kiss on the cheek. None of them could keep Jigme there any longer after that. He quickly untangled himself from their thankful clutches and escaped to the other side of the cave.

"Sherab should not even have seen this!" Dorje exclaimed. "You two are not supposed to be together this morning," he repeated. He put his hands on Sherab's shoulders, spun her around and shooed her away.

"We were starting to think you would sleep all the way through your own wedding!" Dorje told John, after having supervised Sherab's departure.

"Sorry about that, but I do feel a million times better than yesterday. Did Sherab get enough sleep?"

"Not enough for Nyandak's peace of mind, but she slept well, yes. That reminds me, he wants to check your fingers this morning. Nyandak!" Dorje called out in search of the resident doctor. "I'll be right back."

John took this moment of relative privacy to gobble down his breakfast, and then sip some hot tea. The tea his wife brought him, John thought with a smile.

Dorje returned a few minutes later with Nyandak.

"How do you feel, he wants to know." Dorje translated for Nyandak as the doctor began unwrapping the bandages from John's fingers.

"My fingers don't feel like they're burning as much, but they're still not strong. Well, that's not quite right. It's just that my hands are clumsy, I have trouble holding things well."

The sight of his swollen, red fingers began to alarm John. John pulled back when Nyandak pinched the tips of each finger.

"He's very happy John," Dorje announced while Nyandak smiled at him. "The swelling should go down in another day or two. Some of your skin might peel, like if it was sunburned. But your fingers are fine."

"Thank you Nyandak. I don't think they would be fine without your expert care."

Nyandak beamed with pride, slapped John's shoulder and left his bedside. The doctor shot back one last comment before disappearing into the depth of the cave. Dorje laughed before translating.

"He says if you always give such false compliments, he might be tempted to marry you too!" They both laughed this time, John out of embarrassment as well as at Nyandak's sharp wit.

Dorje cleared his throat, and took on a more serious expression.

"Once the wedding ceremony begins, I don't think you and I will have much more time to talk today. I don't want to ruin your festive mood John, but we need to discuss some of the details of your departure."

"No problem, you're not ruining my mood. I'm very interested in details about our departure."

"I have discussed it with Jhampa, and we're sending a double sized party with you, ten men."

"Ten men!" John exclaimed. "What on earth for?"

"Sherab had a long talk with her brother. We know her story, and we have a great interest in getting her to His Holiness the Dalai Lama."

As Dorje had predicted, John's mood did grow somber then.

"It wasn't my business to explain her story to you, I hope you understand that."

"Of course, John. Sherab is among her people now, such information should come from her. But you will never understand how grateful we are, how indebted we are, to you for helping her so much. Jhampa in particular is very uncomfortable with the size of the debt he owes you for Tibet and for his sister."

"I don't understand you people," John said with a smile. "You rescue us and save our lives. You throw a huge celebration for us. And then, the most precious gift you could offer, you marry Sherab and I while she is still in her country. And now you think you owe me a debt?  I never knew Tibetans lacked so much logic!" John slapped Dorje on the shoulder to emphasize the lack of seriousness in his last sentence.

Dorje grinned, but did not change his tone. "We are indebted to you John. Realistically, we all know that we cannot pay you back in this life. But perhaps our situations will be reversed in our next lives, and then we can be equal once again."

"How do you know I'm not just repaying you a previous life's debt?"

Dorje laughed then, shaking his head. "You are catching on to our teachings too quickly. Please, be a more ignorant westerner and make my life easier!"

"Alright, I'll try harder."

"Who will go with us?" John asked after a moment of thought.

"Certainly I will go, to allow you to communicate with the rest of us. Jhampa insists on leading the team. Nyandak wants to keep an eye on your injuries. I'm not sure about the rest, Jhampa and Sonam together will determine the fighters who will go."

"What about Sonam?"

"No, he's getting too old for such excursions. He still goes out on the smaller raids, but not for journeys that may take a week, roundtrip."

"Are you mostly worried about the last checkpoint at the top of the Nangpa La?"

"No, we're not going through that pass. We won't be crossing any checkpoints. Really we don't expect any trouble. But we can't be sure how far the Chinese will go to stop Sherab from escaping Tibet. Our strong force is a precaution, not a necessity."

"But I thought the Nangpa La was the only way out. Our guide told us that."

Dorje snorted at John's comment. "Guides are just country people. They know one or two paths and they stick to them. We are mountain people. We know these mountains better than anyone. If Tibetans knew where to find us, they would come to us for escape, not the country guides."

John smiled at his pride, and the rivalry between mountain dwellers and flatlanders.

"Why don't you let your presence be known, so that they can come to you?"

"Too risky. If the Chinese ever caught someone who knew our location, they would send their army out to destroy us completely. No," he said, shaking his head sadly, "secrecy is our most important factor. Unfortunately, it's even more important than the thousands wanting to escape Tibet."

"What made your raiding party save Sherab and I, then?"

Dorje shrugged his shoulders. "We're human. There's a difference between not advertising your presence to potential runaways, and ignoring two dying people lying in front of you."

Sonam came up to them, interrupting their conversation. He and Dorje spoke briefly.

"It's time to prepare for the wedding now John."

"This early in the morning?"

Dorje smiled at him in amusement. "We ate a light lunch already, you really did sleep all morning. The wedding is in the early afternoon, followed by a feast and then a celebration late into the night."

John felt embarrassed by his extended sleep. Sonam left them alone again, making John wonder what preparations Dorje had meant.

"So what do I do now?" John asked.

"You wait for your bride. Your 'uncle' will return ahead of her, announcing her arrival."

Two women then arrived next to John, smiling shyly. He nodded to them, returning their smile and hiding his confusion. He could barely keep up with the goings-on at his own wedding. Each woman carried an opened bottle of barley beer.

"This is Phuntsok and Tsultrim, they represent your family. Like sisters, or cousins."

John shook their hands then. "Hi sis!" he told each of them. His foreign tongue made them laugh nervously.

The drummer began a fast insistent beat, silencing all talk and capturing everyone's attention.   He stopped when Sonam entered into view, and approached John's 'house'. Sonam boomed out some words, announcing the coming bride's arrival. Sonam stood by John's side then, while the drummer took up a slow, marching beat. John's heart began to pound wildly when he saw Sherab approaching in the distance. Where Sonam had looked silly riding on the yak hide, Sherab looked like a queen. She sat gracefully, using her arms to balance herself against the unsteady movements of the hide as the men carried her towards him. His mind found it difficult to accept what he saw. Could this goddess-like creature riding towards him truly be his wife? He swallowed hard, trying to contain his emotions.

Jhampa walked proudly at his sister's side. When they drew near, John's two 'sisters' went forward and offered Jhampa the beer. The three of them began to sing then, Jhampa's baritone voice providing a pleasant contrast to their soft, angelic song. Sherab dismounted precisely onto the white mat full of barley grain symbols. John could not help but notice that the woman who had lent her the white gown had been smaller than Sherab. The woolen fabric stretched provocatively over her body, showing every curve underneath. As she put her leg down onto the mat, the gown revealed the flex of her muscular calf. She had filled out remarkably since John had first seen her emaciated body. Several weeks of hard exercise and decent nutrition had added beautiful, sculpted muscle tone to her figure. Somehow it seemed wrong to feel physical desire at such a holy and emotional ceremony. Yet Sherab's presence did not give him a choice, as he shifted position to try to hide the obvious sign of his excitement.

Dorje leaned close to his ear. "When your father feels Sherab's 'uncle' and your 'sisters' have sung long enough, he'll invite them into his house."

Much to everyone's pleasure, the singing lasted a full five minutes before Sonam raised his hand. Jhampa and the two women stopped their singing immediately. Jhampa stepped forward, and wrapped a hada around Sonam's neck. In turn, Sonam gave a hada to Jhampa. They chanted small prayers or blessings to each other during the exchange. Jhampa then turned to John, placing a hada around his neck. John looked at Dorje anxiously, for he had no hada in return.

"You aren't supposed to give one," Dorje whispered.

Sonam then spoke loudly, for all the audience to hear.

"He has now formally started the wedding," Dorje informed him. "Now you will go pray while the monks chant for your marriage blessings."

Sherab took John's hand, and led him towards a statue of Buddha. Sonam sat behind the statue, while Sherab and John knelt before it. A row of six men, presumably monks before their forced exile, began to chant behind Sonam. John followed Sherab's lead and lowered his head in prayer. He felt like an impostor going through the motions of these people's religion. Yet the peaceful look on Sherab's face helped him feel like he belonged there, praying at her side.

The monks' chant echoed throughout the cave, making a reverberating, almost haunting sound. John's knees began to ache as time passed. Sherab remained completely immobile next to him. He lost track of time, and could not be sure if half an hour or a full hour had passed when the last chant's echo died in his ears.

"Give her the ring now John," Dorje whispered to him. Dorje knelt to the side of their ceremony, coaching John with instructions.

John took out the ring while Sherab extended her pretty hand to him. He held her hand, and hesitated. Which finger? Hoping not to make a fool of himself, he slipped the bone ring over the traditionally western ring finger. Sherab did not flinch, causing him to breathe out in silent relief. He did not want to let her hand go, electricity seemed to flow from it into his hand. She smiled at him, and pulled her hand away gently. A man had just placed a pot in front of them, with a thick, light brown liquid in it.

"Sherab will now salute heaven, earth and the Buddha with the milk-tea," Dorje explained to him.   John had not yet tasted milk-tea, but Dorje had explained this interesting drink to him. The tea was boiled with milk and sugar, as opposed to the western tradition of adding these ingredients after the brewing process.

John watched Sherab delicately dip her ring finger into the tea, and flick droplets into the air. She repeated this ritual two more times. She then poured some tea into a small cup, and served it to Sonam. At once the crowd burst into a cheer. John looked to Dorje in confusion.

"You are now married John, congratulations!"

In shock at the sudden end to the ceremony, John looked towards Sherab. His wife lifted him to a standing position, put her arms around his neck, and kissed him passionately.

"Come on lovers, you don't have any time to yourselves yet!" Dorje kidded John teasingly. He held a chunk of tsampa towards Sherab and John.

"Take a pinch of tsampa, and toss it into the air for good luck. You're saluting Buddha."

Sherab had already plucked her piece while Dorje explained this custom to John. She threw her piece of tsampa far into the crowd of onlookers, causing another round of cheers. John was brought back in time to when Sherab had first brought him some tsampa at the Same temple. There too she had thrown a pinch of the barley dough into the air.

John followed suit, pinching off a tiny piece of dough and flinging it over the heads of the people closest to them. Another cheer went up and then everyone swarmed around the newlyweds. They were almost carried into the center of the cave where Ngawang labored with her son and two other men over a table filled with food.

John's neck began to feel warm and itchy from all the hadas people decorated him with. Very few of the hadas were made of the fine white material that tradition demanded. In such impoverished settings, people improvised with old pieces of clothing, and even strips of animal hide.

Someone handed John a cup of beer, and disappeared into the crowd before John could even figure out who it was. Sherab also had a cup of beer now, and turned to face him. The crowd made room for them, which told John that they were about to take part in another wedding tradition. Sherab smiled at him, and held her beer near his mouth. She glanced at his other hand, and he immediately brought his beer to her mouth. Amid cheering they drank from each other's cup, exchanging their beer.

Jhampa came forward, and faced John. Dorje stood next to him, ready to translate. The crowd grew silent as Jhampa began to speak.

"Tibetan couples normally get many gifts. I desperately wished that my sister and her new husband could feel the generosity of the Tibetan people. But we have very little to give you, and you still have far to travel. With my greatest apology, I offer you this gift."

Jhampa bowed his head slightly as he handed John a large hunting knife. The intricately carved bone handle had been worn smooth with age. The knife's metal still shone with a thin film of oil. The blade's finely honed edge gave it a deadly, graceful curve.

"My grandfather made that knife and gave it to my father when he was a boy, at a time when Tibet was free," Dorje continued the translation of Jhampa's words. "My father in turn gave it to me. I swore I would use it to liberate Tibet one day. Now I give it to you, and hope that you will help us to freedom using western influences. And perhaps my future nephew will one day have the knife to help protect his country."

The enormity of Jhampa's gift began to sink in. He pinned his hopes of a promising future in John's hands.

"Jhampa, I have never received a finer gift. I'll treasure it always. You can be sure it will be passed down to generations of future Tibetans."

Sonam came forward as Jhampa backed away. He spoke to Sherab in a soft voice, and presented her with a tiny statue. Sherab kept a serious expression on her face, but tears began to form on the corner of her eyes. John put his arm protectively around her waist, trying to give her some comfort. Sonam then handed her a small bead bracelet. The beads varied slightly in size and shape, having been hand-carved from small stones. Sherab returned some words to Sonam in a shaky voice.

"Sonam has given Sherab a small Buddha to carry with her everywhere she goes," Dorje explained. "He told her that nuns, and those who are nuns in spirit, must never be without one. The beads will be used to help her count the number of times she recites her mantras."

Sonam shouted a loud announcement to the captive audience. People relaxed, and began gathering around the banquet table.

"You can calm down now John, your part of the wedding is over. Now we all celebrate together. Come have some food with me."

John tried to stay with Sherab as much as possible, but various people came to show one of them one thing, or speak to the other about another thing. Several times during the evening he saw her in the distance, and watched her longingly while Dorje explained or translated something for him. Finally the demands on the couple began to diminish. Some of the older folks went to bed, thinning out the crowd. John made his way to Sherab, and held her hand tightly so that they would not be separated.

Their moment together did not last long. A young woman approached Sherab, and spoke to her. The woman appeared both nervous and embarrassed. Sherab seemed to hesitate, but the woman tugged on her sleeve to get her to follow her. Sherab looked at John apologetically, and released his hand. He saw the fatigue in her eyes. The day's events had drained her already tired body.

John noticed that Dorje had left his side for the first time that evening. The translator smiled and nodded at John from the other side of the fire pit. That left John alone with his thoughts, since none of the others could come talk to him. He saw Sherab emerge from a dark recess in the cave then. The young woman ran off giggling as soon as they came into the light. Sherab headed straight for John with a wide grin on her face. She took his hand, and led him to the place where the young woman had brought her.

The dark area became a narrow tunnel that snaked perhaps thirty feet away from the main cave. The tunnel ended abruptly against a sheer rock wall. The end of the tunnel had widened slightly, forming a miniature cavern. Someone had laid out some bedding in the one space large enough for a person to lie down in. A small candle provided just enough light for them to see each other.

"This must be the honeymoon suite," he told Sherab, grinning crazily himself now.

She ignored his incomprehensible words, got down into the straw, and pulled him to her. John lay on top of her and kissed her. She kissed him briefly, but then pulled away. He looked at her, puzzled, until she began to undress. John felt something was wrong, because she usually liked to kiss for a while before proceeding.

"Sherab? Are you OK?" he asked.

"Sherab OK," she said tiredly, "come John." She extended her arms to him, inviting John to make love to her on their wedding night. She seemed to be having trouble keeping her eyes open. The semi-darkness of the small cave helped relax her to the point of nearly falling asleep.

John lay down beside her, not on top of her.

"Come John!" she said, now concerned.

"Yes, I will come," he lied. "Wait," he told her softly.

She did not seem to understand why he wanted her to wait, but she accepted his request. He brought his hand to her head then, and began running his fingers through her short hair. She moaned with pleasure at the soothing sensation. He began to massage her scalp, and felt her entire body go limp. After a few minutes he softened his touch so that he gently stroked her head. John blew out the candle when her breathing became slow and regular. The thick animal hides would keep her naked body warm during the night. But his body curled up against her to make doubly sure she never became cold. Within minutes, sleep invaded his senses as he drifted off for the night.

# Chapter 20

Sherab woke John up in the most pleasurable way a man can be woken up. He thought he was caught in another dream, until he opened his eyes and saw her head moving over his body. She knelt crosswise next to him, with her legs close within his reach. He reached between her legs and began touching her. Her hips immediately pressed down on his hand, while her mouth worked rhythmically with a new intensity. He knew he could not last much longer, so he removed his hand from her, cupped her face, and brought her to him for a kiss.

John had hoped to have a few seconds to cool down, but before her lips reached his, she had already straddled his body, and brought him inside her. His resistance collapsed when her tongue burst into his mouth, hungrily seeking out his tongue. John experienced a dizzying climax as she sucked on his tongue, her wet lips crushing his own.

"Jesus!" he breathed, when she lifted her head to smile at him. A numbing afterglow buzzed inside his head.

"Good morning John," Sherab whispered to him with a teasing smile. Laughter poured out of him with a mixture of extreme happiness and embarrassment at how easily she had seduced him. John noticed that she still rocked her hips gently against his, enjoying the sensation of having him in her. She was up on her elbows, looking into his eyes. He reached up, and began touching her breasts. She lost her smile then, and closed her eyes in concentration. His fingertips avoided her hard, protruding nipples. He drew slow, diminishing circles around them, moving quickly when she shifted her body to try to get some contact. Her hips began to grind into his, in an increasingly rapid circular motion.

"Please…" she whispered in a hoarse whisper. Her breathing became more erratic. He stopped touching her, and used the tip of his fingernail to tickle her nipples. She cried out, moving even faster against him. He moved each fingernail more rapidly over her tender nipples.

"John! Please!" she repeated, moving her upper body in vain, trying to get his hands to touch her more firmly. When he felt her approaching her own climax, he pinched them hard. Her eyes opened wide in surprise, and a soft sigh of pleasure escaped her lips. Her movements slowed, her hips pressed hard against his. Her body shuddered, and then collapsed on top of John.

"Good morning Sherab," John finally answered her with a smile. She laughed against his chest, and relaxed her body. His hands began to massage her breasts, relieving the pent up stress from the teasing he had inflicted on them.

When he felt she had relaxed long enough, he began to roll her nipples between his thumb and forefinger. Gentle pinches, alternating with feather light strokes got her moving again. She looked up suddenly, when she realized what he was up to.

"No John," she said with a smile, slapping his hands away. He quickly rolled their bodies over, so that he pressed down on her. He pinned her arms to the floor, and lowered his lips to her breast. She gasped, as if she could not breathe. John moved his hips against hers, trying to press in as deeply as he could. Her hips pushed up against his, matching their motion. He continued to rotate his pelvis into her until he felt her body go limp again.

John moved his head back up, and saw her lying in total relaxation, her eyes glazed and half opened.

"I love you John," she said in a drunken slur of pleasure.

"I love you too my wife," he told her, staring into her beautiful face.

Her hand reached behind his head and brought him down for a soft kiss. They kissed long, exploring each other's mouths tenderly. He felt her move beneath him, so he reached for her breast again. She broke their kiss and began laughing, reverting into Tibetan. With a slap on his shoulder, she struggled out from under him and sat up. John sat next to her, and pulled her against him. She leaned into his arms, allowing him to hold her for several minutes. Eventually the cold morning air in the cave forced them to separate and get dressed.

Perhaps both their eyes appeared glazed, for several people sniggered at them as they emerged from the private area. Dorje seemed a little uncomfortable as he approached them.

"Good morning John, Sherab," he began with a nod towards Sherab. "Today you begin the last leg of your journey. I hope you feel well rested."

"I don't know about Sherab, but I feel great," John answered slyly. "My fingers are pretty good, and I've regained most of my strength."

They ate a hurried breakfast, and began packing for their trip. The amount of people escorting them made John feel uncomfortable. He vowed to find a way to repay these people for their care and kindness. How different this part of the trip would be. For once he could take the role of a simple passenger, not worrying about how to get to their destination. Sherab and John would simply tag along, letting the others make all the decisions.

Immediately after eating a hearty lunch, they gathered at the mouth of the cave to depart. John shook hands with Sonam, warmly laying his other hand on Sonam's shoulder. John hugged a surprised and stiffly embarrassed Ngawang. Several people he barely recognized shook his hand as well. The rest of their party bade farewell to their friends and family. Jhampa, Jigme, Dorje, Nyandak, and the giant Gyan, Ngawang's son, were among those John recognized in the departing group. Five other men that he had seen in the cave before, but had not yet met, also gathered at the cave's entrance.

All twelve hikers walked at a brisk pace once they started the journey. Full of hope and energy, John felt like he could hike for a week without effort. By nightfall, he remembered the incredible fatigue that came with long days of walking in the cold mountains.

The feeling of safety and camaraderie Sherab and John had shared with the group made a pleasant contrast to the long struggle for survival they had previously endured. By force of habit, John prepared their sleeping bag when nightfall came. He felt out of place with a modern sleeping bag when the men took out their animal hides. Then he noticed the pattern with which they laid out the hides. As each man stretched out, he rolled himself once in the hide, and then draped the remainder over his neighbor. The end result was a uniform cover over everyone, which minimized the escape of precious body heat.

"Come John, you two will be warmer in here." Dorje indicated a spot he had saved for them near the tail end of the joined hides. They moved their sleeping bag into position, and slipped inside. Dorje threw an extra hide over them to avoid a break in the uniform coverage.

The next day turned out to be as exhausting as it was uneventful. Jhampa drove the group hard, barely giving them a moment to sit and catch their breaths. If not for the several weeks of unplanned training, John never could have kept up with these sturdy mountain men. With barely a word of goodnight to Sherab, he fell asleep with the comfort of several bodies around him.

"We should cross the border into Nepal some time this afternoon, I think." Dorje seemed to be calculating time and distance as they ate their breakfast.

Sherab seemed sad that morning, and ate her breakfast silently, sitting next to her brother. Without words to comfort her impending loss, John could only hold her hand, or touch her frozen cheek to show he understood. After years of being separated from her brother, she must have deeply regretted having to leave him again.

During the mid-morning they walked along a canyon wall in narrow valley. The wall towered over their right side, while a gentler slope rose to the left of the valley. The soldier's white parka almost made him invisible against the backdrop of the white slope.

John was about to shout a warning when one of the men in his group yelled something in Tibetan. Their column stopped advancing, and turned as one to face the slope. The lone soldier made a signal with his hand, and simply stared at them. Although they could not see his feet from this distance, he obviously had a ski pole in each hand. The dark object poking over his shoulder could not be mistaken for anything but a rifle.

Within seconds from his hand signal, a second soldier glided over next to him. Then another. The fear in the pit of John's stomach threatened to make him fall over in pain. The white ghosts silently lined up one after the other. Like counting the nails for his coffin, John added each new arrival to the deadly sum in his head. An oppressing silence hung over the valley as the twenty-one alpine soldiers looked down at the ragged band of rebel fighters.

With a short command from the officer, the valley became a whirlwind of motion. The soldiers shoved off with their poles, forming a descending line of death rapidly approaching the valley floor. The rebels scrambled all around John, trying to find what little cover that could be obtained. Before John could find Sherab, Dorje grabbed his arm, dragged him several feet, and threw him roughly behind a small cluster of stones. John sat up immediately, and saw Jhampa handling his sister. John's instinct told him to go get her, but logically he saw that Jhampa had found her better cover than John had with Dorje.

The first shots rang out in the valley. A few Chinese soldiers fell, but the others merely increased their downward speed without returning fire. Another soldier fell before John realized what objective they sought. Near the base of the slope, a short mini-ridge formed a long low wall, no more than two feet in height. It would provide a perfect position from which they could engage in battle.

The soldiers literally dived behind their protective ridge when they got to it. Soon the rebels had no targets to shoot at. A flurry of discarded skis and poles could be seen above the cover of the ridge. One soldier made the mistake of lifting his head slightly above the ridgeline while disentangling himself from a tenacious ski binding. Several shots rang out, at least one of which splattered his brains about the surrounding snow. A few seconds later, the other soldiers began returning fire.

With a start John realized that he had been watching the developments as a spectator, while his rifle remained slung over his shoulder. He quickly retrieved the gun and took aim at the ridge. No suitable targets could be found, so he shot ineffectively at the rifle muzzles sticking up over the ridgeline.

John tried to force some calm into his panicked brain, and searched the area more carefully. One of the soldiers must have been taller than the rest. They were all lying flat on their stomachs, but his boots were stretched out far enough behind him to be within John's line of sight. John took aim, and began firing. On his fourth shot, the boot seemed to bounce up like a toy. Perhaps it was his imagination, but John thought he heard a scream of pain above the din of gunshots. The boots quickly disappeared as the soldier tucked himself up against the ridge. John had not killed him, but at least he would be much less effective against the rebels.

"We're pinned down and outnumbered. What are we going to do?" John asked Dorje beside him.

"We'll die if we stay here. Jhampa has ordered us to prepare to rush the soldiers."

"Rush the soldiers?" John asked incredulously. "That's suicide!"

"You stay behind with Sherab then, and try to run away."

John felt humiliated. "Of course not, I'm in this with you. I just don't know what that running into their guns will accomplish."

"What do you think staying…"

Dorje's words cut off abruptly as a loud "whummp" echoed across the valley. A short whistling sounded just before a thunderous explosion erupted fifty feet on their right. Screams of death and suffering followed the explosion. A crater formed in the snow, with three bodies littered around it.

"They've got mortar!" Dorje shouted, showing total panic for the first time since John had met him.

"Jhampa!" Sherab's scream rang above the noise and reached John's ears with frightening clarity. John turned and saw her anguished face safely behind her rocky cover. Jhampa had begun his mad rush towards the Chinese. John watched in fascination as Jhampa miraculously ran at least five yards before one of the many bullets aimed his way tore him down. The rest of the rebels had not even had time to consider joining his rush.

Sherab screamed once more before dashing after her fallen brother.

"No!" John shouted, loud enough to hurt his throat.

Sherab ignored his plea, and ran towards her brother. She had taken just a few steps before her body spun around in the air. She landed hard on the snow, staining the unspoiled white snow with a fine mist of crimson.

A low growling noise started to form deep within John's chest. As the shock of seeing her fallen body wore off, the growl transform into a primeval scream of rage. One soldier lifted himself above the ridgeline to get a better shot at the two fallen siblings. John no longer had any clear conscious thought. The guttural scream seemed to belong to another man's throat, not his. He ran towards Sherab, firing at the exposed soldier. Whether it was his shots or someone else's that hit him did not matter, the soldier's body flew backwards.

Thin wisps of snow danced upwards at his feet as the bullets flew around John. On a subconscious level he understood that over a dozen guns must be firing at him. Yet all he could see was Sherab's body, ever so slowly getting closer to him.

The air came alive with a chorus of defiant roars. The six remaining rebels charged the soldiers with the vigorousness of a small army. Their rush drew fire away from John, undoubtedly saving his life. He dove in front of Sherab's prone body, shielding her from the Chinese guns. He swung his rifle out and began firing wildly into the ridge.

Jhampa held his leg at an awkward position, but managed to fire at the soldiers while lying in the snow. John recognized their ring carver's face just before a bullet tore it apart. The soldiers did not panic from the rebel's attack, but remained hidden and picked out their targets with practiced skill.

Suddenly a soldier stood briefly, and then slumped forward on the ridge. A frenzied commotion ensued behind the ridge, giving the rebels a temporary break from the deadly Chinese fire. The battlefield became a mass of confusion as soldiers tried to fire at the rebels, while others fired behind their position. John's mind struggled to understand what was happening, until he saw the faint outline of men on top of the slope. From their vantage point, they picked off the exposed soldiers with ease. The officer tried to keep his men under control, but most panicked when they realized they were caught in a crossfire. One soldier dropped his rifle, and placed his hands in the air. Someone at the top of the slope shot him, tumbling his body over onto John's side of the ridge. Others stood to run, but were cut down by both the rebels and their strange allies above them.

The shooting stopped as quickly as it had begun. All the soldiers lay dead or dying at the foot of the slope. John quickly turned over to see his precious Sherab. Her eyes looked up at him in shock, unable to comprehend what had happened. A red stain covered her right shoulder, centered about a small hole in her coat.

*** 

Sherab noticed how curiously calm the valley seemed, as she lay in the snow, staring up at the sky. The moans of the dying reached her ears then, destroying the false serenity of the valley floor. At the same time, an intense burning sensation began to stab her right shoulder. She had been shot, she remembered. So this was how she would be punished. She had feared that fate would take away her husband. But instead, after giving her a glimpse of happiness, fate was finally ending this life. Thoughts of her own pain left her as she remembered Jhampa being shot as well.

"Nyandak!" John's voice dispelled her self-absorbed thoughts, bringing her back to reality. She reached for John's arm with her left hand.

"Jhampa?" she asked weakly. The faintness of her voice surprised her.

"Jhampa is OK," John reassured her. "His leg," he added, pointing to his own leg. She nodded contently, knowing that her brother had not perished.

"Sherab is OK too, Nyandak will help you." John seemed to put as much calm as he could muster into his quaking voice.

With a spray of snow, Nyandak landed at Sherab's side. She felt tiny trickles of snow melting on her face after his abrupt arrival. After a moment of inspection, Nyandak pulled out a knife and began cutting her coat away from the wound. Sherab gritted her teeth at his touch, and squeezed John's hand tightly.

"How is she?" Dorje asked breathlessly as he arrived at Nyandak's side.

Nyandak ignored him while he continued his work. Dorje shrugged his shoulders and looked at John. Despite the pain, Sherab smiled at John's glare towards Nyandak. It looked like John was ready to grab Nyandak by the shoulders and shake an answer out of him. Nyandak then spoke in a quiet, firm voice to Dorje.

"We need to lift her into a sitting position."

Dorje moved to her good side, took her arm, and placed a hand under her shoulder. John used one hand to prepare to support her bad arm, while his other hand began to lift her middle back. Despite their careful movements, Sherab cried out in pain. Nyandak quickly moved in behind her to examine the exit wound. He carefully cut away her coat, exposing her bare shoulder. Ironically, the cold outside air seemed to help numb her pain.

"The bullet went through cleanly, and missed her bone." Nyandak began searching through his medical kit while he muttered his findings to Dorje. "You're very lucky, Sherab"

Sherab began to tremble with relief, and cold. Nyandak's words sunk into her consciousness, tearing away her belief of imminent death.

"I need to clean the wound, and I have nothing to take the pain away." Nyandak looked apologetically at Sherab as he spoke these words. Her eyes opened wide in fear and anticipation of the coming pain.

Dorje communicated Nyandak's words to John. John himself seemed in pain as he straddled her legs, leaned on her left shoulder, and held her body in a careful, awkward hug. Her mouth felt dry, she was unable to speak any words to her husband as he held her. Then she felt her body shudder as Nyandak began to work on her. In her mind she imagined Nyandak with a red-hot poker, jabbing into her shoulder. She pressed her face into John's neck, trying to stifle the moans coming out of her mouth. Her hand tugged at his coat while he squeezed her harder against him.

"All done, Sherab. I'm very sorry for having to hurt you."

Sherab leaned back, releasing John. She held her mouth firmly closed, but could not prevent the tears from forming in the corners of her eyes. John leaned forward, kissing each eye to dry them. This seemed to make matters worse, for the tears began to run down the side of her cheeks. Nyandak carefully applied some clean bandages to her shoulder.

"You have to keep her warm," Nyandak instructed Dorje. "And find a way to cover her shoulder so that the skin doesn't freeze."

Nyandak's face appeared in front of Sherab, causing her to flinch in fear that he was going to touch her again.

"I'm going to attend to Jhampa's leg now, Sherab. Your brother will be fine. You try to rest, OK?"

Sherab nodded absently in response, still unable to speak because of the pain in her shoulder.

Dorje pulled out his knife and began slicing strips of hide. John took the first strip, and gingerly laid it over her shoulder. The strip was long enough to reach under her arm, where he tied a loose knot to hold it in place.

Shouts of anger near the ridge interrupted their work on Sherab. She turned to look at the source of the commotion and saw Gyan face to face with one of the nomads. The nomad held his rifle across his chest, barring Gyan's way.

"What's going on?" she asked Dorje weakly.

"Gyan wants to gather some of the Chinese weapons, but the nomads are claiming everything as their victory. They want the valuable weapons."

Gyan stepped forward, but the nomad pushed him back with his rifle. The big Gyan reached across, grabbed the nomad's wrists, and flung his body aside like a toy. Two other nomads immediately stepped forward and pointed their rifles at Gyan. He seemed about ready to fight them when a loud, commanding voice boomed over the valley.

"Stop fighting!"

They all turned to see Jhampa, leaning up against Nyandak for support. In the same loud voice, he addressed his rebels as well as the nomads.

"This is a great day, not to be spoiled by greed. Today, for the first time, nomads and Tibetan Freedom Resistance Fighters have joined forces and defeated our common enemy. We all would have died without the nomad help, they deserve all of the spoils of this victory."

Jhampa's voice never faltered, despite the obvious grimace of pain on his face.

"But I know this soldier is my kill!" Gyan began to argue, gesturing emphatically at the dead soldier and his equipment.

"Gyan!" Jhampa simply roared, silencing the bigger man. He then continued his address to the others.

"We hope that this is the first of many such battles. Together we will free Tibet."

Jhampa held his rifle into the air, and began repeating "Free Tibet". All the rebels took up his chant, until it echoed and rebounded across the entire valley. The nomads stared at this display impassively, neither committing to the movement nor scorning it. Their main interest at the moment was the vast amount of weapons along the ridge.

Gyan reluctantly threw down the Chinese rifle he had salvaged, and began walking towards the rest of the rebels. The nomads remained watchful while the rebels prepared their departure. They gathered around Jhampa, and discussed their strategy within earshot of Sherab.

"Nyandak, Gyan, and Dorje should bring Sherab and John the rest of the way to Nepal," Jhampa informed the group. He did not make it a command, wanting to let the others have some input. When no one objected, the decision was made.

"With Sherab's shoulder, they'll travel slowly. I don't think they'll make it until some time tomorrow. The others will help me and my useless leg get back to the cave."

"Sherab can you walk?" Dorje called to her.

She nodded, and offered John her left hand to help her to her feet. John put her arm around his neck, and lifted her by the waist. She stood shakily, trying not to let the pain show on her face. With slow determination she walked towards her brother, who was now sitting again.

"So we were both punished today, big brother," she smiled weakly at Jhampa.

"You had no reason to be shot today. That was a foolish thing to do!" Jhampa looked at her seriously, but she saw no anger in his eyes.

"Jhampa, can we be a family again? Will you come with us?"

"You know I can't, Sherab." He shook his head slowly, taking her hand. "This is my life. The Chinese have hurt my family, I can't just walk away now."

"I knew you wouldn't come, but I had to ask." Sherab hesitated a moment, before continuing. She looked for Dorje, and found him out of range of her whispers.

"There is another reason for you to be more careful from now on." Sherab smiled warmly at Jhampa, as he returned her look quizzically.

"You're going to meet your nephew or niece sooner than you think!"

After a brief moment of confusion, understanding washed over his face.

"You mean, you're ..." He looked at her nodding face before breaking into a beaming smile.

"How do you know? I mean, how long?"

Sherab laughed at the stream of questions. She enjoyed finally telling someone that she carried a new life within her.

"About four weeks."

Jhampa seemed uncomfortable then.

"Is that why you and John got married?"

"No!" Sherab answered angrily. "John doesn't even know yet, and he's the one who asked me to marry him."

"He doesn't know? Sherab, you're pregnant and you haven't told your husband?" Jhampa looked incredulously at his sister.

"Shhh, not so loud. I don't want Dorje to hear, he is sure to tell John. I just don't want John worrying about it while we travel. When we're safe in India, of course I'll tell him. He just doesn't need the extra burden right now."

"So you will carry the burden by yourself." Sherab recognized Jhampa's disapproving tone simply as concern for his sister.

"Women have to carry that burden all the time, we're tougher than you men."

Her teasing finally broke through his seriousness, and brought a chuckle to his lips.

"If I were John, I would be so angry when I found out you held it back from me."

"Maybe, but I think the news will take away any anger he might feel at first."

"Even without the news, I don't think he could stay angry at you very long."

"I'm going to miss you so much, Jhampa." Sherab squeezed his hand with her left hand, not wanting to lose her brother again.

"I'll come visit you," Jhampa declared. "I don't want you bringing a baby over here. I promise I'll find the time to leave this war and come see your child."

"I can't wait for that day. We'll all be together in peace."

They might have continued their farewells longer if one of the nomads had not come to talk to Jhampa.

"The Chinese will be sending out more soldiers to look for you," the nomad began stiffly. "We will take care of your dead, you may leave immediately."

"Your offer is generous," Jhampa replied. "We thank you very much. And we will leave immediately."

Sherab was amazed at how easily leadership came to her brother. She recognized the nomad's offer as only partly a peace offering. The offer also got the rebels away from the nomads' claimed weapons sooner. She was sure Jhampa knew this too, but he still acknowledged their offer as a gift from them. She felt comforted by his careful judgment. She had enough to worry about with a new husband and a new baby. As she parted from her brother, she sensed that his wits would keep him alive in this barren land. She knew he would keep his promise to visit her in a safer setting.

***

Jhampa and John shook hands one more time before parting company. John thanked Jhampa and his men a final time before Dorje urged him to continue their march out of Tibet.

Like Dorje had warned John, their progress became extremely slow now that Sherab had been shot. They stopped frequently for her to rest, since she had lost a lot of blood. For the first time in their hiking experience, John was not exhausted when night arrived. He snuggled against Sherab, trying to keep her warm without hurting her shoulder.

Sherab must have slept poorly that night. Her red, bleary eyes looked at John bleakly when he woke up in the morning.

"We are almost free Sherab," he told her encouragingly. "You're so strong, I'm proud of how well you're taking the gunshot wound."

She smiled at him weakly when Dorje translated his words. Her smile faded quickly when Nyandak came to her to redress the wound. After that unpleasant experience was over, they ate their breakfast and lost no time in resuming the march.

"How much further to the border?" John asked Dorje tiredly in the late afternoon.

"Hard to say for sure, but I think we crossed over in the last couple of hours."

"You mean it?" John asked with a growing smile on his face.

"Welcome to Nepal," Dorje answered, matching his smile.

"Sherab!" John cried out to her, "we're in Nepal!" She cooled his enthusiasm with a sad, and tired look. In his excitement he had failed to remember that she was abandoning her country, and her brother. In addition, the jolt of each step they took seemed to send stabs of pain into her shoulder. John took up step beside her guiltily, and simply held her good hand as they continued walking.

"We have to avoid the roads near the border," Dorje told John while they ate supper. "The border police here is corrupt, they'll turn us in to the Chinese for a reward. At this rate, I think we have two days before we reach the United Nations refugee camp. That's where we'll separate. We don't want anyone to see us yet. We're still too small a fighting force to expose ourselves. The refugee camp is safe for you, they'll get you to India."

"This trip is taking longer than you planned for, will you be alright for food?"

"We're used to running short of food. We can ration what's left to make it last long enough."

Sherab almost fell asleep during the evening meal. John forced her to finish her food, knowing that she needed the nourishment more than any of them. They quickly prepared their sleeping area, and he helped her into the promised warmth of the sleeping bag.

The next day followed pretty much the same pattern of walking as long and as far as Sherab could handle. By the end of the day, even John felt tired. Sherab must have been near the point of collapsing. She wanted to keep going, but they decided to force a stop, on account of her obvious fatigue.

She slept better on this second night. Either the exhaustion knocked her out or her wound hurt a little less. In the morning, she looked better than she had ever since being shot.

"How are you feeling this morning?" John asked her.

She waited for Dorje before answering. "Sherab OK," she told him. He doubted that she would have said otherwise even if she was dying, but the look in her eyes let John know that she did indeed feel better.

"I think we'll reach the refugee center this afternoon." Dorje confirmed.

"I can't believe we actually made it," John answered him in awe.

"Yes, you've been on the run a long time now. Our Buddha must be watching over you even if you are Christian." Dorje laughed at his own joke. It felt good to hear someone laugh again. John looked forward to a time where he and Sherab could share jokes and laugh without worrying about surviving the next day.

They stopped for lunch, but John refused to eat. Dorje and the others would be running out of food during the return trip.

"I'll have a big juicy steak tonight," he answered when Dorje tried to get him to eat his lunch.

Dorje snorted at John's comment. "You won't get steak, but you'll have a hot soup, which sounds just as good right now."

John had to agree with him, any hot food sounded marvelous at the moment.

Dorje stopped for the last time around mid-afternoon.

"This is it John. Over that hill," he indicated the small mountain ahead of them, "is the refugee center. We'll wait here while you two climb to the top. You'll see the large encampment in the valley on the other side."

"Are you sure you won't come with us? You could rest for a day, and get more food."

"No, Jhampa doesn't want anyone to see us. He's right too, it's an unnecessary risk. You saw the other day how good a leader he is. He turned an ugly situation into an occasion to ally himself with the nomads. I trust his judgment for this also. We'll wait here."

John shook hands with all three men, while they carefully hugged and kissed Sherab.

"I won't need this anymore," he told Dorje, handing his rifle to Gyan. "Is there anything else you want? What about our sleeping bag?"

"Sure, we could use that."

John untied his backpack, the one he had carried for Sherab, and handed it to Dorje.

"Take whatever you think you could use, we don't have a need for it anymore."

"Thank you John," Dorje answered. He went through the contents of the pack and withdrew a few items, such as matches, and sunglasses against the glare of the snow.

Sherab took John's hand as they began the steep climb up the hill. Her fatigue seemed to melt away as the realization truly sunk into her that this was the end of their journey. They soon crested the top of the hill, and saw the refugee camp below them. John nearly wept at the sight of the United Nations flag fluttering in the wind. They had made it. He turned towards Sherab, overwhelmed with relief.

"John help" she said, and smiled at him. Her eyes were moist, and happy. Those eyes again, as in his dream when she had first knocked John unconscious. He had followed those eyes over many obstacles. Looking at them now, wet with gratitude, peace, and happiness he knew that it was not over. If he had his way he would never leave those eyes for the rest of his life. She could not speak fluent English, but her eyes understood his. They seemed to answer that no, they would never let him go either.

Epilogue

# Missing Canadian Hiker Appears in India

**By Laurie Balton**
Tribune Foreign Correspondent

NEW DELHI – After being lost for 6 weeks, a Canadian tourist hiking in Tibet made a startling appearance in Dharamsala, India. Amid a flurry of political accusations, John Pearson, 36, and a Tibetan woman reported to be his wife, have claimed refugee status in this holy Indian city.

Sherab Choezom was treated and released at the city's hospital for a gunshot wound to the shoulder. Pearson and Choezom allegedly have been on the run from Chinese soldiers for the past six weeks. Their dangerous trek often left them without food, and having to survive in sub-zero weather conditions. The couple miraculously left China by crossing the forbidding Himalayan mountains on foot. It is not known how Pearson, who arrived in China alone, met and married Choezom. Nor have any official documents been provided to substantiate their marriage claims.

In a dramatic press conference speech, Choezom admitted to having been held as a political prisoner in Tibet. Like many such escaped prisoners, she described the atrocities suffered onto Tibetans in Chinese jails. Choezom herself claims to have been a victim of torture and rape by her jailers.

Perhaps Choezom's most spectacular allegation pertains to the missing Tibetan Panchen Lama, or "Great Scholar". Tibetan religious beliefs indicate that this second highest-ranking leader is reincarnated after the death of the previous Panchen Lama. After the exiled Dalai Lama proclaimed 6 year old Gedhun Choekyi Nyima to be the reincarnated 11th Panchen Lama, the young boy and his family vanished. In May 1995, Nyima became the world's youngest political prisoner. While Beijing has refused any Western contact with the missing boy, Choezom claims to have seen him. Furthermore, she claims that his Chinese captors are subjecting the boy to severe mental and physical abuse. Choezom's shocking allegations also predict a more sinister plan for later returning the mentally and emotionally damaged boy back into power as a Chinese puppet.

If Choezom's scandalous claims are true, China will suffer enormous embarrassment and political pressure regarding the Tibet issue. Free Tibet organizations around the world are already expressing their rage and calling for economic sanctions against the Chinese government.

Beijing and the local Chinese embassy have thus far been unavailable for comment.

www.ingramcontent.com/pod-product-compliance
Lightning Source LLC
Chambersburg PA
CBHW050549260626
47157CB00002B/494